Shadowmoor

# Shadowmoor

## GARETH PRESCOTT

# CONTENTS

# Chapter one

W ill hurried out the door, the crisp morning air hitting him and causing his stiff hands to fumble with his keys as he tried to unlock his car.

He quickly slid into the creaky driver's seat, turning the key in the ignition, and the engine reluctantly rattled to life in fits and starts, coughing and sputtering. He pulled out of his driveway and began his daily commute. As he merged onto the main road, he turned on the radio, hoping for a distraction. Instead, the dull, disinterested voice of a news reporter spewed out the daily digest of devastation; climate change accelerating at an alarming rate, escalating war in Europe, an economic downturn teetering on the edge of recession, and now a new virus discovered in some distant country that experts feared might lead to another worldwide pandemic.

As he indicated to exit the roundabout, the news reporter continued to convey what sounded like the end of days in a bored tone, dragging down Will's already sagging spirit. "I can't take any more of that shit." he muttered under his breath, and switched the radio off, preferring the silence.

As the volume dial clicked to the off position, a driver in a sleek black luxury car abruptly cut him off, forcing Will to slam on his brakes. The tires screeched in protest leaving vivid black marks on the road, and his car jerked to a sudden stop. Almost instantly, he heard the sickening crunch of metal as the car behind him ploughed straight into the back of his.

"Perfect," Will muttered under his breath, his heart pounding as a wave of shock and frustration washed over him. He put his car into neutral, lifted the hand brake and paused for a second to compose himself, before stepping out to assess the damage as the morning rush hour traffic continued flowing past. The rear of his car was crumpled, and the other driver, an anxious-looking young man, was already approaching, his face pale and apologetic.

"I'm so sorry," the young man said, wringing his hands nervously. "I didn't have time to react."

Will forced a tight-lipped smile, trying to suppress his irritation given that he had noted the young man tailgating him for the last half mile. "It's alright. Let's just exchange insurance information and we can get this sorted."

As they exchanged details, the adrenaline from the collision began to wear off, and Will felt a dull, pulsing ache forming behind his eyes, growing in intensity by the minute. He rubbed his temples, thinking about the hassle this would add to his day. With the formalities done, Will leaned on the steering wheel for a moment, closing his eyes as the ache behind them throbbed steadily. Today was already unravelling, and he wasn't even at work yet.

By the time he finally pulled into the car park of his office building, he was thoroughly drained and giving some serious thought to just turning around and going home. He leaned his head back against the headrest, realising that the bills piling up at home would disagree with that course of action, so instead, stepped out of the car, taking a deep breath and forced himself to walk toward the entrance.

As he locked his car and made his way across the car park, he heard the notification sound from his phone, and like Pavlov's dog, obediently lifted the glowing slab to his face. 'One new message from Reece' read the notification on the screen. "Happy birthday, mate. See you after work—I'll bring the bud." He smiled, as he stowed his phone back in his pocket. He could always rely on Reece to come through.

The dull, gray facade of the office loomed ahead, the location of his voluntary incarceration, where day after day, he went and traded hours of his life, and pieces of his soul, for just enough money to afford to do it all again the next day.

He pushed open the door to his office building and made his way through the sterile, brightly lit hallway. The familiar hum of fluorescent lights overhead accompanied him as he approached the open-plan office area he and his colleagues referred to as 'the hive.' It was an apt nickname; the workers, like bees, were busy buzzing away, plugged into their terminals with headsets on, resembling dairy cows in a milking facility, each face illuminated by the glow of their monitors.

He walked through the maze of identical cubicles, overhearing snippets of conversations about projects, deadlines and budgets. Will glanced at the clock on the wall and realised the accident had made him late. Anxiety prickled at the back of his mind as he hurried to his cubicle, hoping to settle down to work without drawing any attention.

As he logged onto his system, he knew his late arrival would be time-stamped. He grimaced, wishing he could disappear into the background. But before he could even attempt to get into his workflow, he saw the large form of Mr. Johnston waddling across the office, his red face set in a stern, testy expression.

"Preston, you're late!" Mr. Johnston's voice boomed, drawing the attention of several nearby colleagues.

Will turned in his chair, trying to appear calm and collected. "I'm sorry, Mr. Johnston. There was an accident on the way in. Got rear-ended. I know I should have called in, but I was dealing with the insurance details." he said in an easy tone, hoping that would be enough to placate the eternally irritated man before him.

Mr. Johnston crossed his arms over his ample belly and narrowed his eyes. "An accident, huh? Well, you know the policy, Preston. Tardiness isn't tolerated. This will be recorded as a verbal warning on your record."

Will nodded, swallowing his frustration. "Understood, sir. It won't happen again."

"See that it doesn't," Mr. Johnston said curtly before waddling back to his office, his presence lingering like a dark cloud.

Will sighed and turned back to his monitor. He opened his inbox, already flooded with emails marked "urgent" and "important." He knew he couldn't afford to dwell on the morning's misfortunes. Instead, he had to focus on getting through the day, one monotonous task at a time.

As he settled into his work, the buzz of the hive continued around him. He glanced at the cubicle walls, adorned with motivational posters that felt more like a mockery than inspiration, and felt his soul wither a little. The hum of conversation and the rhythmic tapping of keyboards formed a monotonous symphony that gnawed away at his fragile sanity.

By lunchtime, he was more than ready for a break. He headed to the small break room and grabbed his lunch from the communal fridge, hoping for a moment of respite. As he sat down with his sandwich, he overheard snippets of conversations around him—complaints about work, inane discussions about the latest sports games or celebrity antics, and the ever-present background noise of someone watching mindless bite-sized video clips in three second bursts on their phone.

Will closed his eyes, trying to suppress the growl that was rising up in his throat, and considered just finishing his lunch in his car. Just as he began to gather his things, he noticed Alyssa approaching. His heart skipped a beat as she smiled warmly. "Mind if I sit here?" she said, her tone casual.

"Uh, yeah, sure," he said, stammering awkwardly as he half stood and motioned to the chair opposite him.

Alyssa had a way of brightening any room she walked into, and her presence always lifted Will's spirits, even if he struggled to find the courage to talk to her. He'd admired her from afar for years, her easy laughter and gentle nature always illuminating the darkest of days, like a single ray of sunlight in a grey, cloudy sky.

As she settled into the chair, she glanced at him, her kind eyes meeting his. "How's your day going?" she said, her voice soothing in a way that seemed to melt the noise around them.

Will tried to respond, but the familiar knot of self-doubt tightened in his chest, closing his throat. "It's... fine," he said, internally wincing at his lack of eloquence.

Alyssa didn't seem to mind, her warm smile never faltering. "Good. I've been so busy, I didn't think I was going to get time to grab lunch."

He nodded, wanting desperately to say something more but unsure how to bridge the gap between small talk and the flood of thoughts swirling in his mind. As the conversation hung in the air, he compromised by taking a huge bite of his lunch to give him a chance to come up with something else to say.

Alyssa unwrapped her sandwich, glancing at Will with a hint of hesitation before speaking. "I, uh... heard Mr. Johnston yelling at you this morning. The way he spoke was out of line."

Will sighed, his shoulders sagging slightly. "Yeah, that was... not my favourite way to start the day," he said in a defeated tone. "I wouldn't mind, but I was only late because I got rear-ended on the way to work."

Her eyes widened, and she leaned forward, her sandwich momentarily forgotten. "You were in a crash? Are you okay?"

"Yeah, I'm fine," Will said quickly, waving a hand to reassure her. "It was just a fender-bender, nothing serious. Everyone walked away without a scratch. My car, on the other hand..." He trailed off, grimacing.

Alyssa's concern deepened, her brow creasing slightly as she studied him. "Are you sure you're okay?"

"I promise, I'm fine," he said, unable to keep the small smile off his face at her genuine concern. "Just dealing with some dents and an angry boss now. Could've been worse."

She shook her head, a look of exasperation her face. "Mr. Johnston doesn't care about anything but himself, does he? Did you explain what happened?"

Will shrugged, poking at his lunch. "I did, but you know how he is. I think he was more upset that I interrupted his morning coffee ritual."

That drew a laugh from Alyssa, her eyes softening. "Well, I'm glad you're okay. Cars can be fixed."

"Thanks," Will said, his cheeks warming at her kindness. "I appreciate it."

Their conversation continued from there, drifting into lighter topics—work grumbles, shared observations about their coworkers, and even a brief debate over the best lunch spots nearby. Will found himself easing into the flow, his earlier tension melting away.

He was mid-sentence, telling her about the time the office coffee machine flooded the break room, when he caught sight of the clock on the wall. Lunch was over.

"Wow," he said, grabbing his things. "I didn't realise how fast the time has gone."

"Me neither," Alyssa said with a small laugh as she stood. "Thanks for letting me sit with you, Will. It was nice."

"Yeah," he replied, trying to sound casual despite the flutter in his chest. "Anytime."

As they walked back to their desks, Will couldn't help but smile. Despite the crash and Johnston's tirade, the day suddenly didn't seem so bad.

The remainder of the afternoon was uneventful, with the hands of the clock on the wall eventually making their painstaking journey to home time. Will logged off and packed away his workstation, before grabbing his empty lunch-box from the break room and making his way to his car. The crumpled rear end took him momentarily by surprise, but then the memory of the morning's events flooded back, and he remembered he still needed to contact his insurance. Deciding to let himself off that chore for today—after all, it was his birthday—he settled on doing it tomorrow.

He got into his car, the only light coming from a solitary street-light overhead, taking a moment to enjoy the silence there before setting off for home. The road ahead was filled with blinking brake lights. The commute home was usually quite slow-going, as congestion at this time of the evening was quite bad in the city, but sometime during the day, they had also erected cones along the main stretch of road, adding to the already high levels of congestion. He considered flicking the radio on to pass the time but opted against it, instead listening to the chorus of angry drivers honking their horns.

A particularly aggressive driver cut in front of him, forcing Will to brake sharply again. He clenched the steering wheel tightly, trying to suppress the irritation bubbling up inside him.

As he inched forward in the traffic, his phone buzzed in his pocket. He glanced at it, seeing a text from Reece; "Don't forget about tonight! See you soon!"

Despite his dreadful day, Will couldn't help but smile. The thought of spending the evening with his best friend seemed like a welcome beacon of light at the end of a very dark tunnel.

Eventually, he made it out of the congested city centre and into his neighbourhood. He passed familiar streets and houses, slowly making his way home. Pulling into his driveway, he turned off the engine and sat for a moment, taking a deep breath. The day's events had left him exhausted, but at least now he was home.

He gathered his things from the passenger seat and headed inside, the warm light of his living room lamp filling the space with a comforting glow as he moved about in his normal pattern of routines. He set his lunch-box on the kitchen counter, placed his keys on a hook and shrugged off his coat, glancing at the clock. There was still some time before Reece would arrive.

Will took a moment to check his messages again and saw another birthday wish from his brother. They were not on the best of terms in recent years, and the message, though polite, irritated him. He responded with a short, terse "Thank you."

Sighing, he decided to grab a quick shower to wash away the day's stress. As the hot, soothing water cascaded over him, he allowed himself to relax, his muscles slowly unknotting.

Clean and feeling a bit more refreshed, he threw on some comfortable clothes and made his way to the living room. He glanced around, noting the slight disarray of his home, but decided not to worry about tidying up.

Just as he was settling onto the couch, there was a knock at the door. He opened it to find Reece standing there, a grin on his face and a bag of goodies in hand.

"Happy Birthday, mate!" Reece said enthusiastically, stepping inside and giving Will a hearty pat on the back.

"Thanks, Reece," Will said, smiling. "You really didn't have to."

"Nonsense. It's your birthday. How about you crack open a couple of them beers and I'll fire up the console?"

Will looked inside the bag. It contained everything they would need for a good night in. They sat down and immediately rolled up a smoke, cracked open a couple of beers, and started playing the video game.

As the evening unfolded, the tension from the day began to melt away. The rhythmic clicking of the game controller buttons, the vibrant graphics, and energetic soundtrack of the game provided a welcome distraction. Will found himself laughing and joking with Reece, enjoying an unfamiliar moment of relaxation.

A couple of hours passed in a blur of high-speed chases and explosive action. Will actually had a good time, Reece having redeemed his birthday after all. At one point, Will paused the game to grab another beer from the fridge. As he returned, he noticed Reece leaning back on the couch, lingering over the remnants of the joint.

"Thanks for this, Reece," Will said, handing him a fresh beer. "I really needed it."

Reece grinned and took the beer, passing the joint to Will. "Anytime, mate. It's not every day your best mate turns forty."

They continued playing for a while longer, the smoke and the beer continuing to relax them both. Eventually, they set the controllers down and settled into a more laid-back conversation.

"How's work been?" Reece said, a playful smile on his face, knowing full well Will hated his job.

Will sighed, taking a sip of his beer. "Not great. There's talk of lay-offs."

Reece raised an eyebrow. "Really? What's going on?"

"They're moving towards a more internet based system," Will said, frustration creeping into his voice. "All clickbait bullshit. It's not the same. They don't care about real writers anymore."

Reece nodded sympathetically. "That's rough."

Will shook his head. "I hate it. I got into this job to write real news, not this garbage. But it feels like it's just a matter of time before they cut the old-school guys like me loose."

Reece leaned back, considering his friend's words. "You know, Will, maybe it wouldn't be the worst thing in the world if you did lose your job."

Will looked at him, surprised. "What do you mean?"

"You hate that place," Reece said bluntly. "Maybe getting laid off would be a blessing in disguise. It might push you to find something you actually enjoy."

Will sighed, running a hand through his hair. "I don't know... It's not like jobs are growing on trees, and the bills just keep piling up."

"True," Reece said. "But think about it. You've been stuck there for how long now? Years, right? Maybe this is the universe's way of giving you a kick in the ass to find something better."

Will took another sip of his beer, leaning back as he mulled over Reece's words. "Maybe you're right," he said. "I just don't know what else I'd do."

Reece shrugged. "You've got skills, man. You're good with people, and you're really good at writing. There are plenty of opportunities out there. You just need to look."

Will nodded slowly. "Yeah, maybe." he said, not entirely convinced.

Reece clapped him on the shoulder. "You've got people who care, mate. You'll figure it out. Worst case, you come roofing with me." he said with a laugh.

Will shuddered at the thought of working at height. "I think I would prefer staying at the hive, and that's saying something."

Reece leaned back on the couch, taking a sip of his beer before casually changing the subject. "So, have you finally worked up the courage to ask out Alyssa?"

Will felt his cheeks warm with a blush, his gaze briefly darting away. "Uh, no," he said, clearing his throat uncomfortably. "I haven't."

Reece chuckled softly. "Mate, how long are you going to wait? You've had a crush on her the whole time you've been working there, and from what I've seen, she seems to like you too."

Will shrugged, squirming slightly under the pressure of his friends playful questioning. "I don't know. It's just...complicated."

Reece raised an eyebrow, a playful glint in his eye. "Complicated? Come on, Will. What is the worst that can happen."

Will looked pointedly at Reece. "Well... I could destroy what little dignity I have left at work?" he said, only half joking.

Reece nodded understandingly. "Fair enough. Just remember, life's too short to hold back. Think about it?"

Will chuckled softly, shaking his head. "Maybe." he said, sounding entirely unconvinced.

They chatted for a little while longer, but as the night wore on and the effect of the beer and the smokes dulled their minds, they both grew tired. Will helped Reece pull out the mechanism from the sofa-bed before locking up, and heading to his own bed.

# Chapter two

The muffled patter of rain against the window was the first thing Will noticed as he stirred awake. For a fleeting moment, he entertained the idea of staying in bed, letting the gray morning dissolve into an uneventful afternoon. But the promise he'd reluctantly made earlier in the week left him feeling more uncomfortable than the ache in his back.

A glance at his phone confirmed it—Saturday. The word hanging there above the predictably dreary weather forecast on his home-screen, and below it, a reminder from his mother: "Looking forward to seeing you at noon, sweetheart. Drive safe!"

Will groaned, throwing the phone onto the mattress and staring at the ceiling. Visiting his parents had once been a comfort, a chance to escape the chaos of adult life and return to the safety of childhood, if only for a moment. Lately, though, it felt more like a chore—a parade of subtle jabs about his job, his car, and the ever-present spectre of his non-existent love life.

His father's voice already echoed in his head: "When I was your age, I had a house, two kids, and a pension. What's your excuse, son?"

With a heavy sigh, Will swung his legs over the side of the bed. If he left now, he could grab coffee on the way and still arrive on time. Anything to fortify himself for the inevitable inquisition that awaited.

He brushed his teeth, staring at his reflection in the mirror and wondering how all those lines had gotten there. He quickly considered calling Alyssa, inspired momentarily by Reece's pestering last night, but he quickly dismissed the thought as he splashed water on his face. "You're pathetic." he muttered at his indifferent reflection, before continuing.

After a quick shower, he dressed casually and rooted through the fridge for some leftovers to eat. After resealing some packets and throwing out the contents of a particularly pungent smelling tupperware, he finally settled on a couple of slices of pizza left over from their late night take-away delivery. Reece had already folded the sofa away and left before Will got up, so he grabbed his keys and left the house.

The route to his childhood home wasn't long, but there was a significant shift from the gray monotony of the city's urban sprawl, gradually giving way to the comforting greens of suburban streets, where neatly trimmed hedges and blossoming trees swayed gently in the breeze. Will lowered his window slightly, the crisp, earthy scent of the morning mingling with faint hints of freshly cut grass—the familiar scent that always reminded him of visiting his parents.

He stopped at the drive-through of his favourite coffee chain, the hum of idling engines filling the air as he drummed his fingers impatiently on the steering wheel. By the time his order arrived, he grabbed it with a mumbled thanks and pulled away, the first sip of warm, sweet caffeine immediately soothing the edge off his nerves.

By the time his parents' house came into view, Will's coffee was finished, and the caffeine had done its job. He parked on the curb, his hands lingering on the wheel as he stared at the front door, preparing himself for the visit.

His parents greeted him warmly at the door, his mother wrapped her arms around him in a tight hug while his father clapped him on the back. "Good to see you, son," his father said with a smile. "How's life treating you?"

Will forced a smile, hoping to keep the conversation light. "Same old, same old," he said, hoping that would suffice. "How about you two?"

They moved inside, the familiar comfort of his childhood home wrapping around him like a blanket. As they settled into the living room, the usual sense of nostalgia washed over Will as the familiar sights and smells enveloped him, soothing his soul.

His mother brought out a tray of tea and biscuits, laying them on the old coffee table. "So, what's new at work?" she said, her tone deliberately light, but her eyes betraying her real intent. He knew she was referring to the promotion that they had been promising for the last couple of years, but never delivering on.

Will sighed inwardly, but kept his tone even. "Not much, really. Just a lot of worry about the upcoming lay-offs."

His father leaned forward, a look of concern in his eyes. "Is your position safe?"

Will just shrugged.

The conversation continued on through the early afternoon, catching up on each others news. As his mum finished detailing a full and graphic depiction of his dad's recent toenail infection, she suddenly looked thoughtful. "Oh, I forgot to say Will, we've been clearing out the loft and found an old box of your stuff," she said, her eyes wandering towards the dining room. "We put it to one side to see if there was anything you might want to keep. Why don't you have a look through it and anything you don't want just pop it in the bin outside?"

Intrigued, Will nodded and got up, setting aside the nearly-empty coffee mug he had been nursing and making his way to the dining room. On the table sat a dusty, old box, worn and a bit tattered at the edges. He unfolded the lid and began rooting through its contents, pulling out old childhood trophies, trinkets, and mementos. He wondered why he'd ever saved some of it, but other items brought waves of nostalgia that left him staring, bemused into the treasure chest of long forgotten memories.

Eventually, at the bottom of the box, he found an old folder, covered in a thick layer of dust. He pulled it out curiously, wiping the dust away with the sleeve of his shirt. Slowly, he opened it, revealing meticulously drawn maps and a plethora of hand-written notes.

A smile spread across his face as he remembered the summer he broke his arm and couldn't play outside. Instead, he had immersed himself in his imagination, trying to write a fantasy novel. The maps detailed fantastical lands with winding rivers, towering mountains, and mysterious forests. The notes described characters, plot-lines, and magical creatures, all born from the boundless creativity of his younger self.

He sat down at the table, flipping through the pages and marvelling at the intricate details he had once so passionately created. The names of places and characters came rushing back to him, each one like a fragment of a forgotten dream, like the memories of old friends from a past life.

As he continued to leaf through the folder, a pang of longing for those days when his imagination knew no bounds and the world was full of endless possibilities left him with a hollow feeling in his chest.

He chuckled softly, realising how much he had poured his heart into this creation. Sitting there, surrounded by the remnants of his childhood, he felt a tiny flicker of that old excitement, an excitement he hadn't felt in a long time. He had never even come close to finishing the story, but his memories of that summer were perhaps the happiest of his life.

After packing away a few of the items he wanted to keep into the box, Will slipped out the front door to place the box in his car, placing the unwanted items into the wheelie bin at the side of the house. He returned to the living room where his dad had flicked on the TV in his absence and was watching the news.

Will sat with them a while longer, but after staring at the back of his mum's magazine and failing to get his dad's attention away from the TV, he realised it was time to leave. He stood up, stretching slightly. "Well, I should probably get going," he said, trying to sound casual.

His mum looked up from her magazine, a bit surprised. "Already, Will? You just got here."

"Yeah, I've got a few things I need to take care of today," he said, offering a small smile.

His dad turned briefly from the TV. "Alright, son. Drive safe."

Will said his goodbyes, hugging his mum and exchanging a quick handshake with his dad. He got into his car and started the engine, preparing for the short journey back home. He glanced at the box of old memories on the passenger seat, the edges of the folder peeking out. The sight bringing a small smile to his face as he buckled up and prepared to leave.

The afternoon sun cast long shadows on the road ahead as he indulged in a leisurely drive back home. As he neared the city, the familiar sense of tension started building as he hit the Saturday afternoon traffic. The congestion was worse than usual, and by the time he reached home and pulled onto his driveway, his usual air of anxiety and melancholy had wrapped around him like a familiar blanket. He needed to sit for a few moments, gripping the steering wheel tightly as he tried to dispel the accumulated frustration, releasing it slowly to avoid an explosion.

Taking a deep breath, he closed his eyes and leaned back against the seat, letting the silence of the car envelop him.

Finally, feeling a bit more composed, he gathered his things and stepped out of the car. He placed the box on the kitchen table, grabbed a cold beer from the fridge, casually flicking the lid into the open bin. He sank into a chair, staring over at the box, imagining getting his old story out and finishing it off. He shook his head, smiling at the idea that his tired old brain would be able to conjure up any magic instead, flicked on the television.

In bed later that night, Will lay in the darkness, his face illuminated by the bright flickering light from his phone, as he watched a video of some guys build a small house using trees and mud in the jungle, waiting for exhaustion to drag his mind off into slumber. Eventually, he felt his eyelids growing heavy, so he set his phone down, casting the room into darkness. At the last second he remembered to turn off his alarm, lighting up the room again momentarily, before settling down to sleep.

That night, Will's sleep was anything but restful. It wasn't the gradual drift into unconsciousness he hoped for but a violent plunge into chaos. His dreams were fractured and restless, haunted by flickering visions that seemed to shift and swirl like smoke caught in a gust. Voices—some familiar, others foreign—whispered his name, each murmur edged with urgency and dread.

He woke abruptly, his chest heaving as though he'd just surfaced from drowning. Sweat clung to his skin, cold and clammy, as he struggled to pull air into his lungs. The room around him lay shrouded in silence, but the darkness felt alive, menacing—its shadows more absolute, intruding into the corners of his vision like unholy spectres.

Will rubbed his face with trembling hands, muttering reassurances to himself in a trebling voice that lacked conviction in the stillness. He tried to push the creeping dread aside, telling himself it was just his overactive mind playing tricks, but his heart continued to pound in his chest, his extremities tingling.

When sleep claimed him again, it dragged him back into a world even more vivid and cruel. He wandered through landscapes that defied logic—cities crumbling under strange skies, filled with creatures both beautiful and terrifying. The voices were louder now, no longer whispers but a cacophony of desperate cries and wails, merging into a suffocating chorus that threatened to drown him.

Each time he jolted awake, the line between dream and reality blurred further. His eyes darted to the foot of his bed, catching the faint outline of a figure cloaked in mist. For an agonising heartbeat, it felt real—a presence in the room with him. The shape dissolved into nothingness when he blinked, but the phantom chill it left behind crawled over his skin.

Fleeting bursts of light darted across the walls, like distant fireworks flickering through a haze. He pressed his palms into his eyes, willing the visions to stop, but the pressure only made the shadows pulse and shift like living things.

By the time dawn's first light crept through the curtains, Will felt hollowed out. His body ached with exhaustion, but his mind buzzed with an edge of panic he couldn't quite shake.

He wasn't sure how long he lay there, waiting for his trembling limbs to cooperate. When the shaking finally subsided, he forced himself out of bed, every movement slow and deliberate. Pulling the curtains aside just enough to peek through and squinting against the harsh light, he saw the sun hovering above the rooflines across the street.

Stumbling to the bathroom, he splashed cold water on his face, the icy shock biting into his skin, chasing away the lingering fog of the night. He raised his head to meet his reflection in the mirror—a pale version of himself. Dark circles ringed his bloodshot eyes, standing out in contrast to his pale clammy skin.

The rest of the day crawled by in a distorted haze, each minute dragging as Will's sleep-deprived mind struggled to remain focussed on anything. His normal weekend chores became overwhelming, their simplicity now insurmountable. He moved from room to room in a fog, only to pause and realise he'd left cupboard doors open, drawers half-closed, or lights on.

Making a cup of coffee turned into a small quest. He misplaced the spoon twice, scattered sugar across the counter, and squinted at the mug in confusion, trying to remember if he'd already added milk. The hum of the refrigerator and the steady ticking of the clock grew intrusively loud, each sound compounding the fog that was blotting out his thoughts.

Despite his exhaustion, a restless energy gripped him, leaving him unable to sit still. Every movement was sluggish, as though gravity itself conspired against him, but knowing he had work the following day, he persevered with his chores. By evening, his body had reached its limit. His limbs ached with a dull, relentless fatigue, his eyes stung with the rawness that couldn't be soothed, and his mind hummed with a disjointed rhythm that made coherent thought impossible.

When he finally sank into bed, it felt like surrender. The mattress enveloped him, and he sank into its embrace like a stone plummeting to the depths of a lake. Yet even as exhaustion threatened to consume him, a faint, inexplicable tension lingered. It was as though some part of him was still on edge, waiting—anticipating something that hovered just out of reach, at the fragile boundary between wakefulness and sleep.

# Chapter three

The alarm on Will's phone had been sounding for some time when it eventually managed to drag him, reluctantly, from the depths of slumber. As he flopped one arm across to grab the device and silence the alarm, he lifted it to check the time and realised he was already running late. Cursing under his breath, he threw himself out of bed with such agility that he took himself by surprise, the urgency of being late overriding his usual slower approach to starting the day.

Rushing through his morning routine, he dressed hastily, nearly tripping over a pair of discarded shoes as he pulled on his trousers. There was no time for a proper breakfast; he grabbed a granola bar from the kitchen counter and stuffed it into his bag, hoping he would have time to eat it at some point. With one final check to make sure he had everything, he darted out the front door, almost forgetting to lock up in his haste.

He got into his car, the familiar creaks and groans of the ageing vehicle barely registering in his rush. As he pulled out of the driveway and into the morning traffic, his phone pinged from the passenger seat next to him. He grabbed it and cast a quick glance downwards, "Dr Evans appt. after work" read the reminder on his phone screen. He still wasn't feeling himself since his anxiety attack and looked forward to discussing this with her.

He reached work with a few minutes to spare and was thankful that he wouldn't have to face Mr. Johnston's wrath today. With a sigh of relief, he dropped his lunch box in the fridge and made his way to his workstation. The hum of fluorescent lights and the distant murmur of his colleagues greeted him, a familiar soundtrack to the soul-destroying monotony of his day.

As Will settled into his cubicle, and logged onto his system, he glanced at the timestamp and felt a fleeting satisfaction at having made it on time. He sifted through the initial flood of emails and began his tasks, the dreariness of his routine quickly set in, draining away his soul one drop at a time as he churned out writing that was mediocre at best. But somewhere underneath the usual dull desolation the he felt here, he started to feel a subtle, yet profound difference within himself. Although he was in the hive, where souls came to die, something was tugging at the back of his mind, sparking a small sense of excitement. It was such an unfamiliar feeling that it took him most of the day to put his finger on it.

By late afternoon, as the fluorescent lights buzzed overhead and the monotonous clatter of keyboards droned on, Will finally recognised what had been tugging at the edges of his mind all day. In the rare quiet moments between calls and emails, his thoughts kept circling back to the box from his parents' house—and the unfinished story buried within it.

Fragmented plot-lines began surfacing in his imagination, like half-forgotten dreams swimming up from the depths. They wove together tentatively, forming the beginnings of something vivid and alive. Beneath his desk, he found himself jotting notes on a simple note pad, trying to capture the elusive threads before they slipped away. The maps he had drawn as a child, the characters he had created, and the fantastical world he had once imagined all started to reawaken, vibrant with fresh potential.

Yet, every flicker of excitement was quickly dulled by the weight of the ever-present darkness that lived in the back of his mind. Doubt loomed over him like a shadow, smothering each fragile spark before it could ignite. Each time a plot-line began to take shape, a flood of uncertainty surged in, whispering that it wasn't worth pursuing—that it was foolish to even try.

Still, the ideas refused to stay buried. As the hours crept by, his mind kept drifting back to those maps and notes. Something in them called to him, persistent, as though daring him to believe that the worlds he once dreamed of might still be waiting for him to breathe life into them.

By the end of the workday, the lingering effects of his tough weekend left him weary. He logged off his computer, packed away his belongings, and made his way to his parked car, eager to see his therapist.

The journey to Dr Evans' office was not long, and for once the traffic co-operated so he arrived in plenty of time. He parked his car and took a deep breath, preparing himself for what lay ahead. He checked in at the reception, and sat in the waiting room.

There weren't many people here at this late hour, most of the day's appointments having already been seen. Somewhere in the room, a tinny radio chimed out the latest manufactured pop artist, intermittently interrupted by static as the badly tuned radio dipped in and out of signal. Will closed his eyes and rested his head back against the wall, attempting to rest for a few minutes before his appointment.

He was suddenly jolted back into wakefulness by the receptionist shaking his shoulder, informing him that the doctor had already called him. Noticing the clock had jumped forward, Will realised he had dozed off and mumbled an apology, before standing up and walking down the hall.

The doctors door was slightly ajar, and he gave it a gentle knock before stepping inside. Dr. Evans looked up from her desk and gave him a warm, welcoming smile.

"Good evening, Will. Come in, have a seat," she said, gesturing to the chair opposite her.

Will sat down, trying to shake off the lingering haze from his unexpected nap. Dr. Evans studied him for a moment, her expression turning serious as she took in his weary face.

"How have you been feeling since our last session?" she said in a gentle voice.

Will took a deep breath, his hands fidgeting in his lap. "The past few days have been... rough," he said hesitantly. "I've been having these nightmares—they started over the weekend. And... my anxiety's been worse than usual. A lot worse."

Dr. Evans nodded, her pen moving across the notepad. "Nightmares?" she said, looking up at him, gently prompting him to continue.

He shifted uncomfortably in his seat, running a hand through his hair. "They were vivid—like, too vivid. But most unsettling of all was how they stayed with me. Even after I woke up, it's like... they wouldn't let go. I'll saw things—felt things—as though it had all followed me into the waking world. It's hard to explain."

Dr. Evans leaned forward slightly, analysing Will for a long moment. "What sort of things did you see?"

Will hesitated, the words catching in his dry throat before spilling out in a rush. "Shapes... shadows. Sometimes faces."

She nodded again, her pen momentarily pausing as she made notes, the scribbling sound of pen on paper the only sound interrupting the persistent ticking of the clock.

"What had you been doing that day?," she said. "have you had any significant changes?"

Will hesitated for a moment, his fingers fidgeting with a loose thread on the arm of his chair. "My birthday was last week. I went to my parents' house, and I found this old box of stuff I'd forgotten about—maps, notes, bits and pieces from when I tried writing a fantasy novel as a kid."

Dr. Evans tilted her head slightly, a faint smile on her lips. "That sounds like an interesting discovery. How did it make you feel?"

He shrugged, his gaze dropping to the floor. "I don't know. At first, it was kind of nice—a reminder of when I used to dream big, you know? But then... I don't know. It felt like a punch to the gut. Like, what happened to that kid?.. you know? The one who thought he could actually create something meaningful? Now I'm just... stuck in this job I can't stand, living this life that feels so small... so pointless."

Dr. Evans jotted something down before looking back at him. "It's understandable to feel disillusioned, especially when you're reflecting on the past. Revisiting those old memories can stir up a lot—nostalgia, regret, even a sense of loss."

Will nodded slowly, "Yeah. I guess finding that stuff brought it all back. It's the same grind every day. I'm just... tired of it all. Tired of the news, tired of society, tired of..." He trailed off, gesturing vaguely.

Dr. Evans leaned back in her chair, steepling her fingers as she considering his words carefully. "It sounds like this recent episode might be tied to your birthday—a significant milestone like turning forty can bring these feelings to the surface. It's not uncommon to experience anxiety or even panic during these times, especially when you're already feeling disconnected. And rediscovering those pieces of your past... stirring up both memories and questions about where you are now."

Will exhaled a shuddering breath, trying to suppress the tears that were bubbling up. "So I'm not going completely crazy?"

"Not at all," Dr. Evans said, reassuring him as she passed a small box of tissues. "What you're feeling is very real, and it's also very human. These moments of reflection can be uncomfortable, but they're part of the process of understanding ourselves better. That said, I think we need to make sure you're equipped to handle it."

She glanced down at her notes, scribbled a few more lines, and tore off a prescription. "I'm going to adjust your medication temporarily. This should help manage your anxiety and improve your sleep. In the meantime, focus on the breathing exercises we talked about last session. They can be a powerful tool when things start to feel overwhelming."

Will accepted the slip of paper. "Thanks, Doctor," he said, his tone genuinely grateful.

"You're welcome," she said with a reassuring smile. "Please make an appointment with the receptionist for next week so we can check in and see how you're doing."

Will nodded and stood up, feeling a bit lighter as he left the office. He made his way to the receptionist, scheduled his next appointment, and headed out into the cool evening air. It wasn't a complete solution, but it was a start, and for now, that was enough.

Will went home, after making a quick detour to the pharmacy and placed his new meds on the kitchen table. He grabbed a beer from the fridge and then pulled out the contents of the box that still sat there. He spread the old maps and notes out before him, and began tracing his finger across the lines and symbols he had meticulously drawn so many years ago.

As Will poured over the familiar, faded ink, it felt like slipping into an old, half-forgotten dream. The maps, the notes, the sketches of characters—they all drew him in, piece by piece, until the present seemed to fade around him. He traced the delicate lines of rivers and mountain ranges with his finger, his thoughts drifting back to the world he had created so long ago.

The characters came alive in his mind's eye as if greeting an old friend. He could almost hear their voices—faint murmurs just behind him, blending into the soft hum of the house. At first, he dismissed it as the muffled sound of Mrs. Smith's TV next door, turned up too loud as usual. But when the voices rose again, fragmented and urgent, he glanced over his shoulder. There was nothing there.

With a shake of his head, he picked up his beer and took a long sip. "You need sleep, Will," he muttered to himself, forcing his focus back to the maps. His finger resumed its path across the parchment, tracing the roads and trails he had once imagined adventurers travelling.

But the intrusions grew harder to ignore. The distant clash of swords rang out, steel meeting steel, followed by muffled cries of battle. A horn's low, mournful call rippled through the air, so faint he glanced to the window, imagining a passing lorry made the sound. His hands trembled as he rubbed his temples, trying to will the noises away, but they refused to fade.

Anxiety twisted in his chest, a sharp, familiar ache that left him breathless. This felt like something more than just a tired mind playing tricks. He wasn't sure what it was, but it pressed against the edges of his awareness, reaching for him.

He looked around his quiet kitchen, the beer in his hand growing warm. He closed his eyes, running through the breathing exercises that Dr. Evans had suggested, and the sounds faded slightly. When he opened them again, the ink in the maps and notes in front of him seemed to shimmer with a strange light, a slight radiance casting a shimmering reflection on the ceiling above. The noises stopped abruptly, and from the silence came just one more sound; an urgent whisper in a woman's voice, "Will!".

He stood up abruptly, nearly knocking over his chair. He looked over at the box of medication on the kitchen counter and decided it was probably time for bed. But as he gathered the papers and stuffed them back into the box, he felt a distinct sense that something had shifted.

Tomorrow, he would start fresh, but tonight, he needed to rest and let this strange day come to an end. He quickly got himself ready for bed and before long was tucked up, not even needing to go through his usual routine of mindless scrolling on his phone before falling into a deep sleep.

That night, the dreams returned with a vengeance. They were sharper now, more vivid, as though the veil between sleep and the waking world had thinned. Each time Will awoke, gasping for breath, the visions clung to him, bleeding into reality like ink spreading across water.

He was in a vast, shadowy forest, the kind that seemed to stretch endlessly in all directions. The trees loomed above, ancient and gnarled, their branches twisting together to form a dense canopy that smothered the sky. A cold wind whispered through the leaves, making the branches groan as if under some unbearable weight. The air was heavy with fog, and faint, flickering lights danced at the edge of his vision, just out of reach. He could sense a malevolent presence, just out of sight, but the wave of pure hatred reached out and violently crushed his spirit.

When he awoke, his heart was pounding so violently it felt as though it might burst. Sweat drenched his skin, and the air in his room felt thick and stifling. He sat up, trembling, but the dream refused to release him. The shadows of towering trees still loomed at the edge of his vision, flickering lights danced on the walls of his bedroom, always just out of his field of view.

Will fumbled for the bedside lamp, its warm glow finally breaking through the remnants of the dream, dispelling the persistent visions that remained. He stared at the familiar surroundings of his room, willing himself to calm, but the feelings of dread refused to fade.

Lying back down, he stared at the ceiling, his mind replaying the images of the forest and the shadows as he waited for his heart to resume a normal rhythm.

When sleep finally overtook him again, it came with even greater intensity. He saw a massive black monolith on the distant horizon, an impossibly large structure that seemed to pulse with dark energy. The cries of thousands filled the air around him, anguished voices shouting over one another in a rising crescendo.

Though their words were still unintelligible, the raw emotion behind them was unmistakable—pleas for help, for salvation. Will's chest tightened as a wave of compassion washed over him. He wanted to reach them, to understand their pain, to do something—anything—to ease their suffering.

He felt it then—that pull, an almost physical tugging sensation behind his eyes, drawing him forward. It wasn't fear that propelled him, but something deeper; an overwhelming sense that he had to do something, though he didn't yet know what.

When he awoke again, it was almost morning. He sat bolt upright in bed, drenched in sweat and shivering, convinced he was losing his mind. He called in to work sick, making a follow-up call to Dr. Evans' office for an emergency appointment. The receptionist, hearing the urgency in his voice, scheduled him for a slot later that morning. As exhausted as he was, he daren't try going back to sleep, so he went to the kitchen in search of coffee. He slipped into a tatty old robe before staggering, bleary-eyed through the hallway and opening the kitchen door.

Will shuffled into the kitchen, barely able to keep his eyes open. He felt detached, as though he were drifting outside of himself. An eerie, suffocating stillness filled the air, wrapping around him like a thick fog. Even the familiar ticking of the clock sounded wrong—a hollow, distant echo, reverberating unnaturally. When he glanced at it, the hands were ticking backward, the seconds slipping away in reverse. A familiar sense of panic started getting through to his numb brain.

Disorientated, he gripped the edge of the sink, reaching for a glass with shaky hands. He turned on the tap, but the water wasn't right—like the clock, it too seemed to be flowing in reverse, defying gravity and moving up into the tap. Instead of filling the glass, it spilled over his hand, coiling up his wrist in tendrils of ice-cold liquid that twisted and tightened around his arm, pulsing with a life of its own. A biting chill radiated from it, seeping through his skin and into his veins.

He staggered back, his breath shallow and ragged as an inexplicable force began to shift the room. Walls wavered and stretched, bending as though he were looking through warped glass. Panic surged in his chest, and he turned to the door, but before he could even reach for it, a gust of wind ripped through the kitchen, roaring as if from nowhere. The force of it sucked the air from his lungs, and the glass fell from his hand, shattering and scattering in fragments that seemed to float, suspended in the churning air. The wind rose to a crescendo, tearing at his robe, howling with relentless intensity as his surroundings continued to twist and melt, transmuting.

The coiling water had wrapped itself around his entire body, binding him tightly in its freezing grip. The wind whipped around him, the roar reaching a deafening pitch, until suddenly the entire room seemed to implode, every surface pulled into a spiralling, elemental vortex. Everything he knew was swept away in a torrent of raw, swirling energy.

Then came the silence—absolute, suffocating, endless. The darkness pressed upon him, and he felt weightless, suspended in a void. Just as the terror threatened to overwhelm him, a voice pierced the stillness, a whisper so clear it seemed to emanate from within him.

"We need you, Will."

The words hung in the air, vibrating with a calm urgency. And then the energy returned, this time pulling from behind his navel. He was yanked forward, hurled through the darkness with an impossible speed, the distance stretching end-lessly—until, as suddenly as it began, the sensation ceased.

He found himself standing on solid ground, heart pound-ing. Before him stood the towering trees he had seen in his dreams, their ancient trunks stretching skyward, wreathed in thick, swirling fog. The cold mist clung to his skin, and he took a deep, trembling breath.

The forest seemed to close in around him, the trees tow-ering above like silent sentinels. His breaths came in shallow, rapid gasps as a cascade of panic overtook him, each breath fuelling the fire of his anxiety. His heart hammered painfully against his ribcage, a deafening rhythm that only heightened his disorientation. A tingling numbness crept up his arms and legs, prickling his fingertips and toes.

His rational mind tried to surface, reminding him this was an anxiety attack, that he just needed to breathe slowly and re-gain control. But his body betrayed him, locked in a battle be-tween fear and reason, and all he could do was brace himself against the dizzying rush of panic that swelled like an unstop-pable tide.

The panic surged through him, a tidal wave of fear and confusion that left him powerless to think or act. His hands trembled, his knees buckling. With a final, desperate gasp, Will collapsed to the ground, the world around him spinning before fading to black as he lost consciousness.

4

# Chapter four

Will awoke slowly, his hand instinctively reaching for his phone beside him. Instead of the familiar smooth surface, his fingers met something soft and damp. His eyes fluttered open, adjusting to the dim light filtering through the forest canopy above. Branches swayed gently in the breeze, their movements almost hypnotic, but the unfamiliar sight sent a spike of panic through him.

His breath quickened as confusion and panic set in, but he closed his eyes, forcing himself to inhale deeply and exhale slowly. Stay calm, he thought, repeating the mantra until the tightness in his chest began to ease. Sitting up, he winced at the dampness soaking through the back of his robe, the moss beneath him cold and spongy against his hands.

The world around him was shrouded in shadow, the forest dense and still, save for the occasional rustle of unseen creatures in the underbrush or the hooting of an owl somewhere high above.

He got to his feet, brushing moss and dirt from his clothes, and caught sight of a faint glow; a flickering light in the distance. It wasn't bright, just a soft, warm shimmer, but it stood out against the darkness. Despite the fear knotting his stomach, Will felt inexplicably drawn to it. Without fully understanding why, he began to move toward it, hesitantly, cautiously scanning all around him as his eyes slowly began adjusting to the darkness.

His thoughts churned as he walked. No matter how hard he tried, he couldn't piece together a rational explanation for what was happening. Fragmented memories from the morning flickered in his mind—the strange experience in his kitchen, his terrible nightmares—but they only deepened his confusion, leaving him questioning his own sanity.

The forest felt vast and unending, its silence amplifying the creeping panic in his thoughts. A chilling thought crept in: *What if I never find my way out?* He shook his head, pushing back against the wave of fear that threatened to overwhelm him, focussing instead on the light ahead.

As he drew closer, the glow brightened, revealing the outline of a small cottage tucked among the trees. Relief swept through him at the sight—*if there was a cottage, there had to be someone inside. Someone who could make a call, get help, and explain this madness.* The possibility filled him with a glimmer of hope, enough to delay the worst of his fears.

With renewed energy, Will quickened his pace, the thought of finally finding out where he was and how he had come to be here driving him forward. The light on the porch grew warmer and more inviting with each step.

Will hesitated as he stepped onto the creaky wooden porch, the sound breaking the forest's eerie stillness. He glanced behind him, half expecting to see the familiar outlines of houses or streetlights beyond the trees, but the forest remained dark and silent. The soft glow spilling from the cottage's windows was his only anchor in this disorientating night. Swallowing his nerves, he raised his hand and knocked.

The sound echoed unnaturally in the still air, making him flinch. He waited, breath held, unsure what he expected. The door creaked open, and a figure emerged from the golden light inside: an elderly woman with kind, piercing eyes and a serene smile that didn't quite fit the strange circumstances.

"Welcome, traveller," she said in a soothing voice. "You look weary. Come inside and rest."

Will froze, his mind racing. Traveller? What kind of greeting is that? He eyed her warily, noting her calmness despite the fact that a complete stranger was standing on her porch in the dead of night. The situation was bizarre, but the warm light spilling out from behind her and the inviting smell of something earthy and comforting made him pause.

"I... I'm sorry," he stammered, stepping back instinctively. "I think I'm lost. I must've somehow wandered too far in the woods and I don't know how to get home."

The woman tilted her head slightly, her smile deepening as though she found his confusion endearing. "You're not lost," she said gently. "You've simply found yourself in a place you weren't expecting."

Will's grew more uncomfortable at her cryptic response, but the cold air pressing against his back reminded him that his options were limited. With a nod of reluctant gratitude, he stepped inside, the warmth of the cottage immediately wrapping around him like a blanket.

The room was small but inviting, filled with the scents of herbs and woodsmoke. The furniture was rustic, the wooden table and mismatched chairs worn smooth by time. She gestured for him to sit, her movements graceful and unhurried.

As he sank into the chair, the woman shuffled to the hearth, humming softly to herself. She placed a kettle over the fire, her back to him, as if his sudden presence was the most natural thing in the world. That sense of calm unsettled him even more.

"Tea will be ready soon," she said without turning around.

Will shifted in his seat, glancing around the room. "Thank you," he managed, his voice shaking slightly from the adrenaline. His heart was still pounding, and his thoughts raced as he tried to process everything.

"You've had a rough journey, haven't you?" she said as she turned back to him, her kind eyes fixed on his.

He swallowed hard, unsure how to respond. "I... I don't even know how I got here," he admitted, his voice barely above a whisper.

Her gaze didn't waver. "The veil between worlds can be thin," she explained, her tone gentle, as though she were speaking to a frightened child. "Sometimes, those attuned to its shifting sands glimpse through. And when there is a need, destiny can reach across the veil to bring the right pieces together."

Will stared at her, the words barely making sense. "No, this is just... the woods, right? I'm just lost." His voice wavered, his certainty crumbling even as he tried to cling to it.

She didn't argue. Instead, she turned back to the hearth, retrieving the now-whistling kettle. "Perhaps," she said softly, pouring steaming water into two mismatched cups. From a small jar on a nearby shelf, she added a pinch of herbs to each cup, the fragrant aroma filling the air.

"This will help calm your nerves," she said, placing one of the cups in front of him.

Will hesitated, sniffing the tea cautiously. The scent was earthy and unfamiliar, but something about it felt comforting. He took a tentative sip, the warmth spreading through him like a gentle wave. His racing thoughts slowed, and the tension in his shoulders began to ease.

As the silence settled between them, Will studied her more closely. She seemed impossibly serene, her movements fluid and deliberate as she sipped her own tea. It unnerved him—her calmness, her cryptic words, her complete lack of surprise at his arrival.

"You're telling me I'm... in another world," he said finally, his voice much calmer now.

The old lady nodded, her gaze holding his as she set her cup down. "And whether you believe it or not, you were meant to be here, Will."

The sound of his name from her lips sent a shiver down his spine. He hadn't told her who he was.

"Who are you? And how do you know me?" Will asked, his voice rising slightly as a flicker of panic crept through the calm haze of the tea.

The woman's smile didn't waver. "My name is Elysande," she said, her tone as soothing as the tea itself. "I am a healer, of sorts. And I know you, Will, because your arrival here in Aruna was predestined. It is my task to set you on the right path."

Will's heart skipped a beat at the sound of the name. "Aruna?" he repeated, his disbelief sharp and immediate. "Did you just say Aruna?"

Elysande nodded, her eyes gleaming with quiet amusement. "Yes, this is Aruna."

He leaned back in his chair, his thoughts scrambling for purchase. "That's... impossible. Aruna isn't real. I made it up—years ago."

Elysande's smile deepened, her gaze steady and unflinching. "And yet," she said softly, "here you are."

Will absently stroked his beard, pulling a small twig from it as his mind raced. "So, suppose for a moment I believe this," he said, his tone edged with uncertainty. "That this isn't some... elaborate hallucination or proof I've finally lost it. Why me? Why am I here?"

Elysande's expression turned serious, her voice dropping to a more reverent tone. "Among those of my order, you are known as the Traveller. Yours is a rare connection to this world—one that transcends explanation. I do not claim to know why you were chosen, but you are bound to Aruna by destiny. What lies ahead is for you to uncover."

Will felt her words deep in his soul, as though unlocking something that had lain dormant, but that brief flicker was drowned out by his fear. "Look," he said, his voice cracking slightly. "I don't know anything about destiny, or paths, or... any of this. I just want to go home. Please, tell me how I can get back."

Elysande's expression softened, a glimmer of sympathy in her eyes. "To reach any destination, you must first follow the path," she said, her tone warm but firm. "The elves in Silverwood have long been keepers of wisdom. Their great library holds knowledge beyond imagining. Perhaps there, you will find the answers you seek."

Will stared at her, torn between scepticism and the odd sense of calm the tea had instilled in him. "How do I even find Silverwood?" he said in a resigned tone.

Elysande stood with the grace of someone far younger than she appeared, moving to a cabinet on the far side of the room. From within, she retrieved a weathered scroll, its edges frayed with age. She returned and placed it gently in his hands.

"This map will guide you," she said, her voice confident, filled with quiet certainty. "The path is never easy, Will. But it is yours to walk."

Will took the map, his hands trembling slightly. As he unrolled it, he recognised the familiar landmarks and place names from his childhood drawings, but this version was infinitely more detailed and though fear churned in his stomach, a faint spark of curiosity flickered alongside it. Elysande pointed out the location of Silverwood, suggesting a couple of routes he might take, before sitting back to allow him to study the map for a while. His fingers traced the familiar areas of the map as his eyes scanned over the beautiful illustrations that seemed to move, as though animated, until he came to an unfamiliar part. Looking up in confusion, he glanced at Elysande. "What is this?" he asked, pointing.

She looked at the place he pointed to on the map, a look of concern crossing her face. "Do not venture there," she said insistently, "The Shadowmoor has been claimed by the darkness."

"Shadowmoor?" will said, intrigued.

Elysande nodded solemnly. "The curse of Shadowmoor is a force that corrupts and consumes everything it touches. The land you pointed to was once a place of great beauty, but now it is shrouded in shadow."

Will looked back at the map, the darkened area now seeming even more ominous. Lifting his cup to his lips, he drained the last of his tea and then laid the map down on the table, his eyes growing heavy as the overwhelming events of the day left him weary.

Elysande seemed to notice that exhaustion in him and stood up, grabbing their empty cups. "Go now, rest and gather your strength. Tomorrow, your journey truly begins."

"Where can I rest?" he asked, confused.

Elysande gestured towards the bed in the corner. "Rest there, weary traveller," she said.

"But where will you sleep?" Will asked, his concern genuine despite his exhaustion.

Elysande smiled softly. "Do not worry about me. I have a place to rest. You have been through a lot; you need the sleep more than I do."

Too tired to argue, Will nodded gratefully and moved towards the bed. As he lay down, the comfort of the mattress and the soothing sounds of the forest beyond the window quickly began to lull him into a deeper state of relaxation.

Elysande snuffed out the candles around the room and moved to a small alcove, settling herself on a cushioned bench. "Sleep well, Will."

Will's eyes closed, his mind finally allowing itself to drift into the welcoming embrace of sleep. As he drifted off, he could hear the faint whispers of the forest beyond the window, almost as if it were speaking to him, soothing him, preparing him for the journey to come.

# Chapter five

When he awoke, Will found himself once again lying on the forest floor. Sunlight filtered through the canopy above, its warm, golden rays dancing across his face as the gentle morning breeze swayed the branches. He blinked against the soft light, stretching his limbs as the remnants of sleep faded. There was a moment of confusion—he distinctly remembered falling asleep in Elysande's cottage—but for some reason, the disorientation didn't trouble him.

For the first time in a long time, Will felt at peace. The usual weight of his anxiety was conspicuously absent, replaced by an unfamiliar but welcome calm. He sat up slowly, brushing a few stray leaves from his robe, and smiled at the sounds of chirping birds and rustling leaves. The forest around him was alive, vibrant, almost magical in its beauty.

As his eyes scanned the clearing, he realised there was no sign of the cottage. Where it had stood the night before, more trees now swayed gently, as if they'd always been there. He frowned slightly but found it hard to feel alarmed. Instead, he chuckled softly, shaking his head. "Figures," he muttered, his voice light with resignation.

His gaze went to a small leather satchel at his side, inside he found the map Elysande had given him the night before, along with a few other items he might need for his journey. He pulled out the map and smoothed it out, his fingers tracing the lines and markings they had discussed the night before.

Will stood, brushing dirt from his robe and taking a deep breath. The cool, fresh air filled his lungs, invigorating him. His finger hovered over the places Elysande had pointed out, his mind replaying her instructions.

Determined now, he rolled the map carefully and tucked it into the pocket of his robe. *If finding the Elves is my way home, then let's get started,* he thought to himself.

He journeyed in a generally northerly direction, absorbing the rich and vibrant energy of the natural world around him. The forest was alive with creatures he believed to be the stuff of myth and dreams; ethereal sprites that floated between the trees, their wings shimmering like stained glass— tiny, curious faeries that peeked out from behind leaves, and majestic unicorns that galloped gracefully between the trees in distant clearings, their horns glinting in the dappled sunlight. He caught sight of a shimmering creature—a silver-furred fox with iridescent eyes, watching him from behind a bush. Its gaze held his for a long, silent moment before it silently slipped away, vanishing as though it had never been there. At one point, he glimpsed a herd of deer-like creatures with translucent coats that glowed faintly, moving together in perfect harmony through the trees with a fluid grace, completely unfazed by his presence.

After walking for some time, Will's stomach rumbled, reminding him that he had not eaten since he'd been here. He found a quiet clearing and decided it was a good time to stop and rest. Sitting down on a soft patch of moss, he opened the satchel Elysande had given him to find a small, neatly wrapped bundle of bread and cheese, a flask of cool, refreshing water, and some dried fruits and nuts.

As he ate, he let his gaze wander around the clearing. Birds sang beautiful melodies, filled with hope and happiness, and a gentle breeze rustled the leaves. He sighed deeply as a sense of contentment washed over him. He wondered briefly if anyone back home had noticed him missing yet, but after imagining Mr Johnston had probably just sent him a written warning for absence and that the world had simply marched on without him, he leaned back against a tree and smiled.

He lingered in the clearing for a while, but eventually, rested and rejuvenated, he rose to his feet, ready to continue his journey. It was very unlike him, but he had no clear route in mind, instead trusting that the path would reveal itself to him in time.

As he walked, he wondered why he wasn't more disturbed by his abrupt change of circumstances. Was it because deep down he had yearned to be taken away from it all, to escape the monotony and despair that had defined his existence? Or maybe, he mused, it was because deep down he was still harbouring some belief that this was all an elaborate dream, conjured up by his new tablets and that he would soon wake to the familiar grating sound of his alarm.

As he trudged on, the forest seemed to change gradually around him. The trees grew closer together, their gnarled branches twisting into an impenetrable canopy that choked out the sunlight, making the path ahead hard to see in the dim light. The air turned cool and damp, carrying a profound silence, devoid of the sounds of wildlife that had so lifted his spirit earlier that morning.

A sudden rustling in the underbrush shattered the stillness. His heart leapt, and he instinctively reached down, grabbing a sturdy stick from the ground. Gripping it tightly, he scanned the shadows ahead, his breath shallow and rapid.

The rustling grew louder, closer. He raised the stick, ready for whatever was coming—when a figure burst through the trees, stumbling into view.

It was a young woman, her silver hair catching what little light filtered through the dense canopy. Her face was streaked with dirt, her wide, frightened eyes locking onto his. She ran toward him, her steps faltering before she collapsed at his feet.

"Please," she gasped, her voice trembling with desperation. "You have to help me—they're coming."

Will dropped the stick, his own fear momentarily eclipsed by the sight of her panic. He knelt beside her, hands hovering awkwardly before settling gently on her shoulders. "Hey, it's okay," he said, his voice softer than he expected. "Who's coming? What's happening?"

"The shadows," she whispered, her voice cracking. "They... they are attacking my home. Everyone..." Her words broke off into a choked sob, and she clutched at his arm as if anchoring herself to reality.

Will's chest tightened at the sight of her trembling, at the raw terror in her eyes. He didn't know who she was, didn't understand what she was talking about—but something about her vulnerability hit him like a blow to the heart.

"Alright," he said, his voice firmer now. "We can't stay here. Can you stand?"

She nodded shakily, though her legs wobbled as she tried to rise. Will caught her, his hands steadying her by the waist. Her touch sent an unexplainable warmth through him, but he pushed the feeling aside, focusing instead on her safety.

"Lean on me," he said, slipping an arm around her to support her. "We'll figure this out. Just stay with me."

Her gaze met his again, her silver hair falling across her face. "You... you don't even know what's out there," she murmured, her voice filled with gratitude.

"I don't need to," he replied, scanning the forest around them as his pulse quickened. "But whatever it is, you're not facing it alone."

For the first time, a flicker of something other than fear crossed her face—relief, or perhaps hope. She nodded, leaning against him as they began to move through the forest.

Will didn't know where he was going or what they would encounter, but one thing was clear: he would do everything in his power to protect her.

After stumbling along for a short time, Will determined that nothing was pursuing them. He decided to sit the woman down on a fallen tree so he could think for a moment. As she sat down, he noticed her wincing in pain.

"What's wrong with your leg?" he asked, his concern evident in his tone.

She rubbed at her ankle, grimacing. "I twisted it on an exposed tree root a while ago," she said, wincing again.

Will knelt beside her, carefully examining her ankle. It was swollen and starting to bruise. "We need to wrap this up and get you off it," he said. He rummaged around in his pack looking for a piece of cloth but found nothing. Instead he reached down and tore off a section of his robe, tearing it into strips to create a makeshift bandage. As he worked, he tried to keep the conversation light to distract her from the pain.

"What's your name?" he asked, glancing up at her.

"Lyra," she replied, her voice a little steadier now that they had stopped moving. "And you?"

"Will," he said, smiling reassuringly. "I know this is going to hurt, but we need to support your ankle."

Lyra nodded, biting her lip as Will wrapped the cloth around her ankle, securing it as best as he could. When he was done, he looked around, trying to get his bearings.

"We should find somewhere to rest," he said, helping Lyra to her feet again, and pulling out his map.

Silverwood was still some distance, and he knew they would never make it there by nightfall with Lyra injured. Studying the map intently he noticed the terrain markers indicated a ravine nearby.

"Let's make our way to this ravine for now and we can rest there for a while," he said, pointing to a spot on the map.

They moved slowly, Will supporting Lyra as they searched for the ravine. Eventually, they came across a small clearing with a rocky overhang on one side and a small stream cutting through it's centre. Will helped Lyra sit down, and they both took a moment to catch their breath.

"What are these shadows you mentioned?" Will asked eventually, breaking the silence.

Lyra's face darkened. "They're shadow wights, creatures of darkness from the Shadowmoor. They've been venturing north, trying to claim more lands. They've plagued our farm just outside Candleford, and I was on my way to Silverwood seek aid of the elves before Shadowmoor consumes our town."

Will went cold at the description. He didn't fully understand what was happening, but none of it sounded good.

As they rested in the clearing, Will found his gaze drifting to Lyra again. There was something about her—something familiar. Her silver hair caught the light as it tumbled down her back, and the warmth in her eyes reminded him of someone he couldn't quite shake from his thoughts. It wasn't just her gentle nature or her quiet beauty; it was the way she moved, the way her presence seemed to fill the space.

Alyssa. The thought hit him unexpectedly, and his chest tightened. The resemblance was uncanny, and yet... different. He shook his head, trying to dismiss the thought, but not before Lyra noticed his lingering stare.

She gave him a small, curious smile, her voice soft as she asked, "What? I look a mess don't I?"

Will startled, his cheeks heating. "No! No, it's not that," he said quickly, stumbling over his words. "You just—" He stopped, hesitating before finally settling on, "You remind me of someone."

Her expression softened, the hint of a smile still on her lips. "Someone important?"

"Not really," he said, a little too quickly. He cleared his throat, forcing a casual tone. "Just someone I know."

Lyra tilted her head, studying him for a moment before letting it go. She didn't press, but her silence left him squirming. Desperate for a change in subject, he blurted out, "What about you? Do you have family?"

Her smile grew wistful as she looked toward the trees. "Yes, I live on my family's farm," she said, her voice brightening. "It's just a little place, but it's home. My father built the house himself, and we've been tending the land for generations."

Will felt a pang of guilt for asking, though he wasn't entirely sure why. "Sounds nice," he said, his voice softer now.

"It is," Lyra replied, her gaze distant as if picturing it. "I know it's not much compared to somewhere like Silverwood, but it's home."

Lyra's expression grew serious. "My family has lived on our farm for generations. We've always managed to get by, even during hard times. But recently, things have changed. The shadow wights started appearing more and more frequently, blighting the land and making it barren. They don't normally stray far from Shadowmoor except during the hunger."

"The hunger?" Will asked, confused.

"Times when the Shadowmoor expands and consumes more of the surrounding area."

Will realised the implications of that immediately. If Lyra's home town lay just outside Shadowmoor then they were in great danger.

They rested in the clearing until the next day, the forest seeming to cradle them in its quiet, protective embrace. When they awoke, Lyra tested her ankle, finding it much better.

Will noticed her improved condition and smiled. "Looks like you're ready to move. I was heading to Silverwood too, maybe we should travel together for a while?"

Lyra nodded gratefully. "Thank you, Will. I would like that."

As they walked through the woods, Will found himself talking more than he had in years. The conversation flowed effortlessly, and Lyra's curious questions pulled him further out of his shell.

"My world's nothing like this," he said, gesturing to the towering trees around them. "We've got cities made of glass and steel, and people travel in machines—cars, we call them—that don't need horses or anything to move. Everything's fast-paced, like everyone's in a constant rush to get somewhere or do something."

Lyra glanced at him, her silver hair catching the dappled light. "Machines that move without beasts? That sounds... odd. Do you have magical creatures there too?"

Will laughed softly. "Not exactly. We've got stories about dragons, fairies, and stuff like that, but no one actually believes in them past childhood. Magic's just... a thing for books and movies."

Lyra frowned, her expression thoughtful. "That sounds lonely," she said simply, her voice tinged with quiet sympathy.

Will paused, her words catching him off guard. "It can be," he admitted. "I guess that's why I spent so much time daydreaming about places like this when I was younger. It felt better than reality, you know?"

Lyra nodded slowly, a small smile playing on her lips. "Maybe you were always meant to come here. Sounds like your world wasn't quite right for you."

Will chuckled, though her words struck a deeper chord than he expected. "Maybe," he said softly, glancing at her.

"Back home, I work in an office. It's just a tiny cubicle in this big, gray building. It's boring, and... well, soul-crushing, honestly."

Lyra tilted her head, clearly trying to picture it. "That's terrible! Why would anyone want to live like that?"

"Most of us don't want to," Will admitted, kicking a loose rock along the path. "But we get stuck in it, you know? It's this endless loop—wake up, go to work, go home, sleep, repeat. It's hard to break out when you've got bills to pay."

Lyra's brow furrowed. "It sounds like a curse," she said, her voice quiet but intense.

Will blinked, surprised by the word. "A curse? I've never thought of it that way, but yeah... I guess it kind of is. A curse we put on ourselves." He shook his head. "It wasn't always like that though. And I like to think that one day things can get better."

Lyra smiled warmly, her eyes bright with hope. "Maybe one day the curse can be lifted," she said.

"Maybe," Will echoed, smiling back.

As they walked, Will marvelled at how easily he was opening up to this stranger from a world he still didn't fully understand. Her kindness, her quiet strength—all drew him in. It had been so long since he'd felt this kind of connection that he wasn't sure he even remembered how to make one. Yet here he was, talking like they'd known each other forever.

As they trudged through the forest, Will stopped abruptly, his stomach sinking as his eyes landed on a gnarled tree with twisted branches that bore an uncanny resemblance to the face of Steve from work. He groaned, running a hand down his face. "No way."

Lyra paused beside him, her silver hair glinting in the soft light. "What's wrong?"

Will pointed at the tree, his voice tight with frustration. "That tree. I swear we've passed it before. Look at the bark—it's got that weird, face-like shape. We're walking in circles."

Lyra frowned, looking around. "You're sure? I thought we were on the right track."

"I thought we were too," Will said, shaking his head. "But we've definitely passed that tree about an hour ago."

Lyra placed a comforting hand on his arm. "We'll figure it out," she said gently.

After a moment of contemplation, Lyra reached into her satchel and pulled out a small, leather-bound book. "This is my grandmother's journal," she explained, her tone brightening slightly. "She used to visit the elves in Silverwood all the time. Maybe there's something in here that can help us."

Will watched as she carefully flipped through the pages, the faded lettering and detailed drawings catching the light. She paused on a page featuring a rough sketch of the forest and began to read aloud.

"'Beware the hidden paths of the enchanted woods,'" she said, her voice soft, "'for they will seek to waylay you unless you make a sacrifice to the old spirits.'"

Will leaned in, his brow creasing with concern. "Sacrifice? What does that even mean?"

Lyra scanned further. "'You must bequeath something of great value to the spirits, and with a pure heart, declare your intentions. But be warned,'" she continued, her voice growing more serious, "'if the spirits deem you worthy, the hidden path will reveal itself, but another test awaits before you can pass through to the homeland of the elves.'"

Will sighed, leaning back on the log. "Great. Where am I supposed to find something valuable?"

"Valuable doesn't have to be expensive," Lyra said thoughtfully. "It probably means something that holds some importance to you."

Will frowned, thinking for a moment. Finally, he reached up to a simple silver chain around his neck and the pendant that rested there—a tiny compass, its metal dulled with age. "This," he said quietly, holding it up. "It was my grandfather's. He gave it to me before he passed. It's... important to me."

Lyra nodded, her expression encouraging. "That's perfect. Try placing it at the base of the tree. Just... say something respectful."

Will stood, clutching the pendant tightly. He approached the tree, his heart pounding. Kneeling at its base, he placed the compass gently on the mossy ground. Feeling a bit foolish, he cleared his throat and spoke. "Spirits of the forest," he began, his voice cracking slightly. "We mean no harm. We seek guidance and safe passage to Silverwood. Please help us find our way."

For a moment, nothing happened. Will glanced back at Lyra, doubt flickering across his face. But before he could speak, a low, resonant creak rumbled through the clearing.

The gnarled bark at the tree's base began to twist and peel, its tightly woven fibres loosening as if unravelling. The tree groaned and shifted, its movements impossibly fluid, until a dark opening took shape at its core.

Will stepped back, his breath catching as the darkness within the tree began to glow softly. A breathtaking woodland revealed itself beyond the threshold, bathed in the golden light of a late afternoon sun. Rays of warm light filtered through a vibrant canopy of straw-coloured leaves, casting dappled patterns onto the soft moss and scattered foliage below.

Lyra's face lit up, her earlier worry replaced by excitement. "That's it!" she exclaimed, tucking the journal back into her satchel and quickly stepping toward the opening.

Will remained rooted in place for a moment, staring at the enchanted scene. His eyes wide with wonder as the enormity of what had just happened settled over him. "This world is... something else," he muttered under his breath before following Lyra into the glowing path ahead.

They continued their journey down the new path, but Will was less chatty as he tried to remain vigilant. He had not expected the forest to try and thwart them, and it made him realise how little he knew about this land, and that made him feel uneasy.

Lyra, sensing his discomfort, offered a reassuring smile. "The forest can be tricky," she said softly. "But we're not far from Silverwood now."

Will nodded, but he remained on high alert. They continued on in that uneasy silence for some time, making their way north as the sun continued it's steady march across the sky.

Later that afternoon, as they approached the area near Silverwood, clouds rolled in from the east, their darkened edges clawing at the sky as the light faded unnaturally fast. A heavy stillness settled over the trees, and the air grew thicker, clinging to Will's skin.

As they approached a wide clearing, Will slowed his steps. The clearing was unnervingly quiet, the usual rustling of leaves and chirping of birds eerily absent. His chest tightened as he scanned the area, sensing an unseen presence closing in around them.

"Something's not right," he muttered, his voice barely audible.

Lyra's hand brushed his arm, her grip tightening as her gaze darted nervously around the clearing. Before she could respond, a dense fog began to seep in from the forest edges, rolling across the ground like a living thing. It rose quickly, obscuring everything at eye level, but the ground was completely swallowed, an impenetrable white sea that seemed to pulse with a life of its own.

"This isn't natural," Lyra whispered, her voice trembling.

Will reached out instinctively, gripping her hand as if the contact could anchor them both. They moved cautiously forward, the fog dampening their footsteps until even that small sound disappeared.

Then came the whispers.

At first, they were faint, just on the edge of hearing—indistinct murmurs that seemed to rise and fall with the fog's slow movements. But as they pressed deeper into the clearing, the whispers grew louder, clearer. Words began to take shape, insidious and cruel, each one carrying a weight that burrowed into Will's mind.

"Do you hear that?" he asked, his voice tight.

Lyra nodded, her wide eyes betraying the fear she was trying desperately to hide. "Yes," she whispered.

The voices became more insistent, each whisper filled with malice.

Will's breath came quicker as a cold sweat broke out across his brow. The fog pressed closer, thick and stifling—like breathing underwater, until it felt like it was crawling into his lungs. He could see Lyra trembling beside him, her grip on his hand tightening as the whispers grew to an almost deafening crescendo.

Then, the ground beneath them began to writhe.

Will's eyes snapped downward just as dark vines began to slither out of the fog, moving like serpents across the forest floor. One brushed against Lyra's leg, cold and slick, and she screamed, stumbling backward.

"Will!" she cried, her voice breaking with panic as the vines coiled around her ankles, dragging her down.

Will dropped to his knees, grabbing at the vines and trying to pull her free. The tendrils were unnaturally strong, their surface pulsating as if alive. As he struggled, more vines shot out, wrapping around his legs and yanking him down into the suffocating fog.

The whispers became a cacophony, filling their ears with venomous doubt and overwhelming fear. Will felt the world spinning, his vision blurring as the fog thickened, swallowing them both whole. The last thing he heard before the darkness claimed him was Lyra's voice calling his name, fractured and desperate.

Will suddenly found himself stood in a dark landscape, devoid of life, the ground beneath his feet darkened to a sickly gray, the earth cracked and barren, like broken shards of ancient bone. Jagged rocks clawed up from the ground, twisted into shapes that defied reason, while crooked, skeletal trees loomed with brittle branches that reached toward him like hungry hands. A chill clung to the air, cutting through him with an almost unnatural cold, biting past skin and sinking deep into his bones.

Above him, a perpetual storm raged, thunder splitting the sky with a jagged crack as flashes of dark lightning illuminated the swirling clouds. The winds howled, carrying with them a cacophony of whispers that grew louder, until Will could hear them distinctly; cruel voices taunting him, relentless in their accusations.

"Failure. Weak." The words slithered into his ears, filling his head like poison seeming to latch on to each of his deepest insecurities and nurture them into full bloom.

Will stumbled, clutching his head, his heart racing as he tried to drown out the voices. They wormed into his mind, each one a knife twisting deeper, punctuated by the crashing thunder from the raging skies above.

"You act like you have it all together, but it's all a lie, isn't it? You're nothing."

A figure appeared through the shadows, a distorted reflection of himself, eyes hollow and filled with a darkness that seemed to suck in every last shred of light. Its face twisted into a mocking grin as it spoke, Will's own voice, yet drenched in disdain. "You will always fail, just give up now and save yourself the trouble of failing like you always do."

His breathing quickened, his vision blurred, and his heart pounded with a fevered intensity, threatening to consume him. He fell to his knees, struggling to resist the despair clawing its way through his mind. A weight settled on his chest, an unbearable heaviness that made it nearly impossible to draw breath. Panic seized him, his rational mind detaching and drifting towards the abyss, leaving him drowning in the pain he'd tried so hard to bury.

It was too much, too relentless. His heart felt like it might give out, his mind teetering on the edge, ready to shatter under the pressure. A scream built in his throat, raw and desperate, until he felt as though his very soul would splinter.

Meanwhile, Lyra found herself standing in a barren field under a blood-red sky. Shadow wights, like the ones that plagued her family's farm, blinked in and out if sight around her, first it was just a few, but they began multiplying as they slowly started to advanced toward her. She tried to run, but her legs felt like lead, and as the wights closed in she looked down to see the vines wrapped around her legs, tethering her in place.

"Help me!" she screamed, tears rolling down her face in terror, but her voice was swallowed by the deafening silence of the nightmare.

From where he stood, facing his own personal nightmare, Will heard Lyra's scream. In that moment, his overwhelming urge to protect her obliterated any feelings of self-doubt or worthlessness. The illusion that had trapped him shattered into a thousand fragments, like a huge obsidian mirror falling in pieces to the ground around him.

Will found himself in Lyra's nightmare. A barren field stretched endlessly beneath a blood-red sky, the air thick and heavy. Ahead of him, Lyra stood frozen, her legs rooted to the ground as shadow wights closed in from all sides. Their malevolent forms flickered and shifted, their glowing eyes fixed on her with a hunger that made Will's blood run cold.

"Lyra!" he shouted, his voice cutting through the unnatural stillness.

Her head jerked in his direction, her face pale with terror. "Will..." she whispered, her voice trembling, barely audible over the sound of the wights' raspy breaths.

Will didn't hesitate. Fuelled by adrenaline and an unshakable need to protect her, he sprinted toward her. The shadow wights turned their glowing eyes on him, their forms rippling with malice as they shifted focus. But Will didn't stop.

As he reached her, the wights began to close in, their movements slow but relentless. Fear clawed at him, but another sensation burned even brighter—a surge of strength rising within him, unfamiliar and untamed. It built rapidly, like a dam ready to burst, and he felt as if it might consume him.

"Get back!" he shouted, his voice carrying a force he didn't recognise.

He concentrated, his entire being focused on pushing back the encroaching darkness. The power inside him surged, spilling outward in an invisible wave. The shadow wights recoiled, their forms unravelling into tendrils of smoke as that wave washed over them.

Lyra stared at him, her wide eyes brimming with disbelief. "Will... how did you—"

"No time," he cut her off, his gaze darting to the remaining wights, which had begun to regroup and move toward them. He took her hand, gripping it firmly. "Listen to me. This isn't real—it's all an illusion. I think we're still in the forest."

Confusion flickering across her face, but she nodded.

"You just have to see through it. Focus on the truth—the clearing, the trees. This place isn't real." he said.

Lyra took a shaky breath, her hand tightening around his. She closed her eyes, her expression tense as she fought to steady her thoughts. Will's presence beside her, the warmth of his hand, anchored her. Slowly, the field began to waver, the blood-red sky dimming as the nightmare dissolved.

The barren landscape gave way to the forest clearing, the fog lifting in tendrils that evaporated into nothingness. The whispers faded, replaced by the gentle rustle of leaves and the distant calls of birds.

They stood in silence, both breathing heavily as the last remnants of the illusion vanished. Lyra still clung to Will's hand, her fingers trembling slightly.

"Thank you," she whispered, her voice quivering as tears pooled in her eyes.

Will nodded, his chest rising and falling as he struggled to catch his breath. "Are you okay?" he asked softly.

Lyra managed a faint smile, though her tears spilled over. "I think so," she said, her voice thick with emotion.

Will looked away, trembling slightly as the adrenaline began to fade. He couldn't explain what had just happened—how he had pushed back the shadow wights or banished the nightmare—but for now, it didn't matter. They were safe.

# Chapter six

As the sun dipped low in the sky, Will and Lyra pressed onward through the woods. The air grew cooler, tinged with the faint scent of blooming flowers. When the first shining spires of Silverwood appeared above the treetops, their steps faltered, both of them caught in awe.

The spires glimmered in the golden hues of sunset, their surfaces reflecting the deep oranges and purples of the sky. They seemed to stretch effortlessly toward the heavens, casting a soft, shimmering glow over the surrounding forest. Lyra's face lit up at the sight, and for the first time since their journey began, Will felt like he was one step closer to getting home.

They quickened their pace, the anticipation of reaching Silverwood lending strength to their weary legs. The forest began to change around them; the trees grew taller, their trunks broad and ancient, their leaves shimmering with a vibrant green that seemed almost otherworldly. Birdsong filled the air, their melodies weaving into the faint hum of a city alive with energy yet at peace with its surroundings.

Finally, they emerged into a vast glade. Before them lay Silverwood, a city that seemed less built and more grown in harmony with the forest itself. Elegant towers rose above the treetops, their delicate structures entwined with living branches. Winding pathways meandered through lush gardens, and waterfalls tumbled from rocky ledges into crystal-clear pools below. Elves moved gracefully along the paths, their serene expressions and flowing robes radiating timeless wisdom.

As they approached the gates, two elven guards stepped forward, their armour glinting faintly in the fading light.

"Welcome to Silverwood," one of them said, his melodic voice carrying respectful, but commanding tone. "What brings you to our city?"

Lyra stepped forward, with a nervous smile. "I am here to seek an audience with the council. My home is in great peril, and I seek the aid of your people."

The guards exchanged a glance, their expressions unreadable, before one nodded. "Follow us," he said.

As they turned to lead the way, two more guards seemed to materialise from the shadows of a nearby guardhouse, taking their place at the gate as if they had been there all along.

Will and Lyra followed closely, their awe growing with every step. The city unfolded before them like a living masterpiece. They crossed arched bridges over streams so clear they seemed to glow, the water reflecting the last light of day. Exotic plants bloomed in perfectly tended gardens, their colours vivid and almost unreal. The streets were lined with graceful archways, their surfaces carved with designs so intricate and precise they seemed to defy possibility.

Will's eyes darted from one marvel to the next, his mouth slightly agape. "This place..." he murmured, his voice barely above a whisper.

Lyra glanced at him with a faint smile. "It's more beautiful than I imagined."

Eventually, they reached a grand hall at the heart of the city. The guards gestured for them to enter, and they stepped inside, finding themselves in a spacious chamber filled with natural light. At the far end of the hall, a group of elven elders sat in a semi-circle, their expressions preoccupied and aloof.

One of the elders, a tall elf with silver hair and piercing blue eyes, rose to greet them. "I am Elenion, head of the council. We have been expecting you."

Lyra glanced at Will in surprise, but Elenion continued before they could speak. "The trees have whispered of your journey. We have been following your progress and witnessing your trials as you moved through the woods."

Will felt a surge of anger rise within him. "If you've been watching us all this time, why didn't you help us?" he demanded, his voice shaking as he tried to suppress his anger.

Elenion's expression remained calm and composed. "The forest needed to know if you were worthy," he explained. "Only those who prove themselves are allowed safe passage to Silverwood. If we had intervened, the woods would have simply increased the difficulty of the challenges."

Will clenched his fists, struggling to contain his anger as he tried to find fault with Elenion's logic, but looking into Elenion's serene eyes, he saw no malice or indifference—only a deep understanding.

Elenion smiled gently. "There is much to discuss, but first, you must rest and regain your strength. Tomorrow, we will begin our preparations to aid the people of Candleford."

Will and Lyra were led to opulent chambers, their eyes widening at the sheer elegance and beauty of the rooms. The walls were adorned with intricate tapestries depicting scenes from elven history, and the furniture was crafted from rich, dark wood, polished to a gleaming finish. Two soft, inviting beds were covered with silken sheets, and a large, ornate mirror reflected their astonished expressions.

After a chance to clean themselves and refresh, they found elven attire laid out for them. Will's outfit consisted of a deep green tunic with silver embroidery, paired with comfortable, well-tailored trousers and boots. He felt a little out of place in his new attire, but slightly less so than walking all over the place in his pyjamas. Lyra's dress was a flowing gown of rich blue, intricately embroidered with delicate patterns of leaves and flowers in a silver thread. Alongside the clothing was a written invitation to an evening of celebration.

As they dressed, Will marvelled at the craftsmanship of the elven clothing. It felt almost magical against his skin, light and comfortable and softer than any fabric he had ever felt in his life. Lyra looked radiant in her gown, her silver hair complementing the delicate fabric perfectly.

When they were ready, an elf arrived to escort them to the banquet. The hall they entered was grand, filled with the soft glow of hundreds of candles and the sound of gentle, melodic music, the likes of which Will had never heard before. The elves present were dressed in their finest, each one embodying grace and elegance. As Will and Lyra were led to their seats they could barely contain their nerves, both feeling quite out of place.

The banquet began with an ancient elven tradition; a ceremonial toast. "To the forest and our ancestors," Elenion intoned, his voice resonant and clear, filling the room. "May their wisdom guide us, and their strength support us in our times of need." he stood at the head of the table, raising a crystal goblet filled with a shimmering, golden liquid.

Everyone raised their goblets in unison, repeating the words, and took a sip of the golden liquid. It tasted like sunlight and honey, warming Will from the inside out.

As the evening progressed, the formality gave way to a more relaxed atmosphere. Elven musicians played enchanting tunes on harps and flutes, and dancers moved gracefully across the floor. The food was exquisite; platters of fruits and vegetables, freshly baked bread, and succulent meats, all prepared with herbs and spices that were unfamiliar but created complex flavours that made Will wish he would never get full.

Will and Lyra found themselves seated near Elenion, who engaged them in conversation about their journey and the challenges they had faced. Despite the formal setting, the elven leader's genuine interest and kind demeanour helped to put them at ease.

Lyra tried on a few occasions to steer the conversation around to Candleford, but each time Elenion would expertly deflect, refusing to discuss it.

"The issue is complex and needs the full council's approval. It's best we discuss it tomorrow." he replied to her on one such occasion, quickly changing the subject. "What brings you to Silverwood anyway Will?"

Will went on to describe the strange journey that had brought him here and how his search for a way home had brought him to seek the great library of Silverwood. Elenion was thoroughly intrigued by Will's tale, asking a great many questions and promising to show Will to the library the following day after the council meeting.

As Will took in the dazzling sight of the grand hall, he felt quite overwhelmed. The air was alive with music and laughter, the clinking of glasses, and the soft rustle of elegant elven attire. Dozens of joyful faces moved through the golden light of the lanterns, the festivities in full swing. Will swirled the golden liquid in his glass, the warmth of it making him pleasantly light-headed.

But his smile faded when a flicker of movement caught his eye. His gaze was drawn upward to the gallery balcony near the top of the hall. In the shadows stood a pale-faced elf with jet-black hair, his expression cold and severe as he looked down upon the celebration below.

The elf's presence was like a blemish on an otherwise perfect scene. Where others exuded joy and camaraderie, this figure radiated something far darker—disdain, perhaps even contempt.

He nudged Lyra gently, gesturing subtly toward the balcony. "Do you see that?" he murmured.

Lyra followed his gaze, her brow furrowing. "I see him," she said, her voice quiet but sharp. "He doesn't exactly look like he's here to celebrate, does he?"

As they watched, the elf's cold, calculating eyes swept the room. Then, with unsettling precision, his gaze locked onto Will's.

The connection was brief but intense, like a jolt of ice down Will's spine. The elf's eyes held a sharp intelligence, but also a simmering anger that seemed to pierce right through him. Before Will could react, the figure turned and melted into the shadows, vanishing as if he'd never been there.

"Who was that?" Will asked, his voice low and tense as he turned to Elenion, who was seated nearby.

Elenion followed Will's gaze, his expression darkening as he caught sight of the fading figure. "That is Valenor," he said quietly, his tone heavy with regret. "He is one of our kin, but he walks a dangerous path."

Will looked at him inquisitively. "Dangerous how?"

Elenion sighed, his gaze lingering on the empty balcony. "Valenor has grown discontent with our ways and the council's measured approach to combating the darkness. He believes in a more... aggressive strategy, one that many of us fear could cost countless lives. He has no patience for tradition or the old ways that guide us. To him, they are relics—an anchor weighing us down when we should act swiftly and decisively."

Lyra's expression mirrored Will's discomfort as she asked, "And the council? Do they trust him?"

Elenion hesitated before answering. "They tolerate him, but trust?" He shook his head, his voice heavy. "Trust has long been strained. Valenor walks his own path."

Will's mind swirled with questions, his discomfort sharpening into something closer to suspicion. Whatever Valenor's intentions, Will couldn't shake the feeling that this wouldn't be their last encounter.

Eventually, the festivities began to wind down. Elenion stood once more to address the room. "Tonight, we have celebrated courage and hope. Tomorrow, we begin anew. Rest well, for the days ahead will require all our strength and unity."

As Will lay down in bed that night, he replayed the evening's events in his mind and smiled. He had been thoroughly charmed by the ancient traditions of the proud Elven people, but his mind kept wandering back to the strange moment when he had spotted Valenor.

"Do you think we can trust them?" Lyra asked quietly from her bed.

Will turned to look at her. "I think so," he said. "Elenion seems genuine." He paused briefly whilst he thought about her question a moment longer. "I guess we'll see what tomorrow brings."

The next day soon after sun up, Will and Lyra were escorted to the council, the air already buzzing with respectful debate as they entered. Elenion and the other council members were already seated, their expressions unreadable as they welcomed Will and Lyra.

"Please, take your seats," Elenion said, gesturing to the chairs prepared for them. "We have much to discuss."

As they settled in, Elenion began to address the council, beginning the proceedings by outlining the situation. "Shadowmoor has long been a dark wound on South Aruna. Once a mere blight kept at bay by our wards and the strength of our people, but we've all seen the curse changing, growing in strength in recent years. Shadowmoor has undergone hunger cycles in ever increasing frequency, devouring land and life at an alarming rate. Once, it claimed a few acres each decade; now, it advances each season. If left unchecked, the curse will soon consume all of South Aruna, and beyond. We can no longer ignore this threat—it must be confronted directly, or our lands will be lost to shadow."

The debate in the council hall stretched on for hours, voices rising and falling as strategies were proposed, dissected, and ultimately dismissed. Will and Lyra listened intently, contributing where they could, but mostly absorbing the weight of the crisis. The complexity of the solutions—and their limitations—was becoming painfully clear, as was the council's reserved, often painfully conservative approach.

Finally, a consensus was reached: a small contingent of elven mages would be sent to Candleford to strengthen the failing wall of warding. The council members seemed satisfied, their murmured words of agreement giving way to a quiet hum of self-congratulation.

Will was still processing the decision when the chamber doors flew open with a deafening crash. The sound reverberated through the hall, silencing the room and turning every head toward the intruder.

Valenor strode in, his pale face flushed with anger, his dark eyes burning with intensity. The tension in the room was palpable, the atmosphere shifting as his presence disrupted the council's carefully maintained decorum.

"Valenor!" Elenion exclaimed, rising to his feet. "What is the meaning of this intrusion?"

Valenor ignored him, his gaze sweeping the chamber before locking onto the council members. "You sit here, as always, unwilling to do what must be done," he began, his voice sharp and cutting. "While you dither and debate, the hollow, lost to the curse of Shadowmoor continue to suffer!"

Elenion opened his mouth to respond, but Valenor pressed on, his tone rising with each word. "How can you be so blind? So uncaring? Fortifying a crumbling wall won't save us. It won't save them. Every moment you delay, more lives are swallowed by the darkness!"

The council members exchanged uneasy glances, but it was Taegen who stepped forward, his demeanour calm despite Valenor's fury. "Valenor, we have heard your concerns. But we must respect the will of the council."

"The will of the council is a farce," Valenor spat, his contempt palpable. "You talk endlessly, but where is your action? You cling to your traditions and your fear, leaving others to suffer the consequences of your cowardice!"

Will watched, anxiety churning in his gut. He couldn't deny the raw power of Valenor's words, even as they unsettled him. He exchanged a glance with Lyra before stepping forward hesitantly. "I understand your frustration, Valenor," he said cautiously. "But it seems like the council is trying to do all they can."

Valenor turned his piercing gaze on Will, the anger in his eyes flickering briefly into something else—pleading, almost desperate. "I wouldn't expect an outsider to understand," he said quietly, his words deliberate. "None of you do. The solution is right in front of them, and they're too weak to act."

"What solution?" Will asked, his curiosity overriding his discomfort.

Valenor turned back to the council, his voice rising again. "My proposal! We send a force directly into Shadowmoor. We strike at its heart and break the darkness once and for all. But no," he sneered, "that's too bold, too risky for you."

Elenion's expression darkened, his tone firm but regretful. "We've considered your plan, Valenor. It's too dangerous. The risk to our people is unacceptable."

Valenor's fists clenched, his body trembling with barely contained fury. "You call it dangerous, but I call it necessary! If no one else will fight, I will go alone. I will not stand by while more lives are lost."

Taegen stepped forward again, his voice even but resolute. "Valenor, your passion is admirable, but we cannot act recklessly. If we lose our warriors and mages in Shadowmoor, we leave the rest of Aruna defenceless. The wall of warding will hold for now."

Valenor let out a bitter laugh, his voice shaking with rage. "For now? For how long? Until it crumbles completely, and the darkness engulfs us all?" He swept his gaze across the room, his eyes blazing. "You sit in your gilded halls, congratulating yourselves while people die! How many more lives must be sacrificed before you act?"

Elenion's expression softened, sorrow replacing his earlier sternness. "We must protect what we can, Valenor. We cannot gamble everything on a single strike."

Valenor's shoulders sagged, a mixture of frustration and despair etched across his face. His gaze swept the room once more, landing on Will. For a brief moment, his eyes softened, a silent plea for understanding passing between them.

Before Will could find the words to respond, Valenor turned abruptly and stormed out of the chamber. The heavy doors slammed shut behind him, the echo lingering in the silence that followed.

Will exchanged a look with Lyra, both of them unsettled by the confrontation. The weight of Valenor's desperation hung in the air, leaving Will with a gnawing sense that the issue was far from resolved.

Will and Lyra watched for the remainder of the meeting as the council proceeded exactly as they were prior to Valenor's outburst, but as the voices of the assembled council continued on, Will's mind returned to Valenor and the fiery passion with which he had addressed the council. It was clear that he cared, and wanted to help the ones suffering, but Will wondered how reckless his proposal must have been to have been refused by the council.

# Chapter seven

Back in their room later that afternoon, Will sat on the edge of the bed, his elbows resting on his knees as he stared at the floor, lost in thought. Lyra sat nearby, watching him carefully. The sombre mood of the council's meeting still lingered between them, heavy and unspoken. Finally, Will exhaled deeply and broke the silence.

"I've been thinking about what Valenor said in the council chamber," he began, his tone measured but tense. "I can't shake the feeling that there's more going on than they're letting on. Maybe he knows something the council doesn't want us to know."

Lyra nodded slowly, her expression thoughtful. "You could be right, but he's... unpredictable. Reckless, even."

Will looked up, meeting her gaze. "I know. He's a loose cannon, but he's passionate, and that kind of anger doesn't come from nowhere. If there's even a chance he has answers—answers that could help us protect your home—we can't just ignore it."

Lyra bit her lip, considering his words. "It's risky, Will," she said after a pause. "If the council catches wind of us poking around, they might see us as untrustworthy. Or worse."

"I get that," Will said, his voice firm. "But we didn't come all this way to sit on our hands. Your family's at risk, and so is everyone in Candleford. We can't afford to just wait and hope the council has it under control—because right now, it doesn't feel like they do."

Lyra sighed, rubbing her temples. "Alright," she said reluctantly. "Let's find him and see what he knows. But we have to be careful. If we're caught sneaking around, we might lose what trust we've built with the council."

Will nodded, standing and stretching out his shoulders. "Agreed. We'll keep it low-key. No unnecessary risks."

The two of them moved through the halls of Silverwood, their pace casual and their expressions calm, doing their best to appear unremarkable. They exchanged polite nods and smiles with passing elves, blending into the serene hum of activity around them.

Occasionally, they paused to ask discreet questions about Valenor's whereabouts, framing their inquiries with curiosity rather than suspicion. The name "Valenor" drew mixed reactions—some responses were hesitant, others tinged with disdain or concern.

Eventually, their quiet probing led them to the library, a place spoken of with quiet reverence by those they'd questioned. The massive doors loomed ahead, intricately carved with twisting vines and symbols that seemed to hum faintly with magic.

Will glanced at Lyra. "Ready?"

She gave him a small, resolute nod. "Let's hope he's as willing to talk as he was to yell."

As they passed through the massive, ornate, carved wooden doors that led to the library, Will and Lyra were immediately struck by its grandeur. The room was vast, with high vaulted ceilings supported by intricately carved wooden beams. Rows upon rows of beautifully crafted wooden shelves stretched out before them, each one meticulously finished with stunning brass rails and finials that gleamed in the soft afternoon light pouring in through the leaded glass windows that stretched from floor to ceiling.

The unmistakable vellichor of ancient parchment filled their nostrils, a comforting and almost magical scent that spoke of untold knowledge and centuries of accumulated wisdom. The books and scrolls themselves varied in size and colour, their spines bearing the wear of countless generations. Some volumes were bound in rich, dark leather with gilded lettering, while others were more modestly covered, their contents no less valuable.

As they wandered deeper into the library, their footsteps softened by the plush rugs that lined the wooden floors, they found Valenor at a large, ornate table near the back of the room. He was surrounded by stacks of books and scrolls, his attention focused on a particularly ancient tome laid out before him.

Will and Lyra approached cautiously, their footsteps quiet. Valenor sat hunched over the massive leather-bound book, his dark hair falling into his face as he scrawled notes onto a piece of parchment. He seemed entirely absorbed in his work, the warm afternoon sunlight from the window to his side casting sharp shadows across his sharp features.

Will glanced at Lyra, and she gave a small nod, silently encouraging him to speak. Clearing his throat softly, Will announced their presence.

Valenor's head snapped up, his piercing gaze narrowing as he recognised them. "What do you want?" he asked, his tone sharp but not outright hostile.

Will stepped closer, trying to keep his posture non-threatening. "We need to talk," he said evenly. "We think you might have answers—about Shadowmoor and the darkness spreading through the land."

Valenor leaned back in his chair, his expression guarded. His dark eyes flicked between Will and Lyra, suspicion clouding his features. "And why, exactly, should I trust either of you? You're outsiders to this council and to this city. What's to stop me from assuming you've come to spy for the elders?"

"Because we're trying to help," Lyra interjected, her voice rising with urgency. "We heard what you said in the council chamber. We... we think there's more to this than the council is letting on, and we want to understand the truth."

Valenor studied her intently, his gaze flickering with something unreadable. For a long, uncomfortable moment, the tension hung thick in the air. Finally, his posture relaxed slightly, though his expression remained sceptical. He closed the book in front of him with a soft thud and folded his arms.

"What do you know of the curse?" he asked, his tone probing. "And how it began?"

Lyra and Will exchanged a glance, both of them shaking their heads. "It was before my time," Lyra admitted. "And Will... well, he's not from Aruna."

A faint flicker of amusement crossed Valenor's face before he sighed and leaned forward. "Then listen carefully," he said, his voice low. "The curse is Malakar's creation—a blight he cast upon this land. He is no mere sorcerer; he is cunning, ruthless, and consumed by a hunger to claim all of Aruna. His magic doesn't just destroy; it corrupts. Everything it touches is twisted into a reflection of his darkness."

Will leaned closer, Valenor holding his full attention as the devastating effects of the curse were explained.

"The souls of those trapped within Shadowmoor still exist, but they are no longer what they were. They are hollow now, stripped of their humanity and driven by malevolence. Even the land itself is tainted. Trees that once stood tall and noble now grasp and strangle anything they can reach. Flowers that once bloomed with vibrant beauty now drip poison, luring the unwary to their deaths."

Lyra shivered, her hands clasping the edge of the table as she tried to process his words. "But the council's wards," she began hesitantly, "they're holding it back, aren't they?"

Valenor's expression hardened, his gaze piercing. "The council's wards are a patchwork solution, a bandage over a wound that continues to fester. They hold back only the weakest tendrils of Malakar's power. The truth is, they're delaying the inevitable, not stopping it."

Lyra frowned, her voice cracking slightly as she asked, "But why? Why would the council hide this? My people have always held the elves in the highest regard."

Valenor's jaw tightened. "Because the truth would break them," he said bitterly. "Imagine the panic, the chaos, if the people of Aruna knew that their protectors—the great and wise elves—cannot hold the darkness back forever. They cling to the illusion of control because it's the only thing that keeps fear from spreading like wildfire."

Lyra recoiled slightly, her breath catching as the weight of his words hit her like a blow to the stomach. Will saw her expression falter, a maelstrom of emotions playing across her face—disbelief, sorrow, and anger warring for dominance.

Valenor turned his gaze to Will, his tone colder now. "So tell me, outsider. Do you still think the council has it under control?"

Will hesitated, feeling the pull of both sides of the argument. He met Valenor's gaze, searching for the cracks in his hostility. "No," he said finally, his voice low. "But that's why we're here—to figure out what to do about it."

Valenor studied him for a long moment, his expression unreadable, before he gave a curt nod. "Then perhaps you're not as blind as others," he muttered. "But be warned—the truth is not a burden easily borne."

Will stepped closer, his gaze flicking toward the scattered texts Valenor was poring over. Their worn pages and faded ink seemed ancient, steeped in history. "So," Will began cautiously, "you believe there's a way to break this curse?"

Valenor's eyes gleamed with that same fervent intensity he had displayed in the council chamber. He nodded, his voice measured as he continued. "There are texts—obscure fragments of prophecies. They speak of a hero who will rise to confront the darkness, a force strong enough to challenge Malakar's curse. The council fears the risk of direct action, worrying it will provoke him into moving faster, maybe targetting the elven homeland next. But doing nothing only delays the inevitable."

Will studied him carefully. There was no doubting Valenor's passion, but beneath it, he sensed something else—a restraint, a hesitation that didn't quite match his fiery words.

Lyra, still absorbing the weight of his revelations, nodded slowly. "How can we help?"

Valenor closed the ancient tome with a resounding thud and turned to them, his expression grim. "There is a place deep within Shadowmoor where the darkness is strongest. According to old accounts, Malakar constructed a conduit there—a dark altar that serves as the foundation of his enchantment. If we destroy it, we might sever the curse at its source and, just maybe, free those lost souls who have been trapped."

The thought of freeing those lost souls sent a shiver of excitement through Will, a powerful sense of being on the right path, though he couldn't shake the sense of apprehension gnawing at him. "And if we're wrong?" he asked quietly. "What happens then?"

Valenor's jaw tightened. "If we're wrong, then the curse will remain. But if we do nothing, we already know the outcome."

Will hesitated, before pulling out the map still tucked into his satchel, and unrolling it on the table. "Show me," he said.

Valenor studied the map, his finger pausing at a point that seemed to pulse with dark energy, even on paper. "There," he said firmly, jabbing the heart of Shadowmoor.

Will leaned over the map, considering the terrain and the distance they would need to traverse. After a moment, he asked the more pressing question. "And how exactly are we supposed to destroy this altar?"

Valenor took a long breath before answering. "The altar is said to be protected by powerful seals. The prophecies speak of three ancient relics—artifacts imbued with magic capable of breaking those seals when brought together. The Sword of Light, the Amulet of Purity, and the Stone of Wisdom."

Lyra's eyes narrowed as she absorbed the information. "Then the relics are our first priority. Where can they be found?"

Valenor pointed to three different locations marked on the map. "The Sword of Light lies in the Sunfire Peaks to the south of Stonehelm—a realm of blistering heat and treacherous climbs. It's guarded by an ancient creature of fire and wrath."

Lyra shuddered slightly but pressed on. "And the Stone of Wisdom?"

Valenor's finger moved to another location, this time west of Stonehelm. "In the Whispering Caverns. Many have tried to retrieve it and failed, driven mad by the whispers of restless spirits that plague that place."

Will nodded, feeling less and less sure of their chances of success by the moment. "That's two. What about the Amulet of Purity?"

For the first time, hesitation flickered across Valenor's face. His confident tone faltered slightly as he said, "That one is… complicated. The Amulet is said to rest in the depths of Crystal Lake to the west. But its exact location is unknown, lost to the shimmering waters."

Will caught the flicker of doubt in Valenor's eyes and felt his own uncertainty deepen. Was there more Valenor wasn't saying? Or was his confidence in the plan starting to waver? Either way, Will's own reservations about the scope of this undertaking were growing.

Still, what choice did he have? He didn't have a better plan, and the stakes were far too high to do nothing. Folding the map, he tucked it away and met Valenor's gaze.

"I don't know how much help I'll be," he admitted, his voice quieter now. "But count me in."

Valenor nodded, his expression unreadable. Lyra looked between them, her own doubt visible, but she gave a firm nod.

As the tension settled over the room in the silence that followed Valenor's explanation, Will's mind churned. The plan might be their best chance to stop Malakar, but doubt nagged at him. Could Valenor be trusted? And more importantly—what chance of success did they have where so many others had failed?

Valenor's expression softened slightly. "Thank you, both of you. We'll need to gather supplies and prepare for the journey. Meet me at the south gate at dawn. From there, we head south-west into dwarven territory."

Feeling good about their plan, Will and Lyra made their way back towards their room. As they approached their door, the sight of armed guards waiting outside brought them to an abrupt halt. The elves stood in silence, their ornate armour catching the torchlight.

Will's heart began to pound. "What's going on?" he asked, glancing at Lyra, who looked equally alarmed.

One of the guards, an imposing elf with a stern demeanour, stepped forward. "By order of the council, you are to be detained. You will accompany us to the holding chambers immediately."

Lyra's eyes widened. "Detained? On what grounds?"

The guard's expression didn't waver. "You are suspected of conspiring with Lord Valenor to undermine the council's authority. Your conversations in the library were observed."

Will's mind raced. "We weren't conspiring," he said quickly. "We're only trying to help!"

"You'll have the opportunity to explain yourselves before the council," the guard replied curtly. "For now, you will come with us."

Realising there was no other choice, Will and Lyra exchanged a worried glance before allowing themselves to be escorted away.

The journey through the grand halls of Silverwood had a much more foreboding mood than their earlier walks. The once welcoming marble corridors now felt cold and hostile.

They were led down to the lower levels, where dimly lit holding chambers awaited. Heavy wooden doors creaked open, and Will and Lyra were separated, each placed in a narrow cell.

The silence was stifling as Will sat on the cold stone bench, his thoughts a whirlwind of confusion and anger. He had come to Aruna to help, not to end up imprisoned by those who claimed to protect the land.

Before the day was out, Will and Lyra were escorted to the council chamber, their steps echoing ominously in the vast, gilded hall. The room, normally a place of grace and harmony, was heavy with tension as the council members took their seats, their gazes sharp and unforgiving.

Elenion, seated at the head of the council, regarded them with a measured expression. At his side sat Taegen, whose calm demeanour masked the weight of his influence, and on the far end of the table, Lord Maedryn, a staunch conservative whose disdain for Valenor's radicalism was barely concealed.

Valenor stood to one side of the chamber, apart from both the council and Will and Lyra. His expression was unreadable, but his eyes glimmered with quiet defiance.

Elenion began, his voice carrying an even tone, but with an edge that hinted at deeper calculations. "Will and Lyra," he said, addressing them directly, "you stand accused of conspiring with Lord Valenor to undermine this council's authority. Your actions in seeking out private counsel with him were observed, and your intentions, while perhaps noble, have created significant concern."

Lyra stepped forward, her voice steady despite the intimidating weight of the council's collective gaze. "We never intended to conspire against you," she said. "We were just looking for answers—answers that might help us understand the curse and how to stop it. If anything, it feels as though the council has been withholding the truth."

A dissatisfied murmur rippled through the chamber, subtle but telling. Elenion raised a hand to silence it, his eyes narrowing slightly. "And yet, by defying our edicts, you have raised difficult questions about trust and loyalty. Trust is the foundation of this council, and a breach of this nature cannot be ignored."

Will stepped forward now, emboldened by Lyra's words. "With respect, your trust cannot rest on silence and secrecy. The darkness doesn't wait while we debate. If Valenor's plan has merit, isn't it worth at least hearing him out?"

At this, Maedryn leaned forward, his voice sharp. "Hearing him out? We have heard Valenor's plan on countless occasions. It is reckless—foolish, even. You have no understanding of the delicacy required to manage the balance of power in Aruna. This is why outsiders have no place meddling in our affairs."

Valenor's lips curled into a bitter smile, but he remained silent as Elenion raised a hand again, this time directing his gaze at Maedryn. "Enough, Lord Maedryn," he said, his tone firm. "The accusations against these two are serious, but so too are the consequences of our inaction. You speak of balance, but how long can we maintain that balance while the darkness continues to spread?"

Taegen inclined his head slightly, a silent signal of agreement. Maedryn's mouth pressed into a thin line, but he did not respond.

Elenion stood, his movements slow and deliberate as he addressed the chamber. "For years, this council has debated Valenor's proposals. Each time, we have come to the same conclusion: the risks outweigh the potential rewards. And yet..." He let the words hang for a moment, his eyes sweeping the room, "the darkness has not abated. The wards weaken, the lands fall, and still we cling to our caution. Perhaps it is time to reconsider."

The council erupted into murmurs, some members nodding thoughtfully while others whispered their dissent. Maedryn shot to his feet, his voice cutting through the noise. "This is nothing more than a veiled attempt to legitimise Valenor's recklessness. You cannot expect us to endorse such folly!"

Elenion turned to Maedryn, his expression calm but his eyes flashing with barely veiled contempt. "And I am not asking for endorsement, Lord Maedryn. I am merely suggesting an opportunity—a chance for these individuals to act outside of this council's authority. A deniable action that does not compromise us should they fail."

The chamber fell silent as the significance of his words settled. Elenion continued, his tone measured as he sensed the shifting sentiment. "Will and Lyra have already chosen to follow Valenor. Let them take this quest upon themselves. If they succeed, they will vindicate Valenor's plan and demonstrate the wisdom of our oversight. And if they fail…" He paused, his voice dropping. "Then they bear the consequences alone."

Maedryn's face darkened, but he did not interrupt again. Around the table, council members exchanged glances, their expressions betraying the delicate calculus of their positions.

Elenion scanned the assembled nobles around the council chamber, waiting for the right moment before lifting his voice once again. "Let us vote. Who votes to approve this expedition, on the basis of an unsanctioned quest?"

One by one, hands began to rise. Some were hesitant, others resolute. Taegen and those who voted with him were amongst the first to vote in favour. Maedryn remained stubborn, his arms resolutely folded across his chest, but enough of his followers voted in favour to swing the vote.

Elenion's gaze swept the room with satisfaction before he spoke again. "It is settled. Lord Valenor, Will, and Lyra will proceed. This council's reputation remains intact, its hands clean."

The tension eased, though an undercurrent of uncertainty lingered. Valenor approached Will and Lyra, his smirk laced with irony. "Well, it seems we've been granted the council's begrudging approval. Shall we make the most of it?"

Will exchanged a glance with Lyra, anxiety knotting in his stomach. They had earned the council's leave, but the cost of that victory was written in the calculating glint in Elenion's eyes. This was no triumph—it was a gamble, one with stakes higher than he'd imagined.

"So," Valenor continued, his voice low, "dawn it is, then."

8

# Chapter eight

The companions met as the city of Silverwood was bathed in the soft pastel hues of sunrise. The crisp air carried the scent of morning dew, and the distant chirping of birds lent a serene energy to the start of their journey. As they left the towering spires behind, Will glanced back one last time, the city fading into the distance as they followed the winding forest paths south-west toward the dwarven kingdom.

Their conversation was light at first, an easy rhythm forming between them as they walked. They each shared stories of their past, slowly getting to know one another, and as they opened up more, they found that conversation flowed easily.

By mid-morning, they paused in a shaded glade to rest and share a meal of bread, dried fruits, and cheese. The conversation shifted naturally to the task ahead.

Valenor leaned in. "Our first stop must be Stonehelm. Before we can hope to traverse the dwarven realm, we need King Thranin's blessing. Entering his lands without permission would be a grave insult."

Lyra nodded, though her expression darkened. "The dwarves have changed in recent years. They've grown... distant. Suspicious, even. They rarely deal with other races anymore, let alone grant an audience to outsiders."

Valenor sighed, his gaze thoughtful. "You're right. Their isolationism has grown deeper, but the old bonds between our people remain. The elves and the dwarves have always shared mutual respect, if not outright friendship. Thranin may be reluctant, but once he understands the importance of our mission, I believe he'll grant us passage."

Will frowned, his brows knitting. "And if he doesn't? What's the plan then?"

For the first time, Valenor hesitated, taking a deep breath. His usually confident expression faltered, and he glanced away, considering his words carefully. "Let's hope it doesn't come to that," he said finally.

The uncertainty in his voice wasn't lost on Will, who exchanged a glance with Lyra. Neither of them said anything, but the unspoken worry hung between them.

After a moment, Valenor straightened, his composure returning as he packed up the remains of their meal. "Best not linger too long," he said briskly. "We have much ground to cover if we want to reach Stonehelm, and the day won't wait for us."

They journeyed on for the remainder of the day, making camp in a clearing long after dark, and rising again before the sun, eager to make their destination.

By noon, the path had started to turn rocky and uneven beneath their feet. Trees gave way to sparse patches of grass clinging stubbornly to the rocky soil, and the trail inclined sharply, winding upward through jagged foothills. The air grew thinner, cooler, carrying the crisp, mineral scent of the mountains.

Mid-afternoon found them standing at the base of an imposing cliff, where the path abruptly vanished into a sheer wall of stone stretching skyward. Valenor tilted his head back, scanning the vertical expanse with the practised eye of someone who had made such climbs many times before. "The trail doesn't get any easier from here," he said quietly, his tone more matter-of-fact than reassuring.

Will stared at the cliff face, his stomach knotting as vertigo crept in at just the thought of the climb. The jagged rock seemed to loom over him, indifferent to his rising fear. Memories surfaced unbidden—his friend Reece jokingly badgering him to take up roofing work, Will laughing it off but never admitting the truth; he was deathly terrified of heights.

"This is impossible," he muttered under his breath, his voice barely audible over the whisper of the wind.

Lyra noticed his hesitation, stepping closer to him. "You can do this, Will," she said, her voice soft, soothing. "Just take it one step at a time. We'll be right here with you."

Valenor, already scouting the first handholds, glanced over his shoulder. "Once you begin the climb, don't look down. Just focus on the next grip and the one after that. The rest will take care of itself."

Easy for you to say, Will thought, his pulse pounding in his ears.

He wanted to protest, to suggest another route—any route that didn't involve scaling this towering wall—but Lyra was already tying her satchel securely, and Valenor was reaching for the first handhold. Will swallowed hard, his throat dry, and forced himself to step forward.

The first few feet were manageable, the rock cool and rough under his palms. But as they ascended, the reality of the climb set in. Every slip of his foot sent loose stones tumbling down the cliff, the sound echoing ominously in the quiet. His arms began to ache, his breaths coming shallow and fast as panic clawed at the edges of his mind.

"Don't stop," Valenor called from above, his voice calm but firm. "You're doing fine."

Will clenched his jaw, his knuckles white as he gripped the rock. Fine wasn't the word he'd use. His thoughts swirled, vivid memories of every excuse he'd ever made to avoid high places flashing through his mind. The ladder he refused to climb, the rooftop parties he'd declined—all moments when his fear had dictated his choices.

Not this time, he told himself. Not here.

He took a shaky breath, forcing himself to focus on the rock directly in front of him. One handhold. Then another. Then another. He shut out the open void below him, the scrape of stone, the ache in his muscles—all of it reduced to the singular task of moving upward.

Lyra's voice came softly from below, her soothing presence grounding him. "You're almost there, Will. Just a little farther."

Finally, after what felt like an eternity, his hand found the edge of the cliff. Valenor reached down, gripping Will's wrist and hauling him up the last few feet. Will collapsed onto the flat ground, his chest heaving as he stared up at the sky, his arms trembling with exertion.

The view from the top was breathtaking. Jagged peaks stretched endlessly into the horizon, bathed in golden sunlight. The air was fresh, filling his lungs with a clarity he hadn't felt in years.

Lyra pulled herself over the edge moments later, her face flushed but triumphant. She glanced at Will, her smile wide and genuine. "See? You did it."

Will gave a weak laugh, his fear slowly ebbing away, giving way to pride. "I did, didn't I?"

Valenor stood a few steps ahead, already scanning the next part of their path. "We're not done yet," he said, his tone pointed.

Will sat up, his legs still shaking but his resolve stronger now. He was physically exhausted but he felt so euphoric at having overcome such a deep seated fear. He still didn't like heights, but he would never let it rule him again. "Let's keep moving," he said, pushing himself to his feet.

As the sun dipped below the horizon, casting the land in deep purples and golds, the great gates of Stonehelm came into view. Set seamlessly into the mountainside, the gates rose hundreds of feet high, their colossal size awe-inspiring. On either side, towering stone columns were carved directly into the rock, their surfaces etched with intricate depictions of ancient dwarven conquests. Warriors frozen in mid-battle seemed to leap from the stone, their axes raised, their faces fierce. Will found himself captivated by the craftsmanship, each detail so precise it seemed almost alive.

Flickering torches lined the gates, their warm light dancing over the carvings and casting long shadows across the rugged terrain. The combination of artistry and raw strength spoke of a civilisation that valued both beauty and power.

At the base of the gates, two dwarven guards stood sentinel, their stout frames clad in ornate armour, axes resting at their sides but ready in an instant. Their sharp eyes assessed the approaching trio with practised ease of trained professionals.

Valenor stepped forward, speaking in the deep, resonant tones of the dwarven tongue. His words were measured and respectful, and though Will couldn't understand them, the sincerity in Valenor's voice was evident. The guards exchanged a glance, their expressions softening slightly, before one nodded and motioned for them to follow.

The gates groaned as they opened, vibrating through the ground beneath their feet. As they stepped inside, Will's breath caught.

The heart of Stonehelm unfolded before them in a vast, awe-inspiring cavern, its size defying anything Will could have imagined. The cavern walls rose so high they seemed to disappear into darkness, and along their surfaces, tiers had been carved, forming a sprawling city built into the rock itself.

Each tier was alive with activity. Rows of living quarters stretched outward, their stone facades illuminated by glowing lanterns. Market squares bustled with dwarves haggling over goods, their deep voices echoing through the cavern. On another level, work areas hummed with industry. Blacksmiths hammered molten metal into shape, the rhythmic clang of hammers on anvils reverberating like a heartbeat that echoed through the cavern. Sparks flew in dazzling bursts as blades were honed against spinning stones, casting fleeting flashes of brilliance into the smoky air.

The scent of molten metal and forge fires filled the space, warm and heavy, mingling with the earthy aroma of stone and minerals. Massive forges glowed red-hot, their roaring flames sending waves of heat across the cavern. Dwarves worked with precision and care, their tools extensions of their hands, their movements quick and efficient.

Will craned his neck, his gaze drawn upward to an ornate stone bridge spanning the cavern, connecting two tiers. Beyond it, a grand hall carved from the mountain itself loomed, its entrance flanked by towering statues of ancient dwarven kings. Statues that seemed to watch over their people, guardians of a legacy carved into the very bones of the earth.

"This is incredible," Will murmured, his voice barely audible over the cacophony of life around them.

Lyra, walking beside him, nodded, her expression mirroring the awe and reverence that Will felt. "I've heard stories," she said softly, "but nothing could have prepared me for this."

Valenor glanced back at them, his lips curving into a faint smile. "Stonehelm does have the ability to take one's breath away. But remember, we're not here as spectators. We need King Thranin's blessing to continue."

The reminder brought Will back to the task at hand, though he couldn't help but glance around once more as they were led deeper into the city. The overwhelming scale and tireless industry of Stonehelm left an indelible mark on him.

The guards led Will, Lyra, and Valenor through the towering statues flanking the grand hall and into King Thranin's throne room. The cavernous space had an air of majesty, the walls lined with intricate carvings of ancient dwarven battles. At its heart, King Thranin sat on a throne hewn from the mountain itself, its form so perfect it seemed almost like a natural formation.

Thranin was stout and solid, his long, braided beard falling down over his ample frame. His sharp eyes, gleaming beneath bushy brows, scanned the trio as they entered, his expression unreadable. Around him stood a group of heavily armed dwarves, their hands resting on the hilts of axes and hammers, each watching the newcomers with suspicion.

Valenor stepped forward and bowed deeply, his movements respectful. "King Thranin, we seek your aid. Our mission is to end the curse of Shadowmoor and restore peace to Aruna. To do so, we must pass through Sunfire Peaks. We humbly request your blessing and support."

Thranin leaned forward slightly, his gaze narrowing. "A noble quest," he said, his gravelly voice filling the chamber. "The dwarves of Stonehelm have long defended against the darkness. We know its cost, its pain, its unyielding hunger."

For a moment, Will thought the king might actually sympathise, but then Thranin's tone shifted. A cunning glint lit his eyes, and he stroked his beard as though savouring an unspoken thought. "And yet," he continued, his voice slowing to a deliberate drawl, "I cannot simply grant such a favour without consideration. The needs of my people must always come first."

Will stiffened, sensing the trap before it was fully sprung. Thranin let the silence stretch, the weight of expectant silence almost unbearable.

"Unless?" Lyra ventured, her voice wary.

Thranin glanced theatrically to the side, his fingers tapping the armrest of his throne as though in deep contemplation. "Unless," he said finally, his gaze snapping back to them, "you were willing to assist us with a certain… predicament."

Will exchanged a glance with Lyra, his stomach tightening. Valenor's jaw clenched, but his tone remained measured. "What sort of predicament, your majesty?"

Thranin's lips curled into a faint smile, and he cast a quick glance at his courtiers. The performance was for their benefit as much as for his own. "A Rock Wyrm," he declared, his voice carrying a theatrical weight. "A monstrous beast that has made its lair in our lower caverns. Vicious and cunning, its hide as tough as the iron it devours. It has slaughtered my miners, terrorized my people, and brought my operations to a standstill."

Will felt a shiver crawl down his spine as he imagined the creature lurking in the dark, its eyes gleaming and its maw dripping with malice. "And you want us to kill it?" he asked, trying to keep his voice steady.

Thranin nodded solemnly, though the gleam in his eyes betrayed his conceited satisfaction. "Precisely. My warriors have refused the task—too costly, they say, too dangerous.

And perhaps they are right. But you..." He let his gaze drift over the three of them, assessing and calculating. "You are outsiders. Capable. Desperate enough to take risks."

Valenor's eyes narrowed. "And if we succeed?"

Thranin leaned back, his expression softening just enough to feign magnanimity. "Should you slay the beast, you will have my blessing to pass through Sunfire Peaks. More than that—I will see to it you are provisioned with what you need for the journey ahead. Do this, and you will have the goodwill of the dwarves at your back."

Will's stomach twisted as he realised how neatly they had been cornered. To refuse would mean losing the chance to move forward, leaving their mission stranded. To accept was to risk death at the hands of a creature even Thranin's warriors feared.

"And if we fail?" Will asked quietly.

Thranin's expression hardened, and his voice echoed ominously through the stone hall. "Then your bones will lie forgotten in the dark, and no one will mourn your passing."

The silence that followed was heavy. Thranin's shrewd gaze darted between them, a predator savouring his advantage. Finally, Will nodded, his voice resolute despite the feelings of frustration gnawing at him. "We will do it," he said. "Will you provide a guide though? Someone who knows the beast, that we may learn of it as we descend to it's lair? And perhaps some weapons?"

Thranin nodded, a pleased expression on his face. "I applaud your wisdom and bravery. I will assign Lolmig, one of our most seasoned warriors to aid you. He knows the tunnels well and can guide you to the right place."

He gestured to one of the guards, who immediately left the room. Moments later, a stout dwarf with a rugged, weathered face and a thick, silvery beard entered. He wore practical, sturdy clothing and carried a large war-hammer slung across his back. Despite his years, his eyes were sharp and he carried himself with a strength and confidence borne of his years of experience.

"This is Lolmig," Thranin said. "He will be your guide."

Lolmig stepped forward and bowed slightly, greeting each of them in a gruff voice, but wasting no more words before leading them from the throne room.

Thranin's lips curled into a sly smile as he dismissed them, his final words following them as they left his chamber. "Go well, brave souls. And may the Rock Wyrm's bones pave your path to glory."

Lolmig led the trio through the labyrinth of caverns of Stonehelm, the air thick with the rhythmic clanging of hammers and the warm glow of forge fires. Dwarves bustled about, their faces set with determination as they worked on weapons, armour, and trinkets, the very essence of their craft alive in every corner of the city.

As they neared the armoury, Lolmig glanced back at the group, a mischievous glint in his eye. "So, our esteemed king has managed to rope the lot of you into this little suicide mission, has he?" His tone was casual, but the grin that followed softened his words into something almost friendly.

Valenor raised an eyebrow, the corner of his mouth turning up slightly. "Not exactly a glowing endorsement. Are you trying to scare us off?"

Lolmig chuckled, a rich sound that echoed down the stone corridors. "Scare you off? Oh no, laddie. If you've agreed to take on a Rock Wyrm, you're either braver or dumber than most. Probably both. I'm just here to make sure you don't get yourselves killed... too quickly."

Will couldn't help but smile at the dwarf's blunt humour, though the mention of the creature sent a chill through him. "So, what's the story with this wyrm?" he asked, his voice tinged with apprehension.

Lolmig's grin faded, replaced by a more thoughtful expression. "Rock Wyrms are rare beasts," he began, his tone quieter now. "They're ancient creatures, formed of stone and shadow. They usually stick to the deepest parts of the mountain, far below where even we dwarves venture. They've no need to bother us, and we've no need to bother them. That's how it's always been—until now."

Lyra frowned. "What changed?"

Lolmig sighed, glancing around as if to ensure no prying ears. "Greed changed it. Our dear King Thranin, in his infinite wisdom, decided he wanted a rare gem found only in the lowest caverns. Beautiful thing, they say—gleams like a star and worth a fortune. Trouble is, those lower tunnels have always been sacred ground for creatures like the wyrm. It was against the advice of every dwarf lord, every elder worth their salt, but Thranin wouldn't listen."

Valenor crossed his arms, his expression hardening. "And now the wyrm's lashing out because you disturbed its territory."

"Aye," Lolmig said, nodding grimly. "It's tearing through the lower tunnels, attacking anyone it comes across. Good dwarves—miners, smiths—gone in an instant. Thranin's gamble has cost us dearly, but of course, it's the people who pay the price, not him."

Will exchanged a glance with Lyra, the weight of Lolmig's words settling over him. "And he expects us to clean up his mess," he muttered.

Lolmig gave him a sharp look, his gaze softening as he studied the three of them. "I won't lie to you—it's a fool's errand. But fools or not, you've got guts to take it on. That counts for something in my book."

There was a brief silence as the companions absorbed his words. Then, with a sudden clap of his hands, Lolmig grinned again. "Well, if you're set on doing this, you'll need more than guts. Let's get you kitted out properly. No sense going after a wyrm without a bit of dwarven steel to keep you breathing."

"Thank you, Lolmig," Lyra said, her voice earnest.

"Don't thank me yet, lass," he replied, leading them into the armoury. "Let's just hope you make it back in one piece so I don't have to say 'I told you so.'"

As they stepped into the armoury, the group found themselves warming to Lolmig. Beneath his sarcasm and cynicism was a genuine concern for their survival.

The three of them fanned out, browsing the weapons and armour on display there. Valenor gravitated toward a sleek, elegant bow with intricate engravings and a quiver of arrows tipped with gleaming metal. Will selected a sturdy sword, its blade perfectly balanced. Lyra, drawn to the agility and precision offered by smaller weapons, chose a pair of small daggers, their blades honed to a razor's edge.

Once fully armed they felt better prepared and descended deeper into the lower tunnels, the air growing cooler and the light dimmer.

"The rock wyrm is a massive, serpent-like creature," Lolmig began explaining as they walked. "Its scales are as hard as stone, and it can burrow through rock with ease. It's attracted to the vibrations of mining, which is why it's been attacking our workers. It has a weak spot, though—just behind its head, where the scales are thinner."

"Any advice on how to approach it?" Will asked, trying to absorb as much information as possible.

"Carefully" Lolmig replied with a chuckle. "But seriously, the wyrm senses movement and sound through the ground. We need to tread carefully and slowly. We've lost a lot of workers to this beast."

The descent into the mountain was suffocating. Each step deeper into the labyrinth of tunnels brought colder air and a growing sense of apprehension. The narrow shafts creaked under the strain of ancient wood braces, and the occasional drip of water echoed like distant footsteps, keeping Will's nerves on edge. The scent of damp earth and metallic tang of ore filled the air, heavy and cloying.

Will tried to focus on the path ahead, but his thoughts churned with dread. The stories Lolmig had told of the Rock

Wyrm played over and over in his mind—a beast of stone and shadow, a creature that hunted in the dark. His hand tightened on the hilt of his sword, slick with sweat despite the chill.

"Steady, lad," Lolmig whispered as they reached the cavern. The dwarf's calm demeanour betrayed a hint of tension in his eyes. "We're close."

The cavern Lolmig led them to was immense, its walls glimmering faintly with embedded crystals that cast an eerie, pale light. Broken mining equipment lay scattered across the floor, twisted and half-buried in rubble. The smell of decay was faint but unmistakable.

"This is it," Lolmig murmured, raising a hand to signal silence.

The companions spread out, moving cautiously across the cavern. Will's pulse thundered in his ears, drowning out the faint dripping of water and the occasional creak of rock settling. His every step seemed too loud, every breath a betrayal of their presence.

Then, a low rumble began to build, growing into a trembling vibration beneath their feet. The sound was primal, as if the mountain itself were groaning in protest. From the shadows of a massive tunnel, the wyrm emerged.

The creature was enormous, its body undulating as it moved with terrifying grace. Its scales gleamed like polished granite, and its glowing eyes scanned the cavern, casting a sickly light over the walls.

Will froze, his breath catching in his throat as he gripped his sword tighter. The wyrm swung its head back and forth, tasting the air, its jagged maw opening slightly to release a low, guttural growl.

Valenor motioned for them to hold position, drawing an arrow from his quiver and nocking it silently. But the faint creak of his bowstring was enough. The wyrm's head snapped toward him, its glowing eyes narrowing as it let out a deafening roar.

With terrifying speed, its massive tail lashed out, striking Valenor and sending him hurtling into the cavern wall. The impact knocked the wind from him, as he crumpled to the ground, clutching his side.

"Valenor!" Lyra shouted, but her cry only drew the wyrm's attention.

Will's heart raced as he saw the beast coil, preparing to strike. Without thinking, he sprinted forward, raising his sword. "Over here!" he yelled, his voice echoing through the cavern.

The wyrm swung its head toward him, jaws snapping. Will barely managed to dive to the side, rolling across the rocky floor as its teeth clamped shut on empty air.

Lolmig seized the opportunity, letting out a roar as he charged. His war hammer struck the wyrm's side with a resounding crash, the force of the blow making the creature recoil.

"Keep it distracted!" Valenor shouted, staggering to his feet with Lyra's help. "I'll get behind it!"

Lyra nodded, drawing her dagger and darting forward to join the fray. Together, she and Lolmig flanked the beast, forcing it to divide its attention.

Will dodged another snap of the wyrm's jaws, his muscles burning with exertion as he swung his sword at its neck. The blade glanced off the hardened scales, but the strike bought him precious seconds.

The companions moved in a deadly rhythm—Will's feints, Lolmig's crushing strikes, and Lyra's swift, precise cuts keeping the wyrm off balance. All the while, Valenor crept silently around the perimeter, bow in hand, his eyes fixed on the beast's vulnerable spot.

Finally, Valenor found his opening. He drew his bowstring back, aiming for the base of the wyrm's skull where the scales were thinnest. With a deep breath, he released.

The arrow flew true, piercing the wyrm's hide. The beast reared back, letting out a blood-curdling screech as it thrashed wildly. Dust and debris rained down from the cavern ceiling, and the ground shook violently.

"Nice shot!" Will called, adrenaline surging through him. "Let's finish it!"

As the wyrm thrashed, Lolmig brought his hammer down with a mighty swing, striking its head. The blow stunned the creature, but its thrashing continued.

With one final roar, the wyrm lunged at Lyra, its jaws wide and razor-sharp. Time seemed to slow as Will saw the beast descending on her, and without hesitation, he leapt.

His sword plunged into the top of the wyrm's skull, the blade glowing with a blinding radiance that illuminated the entire cavern. The light pulsed, flooding the space before fading as the blade sank deep into the creature's head.

The wyrm let out a final, ear-splitting cry before collapsing, its massive body hitting the ground with a thunderous crash. Dust filled the air, and the cavern fell eerily silent.

Will staggered back, pulling his sword free and gasping for breath. His arms trembled, and his vision blurred from the sudden brightness.

Lolmig let out a low whistle. "Well, lad," he said, his voice breaking the silence. "That was one hell of a move."

Will looked at his sword in awe, the blade now appearing ordinary once more. He turned to his companions, whose expressions mirrored his astonishment.

"What... what just happened?" Lyra asked, her voice trembling slightly.

Valenor approached, his eyes fixed on the sword. His eyes shifted back to Will and there was a flicker of realisation, but he said nothing.

Lolmig, still clutching his war hammer, nodded. "Nice little fight." he said, brushing the dust off his tunic.

Will, still in shock, simply nodded. "Trust me to pick up a magical weapon." he said with a nervous laugh, as the initial adrenaline rush began to fade.

Lolmig chuckled again. "We don't make magical weapons lad. I don't know much about such things, but your fine elven friend there would be the one to ask."

As they stood over the fallen beast, and as the dust began to settle, they slowly gathered their things and began the short journey back to the main caverns.

9

# Chapter nine

Covered in grime and exhausted, but victorious, the four trudged back through the winding tunnels leading to the heart of the dwarven city. As they neared the main caverns, their spirits lifted tremendously as the reality of their success began to sink in.

When they emerged into the main caverns, the bustling marketplace was alive with dwarves haggling with traders, and laughing around tables laden with food and ale. They exchanged tired smiles as they wove through the crowd, their weariness eased by the warmth of the bustling city around them.

"Back already?" a dwarf called out, raising an eyebrow in surprise as he spotted the group. Word spread quickly through the crowd, and soon dwarves were stopping their work to nod respectfully or clap them on the shoulder as they passed.

Lolmig looked over at the others, a glint of pride in his eyes. "Nothing like a bit of glory among friends, eh?"

Will chuckled, feeling the weight of the battle dissipate. "Nothing like it," he agreed, glancing at Lyra, who returned his smile with a weary but radiant one of her own.

As they approached the grand doors, they composed themselves, preparing to meet with King Thranin. They straightened their clothes and weapons, brushing off the dust and debris and exchanging solemn nods before moving forward.

The doors to the throne room opened before them as they approached and they stepped inside, the euphoria of their accomplishment lifting them up as they faced Thranin and the gathered dwarves in his cavernous throne room. There was a palpable tension as they approached as the anticipation of their news left everyone present waiting with silent expectation.

Thranin turned to face them as they approached the throne. "Well?... can the miners return to work?"

Valenor stepped forward, his head held high. "Yes, King Thranin. The rock wyrm has been slain. Your miners can return to their work without fear."

A murmur of approval rippled through the gathered dwarves. Thranin's stern face softened slightly, a hint of relief in his eyes. "You have done well. The courage and skill you displayed are commendable. The dwarves of Stonehelm owe you a debt."

Valenor took another step forward, his expression earnest. "Thranin, if I may, I ask a favour of you. We do not know the terrain around our intended destination. Lolmig's guidance has been invaluable and he works well with our group.

We request that he join us to help guide us through the mountains."

Thranin's eyes flickered with surprise before he glanced at Lolmig, who stood proudly among the companions. "Lolmig's knowledge of the terrain is unparalleled. If he is willing, I will allow it."

Lolmig nodded briefly. "I will go with them, Thranin. They have explained their quest to me as we descended to the encounter with the rock wyrm, and if I can be of any assistance it would be my honour."

Valenor continued, "Thank you. We also request to keep the weapons we have chosen from your armoury. All the world knows that dwarven weapons are the finest in the land, and I fear we may have further need of weapons before our quest concludes."

Thranin regarded them for a long moment before nodding. "You have earned that right. Keep your weapons and may they serve you well. Use them wisely and with honour."

Will glanced at his companions, their faces reflecting the same sense of pride and relief he felt. "Thank you, Thranin. We will not forget your generosity."

Thranin's stern expression softened slightly, a hint of a smile playing at the corners of his mouth. "I get a strong sense of destiny from your group. I just want to make sure that when the history books record these moments, everyone knows that this old King of the Aruna dwarves played his part."

Valenor bowed deeply. "Rest assured, Thranin, your contributions will not be forgotten."

Thranin gave a satisfied nod. "Good. Will you rest here within our mountain for the night?"

Valenor glanced at his companions, and a single look between them was enough to confirm that they all shared the same yearning—to be free of these caves and back under the open sky. "Thank you for the kind offer, your majesty, but we would like to cover a bit more ground before we rest for the night."

The group waited while Lolmig gathered a few things he would need for the journey. They took this time to ensure their own gear was in order, talking of what might lie ahead in hushed tones. When Lolmig returned, his pack slung over his shoulder, they said their farewells to Thranin. "May the gods watch over you," Thranin said, intoning a ritual dwarven farewell as he clasped each of their hands in turn. "And may your path be clear."

"Thank you, Thranin," Will said.

With a few final words of gratitude, they made their way back to the main gates of Stonehelm. As they stepped outside, the fresh mountain air filled their lungs, invigorating them after the musty air that had seemed to settle in their chests during their brief sojourn in the caverns. The moon was high in the sky, casting a pale glow over the rugged landscape. The companions decided to make camp for the night, exhausted from their fight with the wyrm.

They found a sheltered ravine, its walls offering some protection from the wind. Valenor, They all worked together to gather firewood, piling the dry branches and twigs into a small clearing. Lolmig kindled the fire, the flames soon dancing and casting a warm light that flickered against the rocky walls of the ravine.

As they sat around the campfire, eyes heavy with exhaustion, Will's mind drifted through the strange whirlwind of the past few days. He replayed each incredible twist, each brush with danger since he'd been plucked from his quiet, predictable life and cast into this incredible world. A pang of guilt hit him briefly as he realised he hadn't thought much of home—or of the people waiting there for him. He wondered how they were, what they thought of his sudden absence.

But the thought was quickly overtaken by a revelation that stunned him. He hadn't taken his prescription meds since arriving here, yet he felt an unfamiliar sense of well-being. The familiar weight of his anxiety rarely concerned him since his arrival, but instead was replaced with a rare clarity and strength that felt as foreign as it did liberating. He stared into the fire, wondering if it was the thrill of purpose or the magic of this land—or perhaps both—that had somehow filled the void he'd felt for so long.

Will looked up to see Lyra watching him intently, her eyes reflecting the firelight. He smiled at her, and she smiled back. He looked around at the others, feeling a warmth in their burgeoning bond that gave him fortitude.

Valenor looked up at them as he poked the fire with a stick, releasing a plume of embers into the night sky. "We should get some rest. At first light we will make the ascent to Sunfire Peak."

Lolmig grunted in agreement. "Once we're on our way tomorrow I will cover what you need to know about the trail."

The fire burned low as one-by-one they settled down to sleep, the comforting warmth lulling them into a much-needed rest.

* * *

The following day, the companions set off before dawn, hoping to cover as much ground as possible before the sun reached its zenith. But as they climbed higher into the region of Sunfire Peaks, the temperature soared. The rocky terrain reflected the heat like a furnace, and the air shimmered with waves of heat that made the path ahead appear like a distant mirage.

The land was harsh and barren, a blistering desert of jagged stone and cracked earth. The few lizard-like creatures they'd seen skittering about at dawn had long since vanished into crevices, escaping the punishing sun. The companions had no such luxury.

Lolmig, leading the way, wiped sweat from his brow with a small square of linen. Even his thick beard, usually a point of pride, now clung uncomfortably to his face. "There's a cluster of caves up ahead," he announced, his voice rough from the dry air. "Not on any maps, but they'll give us a place to rest. You'll not last long out here otherwise."

Will, already feeling light-headed, squinted against the blinding light. Every step felt like trudging through an oven, and even the air seemed to sear his lungs. "Sounds good to me," he muttered, earning a grunt of agreement from Lyra.

It wasn't long before the rocky landscape revealed the caves—a small, unassuming cluster of dark openings in the stone. The entrance was narrow, forcing them to duck as they slipped inside, but the cool air within was an immediate relief, the intense heat giving way to a welcome chill.

"We're close now," Valenor said, his voice breaking the quiet.

Will looked up, his curiosity piqued despite his fatigue. "How close?"

Valenor leaned back against the stone wall, his expression guarded. "According to the prophecy, the Sword of Light lies beneath the highest peak in the region, guarded by the most ancient of beasts. We're very close to the highest peak."

The words hung between them, as the others absorbed their implications.

"What kind of beast? Does the prophecy say?" Lyra asked, her tone curious.

Valenor hesitated, his eyes flickering away. "The prophecy doesn't say outright. It's vague, like they all are. But..." He paused, popping a berry into his mouth and chewing slowly. "If I had to guess... it could be a dragon."

"A dragon?" Lyra's voice rose, her eyes going wide with disbelief. "But no one's seen a dragon in generations!"

"That doesn't mean they're gone," Valenor replied, his tone careful, though he refused to meet her gaze.

Will straightened, his exhaustion momentarily forgotten. "Wait a second—you guessed it might be a dragon? Did you know this before we agreed to come here?"

Valenor shifted uncomfortably but didn't respond immediately.

Lolmig let out a low chuckle, shaking his head. "And here I thought Thranin was the master of conveniently leaving out details."

"It's not like I'm hiding anything," Valenor said defensively. "The prophecy doesn't confirm what we're dealing with, only that it's ancient and powerful. I didn't want to alarm anyone unnecessarily."

Lyra crossed her arms, her voice turning slightly sharper. "This feels like the kind of thing you might have shared."

Will leaned back, rubbing his hand down his face. "Great. A dragon. How exactly are we supposed to get past that?"

Lolmig shrugged, his tone almost amused. "Assuming we even get close enough to fight, lad. Dragons don't tend to take kindly to visitors. But hey," he added, flashing a wry grin, "at least you'll have a good story to tell—*if* you survive."

The conversation dissolved into tense murmurs as they tried to piece together a plan. Each suggestion seemed more desperate than the last.

As the sun dipped below the horizon, they packed their belongings and stepped back out into the open. Though the sun was gone, the ground still radiated the day's heat like an invisible fire, and the air clung to them like a second skin, drying their sweat almost as soon as it beaded up.

Will glanced at the dark silhouette of the towering peaks ahead, his chest tightening. A dragon. He'd barely survived the Rock Wyrm, and now this? He took a deep breath, forcing the doubt from his mind. There was no turning back now.

Lolmig led them deeper into the mountains, navigating through valleys and ravines, but always steadily climbing. At one point, he led them once again into a network of caves, now moving deep under the mountain. He had an uncanny ability to navigate through the dark subterranean world, using senses that were inherent to his race. The others, however didn't have dwarven sight and had to stop to light torches after stumbling about in the dark for a while.

They continued through the tunnels like this for what felt like an eternity, until suddenly Lolmig stopped in his tracks. "We're nearing the main cavern soon." he whispered back over his shoulder to the others. "As far as I can tell, we will be almost directly beneath the highest peak. Does that sound like the place you're looking for Valenor?"

Valenor nodded in approval, pulling out some old texts from his bag and moving his torch overhead so he could read. Satisfied, he packed the book away. "I think this is it," he said, "we should move more carefully now. Whatever beast guards the sword, we have to assume it will have the advantage if we alert it to our presence."

They all pressed on, being more mindful of their movements and keeping any conversation to a minimum. As they emerged from the last of the tunnels, the companions found themselves standing at the edge of a vast, multi-levelled cavern. The walls were riddled with openings, almost like a honeycomb, leading up to a large aperture at the top that allowed beams of moonlight to spill in, selectively illuminating areas of the cavern below. The air was thick with an ancient presence, and the smell of sulphur was strong.

At the centre of the cavern in a single beam of moonlight that cascaded from the opening above, the Sword of Light rested atop a stone pedestal, its blade glowing faintly as if it were alive. The companions moved with deliberate care, each step placed deliberately to avoid the loose rocks and debris littering the ground.

"Quietly now," Valenor whispered, his voice barely audible over the faint hiss of steam escaping from fissures in the rock.

But the silence shattered as Lyra's foot made contact with one of the loose stones. It skittered across the cavern floor, the sound echoing and reverberating in the stillness of the cave. All four froze, tension gripping them.

From the shadows beyond the sword, a pair of massive, glowing eyes snapped open, cutting through the darkness like twin beacons, as two puffs of dust kicked up on the cave floor in front of it's nostrils. Their blood ran cold as the beast stirred.

The dragon rose slowly, its gargantuan form emerging from the darkness. Its scales covered in dust, blended perfectly with the surrounding stone. A low, guttural growl rumbled from deep within its chest, the sound vibrating through the cavern and into their bones.

"Move!" Lolmig barked, shoving Will behind a boulder as the dragon stretched its wings, sending a powerful gust of hot wind rippling through the cavern.

The companions scattered, seeking cover as the dragon reared back and let out a deafening roar. Its glowing eyes scanned the cavern, locking onto Will, who crouched behind a jagged rock.

The beast lunged with terrifying speed. Will barely had time to roll out of the way, the heat of the dragon's breath singeing his skin as its jaws snapped shut inches from him. Scrambling to his feet, he swung his sword in a wide arc, but the blade glanced off the creature's iron-like scales, sending a jarring vibration through his arms.

"Over here, you great lizard!" Lolmig bellowed, charging in with his war hammer. He struck the dragon's foreleg, the impact resounding like thunder, but the beast barely flinched.

Lyra darted in from the side, her daggers glinting in the faint light as she aimed for the softer flesh in the dragon's underbelly. Her strikes landed, drawing a thin line of dark blood, but it only seemed to enrage the creature further, causing her to dodge for cover as it stomped around.

The dragon swung its massive tail, catching Lolmig mid-stride and sending him crashing into a wall. He landed with a grunt, clutching his ribs as he struggled to rise.

"Valenor, grab the sword!" Will shouted, seeing that Valenor was closest to the pedestal.

But Valenor hesitated, his eyes fixed on the glowing blade as if it were a venomous serpent. "I... I can't!" he stammered, backing away.

"Damn it, Valenor!" Will yelled, his frustration mounting. But before he could say more, the dragon inhaled deeply, its chest expanding as a fiery glow built within its throat.

"Take cover!" Lolmig roared, diving behind a boulder.

The dragon unleashed a torrent of fire, the heat so intense it warped the air and turned loose rocks into glowing, molten pools. The smell of sulphur and burning stone filled the cavern, choking the companions as they pressed themselves against the rock faces they were hiding behind, shielding their faces from the searing blast of air.

From his crouched position behind the crumbling rock, Will peered through the haze of heat and ash, his heart pounding in time with the thunderous roar of the dragon's fiery breath. With a deliberate motion, he gestured silently to the others, signalling that they should coordinate their attack the moment the flames ceased.

Lyra, tucked behind a jagged outcropping, held a dagger in each hand, their edges gleaming ominously in the firelight. She nodded sharply, her eyes locking with Will's. Valenor, crouched nearby, raised a hand in acknowledgment. Lolmig was pressed against a rock wall, his massive war-hammer resting against his shoulder. He flashed a grin at Will, his teeth white beneath his soot-streaked beard, before giving an enthusiastic thumbs-up.

Without wasting another moment, Lolmig let out a fierce battle cry, and charged out from behind his cover, swinging his war hammer and landing a heavy blow on the dragon's side. The beast roared in fury, its fiery breath ceasing as it turned to face this new threat. Taking advantage of the distraction, Will and Lyra moved into position. Will's mind raced, searching for a way to reach the sword. "Valenor!" he called, trying to cut through the noise with his voice. "We need that sword."

Before he could say more, Valenor started climbing to the higher areas of the cavern. "I'll provide a distraction!" Valenor yelled down. "You grab the sword!" Will watched as Valenor scaled the rocky walls, moving with surprising agility. Will didn't have time to wonder about Valenor's strange reluctance, so he concentrated on the task at hand instead.

"Over here, you ugly brute!" Valenor shouted, hurling rocks at the beast to draw its attention.

The dragon roared and turned its massive frame toward him, flapping its wings to ascend toward the ledge.

Will seized the opportunity, sprinting toward the pedestal. The heat from the molten rock made his skin prickle, but he pressed on, his eyes fixed on the glowing sword.

As his fingers closed around the hilt, a surge of energy coursed through him, flooding his body with warmth and power. The sword felt impossibly light, and its glow intensified, illuminating the cavern in a brilliant light.

The dragon roared again, its eyes locking onto Will as it dove toward him.

"Will, watch out!" Lyra cried, darting forward to distract the beast. She slashed at its tail, drawing its ire.

Lolmig, still winded but determined, swung his war hammer with all his might, striking the dragon's hind leg and causing it to stumble.

With the beast momentarily off-balance, Will raised the Sword of Light high, its radiance cutting through the smoke and ash. He stepped forward, the blade shimmering like a beacon as the dragon turned its glowing eyes on him.

The creature froze mid-lunge, its massive frame trembling. The furious roar that had been rising in its throat caught, and instead, it let out a deep, rumbling growl that shook the cavern walls. Its glowing eyes locked on the Sword of Light, and something shifted in its gaze—fury melting into something almost akin to reverence.

Will stopped, his breath catching in his chest. The cavern grew eerily silent, save for the faint hum of the sword. The dragon, towering above him, began to lower its massive head. Its wings folded against its body, and it crouched low, its sharp talons scraping against the rocky ground.

"What... what's it doing?" Lyra whispered, her voice barely audible as she stood frozen, daggers clutched tightly in her hands.

"I think..." Will's voice trailed off, his eyes never leaving the dragon. "I think it's... bowing."

The dragon lowered its head fully, its massive, scaled brow nearly touching the cavern floor. Its golden eyes flicked back to the sword, and then to Will, as though it had made some sort of judgment and found him worthy.

Will took a hesitant step forward, his heart pounding. The Sword of Light pulsed in his grip, its glow steady. He raised it slightly, the light catching the dragon's scales in a dazzling display of gold and crimson.

The dragon released a deep, guttural rumble—not a growl, but something softer, almost respectful. Then, without warning, it spread its wings wide, the gust of air nearly knocking the companions off their feet. With a single powerful beat, the dragon launched itself into the air, climbing rapidly through the opening at the top of the cavern and disappearing into the night skies above.

The silence that followed was deafening. Dust swirled in the dim light, and the companions stood rooted in place, their weapons still drawn, their breaths shallow.

"What just happened?" Lolmig finally broke the silence, his voice rough and disbelieving.

"I... I don't know," Will murmured, lowering the sword. He stared at the cavern roof where the dragon had vanished, his mind racing.

"It saw the sword," Valenor said, stepping down from his ledge. His expression was unreadable, but his voice carried a quiet awe. "It recognised it. Recognised you."

Lyra sheathed her daggers, her brow furrowed in confusion. "But why? Dragons don't bow to anyone. Not even the gods themselves in the old legends."

The cavern fell silent, save for the faint crackling of cooling molten rock. For a moment, none of them spoke, each grappling with the enormity of the short, but intense battle.

"Well... I am just glad it left when it did. I was starting to have my doubts we were gonna come out of this one alive." said Lolmig.

As his mind reeled, Will looked down to admire their hard won prize. The sword was a thing of beauty. The hilt appeared like entwined trees in different coloured metals, blending together in weave so complex that it was impossible to fathom. The blade itself was adorned with intricate etchings of ancient battles, each scene depicted in exquisite detail on its mirror-like surface. The whole weapon seemed to pulse with a radiant energy that emanated from within, although it was more subdued now.

There was one peculiarity, though. The sword seemed to be missing a pommel stone. It was an odd oversight in what was otherwise a perfect weapon, but Will didn't give it a second thought.

# Chapter ten

The light from the rising sun began to cascade down into the cavern from the opening by the time they had gathered their wits, but the battle with the dragon had left them all completely drained, so they decided to rest in the caves for the remainder of the day. The adrenaline that had fuelled them during the fight began to wane, replaced by a heavy fatigue that settled into their bones.

They found a secluded nook within the vast cavern, away from the debris and remnants of the battle. Lolmig knew the caves well and wandered off by himself, returning a short time later having found a small underground spring which provided them with fresh water to drink and clean their wounds.

Valenor took the first watch, but they were confident that no other threat would be found anywhere near a dragon's lair. Lyra prepared a simple meal from their provisions, as she tried to shake off the lingering shakes that had settled into her muscles in the wake of the fight.

Will sat apart from the others, the sword resting across his lap. He turned it over in his hands, marvelling at the craftsmanship and the power he could feel emanating from it.

Lyra joined him, offering him a portion of their meal. "You did well today," she said softly.

Will nodded, accepting the food. "It was pretty intense there for a moment. I thought we were done for when it unleashed it's fire breath."

"It was a little toasty, wasn't it?" Lolmig chuckled, joining them after taking a plate to Valenor.

The companions ate in comfortable silence, each lost in their own thoughts. After the meal, they took turns resting, sleep coming easy under the weight of exhaustion.

After resting for several hours, the group gathered their belongings and readied themselves for the journey ahead. They climbed up through the tiers of this massive central cavern, slowly making their way to the irregular opening at the top.

The a climb took a lot longer than expected, but they eventually emerged into the scorching air, just as the sun was setting. As they looked around, the stunning vista took their breath away. From this elevation, they could see nearly the entire region laid out like a living map—forests sprawling like green oceans, as rivers cut through the landscape like silver ribbons, and distant towns nestled against the earth like scattered jewels.

"Well," Will said softly, his voice filled with awe, "it's all downhill from here."

Lolmig let out a hearty laugh, clapping Will on the shoulder. "Aye, lad. That it is."

The group chuckled as they adjusted their packs and prepared to descend, each silently preparing themselves for the journey ahead.

Even with the sun setting, the heat radiating from the ground was already making them sweat uncomfortably as they clambered down the mountain trail. "Where to next, Valenor?" asked Will as he carefully scanned the uneven trail ahead.

Valenor's eyes grew distant as he considered the question for a moment, before answering. "We should find the Whispering Caverns and search for the Stone of Wisdom."

The colour drained from Lolmig's face, "We cannot venture there! It is forbidden!"

Will looked sharply at him, taken aback by Lolmig's violent reaction to Valenor's suggestion. "Why, Lolmig? What's the problem?"

Lolmig's eyes darted between his companions, his face pale with dread. Finally, he drew in a shaky breath. "What do you know of the caverns, and how they came by the name?"

Will and Lyra shrugged, but Valenor smirked at Lolmig, "Surely a mighty warrior such as yourself isn't afraid of a ghost story?" he teased.

Lolmig continued, unfazed by Valenor's teasing. "It's more than a ghost story. I have seen the effects of it first hand.

Will was watching this exchange, his concern growing as he remembered how Valenor had kept certain facts about the first relic from them until the last moment. "Tell me more about this whispering cavern Lolmig." he said eventually.

"Centuries ago, there was a king of our people—Durmalian the Bold—renowned for his ambition. He ruled during the golden age of the Aruna dwarves, when our kingdoms stretched from mountain to mountain, and our halls glittered with wealth that rivalled the heavens themselves. But Durmalian's thirst for glory was insatiable. He heard whispers of a treasure hidden deep within those caves, a hoard so vast it would make even the wealth of Stonehelm seem like mere trinkets."

Lolmig's voice lowered, trembling. "Against the counsel of his advisors, Durmalian gathered his bravest warriors and ventured into the caverns. They believed themselves unstoppable, armed with the finest weapons and magic of our kind. But what they found there... was no treasure. It was a curse. A dark force beyond understanding guarded those depths, and it claimed them all. Their bodies were never found, but their souls—" Lolmig paused, shivering. "—their souls were bound to the caverns, twisted into eternal guardians of whatever lies in those forsaken depths. Now, their spirits wander, filled with rage and sorrow, attacking any who dare to trespass."

Will's eyes widened as the tale unfolded, but Lolmig wasn't finished. "The stories say that those the spirits kill are claimed by the curse, joining their ranks. Those who escape are left scarred—physically and mentally—driven mad by the whispers of the lost. Only the most desperate or foolish would dare venture there."

Valenor crossed his arms, his expression grim. "You're certain that this is more than ghost stories, designed to scare children away from playing in dangerous places?" he asked Lolmig.

Lolmig simply nodded, the colour still drained from his face. "A few years ago, a group of foolhardy youths set out to bring back the treasure. Like you, they thought it just ghost stories. Only one returned, and he had completely lost his mind."

Will frowned. "Why would they go there? Did you not say there was no treasure there?"

Lolmig nodded solemnly. "Aye lad, that is the belief among most of my kin. But there are those who believe that Durmalian and his men simply didn't find the treasure before succumbing to the curse."

They all stood there in the blazing heat for a moment, feeling defeated. The silence stretched as the weight of Lolmig's tale settled over them like a heavy blanket.

"Could it be that the Stone of Wisdom *is* the treasure in the legends? That Durmalian never found the treasure because he was searching for gold and riches?" asked Lyra in a quiet voice.

Lolmig and Valenor exchanged a look, and then shrugged. "I suppose." said Lolmig.

Will frowned, gazing across the endless vista as if searching for the answer. "After everything we've been through... it can't just end like this. There has to be a way," he murmured, though his voice carried little conviction.

Valenor rubbed his temples, his expression weary. "The dwarves are masters of resilience," he said finally. "Legends always have more to them than what's written in the songs."

He turned to Lolmig, his tone pragmatic. "Lolmig, you're the closest to this history. Is there anything in the old tales that speaks of overcoming this curse?"

Lolmig hesitated, his hand drifting to his beard as if tugging on it would untangle his thoughts. "The Whispering Caverns are sacred to us... few dare to speak of them anymore. The stories are old, even for dwarves."

"There must be something!" Lyra said, her tone edged with desperation. "Anything we can use!"

The dwarf sighed, his expression conflicted. "There is... one thing. It's just a story, mind you."

Valenor's eyes narrowed. "We don't have the luxury of dismissing stories, Lolmig. What does the tale say?"

Lolmig's gaze flickered around at the faces of his comrades, taking a breath before speaking. "It's about Durmalian. When he led his army into the caverns, he carried with him a relic—a medallion forged in the heart of Stonehelm itself, blessed by the first dwarven priests. The Sovereign's Medallion. It was said to hold the power of his authority, a symbol of his divine right to rule."

Will studied Lolmig as he processed what this might mean for their quest. "And what does that have to do with the curse?"

"The legend says that the medallion can command loyalty from the spirits of the ancestors," Lolmig explained, his voice sombre. "That it carries the will of Durmalian himself. If it truly exists, it might be the only thing that can grant us safe passage through the caverns."

"Do you think it's real?" Lyra asked, her voice filled with a spark of hope.

Lolmig nodded slowly, though his expression remained reluctant. "If it is, it would be in the royal vaults of Stonehelm. Guarded, of course, and accessible only with the king's permission. The legend says that after the king and his men were taken by the curse, one escaped with the medallion, turning back up at the gates of Stonehelm gibbering words of madness, but carrying the medallion."

Will's jaw tightened as he set his gaze on Lolmig. "Then we go back. Time to see how much King Thranin wants to be remembered for being on the right side of history."

"It won't be easy," Lolmig replied, shaking his head. "Asking for a relic of that importance is no small thing. The king values tradition above all else."

Valenor turned and continued down the trail. "Then we'll make him see that this is no ordinary circumstance. Without that medallion, our quest is doomed, and all of South Aruna could fall... Stonehelm included."

The journey back to Stonehelm was a gruelling one, though the familiarity of the path made it slightly less treacherous. They moved carefully down the mountain trails, retracing much of the route they had taken to reach Sunfire Peaks. During the sweltering midday heat, they sought refuge in cool caves, their bodies grateful for the respite from the relentless sun. Conversation was sparse, each of them lost in their thoughts. Lolmig often took the lead, his intimate knowledge of the terrain ensuring their passage remained as smooth as possible. By nightfall, they resumed their trek, guided by the pale glow of the moon and the faint shimmer of starlight reflecting off the mountain rocks.

Two nights later, the towering gates of Stonehelm came into view. Lanterns cast a golden glow over the entryway, and the sturdy dwarven guards stationed at the gates eyed them with suspicion.

Lolmig stepped forward, raising a hand in greeting. "We've returned with news for King Thranin," he announced, his voice carrying an authority that seemed to ease the guards' initial wariness.

One of the guards squinted at the group before recognising Lolmig and stepping aside. "Go on, then. The king's likely to be in his personal quarters at this hour."

With a nod of gratitude, the companions passed through the gates and into the bustling heart of Stonehelm. The familiar sights of the cavern city greeted them. At this hour the markets were empty and the taverns full, Dwarves spilled out into the streets, their voices loud and slurred.

Once they had passed through the heart of the city, the companions ascended a winding staircase that led to the private quarters of King Thranin. Two stout guards clad in intricately forged armour stood at attention outside the double doors, their eyes narrowing as the group approached.

"Halt," one of the guards barked, crossing his axe before the entrance. "State your business."

Lolmig stepped forward, drawing himself up to his full height. "We've returned to speak with King Thranin. He'll want to hear what we have to say."

The guard exchanged a glance with his companion before turning to open the door a crack. After a brief murmured exchange with someone inside, he nodded and gestured for the group to wait. A moment later, the doors swung open, and they were granted leave to enter.

The companions stepped into Thranin's quarters, a grand but practical space carved deep into the mountain stone. The room was warmly lit by glowing crystal sconces, their light reflecting off a long table covered in maps, ledgers, and goblets of ale. Thranin himself stood at the head of the table, his stout frame draped in a cloak trimmed with fine fur. His sharp eyes softened as he took in the sight of them.

"Well, well! You've returned," he boomed, spreading his arms in a welcoming gesture. "Come in, sit! Tell me, how did you fare? And more importantly, did you find the relic you sought?"

The group settled themselves before the king, gratefully accepting a drink off a server who officiously moved around the room. Taking it in turns, they began to relay the story of their journey.

"A dragon, you say?" Thranin interrupted, his eyes widening. "In my lifetime, I've heard tales of them, but none who've faced one lived to tell the tale. And here you are before me." He gave a deep chuckle, though there was clear respect in his tone. "Remarkable!"

Eventually, the tale came to an end, and Thranin clapped his hands together, the sound echoing off the stone walls. "Well done! You've had quite the adventure these last few days. Now, what brings you back here? Surely, you've earned some rest after such a feat."

It was Lolmig who stepped forward, his expression serious. "We come seeking your aid once again, King Thranin. We require the Sovereign's Medallion."

The warmth in Thranin's expression faltered, replaced by a look of suspicion. "The medallion? Do you have any idea what you ask of me?"

"I do," Lolmig replied evenly. "But without it, we cannot proceed. The medallion is the only way to enter the Whispering Caverns without succumbing to the curse of the ancestors that lies within."

Thranin frowned deeply, his fingers drumming against the edge of the table. "The medallion is not a trinket to be loaned out at whim. It is a relic of great significance, tied to the very sovereignty of our people. I cannot part with it lightly."

The conversation grew tense as Valenor and Lolmig took turns trying to reason with the king, while Lyra and Will remained silent, watching the exchange unfold.

"You speak of duty and significance," Lolmig said, stepping closer, his tone growing sharper, "but have you forgotten the debt you owe me, Thranin?"

Thranin stiffened. "You dare—"

"I dare remind you," Lolmig interrupted, his voice like the rumble of distant thunder. "When the mines of Korruk collapsed, who stood beside you and led the charge to save the lives of your miners? When the Stonehelm defences faltered, who stood at your gates, keeping your people safe while others fled? I did, Thranin. And you swore a debt to me for those acts. Now, I ask you to repay it—not with gold or titles, but with the medallion that could save countless lives."

The room fell silent as Thranin glared at Lolmig, his jaw tight. Finally, the tension broke as the king let out a low growl of frustration. "Fine. You'll have the medallion. But mark my words—return it, or you'll find no sanctuary in Stonehelm ever again."

Lolmig inclined his head in acknowledgment. "You have my word."

Thranin sighed heavily, gesturing dismissively toward the door. "Return tomorrow morning. The medallion will be prepared for you then. Now go—before I change my mind."

With that, the companions filed out of the room, leaving the king to brood over the decision he had just made.

# Chapter eleven

The following morning, the companions made their way through the winding halls of Stonehelm. They returned to Thranin's throne room, their mood sombre as they approached the imposing double doors, given the heavy handed method used to persuade the king.

Inside, Thranin sat waiting on his granite throne, the Sovereign's Medallion resting in a small chest at his side. His expression was frosty, his demeanour formal and distant, but the room was filled with dwarven courtiers and guards, all gathered to witness the rare handing over of such a sacred artifact.

As the companions entered, Thranin stood, his deep voice commanding the attention of everyone present. "You return as promised, and as agreed, the Sovereign's Medallion is here. But understand, Lolmig"—he fixed the dwarf with a piercing stare—"its safety is your responsibility. It is to you that I will impart this sacred relic, and you are to safeguard it with your life, for should it be lost, it will not only be your name that bears the shame but all of Stonehelm."

Lolmig stepped forward and bowed deeply. "Aye, Your Majesty. I will carry it with the utmost care and return it to its rightful place as soon as our quest is concluded."

Thranin regarded him a moment longer, then gestured for the chest to be opened. With careful hands, he retrieved the medallion, its golden surface gleaming with intricate dwarven runes that seemed to shimmer faintly with their own inner light. He held it aloft for all to see.

"Let it be known," Thranin boomed, his voice echoing through the chamber, "that the sacrifices of the dwarven nation in the fight against the curse of Shadowmoor shall not go unrecognised. History shall remember this day and the lengths to which we have gone to aid in the salvation of Aruna."

The assembled dwarves all boomed "For Stonehelm, and the salvation of Aruna!" in unison, their faces filled with pride as Thranin stepped down from his throne. He approached Lolmig and placed the medallion into his hands, his expression softening just slightly. "Our debt is settled, old friend. Now go, and see that it is returned."

Lolmig straightened, his grip on the medallion firm. "Thank you, Thranin. We won't fail."

Thranin turned his gaze to the others. "See to it that he doesn't. And may the ancestors watch over you all."

Will, Lyra, and Valenor each inclined their heads in respect. "We are grateful, Your Majesty," Valenor said. "We'll return the medallion to you as soon as we are able."

With that, the companions turned to leave, their mood significantly improved now that they had a means of reaching the next relic. They quickly made their way to the south gate, and tried to cover as much ground as possible, trying to make up for the time lost to this unexpected detour.

The journey to the Whispering Caverns, though less than a day's walk from Stonehelm, proved to be an arduous trek. The trails were narrow and uneven, seldom used by even the most steadfast of travellers. Every now and again, they would encounter huge rocks blocking their way where the mountainside had crumbled into the ravine they were trying to pass through, forcing them to turn around and find another path.

They paused often, sitting in silence to catch their breath. Every delay brought a sense of frustration, but they all understood the importance of conserving their strength for what lay ahead. The Whispering Caverns would demand everything they had, and none of them were willing to risk entering it in less than peak condition.

By the time the sun dipped below the jagged peaks, the entrance to the caverns was almost within reach, shrouded in ominous shadows that seemed to stretch unnaturally long. Lolmig came to an abrupt halt, planting his feet firmly on the trail and crossing his arms. "I have no intention of entering a haunted cavern after sundown!" he declared firmly, his voice echoing faintly off the rocky walls.

Will looked at the darkening sky and nodded in agreement. "I don't think any of us do," he said. "We're better off waiting until morning. Whatever's in there… let's face it after a good night's rest, in the light of a new day."

The group silently agreed and began setting up camp. After so many nights on the road together, the routine of making camp had become second nature. Without needing to speak, each member set about their task.

Lyra scouted the surrounding area for firewood while Valenor cleared the ground, sweeping aside loose stones and laying down their bedrolls. Lolmig pulled provisions from his pack, muttering to himself as he counted rations, while Will focused on gathering water from a nearby stream. Within a short time, a small fire crackled at the centre of their camp, casting flickering light on their weary faces.

They ate in relative silence, the tension of their proximity to the Whispering Caverns reminding them what the following day would bring. Even Lolmig, who usually filled the evening with his gruff humour, seemed preoccupied. Every so often, one of them would glance toward the cavern entrance, a gaping black maw in the distance, as if expecting something to emerge from its depths.

As the fire burned low and the stars blinked into view above them, they settled into their bedrolls one by one. Sleep came fitfully, their dreams filled with shadowy figures and distant whispers crafted by their deepest fears and given life by their imaginations. The caverns waited, and the morning would come all too soon.

The next morning, they broke camp in grim silence. Each of them burdened by their own unspoken fears about the task ahead, yet none voiced them. Instead, they exchanged fleeting pats on the shoulder or met each other's eyes with brief, knowing glances. Words weren't needed. They all understood the stakes.

When they were ready, the companions paused to take one final look at their surroundings, a silent farewell to the open world they might not see again. Then, as one, they turned to face the gaping chasm that awaited them.

The cavern loomed like the mouth of a great beast, cold air flowing from its depths in sporadic gusts. Shadows seemed to cling to its edges, defying the sunlight's reach. The companions hesitated at the entrance for a moment before Will took the first step, his boots crunching on loose gravel as he led the way.

Inside, the cave greeted them with a deceptive sense that it was just like any other cave. The air was damp and cool, carrying the faint musty scent of stone and earth. Water dripped rhythmically into unseen pools, and their footsteps echoed softly against the cavern walls.

But there was a sense of an unfriendly presence that they all felt. Something was not right here. The deeper they ventured into the darkness, the stronger the malevolent presence became, watching, waiting. They continued on, remaining vigilant with their hands never far from their weapons, although they were unsure what good they would do.

Valenor broke the silence. "Lolmig, when do we use it? The medallion—how does it work?" he asked in a hushed tone.

Lolmig frowned, his fingers tightening around the relic as he considered the question. "I... I don't know for sure," he admitted, his tone unusually uncertain. "The stories don't say much about how it's meant to be used. I guess... when we first see the spirits?" He shrugged, the slight questioning tone doing little to re-assure the others.

"That's comforting," Lyra muttered under her breath, earning a faint chuckle from Valenor.

As usual when they were navigating caves, Lolmig took the vanguard, using his uncanny ability to know his way around, no matter what cave they were in, whilst the others, remained nearby, trying to hold the darkness at bay with lit torches.

After a time, Lolmig halted abruptly, holding up a hand to signal the others. "Bring a torch closer," he said, his gravelly voice cutting through the silence. He pointed to the wall beside him, where faint markings were etched into the stone. "There's something here."

Will stepped forward, holding his torch high to illuminate the surface. The carvings became clearer—a series of angular runes, their edges softened by the passage of countless years.

"What does it say, my friend?" Valenor asked, his brow furrowing as he studied the markings. "I don't recognise the words."

Lolmig's face darkened as he examined the runes, his fingers brushing lightly over the grooves. His shoulders stiffened, and he turned back to them with a grim expression. "It's written in old dwarven," he said, his voice heavy. "A warning message to turn back now. I'll spare you the details, but it speaks of... unpleasant ends for anyone foolish enough to continue."

A heavy silence fell over the group. Even the flickering torches seemed dimmer, the shadows lengthening around them.

Will was the first to break the silence. "Is there any indication of who might have written the message?"

Lolmig looked back at the message on the wall for a moment, and then turned back, shaking his head. "The warning's old, as old as the curse itself. Maybe older. No sign of who wrote it or when."

"Then let's keep moving," Valenor said, his voice firm. "We knew the risks before we entered. Let's get this over and done with."

As they delved deeper into the caves, the air seemed to thicken around them, carrying with it a chill that seeped into their very bones and left them numb. That strange, malevolent presence grew stronger with every step, a crawling sensation prickling at the back of their necks. It clawed at their senses, leaving them feeling light-headed and queasy.

The shadows around them seemed to stretch and shift unnaturally, tricking their eyes into seeing faint flickering forms that danced just beyond their field of vision. Whenever they turned to catch a better look, the apparitions dissolved into the surrounding gloom, leaving behind only a cold, crawling emptiness. A persistent sibilant whisper wove through the air, snaking into their ears. It was indistinct, like a thousand voices murmuring just beyond comprehension.

Valenor paused mid-step, his sharp eyes scanning the path ahead. "I think we must be getting close," he said confidently, his voice shaking slightly with the chill that was affecting everyone. "We have to assume that the Stone of Wisdom will be nearby when we encounter the spectres. If they were cursed to guard something, it would make sense that their vigil centres around it."

Will nodded, swallowing against the tightness in his throat. "Then we need to stay sharp. Whatever's waiting for us, we need to be ready for it. Are you ready with the medallion Lolmig?"

"Aye lad, whatever happens next I'll be ready." he said.

The companions rounded a corner, stepping into a massive cavern that opened up before them like an ancient, forgotten cathedral. It should have been stunningly beautiful—perhaps the most extraordinary place any of them had ever seen—but the moment they crossed the threshold, an overwhelming wave of hatred crashed into them, almost knocking them to their knees. The malevolent energy was suffocating, wrapping around them like an invisible vice that seemed to reach into their very souls.

On the far side of the cavern, a vast underground lake stretched out, its surface eerily still and serene, as though frozen in time. It gleamed with an ethereal sheen, reflecting the kaleidoscope of light that danced from above. The ceiling of the cavern was a breathtaking spectacle—a sprawling array of crystalline formations that shimmered with every imaginable hue. Sunlight filtered through the crystals from the surface, casting a mesmerising dance of colours on the stone floor and sending rippling rainbows across the lake's glassy surface.

Despite the beauty, the cavern felt profoundly wrong. The light, no matter how dazzling, couldn't banish the intense darkness that clung to the air. The whispers that had plagued them earlier were now a constant, dull roar, as though the cavern itself had come alive to voice its loathing of their presence.

Lyra took a cautious step forward, her eyes wide as she took in the hauntingly beautiful scene. "It's... incredible," she said, her voice barely above a whisper.

"Stay back Lyra," Lolmig growled, his knuckles white around the grip of his war-hammer. "When the spectres show up none of you should be in the way."

Will looked around uneasily, his every nerve on edge. The interplay of light and shadow seemed to mock them, as if the cavern were toying with their senses. "The stone must be here," he said, his voice steady despite the tension curling in his chest.

Valenor nodded, his keen eyes scanning the lake and the far reaches of the cavern. "Stay vigilant," he warned.

As they approached, a ripple passed across the surface of the lake, subtle but unmistakable. The companions froze, their eyes locked on the disturbance as the whispers around them grew louder, more insistent. Whatever resided in this cavern knew they were here.

"There!" Will said suddenly, his voice cutting through the deafening whispers as he pointed toward the far side of the cavern. His finger aimed at a raised area, seemingly carved directly from the cavern floor, as if the earth itself had risen to hold its treasure aloft. The pedestal stood just at the edge of the still lake.

Nestled atop the pedestal, in a small, perfectly carved niche, rested a stone about the size of an egg. It glowed with an internal radiance, as though an energy pulsed within.

But before they could take another step, something flickered in the corner of their vision. A distortion, faint at first, like heat rippling off sun-scorched stone. Will squinted, trying to discern if his mind was playing tricks on him, but the flickering grew stronger, more pronounced. The companions tensed, their gazes snapping to the disturbance.

And then it happened.

Out of the shifting light, shapes began to materialise, flickering in and out of sight. At first, there were only one or two—vague, ghostly outlines with eyes that glowed like embers in a dying fire. But within moments, more began to appear, their spectral forms coalescing from the very air around them. A dozen. Then fifty. Then hundreds.

The spectres hovered between the companions and their goal, their translucent forms shifting and swaying like leaves caught in a breeze. Each figure bore the unmistakable silhouette of a dwarf—ancient warriors clad in spectral armour, edged in a faint green glow, their faces locked in eternal grimaces of pain and rage.

"What are they doing? They're just standing there... watching," Lyra whispered.

Valenor's bow was drawn instinctively, but he immediately knew that it would do little good against this foe. "They're waiting," he said grimly. "For what, I don't know."

Will swallowed hard, his throat dry as dust as he glanced toward Lolmig. "Do you think it's time?"

Lolmig didn't respond immediately. His sharp gaze remained locked on the horde of spectres, their flickering forms shifting like storm clouds in the cavern's unnatural glow. At last, he nodded, gripping the medallion tightly in his hand. "If this doesn't work," he said grimly, "nothing will."

Lolmig stepped forward deliberately, planting himself firmly in front of his companions. The others watched as he raised the medallion high above his head. It seemed to pulse faintly, catching and amplifying the light from the crystalline ceiling.

In a deep, resonant voice, Lolmig began to chant in dwarven, the words guttural and melodic, ancient words resonating power. The language was foreign to the others, but its cadence sent a shiver down their spines.

As the final word left his lips, Lolmig lowered the medallion and turned back to the group, his expression tense.

"What was that?" Lyra asked, her voice tense.

"I called out Durmalian," Lolmig said simply, his voice steady though his grip on the medallion tightened. "He will have to come forward now."

No sooner had the words left his mouth than a deep, guttural roar echoed through the cavern, shaking the very ground beneath their feet. It was a sound that made the spectral dwarves retreat momentarily, their translucent forms swaying and flickering as though buffeted by an unseen wind.

From the midst of the spectral horde, a shadow began to swell, twisting and rising into a colossal form. The air grew icy, the dim light from their torches flickering as if cowering from the powerful force now taking shape. King Durmalian emerged, his towering figure wreathed in spectral fire. The once-proud lines of his dwarven features were now warped into a grotesque mask of fury and despair, his presence radiating an overwhelming malevolence.

"How dare you summon me!" Durmalian's voice roared, his words crashing against them like a hurricane. The sheer power of his presence made them stagger back, their breath ripped from their lungs by the force of his wrath.

The cavern seemed to shrink around him, the weight of his gaze pinning them in place as his fiery eyes bore down upon them. "Who dares to disturb the guardians of the treasure?"

Lolmig stepped forward, the Sovereign's Medallion held high in his trembling hand. "I summoned you, Durmalian! I am Lolmig Nightforge of Stonehelm, and by the power of the Sovereign's Medallion, I command you to grant us passage!"

Durmalian's laughter boomed through the cavern, shaking its very foundation. "Dwarves have grown puny and weak since my time in Stonehelm it seems. You... you poor excuse for my descendant, seek to wield the medallion's power against me?" His spectral form loomed over Lolmig, fiery eyes blazing with disdain. "The Sovereign's Medallion was forged for the pure of heart, the resilient of spirit—you are none of these. You, bound by greed and pride, are unworthy!"

The medallion dimmed in Lolmig's hand, its glow fading like a dying ember. A bead of sweat rolled down his temple as he gritted his teeth and tightened his grip, but the artifact grew heavier, slipping through his fingers. With a snarl of frustration, he turned to Will.

"Catch!" Lolmig shouted, tossing the medallion in an arc toward him.

Will's eyes widened as the artifact hurtled toward him. Reflexively, he caught it, the cold metal searing into his palm.

Durmalian's blazing eyes fixed on him, the king's laughter turning into a sinister chuckle. "And what is this? A broken soul draped in fragile flesh? You are no hero."

The spectral form leaned closer, the flames of his presence licking at Will's resolve. "I see your doubts, your fears, your failures. You are nothing. You don't even believe in yourself—why should anyone else?"

Will staggered back as the cavern seemed to twist around him. Shadows stretched and warped, their whispers mocking him, dragging him into the depths of his own despair. The weight of his past pressed down on him, suffocating and relentless. The familiar sense of crushing self doubt weighing heavily on his soul and threatening to pull him under as he fought against the waves of darkness that pulsed out from Durmalian's towering form.

He saw it all—his failures, his regrets, the days he couldn't get out of bed, the nights spent wondering if anything he did mattered. The walls he had built to keep those feelings at bay crumbled under the weight of Durmalian's presence, leaving him exposed and vulnerable.

"Will!" Lyra's voice cut through the maelstrom. She stood beside him, her hand gripping his shoulder with a warmth that pierced the cold void enveloping him. Her kind eyes met his, steady and unwavering. "You're stronger than this," she said, her voice firm yet gentle. "I believe in you."

Her words ignited a spark within him. The medallion pulsed in his hand, its faint glow intensifying as he clutched it tighter.

Will took a shuddering breath, his chest heaving as he forced himself to stand proud. He met Durmalian's fiery gaze, his voice now filled with confidence. "You're right. I am flawed."

The medallion's light grew brighter, pushing back the shadows that swirled around him. "I've learned that my flaws don't define me. They're part of me, but they don't control me."

Durmalian roared, the gale of his fury whipping through the cavern. But the medallion responded to Will's words, radiating light that pushed back against the spectre's darkness.

As the glow enveloped him, Will felt the weight of his burdens lift—not vanish entirely, but transform into something he could carry. The medallion pulsed in his hand, and he stepped forward, its light carving a path through Durmalian's spectral form.

"You cannot defeat me," Durmalian hissed, his rage now reaching a fever pitch.

"No," Will said, his voice steady. "I don't want to defeat you. I want to release you!"

The light erupted from the medallion, a wave of pure energy that surged forward, engulfing Durmalian and the cavern in its brilliance. The whispers fell silent, the shadows dissipated, and for the first time, the air felt still and calm.

The brilliance of the medallion's light receded, leaving a newfound stillness in the cavern. The spectres were gone, their whispers silenced, and the darkness had lifted, replaced by an almost sacred calm. Will stood in the centre of the chamber, the medallion still glowing faintly in his hand. He felt different—lighter somehow. The weight of doubt and despair that had burdened him for so many long years had transformed, no longer dragging him down.

The cavern fell silent as the last traces of Durmalian's presence vanished. The medallion's glow dimmed, leaving Will standing in the centre of the chamber, his breathing heavy but his mind clear.

Lyra stepped forward, her eyes full of concern and admiration. "Will, are you alright?"

He nodded, a small but genuine smile breaking across his face. "Yeah," he said quietly. "I think I am."

He turned his gaze to the pedestal, where the stone of wisdom rested, its radiant glow pulsing like a heartbeat. Stepping forward, he felt no hesitation, no trace of uncertainty as he reached out. The moment his fingers brushed the smooth surface of the stone, a wave of warmth coursed through him.

As he lifted the stone from its niche, a connection formed in his mind—a symbiotic bond that felt both alien and familiar. Images flooded his thoughts, scenes of ancient battles, legendary heroes, and the history of Aruna stretching back millennia. He saw the creation of the stone itself, forged from the essence of the land, and imbued with the power to guide its bearer.

The stone's knowledge filled his mind, each piece clicking into place like a puzzle being solved. He saw the purpose of his journey with newfound clarity and, most importantly, the next step. Will instinctively looked at the weapon strapped to his side. The pommel was incomplete—a deliberate design waiting for this very moment.

"This...this is what it's meant for," Will murmured, his voice steady.

"What is it, Will?" Lyra asked, stepping closer, her daggers still drawn in caution despite the peace that now filled the cavern.

"The stone," he said, holding it aloft, its light dancing across the walls. "It's meant to complete the sword of light. Together, they become the key to defeating the Shadowmoor."

Lolmig, though visibly weary, grinned. "Then let's finish it, lad. We've come this far."

Will knelt, placing the sword before him. The stone seemed to vibrate in his hand, eager to fulfil its purpose. Carefully, he aligned it with the empty space on the pommel. The moment the stone touched the hilt, there was a sharp, resonant hum, and then—

A blinding brilliance erupted, illuminating every corner of the cavern with a radiance that felt pure and cleansing. The companions shielded their eyes, but Will couldn't look away, captivated by the union of stone and blade.

When the light subsided, the sword lay in his hands, transformed. The keen elegant steel gleamed with a brilliant, iridescent sheen, and the stone of wisdom was embedded perfectly in the pommel, pulsing with a steady glow.

# Chapter twelve

Will sat a short distance from the others, the Sword of Light resting across his lap, its newly rejoined form radiating energy that opened Will's mind. The blade's etchings shimmered faintly in the dim light of the cavern, their intricate patterns appearing to move and shift, as though alive with the power of the Stone of Wisdom now embedded in its hilt. He ran his fingers gently over the cool surface, feeling the faint ripple of energy beneath his touch, a steady pulse that resonated with something deep inside him.

He studied his reflection in the polished steel, distorted and fragmented by the blade's subtle curve. For a fleeting moment, he didn't recognise the man staring back at him—there was a confidence in those eyes that he hadn't seen in such a long time.

But now... something had shifted. The darkness within him hadn't disappeared—it still lingered at the edges of his thoughts, a shadow that would always be part of him. Yet, it no longer consumed him. It felt smaller, less overwhelming, and for the first time, manageable. He wasn't running from it anymore.

His chest swelled with a quiet pride, a feeling so unfamiliar it was almost foreign. It wasn't a boastful pride, but something deeper, more pure—a recognition of his own resilience. He had made it this far, not because he was fearless, but because he had chosen to keep moving despite his fears.

He glanced at his companions—Lolmig sat with his back against a stalagmite, his huge warhammer resting across his knees, as he quietly muttered a prayer of thanks to the ancestors. Valenor leaned against the cavern wall nearby, his eyes closed, his expression unusually soft. Lyra crouched near the lake, dipping her hand into the cool water and watching the kaleidoscopic light dancing across the ripples that radiated out across it's surface.

For the first time, Will felt like he belonged; connected to this world. He wasn't just an outsider fumbling his way through an unfamiliar world—he was part of this group, this mission. He traced the glowing etchings on the blade again, marvelling at the way they seemed to respond to his touch.

A smile crept across his face, unbidden and effortless. It felt easier than it had in years, more natural, as though some invisible weight had been lifted from his shoulders.

Lyra was the first to rise, stretching and rolling her shoulders. "We can't stay here forever," she said, her voice tinged with regret.

"Pity," Lolmig grunted, getting to his feet and brushing dust from his tunic. "I feel like I could sleep for a week."

Valenor simply nodded, and began gathering his things.

Will stood, sheathing the sword with a soft hiss of steel. "Then let's not waste any more time," he said, his voice carrying a newfound confidence.

The group gathered their belongings and began retracing their steps through the warren of tunnels, climbing steadily upward, their torches casting long shadows on the stone walls.

As they ascended, the air grew fresher, and the faint scent of the surface reached their noses, carried on a gentle breeze. By the time they emerged into the open air, the sun was high, bathing the mountains in golden light. Each of them paused at the cavern's mouth, taking a moment to breathe deeply, and relish the unexpected blessing of returning to the surface relatively unscathed.

There was no need for further discussion on their next destination. Having retrieved two of the three artifacts they needed, they all knew that their next destination would be Crystal Lake. Securing the second artifact had notably lifted everyone's mood. There was a sense that they had turned a corner in their quest. What had seemed daunting and insurmountable, now suddenly seemed to be within reach and that put a spring in their step as they set their sights to the southwest and began the journey. Will smiled as he looked around at this unlikely group of friends, talking and laughing as they travelled. He was still no closer to understanding what had brought him to this strange land, but whatever it was, he was thankful it had.

The journey southward through the mountain range was gruelling, though the trails in this part of the region were gentler than the jagged paths of the Sunfire Peaks to the north.

The group moved steadily, covering the distance in good time. Even so, the distance was significant, and by the end of each day, they were bone-weary, their muscles aching from the relentless travel.

As they descended further, the stark, barren crags were gradually replaced by gentler slopes, and the air grew warmer, losing the sharp bite of the higher altitudes. Patches of green began to dot the landscape—first as hardy shrubs clinging to the rocky soil, and later as clusters of trees forming small, shaded groves.

By the second day, the mountains loomed behind them, while the horizon ahead opened up to rolling hills that stretched as far as the eye could see. The trails wound through vibrant meadows, alive with the hum of insects and the occasional flash of colour from wildflowers swaying in the breeze. The scent of earth and fresh grass replaced the dry scents of stone and dust, and the warmth of the sun on their backs was a welcome reprieve.

At night, they camped beneath a vast canopy of stars, talking quietly whilst absorbing the beauty of the cosmos, and then the soft rustle of leaves and the distant call of nocturnal creatures would lull them into a restful sleep. Around their small campfire they shared stories, enjoying the simple pleasure of each others company—and their friendship grew stronger with each passing mile.

On the third day, the landscape began to change once more. The hills became gentler, sloping downward toward the distant horizon. By midday, as they crested a final rise, the shimmering expanse of Crystal Lake came into view. The sight took their breath away—its surface sparkled like liquid silver reflecting the sky above, stretching wide and calm.

"That's it," Lolmig said, his voice tinged with awe as he pointed toward the glimmering waters. "I can't wait to find an inn and spend a night in a proper bed."

Lyra shaded her eyes, her gaze fixed on their destination. "It's beautiful," she murmured, a note of relief in her tone.

Will found himself smiling, despite the ache in his legs and the fatigue resting heavily on his shoulders. Yet beneath the beauty that lay before them, he couldn't shake the growing sense of anticipation—of the challenge that awaited them beneath its deceptively calm surface.

As they began their descent into the foothills that surrounded the lake, Will slowed his pace and turned to Valenor with a furrowed brow. "Have you considered how we're going to retrieve the amulet yet?" he asked.

Valenor paused and glanced over at Will. A flicker of frustration crossed his sharp features as he sighed. "I haven't," he admitted, a wry look on his face. "The prophecy is frustratingly vague on the matter. It speaks of the amulet's significance, but other than a cryptic passage about it being lost to the cold depths, nothing about it's location."

Will's frown deepened. "Then we're heading there blind?"

"Not entirely," Valenor replied, his tone confident. "These artifacts have a way of embedding themselves in the local folklore. Over the years, bits and pieces of the truth tend to resurface in the form of stories and legends. Someone in the area is bound to know something, and I'm sure we'll be able to find someone willing to talk once we arrive."

Lolmig grunted from behind them, his heavy boots crunching against the gravelly path. "That's a lot of hoping for something so important," he muttered.

The clouds started rolling in during the afternoon as they made their final approach to the small fishing village Valenor had pointed out on Will's map. The wind picked up and dark clouds hung low in the sky, shrouding the far shore in an impenetrable mist. The storm's chill wind whipped across the surface, carrying sheets of stinging rain that forced them to walk with their heads bowed.

The village stretched out in a patchwork of sturdy but unremarkable buildings, their wooden walls stained dark by years of hard weather and neglect. It was a place that spoke of quiet endurance rather than prosperity. The docks jutted into the lake in uneven lines, the weathered planks creaked and groaned under the strain of battered fishing boats bobbing restlessly in the rising waves.

The storm had driven most villagers indoors, leaving only a few hardy souls working near the shore. A fisherman hunched under the hood of his tattered cloak, securing a tarp over his boat, while another tended to a stack of nets beneath a makeshift awning. A few children ran through the narrow, muddy streets, their laughter carrying on the wind, their bare feet splashing in puddles.

The companions were drawn to the faint glow of a lantern hanging outside a modest inn. A simple sign hung above the entrance, bearing the name "The Fisherman's Rest" in peeling paint and smoke curled from its crooked chimney, promising warmth and shelter. As they approached, the wind shifted, carrying with it the rich, savoury scent of stew, and they could hear the sound of friendly chatter and music through the heavy wooden door.

Lolmig grunted in appreciation. "Smells like they've got something cooking. Best we get inside before this storm does us in."

"Agreed," Valenor said, shaking rain from his hood. He glanced at Will and Lyra. "We can start asking around once we've dried off and eaten."

Lyra nodded, her face flushed from the cold. "Let's hope the locals are more helpful than the weather."

Pushing open the door, they stepped into the inn's warmth, the soft murmur of conversation and the crackling of a fire providing a comfortable respite from the storm outside. The room fell quiet as the soaked travellers entered, all eyes turning toward them. They were strangers here, and in a village this small, strangers were rarely ignored, but after a moment of scrutiny, the patrons soon lost interest and returned to their conversations.

Several fishermen were clustered around a large table near the hearth, their faces flushed with the effects of both the fire and the ale. They gestured wildly as they recounted tales of their biggest catches, their laughter rising above the general din. Nearby, a fiddler played a cheerful tune, his foot tapping rhythmically against the floorboards, keeping time.

The companions made their way to the bar, where a friendly innkeeper with a ruddy face and a wide grin greeted them. His eyes twinkled with the mirth of a thousand shared jokes as he wiped a mug with a well-worn cloth.

"Welcome to The Fisherman's Rest!" he boomed, his voice carrying above the noise. "What can I do for you fine folk tonight?"

"We'd like to arrange for a room," Valenor said, stepping forward. "And some food, if you have it."

"Of course, of course!" the innkeeper replied, nodding enthusiastically. "We've got the finest beef stew in the area, and fresh bread just out of the oven. As for rooms, we've got a cosy one available upstairs. That'll be one silver for the night, and another for the food and drink. How's that sound?"

"That sounds perfect," Will said, exchanging a look with his companions, who nodded in agreement. Lolmig handed over the coins, and the innkeeper pocketed them with a smile.

"Right then! Your room is ready whenever you are, just up the stairs and the first door on the left. But sit yourselves down first, and I'll have the food brought to you. What'll you be drinking?"

"Ale for all of us," Lolmig answered with a grin. The innkeeper nodded and turned to fill their order.

The companions found an empty table near the back of the common room and settled into the wooden chairs, which creaked under their weight. The innkeeper soon returned with a tray laden with mugs of frothy ale, bowls of steaming stew, and thick slices of fresh bread.

As they began to eat, the warmth of the inn and the hearty food did wonders to lift their spirits. They chatted quietly among themselves, discussing their plans for the next day.

As they talked, a grizzled old fisherman at a nearby table suddenly looked up, his eyes sharp and interested in their conversation. "You're going after the Amulet, are you, adventurers?"

A few people nearby stopped talking to listen, their curiosity piqued. The lively chatter and music softened as the attention of many of the inn's patrons shifted to the old man.

Will exchanged a glance with his companions before nodding. "We are."

The old fisherman chuckled, a sound more like the creaking of an ancient door. "Many have tried and failed, you know. Brave souls, the lot of them, but none came back."

Will looked around his companions, and then turned and invited the old fisherman to sit with them. "Can you tell us more about it? How did the Amulet end up at the bottom of the lake?"

The fisherman stood and moved to their table. He took a long sip from his mug, his eyes distant as he delved into the past. "Ah, the tale of the Amulet is as old as these waters themselves. It is said that many years ago, a powerful sorceress named Elowen lived in these parts. She was a mage of the order of the burning torch, sworn to protect the land from darkness."

He paused, his gaze sweeping across the room, ensuring everyone was listening. "When Malakar sought to enact his dreadful curse upon the land, Elowen fought bravely to stop him. But she was not strong enough to defeat him." The fisherman went to take a drink from his empty cup and looked disheartened. He looked at Will hopefully, and Will called the bartender over to refill the man's cup. Lolmig grumbled as he reached for his purse once again.

When the fisherman had a full cup he took a big gulp of ale and Will urged him to continue. "And the Amulet?"

The fisherman nodded, his face solemn. "As Malakar tracked her down to the shore of Crystal Lake, Elowen used her remaining strength to cast it into our lake, knowing that its magic would be safe from Malakar's reach, binding it with powerful enchantments to protect it from falling into the wrong hands. Legend has it that the Amulet is guarded by the very waters and creatures of the lake, a test for any who would seek it."

Lyra leaned in, her eyes wide with wonder. "Has anyone ever seen it?"

The old man shook his head. "Not since it was lost to the waters. Many have tried to recover it, but none have returned."

The companions sat in silence for a moment after the fisherman finished his tale, absorbing everything he had just told them.

"We understand the dangers, but we must find it," Valenor said quietly, his eyes glinting with an intense fervour.

The old fisherman nodded, but the look he cast at Valenor seemed to bear some malice. When he noticed Will looking at him, he broke off his scrutiny of Valenor and smiled, standing and moving back to his own table, "Then may Elowen's spirit guide you, brave souls. The lake will test you. I wish you better luck than those who came before you."

Will looked intently at the face of the fisherman, trying to read his intentions. There was something to the way this old fisherman presented himself; something Will couldn't quite put his finger on. He had a sense that the old man was hiding something. Unable to put his finger on it, he dismissed the thought and turned back to the group to continue their conversation.

"We'll head down to the lake first thing in the morning," Valenor said. "We need to see what we're dealing with in the light of a new day."

They talked for a while about how they might search the vast body of water, eventually settling on this plan and shifted into a more relaxed conversation, discussing their adventures and sharing a few laughs. Despite the levity, Will couldn't shake the feeling that they were being watched. He glanced back at the old fisherman and found him watching intently, his eyes flicking between Will and his companions.

What does he find so fascinating? Will wondered. There was something about the old man's gaze that unnerved him, but he couldn't place what it was.

As the evening wore on, the inn gradually emptied. The companions finished the last of the drinks they had been nursing and headed upstairs to their room.

# Chapter thirteen

The following day, the group awoke before sunrise and met in the common room, talking in the hushed tones that people use when they rise before the sun. They went over the plan one last time while they waited for the sky to lighten, taking the time to eat some food and enjoy some hot tea.

The common room was already full of local fishermen who sat huddled in groups, planning their day's work before filing out to prepare their boats. The atmosphere buzzed with quiet activity, the low murmur of conversations creating a background hum.

The companions were seated at a corner table in the common room, their breakfast mostly untouched as they debated the best way to search the lake for the Amulet of Purity. The morning sun streamed through the windows, casting warm light on the worn wooden floors, but their mood was clouded by uncertainty.

As Lyra was about to suggest searching the lake in shifts, the innkeeper approached, his expression puzzled. He carried a bundle wrapped in burlap, holding it delicately. "This was left for you at the bar before you rose this morning," he said, setting it carefully on the table.

"For us?" Will asked, frowning as he glanced at the package. "Who left it?"

The innkeeper's brow furrowed, his face a picture of confusion. "That's the strange thing. I can't remember. Normally, I never forget a face, but whoever left this... it's like they vanished from my mind the moment they walked away." He shook his head apologetically.

Will thanked him and watched as the innkeeper wandered back toward the bar. The group turned their attention to the package, their conversation momentarily forgotten.

The burlap had slipped slightly, revealing the corner of an old leather-bound book beneath it. The cover was embossed with a strange arcane seal, the markings faded. Will pushed back the cloth further, fully revealing the tome. The leather was cracked with age, and the title was scrawled in what appeared to be elvish.

The group exchanged wary glances. "What do you think?" Lyra asked, her voice low.

Will hesitated before flipping the cover open, revealing pages filled with text in the flowing script of the elves. Without a word, he slid the book across the rough wooden table toward Valenor.

Valenor studied the text in silence, his eyes moving swiftly across the pages. The faint crease in his brow deepened as he read on, his fingers absent-mindedly tracing the edges of the parchment. The others watched him closely, the tension at the table growing with each passing moment.

Finally, Will broke the silence, unable to contain his nerves. "Well?"

Valenor glanced up, his expression unreadable at first. Then, a small smile tugged at the corners of his mouth. He closed the book gently and pushed it back to the centre of the table. "Whoever left this... I believe they meant to help us."

Lyra leaned forward eagerly. "What does it say?"

Valenor's tone was calm but edged with gravity. "It's a collection of local legends, passed down over centuries. One in particular caught my eye. It speaks of a realm beneath the lake—a place called the Heart of Eryndor."

Lolmig folded his arms, his scepticism evident. "And we're supposed to take this on face value? A random book about the exact place we're searching for, dropped off by someone the innkeeper conveniently can't remember?"

Valenor met his gaze evenly. "Coincidence or not, it's here. And what it describes fits too well to ignore." He reopened the book, flipping to a page near the middle. "The Heart of Eryndor is said to be a nexus of magical energy, hidden beneath the lake's surface. It's protected by an ancient guardian that tests all who enter. Only those with pure intentions are allowed to proceed. Those who fail... are consumed, claimed by the water."

Lyra shivered at the weight of his words. "You think the amulet is down there?"

Valenor nodded slowly. "It makes sense. If Elowen, or anyone from the Order, wanted to hide something from Malakar, they would choose a place like this—somewhere only the worthy could access."

Lolmig squinted at the book, his expression darkening. "Pure intentions, huh? That doesn't sound ominous at all." He gestured toward the bundle. "Still feels like a trap."

Will leaned back, his arms crossed, his gaze fixed on the leather-bound book. "Trap or not, we're running out of options. If this book can point us toward the amulet, I say we've got to see where it leads."

As they talked over the benefits and drawbacks of the plan to seek the heart of Eryndor, Will noticed Valenor begin to pale visibly. "Valenor, are you alright?" Will asked, noticing his friend had paled and was sweating profusely.

Valenor forced a weak smile. "I'm fine, just... not feeling my best."

Will wasn't convinced. Concerned, he pressed the matter further. "If you're not well, just say Val. We need you at your best."

Valenor sighed, realising Will wasn't going to let it drop. He leaned over, conspiratorially and whispered to Will, "The thing is... I'm deathly afraid of open water. The thought of being out there... it terrifies me."

Will placed a reassuring hand on Valenor's shoulder, shooting his friend a reassuring smile. "You'll be fine, we'll go at your pace."

As the first light of dawn began to filter through the windows, Will stood up and stretched, indicating that it was time to leave. The group gathered their belongings and made their way to the door, stepping out into the cool, crisp morning air. The remnants of the previous night's storm were dissipating, but the water was still anything but calm, and a persistent drizzle quickly started to soak them through as they headed down to the lake.

The docks were a hive of activity, with fishermen loading their boats and preparing for the day ahead.

As they neared the edge of the lake, Valenor's face went even paler. He stopped short, his eyes wide with fear as he looked out over the vast expanse of water.

Will noticed his friend's distress and stepped closer. "Valenor, maybe it's best if you stay back at the inn. We need you at your best, and we can handle this part."

Valenor hesitated, apparently torn as he considered Will's suggestion. Finally, he nodded. "If you're sure..." he left it hanging.

Will gave him a reassuring pat on the back before turning to the others. "Let's find someone who can take us out onto the lake."

Lolmig pointed to a sturdy-looking boat moored nearby. "That one looks like it could fit us all," he said. "Let's see if the owner is willing to help us."

They approached the boat, and a burly fisherman looked up from his preparations, eyeing them with suspicion. "Can I help you?" he asked, his voice gruff.

"We need to get out onto the lake," Will said, his voice steady. The burly fisherman looked up from his preparations, his eyes narrowing as he sized up the group.

"I lost time to the storm yesterday, I have to get out and fish," the fisherman grumbled, turning away again and looking back to his task. "I don't have time to be ferrying tourists around."

Will glanced at Lyra and Lolmig before turning back to the fisherman. "Maybe if we help you row, it might save you some time. Please, this is very important to us."

The fisherman's eyes flickered with interest as he considered fishing a deeper part of lake, not often frequented by the others. He hesitated, eyeing the heavy looking purse at Lolmig's waist. "Maybe if I were compensated for my time a bit?" he suggested, raising his bushy eyebrows.

Lolmig grumbled a bit, but pulled a couple of coins out and showed them to the fisherman, who shook his head. Lolmig pulled out another coin, "That's all you're getting." he said.

With a reluctant nod, the fisherman grabbed the coins from Lolmig's outstretched hand and gestured for them to climb aboard. The companions quickly complied, finding seats and picking up the oars. The boat rocked gently as they settled in, the sound of water lapping against the hull.

"Let's get moving then," the fisherman said gruffly, taking his place at the stern. "Row steady, and we might get this done quicker than expected."

As they began to row, the rhythmic motion of the boat cutting through the water created a soothing, almost hypnotic motion. The rain let up a little and the sun slowly broke through the clouds, casting a golden path across the lake and illuminating their way. The village and its bustling docks slowly faded into the distance, replaced by the vast, open expanse of water.

The fisherman kept a wary eye on the companions, occasionally muttering under his breath about the lost time.

Despite his grumbling, he guided them skilfully across the lake, steering them toward their destination that they had described to him.

As they approached the area above where the heart of Eryndor was supposed to be located, the fisherman called out, "Alright, this is as far as I go. You'll have to take it from here."

Will nodded, looking over the side of the boat at the water below. "Thank you for bringing us this far."

The fisherman gave a reluctant nod, then turned his attention back to his own tasks. The companions took a deep breath, preparing themselves as they swung their legs over the edge of the boat and slipped into the icy waters, catching their breath as the chill shocked them.

The three bobbed there in the water, watching the fisherman's boat move off into the distance. They waited for their bodies to become accustomed to the cold water, shivering as they adjusted to the frigid temperature.

The three of them decided on a search pattern and then began diving the depths, searching for any signs of the stone archway Valenor described from the book. The underwater world was dimly lit and eerily quiet. The deeper they went, the less sunlight penetrated from the surface, and they could see only a short distance ahead, the murky water obscuring their vision. They moved slowly, scanning the lakebed for any signs of the archway. Every few minutes, they surfaced, gasping for air and exchanging quick, whispered updates before diving back down to continue their search. The cold water sapped their strength, but they were fiercely determined and persevered, even as their bodies began to protest.

Finally, after what felt like hours of searching, Lyra burst to the surface with a wide grin on her face. "I think I have found it!" she exclaimed. "Follow me!"

They dove back underwater, with Lyra leading the way.

The group followed Lyra in single file, diving deeper and deeper into the dark, icy water. Lyra swam smoothly through the water, her movements graceful, but after a moment she hesitated, glancing around the murky depths as if retracing her memory.

She signalled for the others to wait as she briefly glanced about, scanning the rocky expanse of the lake bed to get her bearings. Then, with a sudden flick of her hand, she beckoned them forward. With quick, deliberate strokes, she led them around an outcropping of jagged rock that loomed out of the shadows.

Beyond the rock, on a wide dais carved from smooth stone, stood a perfectly formed archway that rose from the lake bed, its surface etched with glowing runes that pulsed with light. The runes seemed alive, shifting subtly as though reacting to the water's current.

In the opening of the archway stood a vertical threshold, like the rippling surface of the lake, impossibly contained within the frame.

Will's heart raced as he took it all in. Though the others couldn't speak, the awe on their faces matched his own. This was it. He had no doubt they had found what they were looking for.

But his lungs burned, reminding him how long they'd been submerged. He glanced around at the others, signalling for them to return to the surface. One by one, they turned, swimming back toward the distant light above.

The three companions broke through the surface of the water almost simultaneously, gasping desperately for air, and pushing the water away from their eyes. They bobbed in the choppy waves, their breaths ragged as they filled their aching lungs, their wet hair clinging to their faces.

For a moment, they simply floated there, blinking against the rain that pelted down from the cloudy sky above, waiting for the dizzying pinpricks of light in their vision to fade.

Lyra was the first to recover, pushing wet strands of hair back from her face as her lips curved into a grin. "That was incredible," she said between breaths, her excitement barely contained.

Lolmig let out a short, breathy laugh, shaking his head in disbelief. "Aye, I've never seen anything like it in all my years."

Will wiped the water from his face, his own grin spreading as he glanced between them. "That archway... it has to be the way in." he said, his voice shaking with excitement.

After several long moments spent waiting for their heart's to calm and their breathing to become more measured, the three companions exchanged a silent nod. They couldn't afford to waste any more time. Without another word, they each took one final, deep breath, filling their lungs to capacity, and then dove beneath the surface.

The descent was swift, their strokes strong and deliberate as they cut through the water. The lake grew darker as they sank deeper, the light from above fading, but the faint glow of the runes on the archway guided them like a beacon.

The shimmering, rippling veil of the threshold loomed before them, mesmerising even in the dim light. They didn't hesitate. Lyra led the way, plunging through the watery surface of the archway, her form disappearing into its undulating ripples without resistance.

Will followed close behind, his heart pounding as he breached the veil. There was a moment of strange pressure, like the lake itself pressing in on him, and then he was through.

Lolmig came last, his powerful strokes carrying him forward as he braced himself for what lay beyond.

As they breached the surface, gasping for air, the three companions were struck by an immediate sense of vertigo. The archway had somehow flipped their perspective—what had been a vertical threshold now lay horizontal beneath them, the shimmering water forming the surface of an impossibly large pool inside a cavern.

Will clutched at his head, trying to steady himself as the dizzying disorientation threatened to overwhelm him. "What just happened?" he gasped, glancing back at the surreal archway, now below them in the pool.

The cavern itself left them speechless for a moment. The water emitted a soft glow, a cool, blue-green light that danced across the jagged ceiling like liquid stars in constant motion. Shadows rippled in patterns that shifted with every gentle ripple of the pool's surface.

"This... this is incredible," Lyra whispered, her voice filled with wonder. She spun slowly in place, taking in the cavern's immensity.

Lolmig, ever practical, squinted at their surroundings. "There," he said, pointing to a ledge of rock that jutted out from the side of the cavern. "We can climb out over there."

Wasting no time, they swam toward it, the glowing water strangely buoyant, almost as if it were helping them along. The trio hauled themselves onto the rocky edge, collapsing onto the rough stone with tired grunts.

They sat for a while, water dripping from their clothes and pooling beneath them as they caught their breath. The glow of the pool bathed them in its strange light, and the cavern echoed faintly with the sound of their breathing and the occasional distant drip of water.

Will looked around, his eyes narrowing as he tried to make sense of what he was seeing. "This place... There's a presence here, can you feel it?"

Lyra nodded, her sharp eyes scanning the cavern's expanse. "If the amulet is here, it's going to be guarded. No way a place like this is just sitting empty."

Lolmig grunted, wringing water from his beard as he rose to his feet. "Aye, let's not waste time. Whatever's waiting for us, it'll find us soon enough if we sit here like wet trolls."

The others nodded reluctantly, slowly hauling their aching bodies off the smooth stone and brushing water from their gear. Despite their exhaustion, they worked carefully, methodically ensuring no stone went unturned and no corner unexplored. That feeling of being observed lingered, prickling at the edges of their awareness, but they tried to ignore it as they pressed on.

At first, it seemed as though the cavern was entirely empty, but just as despair began to creep in, Will's eyes caught something at the far end of the cavern—a faint shimmer of light similar to that being emitted from the glowing pool they arrived through. He clambered over a pile of rocks to find another glowing pool, filled with the same glowing water that moved as though it was alive. He called the others over, keeping his voice low.

"There," he said, pointing towards it. "That's it. I can feel it."

"Feel what?" Lolmig asked, his brow furrowing as he stared at the glowing pool.

Will hesitated, trying to find the right words. "I don't know how to explain it... but this is the way. I just know it."

The other two exchanged uncertain glances but didn't argue. Will took a step closer, the pull toward the water growing stronger with every heartbeat. He turned back to them, his expression resolute. "Stay here. I'll go down first and see where it leads."

Lolmig opened his mouth to protest but stopped short, "Be careful, lad," he grumbled instead, his tone tinged with begrudging approval.

Lyra nodded, her expression concerned. "If you're not back soon, we're coming after you."

Will gave them both a quick nod before plunging into the glowing pool. The moment he submerged, the world shifted again. The water here felt denser, almost alive, pushing against him, but slowly guiding him forward. As he swam deeper, he realised he was swimming through an intricate maze of underwater tunnels.

The passages twisted and turned, the glowing light pulsing faintly along the walls to guide his way. The currents shifted subtly, as though the water itself was directing him, and he let it carry him deeper. The tunnels eventually opened into small, hidden chambers. He would briefly take a look around these smaller chambers, satisfying himself that the amulet wasn't present before heading back into the underwater labyrinth.

He paused, his lungs burning, and the realisation struck him that he had ventured some distance from the others. The scale of this labyrinth was vast, and the risk of losing his way too great. Kicking hard against the current, he retraced his path, following the glowing threads back to the pool where he had left them, stopping occasionally at side chambers for air before continuing.

Bursting through the surface, he gasped for air and clambered onto the bank where Lyra and Lolmig waited, their faces tense with concern.

"We're going to have to do this together," Will said, still catching his breath. "It's a maze down there—tunnels and chambers. It's too much for one person, but I think..." he paused for a moment, "There's something strange about this water."

Lolmig and Lyra both looked at him, and then back at each other.

Will caught their sideways glance. "I know how it sounds, but... well, you'll see. Come on, let's go!" he said, before diving back below the surface.

He could sense the others right behind him as he led the way back to the furthest point he had explored, navigating back through the tunnels, trusting in the pull of the current. They stopped occasionally in openings to refill their lungs with air before submerging again and continuing deeper into the maze.

They continued for what seemed like an eternity, splitting up to explore the network of chambers, until eventually they surfaced in a larger cavern, much larger than the one they first entered. They stepped cautiously onto the smooth stone floor, their boots dripping water and echoing softly in the vast space. As they moved away from the glowing pool behind them, a sudden shift in the air hit them like a shock-wave. It was as though the cavern itself exhaled, in response to their presence.

Without warning, the stillness shattered into a display of breathtaking beauty. Rows and tiers of shallow pools, hidden in the shadows moments before, began to illuminate one by one. Each pool glowed with a unique hue—brilliant blues, fiery oranges, tranquil greens—casting shimmering works of art onto the cavern walls. The colours danced and merged, creating swirling patterns more vivid and intricate than the finest sunrise.

At first, there was silence, broken only by the soft trickle of water flowing somewhere, out of sight. Then, as the light spread, each pool began emitting a subtle note, faint and resonant, like the sound of tuning forks in every key. The notes wove together, harmonising into a perfect chorus that seemed to vibrate through their very bones.

Will, Lyra, and Lolmig stood frozen, their expressions filled with wonder. The wall of sound filling every fibre of their being, a symphony that seemed to reach deep into their souls, evoking emotions they couldn't fully grasp.

"This is…" Lyra began, her voice barely above a whisper, but she trailed off, unable to put her feelings into words.

Lolmig, normally stoic, rubbed his beard absently, he said nothing but tears rolled down his cheeks as the emotions he was feeling completely overwhelmed him.

As their eyes adjusted, they began to notice the true peculiarity of the scene. The water in the pools defied all logic. In some, it seemed almost solid, shimmering like polished glass. In others, it floated freely in perfect, wobbling spheres above the pools, glowing faintly like stars caught in a net. Streams of liquid ran upwards in defiance of gravity, forming waterfalls that cascaded into pools above them. Droplets spiralled lazily into the air, drifting toward the ceiling before vanishing into the glowing mist.

"It's like the water is alive," Will murmured, his voice filled with wonder.

Lyra reached out hesitantly, touching a sphere of floating water. It rippled at her touch, a soft hum accompanying the movement before it gently recoiled, as though acknowledging her presence.

Lolmig took a step forward, his boots splashing in a thin stream that flowed upward past his feet. He turned to Will, his expression unusually serious. "If the amulet's here, lad, whatever power protects it won't give it up easily."

Will nodded, his gaze fixed on the centre of the cavern, where the colours and sounds seemed to converge into a mesmerising vortex of light.

In the very centre of the dazzling array of shifting colour and sound stood a column of what seemed to be pure light energy, pulsing, it seemed, from the very core of the earth, up through the centre of the cavern. As they got closer, they realised that once again it was the same living water that seemed to inhabit every corner of this strange underwater realm. Will knew immediately, without any doubt in his soul, that this was the heart of Eryndor.

The companions froze, their breaths catching as the cavern itself seemed to come alive with a forceful sentience. The harmonious symphony that had surrounded them turned uneasy, the notes turning discordant, ominous. The dazzling array of colours converged, flowing together like streams of paint until the entire cavern was bathed in a pulsating crimson light.

At the very centre of the column of light, a massive, transcendent eye formed—a deep, liquid red, ringed with glowing gold. It blinked slowly, deliberately, a movement that seemed to ripple through the cavern in a wave of energy that penetrated into their very souls.

Will's mouth went dry, and his hands instinctively reached for the hilt of his weapon. He glanced at Lyra and Lolmig, both standing rigid, their expressions mirroring his feelings, a confusing mix of awe and fear.

A voice resonated from the column, not spoken aloud but vibrating in their chests, in their minds. It was neither male nor female, neither harsh nor gentle, but carried an undeniable power of authority.

**"Only those who are true of heart may enter the Heart of Eryndor,"** it intoned, the words reverberating through the cavern. **"Who dares approach?"**

Will stepped forward before he could think, as though the hand of fate was guiding his steps. He felt his companions' gazes on him but didn't dare turn away from the eye. "We do," he said, his voice trembling. "We seek the Amulet of Purity, to aid in the fight against the curse of Shadowmoor."

The eye narrowed slightly, as though scrutinising his every word, his every thought. **"Many seek power for selfish ends. Few understand the weight of their quest. Do you understand what it is you ask of Eryndor?"**

Will swallowed hard nodding slowly. "I do. We've faced trials, dangers beyond what I thought possible. But this isn't about us. It's about saving our world from a darkness that will consume everything if we fail."

The eye shifted, the light within the column flickering, casting dancing shadows across the cavern walls. **"Your words are bold. But words alone do not prove worthiness. You must face the trials of the heart, the mind, and the soul. Only then shall the Amulet reveal itself."**

The eye regarded all three of them in silence for what felt like an eternity. Then the voice rang out again, louder, commanding, filling the cavern.

**"Enter, if you dare. But know this—only the true of heart will leave unbroken."**

The light column pulsed once, twice, then parted slightly at its base, revealing an opening into a swirling vortex of glowing water.

Will glanced at his friends, his expression determined. "Together," he said.

"Together," Lyra and Lolmig echoed.

They stepped forward, side by side, into the unknown.

# Chapter fourteen

As Will stepped into the swirling vortex, he felt the familiar pull of water against his skin but in reverse—drawing him forward instead of resisting him. For a moment, his senses blurred; sound dulled, sight dissolved into liquid light, and touch became a confusing meld of pressure and warmth. Then, all at once, the world around him sharpened into focus.

He stood in an alien water world unlike anything he had ever imagined. The ground beneath his feet shimmered like liquid silver, with every step sending ripples cascading outward. Towering columns of water stretched endlessly upward, flowing against gravity into a vast, undulating sky that resembled the churning surface of the ocean more than it did atmosphere. Schools of luminous creatures darted and danced in every direction, their movements painting patterns of light in their wake.

From nowhere and everywhere at once, the voice once again resonated. **"Your heart has brought you far. Now, let us see its true depth."**

The ground beneath him shifted, rippling until it formed three archways of glowing liquid. Each emitted a soft, resonant tone, pulling at different corners of his mind. A faint whisper brushed against his ear. **"Choose."**

Will hesitated, knowing somehow that this was a significant decision, and not wanting to get it wrong. Each archway seemed to radiate a different emotion—pain, love, sacrifice. He stepped forward, not knowing where he was going but trusting his heart to guide him.

When Will stepped through the archway, the alien beauty of the water world faded, replaced by an urgent scene of desperation. He stood on the edge of a chasm filled with crystalline water, its depths glowing faintly with a strange radiant light. Before him, a mother and her child clung to the edge of a precariously balanced outcrop of rock. Above them, jagged stalactites, held aloft by nothing but threads of shimmering liquid, trembled ominously.

The ground beneath Will's feet shuddered, and once again the voice of the guardian echoed: **"You can only save one. The other must fall."**

The words froze Will in place. His gaze darted to the mother, her wide eyes meeting his with fierce determination. "Save my child," she cried, her voice trembling but resolute. "Let me go."

Will's mind raced, his heart pounding in his chest. The child's tiny hands were slipping, his cries weak and panicked. But the mother's unyielding love burned through her desperation, a strength so raw it cut into Will like a blade.

"No!" he shouted, stepping toward the edge. "There has to be a way to save both of you!"

The voice returned, detached, emotionless: **"Choose, or they both fall. The balance cannot hold under the weight of indecision."**

Will glanced down at the outcrop and saw the crystalline threads that tethered it to the cliff edge splintering. With each second, the threads frayed further, the rock tilting precariously. The shifting weight of even a single movement was enough to strain the delicate structure; time was running out.

His breath caught as he darted to a nearby ledge, scanning desperately for something—anything—that could hold them. His eyes landed on a branch, jagged and brittle but long enough to reach. He grabbed it, dragging it into position.

"Hold on!" he yelled, wedging the branch into place and extending it toward them. His fingers scraped against stone as he reached for the mother's hand.

The ground beneath him shuddered violently, sending splinters of rock tumbling into the glowing chasm below. The stalactites above trembled, shards of glistening crystal falling with deafening cracks.

The mother shook her head fiercely, her grip faltering. "It's too late for me," she said, her voice thick with emotion. "Save him. Please."

"No!" Will shouted again, desperation choking his voice. But her gaze, steady and full of love, locked onto his as she released her grip.

Will lunged forward, the crystalline branch snapping under the strain as the child slipped further. With every ounce of strength, Will grabbed the boy and pulled him to safety. His chest heaved as he turned back toward the ledge, his heart screaming for one last chance.

But the mother was gone. The outcrop crumbled, fragments tumbling into the abyss. Her final, grateful smile etched itself into Will's memory, a moment seared into his soul as she vanished into the chasm below.

The voice returned, quieter now: **"Your choice was made. This is the burden of the living."**

Will sat back, cradling the child, his chest hollow and aching. Tears stung his eyes as he whispered, "I'm so sorry."

He barely had time to process the guilt crushing him when the scene shifted abruptly. He now stood in the centre of a circle of people, their faces filled with desperation. In the centre of the circle hovered a single glowing drop of water, radiant and perfect, pulsing with a soothing hum.

The voice returned, low and sombre. **"This drop can heal one. Choose."**

Around him, the pleas began. An elderly man with trembling hands stepped forward. "I've served my village for fifty years. I only want to live long enough to see my grandson born."

A young girl, clutching her stomach, gasped through tears. "Please... I'm so sick. My parents can't lose me too."

A father knelt at Will's feet, his son limp in his arms. "He's all I have left," the man whispered, his voice breaking.

Will felt the weight of their gazes, their need crashing over him like waves. He tried to think logically, to weigh the worth of each life, but his heart rebelled against the idea. "There has to be another way," he said, his voice trembling.

He reached out to touch the drop, willing it to divide, to multiply, to give enough to heal them all. But the drop resisted, glowing brighter as though scorning his effort.

"Why are you doing this?" he demanded, looking to the unseen force he knew was watching. "Why force me to choose? No one should have to make this decision!"

The voice did not answer. The drop hovered, teetering, as though it might drop at any moment.

His vision blurred as tears filled his eyes. Finally, he reached out and touched the young girl's shoulder, guiding her hands to the drop. The moment it touched her lips, its glow faded, and colour returned to her pale cheeks.

The young girl wept with joy at being released from her torment, but Will could only feel the weight of the old man's resigned nod and the father's grief racked sobs.

Will's heart felt as though it had been shattered into a thousand pieces when the ground beneath him shifted again. He found himself before a pool of water so still it seemed solid. His own reflection stared back at him, but there was something wrong.

The figure in the water stepped forward, emerging from the pool like a ghost. It looked exactly like him, but its eyes burned with accusation. "You've failed," the reflection said, its voice harsh and cutting. "You let a mother die. You abandoned the others. You're weak."

"I didn't abandon them!" Will shouted, his fists clenching. "I did what I could!"

"And was it enough?" the reflection sneered. It stepped closer, its voice lowering. "Your efforts always seem to fall short of the mark, don't they?"

The words struck like daggers, slicing through his defences. He dropped to his knees before the pool, staring into his reflection's accusing gaze. But a small flicker of light inside him remained and began to swell, warming the coldness that had gripped him, thawing his soul. "I don't know if it was enough," he whispered. "But I did my best... and that's all I can do."

The reflection softened, its gaze losing its malice. His reflection suddenly smiled, before turning to wisps of smoke and vanishing.

As the final trial faded, his surroundings began to shimmer and he found himself back before the three arches which now stood completely still and quiet. The water around him swirled into a towering figure, and Will found himself face to face with Eryndor.

**"You have faced what many could not,"** the elemental said, its voice flowing with a deep, resonant warmth. **"You sought to save everyone, even when the rules forbade it. You fought not with self-serving pride, but with love and empathy. Such empathy is rare, but it can also be dangerous."**

Eryndor stepped closer, its eyes glowing like twin stars. **"You suffer when you take on too much of the pain of your world. You absorb it, bottle it up, and it dims your light. You have great potential, Will, but your power can** be perverted by the forces of darkness if you allow your pain to consume you.”

Will nodded, his throat tight. “I just... I don’t want to fail anyone.”

**“And that is why you will succeed.”**

Eryndor’s form began to dissolve, its light dimming. **“Carry this wisdom with you. The Amulet of Purity lies ahead. Go forth. Your journey is far from over.”**

With that, Will was propelled backward, landing on the cavern floor abruptly beside Lyra and Lolmig. As they stirred, their wide eyes met his, and he knew they had faced their own trials.

He stood, his heart still aching from what he had just endured, and turned toward a faint glow. The column of flowing water had completely parted and at its centre, floating in a curtain of pure light, stood the amulet. **“Let’s finish this.”**

Will’s fingers closed around the amulet, its surface warm despite the cool air in the cave. The moment his grip tightened, the cavern was flooded with radiant, liquid light, spilling from every pool and filling the air with a luminous mist. It felt as though the water itself was alive, rejoicing at the amulet being claimed.

A harmony of sound erupted from the glowing pools, weaving together like threads of an ancient melody. The notes were achingly familiar, resonating in their very souls, as though echoing from the heart of existence itself. It pulsed in perfect time with their beating hearts, carrying away pain, doubt, and fear.

As the harmony reached its crescendo, Will's body felt weightless, his mind expanding in ways he could never have conceived. His vision blurred, but not from tears—it was as though the very essence of the universe was flooding through him, unravelling and revealing itself as it formed new pathways in his mind. He gasped, his breath catching in his chest as the relics surged with light, binding to him, their energy merging into one cohesive whole.

The knowledge that filled his mind wasn't so much data and information as it was empathy. The pulse of the earth beneath his feet, the lifeblood of ancient forests, the whisper of winds carrying the memories of civilisations long past. He could feel the joy of a newborn's first cry, the grief of a widow's final goodbye, the shared heartbeat of all living things stretched across time and space, woven into an unbreakable tapestry of existence.

For the first time, Will truly saw. He saw how every choice rippled outward, how every life touched another, how the energy of generations was never truly lost but flowed endlessly, shaping the world. This wasn't power—it was responsibility. A delicate, ever-shifting balance between light and shadow, creation and destruction, joy and sorrow. He felt the weight of it settle on his shoulders, but it didn't crush him. Instead, it steadied him, centred his soul in a way that felt like something being put right, something that had always been out of place.

The light within the cavern dimmed, settling into a soft, warm glow as the relics' energy stabilised. Will stood at the centre of it all, his hands trembling as the profound connection within him settled. He turned to his companions, his gaze steady, his voice filled with quiet determination.

"We're all part of this," he said, the words carrying an unshakable conviction. "The fight ahead isn't just about defeating the darkness. It's about protecting the balance—protecting everything."

They nodded, not quite understanding, but seeing the change in him, sensing the shift. They stood for a long moment, absorbing the sense of peace, casting small smiles at one another. They were so absorbed in the moment that they almost didn't notice the subtle, but profound change until it was too late.

The immense sound filling the cavern started to have an unforeseen and terrifying side effect. Rocks and stalactites began shaking loose from the ceiling as the whole place started to shake apart. It's purpose fulfilled, the cavern was coming undone and huge cracks started forming in the ceiling, lake water pouring in rapidly.

Lolmig and Lyra looked about in terror. "We've got to get out of here!" yelled Lyra, looking towards the pool they had arrived though. As she started to move towards it, Will suddenly grabbed her by the arm. "Not that way." he said, grabbing Lolmig's arm with his free hand.

The cacophony of the collapsing cavern roared around them, the ground shaking violently as chunks of rock and cascades of water rained down. Will's heart pounded as he tightened his grip on Lyra and Lolmig, his mind racing to find a way out. The amulet thrummed against his chest, its energy surging in response to his fear and desperation.

Lyra jerked her arm, trying to pull free. "Will, we don't have time for this! That's the only way back!" she shouted, her voice barely audible over the chaos.

"No, it's not safe!" Will yelled back, his voice firm despite the panic rising in his chest. He locked eyes with her, his determination cutting through her fear. "Trust me!"

Without waiting for a response, he turned his focus inward, reaching deep into the well of power the amulet had awakened. He felt the relic's energy pulse, wild and immense, as he visualised the dock where their journey had begun that morning—the weathered planks, the gentle lapping of the lake's waves, the distant cry of gulls. He held the image in his mind with absolute clarity, letting it consume every thought.

The amulet grew hot against his skin, a searing connection to his core. The power built inside, threatening to overwhelm him, but he refused to let it. Beads of sweat began standing out on his forehead as he battled to contain the energy building up in him. He funnelled everything he had into a single thought: *take us there.*

The release came like a thunderclap, an explosion of energy that seemed to ripple through the fabric of reality itself. The deafening sound of the cavern's collapse vanished in an instant, replaced by the much gentler sounds of the outside world. The cool, damp air of the lake shore enveloped them, and their feet landed unsteadily on the familiar wooden boards of the dock.

Will barely registered the sudden shift before his knees buckled. His vision blurred, and a wave of nausea hit him like a blow, his body trembling from the strain of what he had just done. He barely heard Lolmig's startled cry or Lyra's panicked voice as the world tilted and faded to black. The last sensation he felt was the solid wood beneath him, before he surrendered to the darkness.

# Chapter fifteen

Will's friends took turns watching over him during the night. Valenor explained to the others that the first time an elf works magic, it leaves them feeling exhausted for several hours. "Of course, this is the first time someone who is not of this world has ever been known to wield magic, so we really have no way of knowing what the consequences will be." he added.

It was late the following morning when Will eventually awoke from his deep sleep. He stirred slowly, feeling a deep weariness in his limbs, and a fogginess in his mind. As his eyes fluttered open, he saw Valenor sitting by his bedside, reading from an ancient looking book. As Will awoke, Valenor turned to look at him.

"You're awake," Valenor said softly, leaning forward.

Will tried to sit up, but Valenor gently pushed him back down. "Take it easy, Will. You've been through quite a unique experience."

Hearing conversation, Lyra and Lolmig entered the room, their faces lighting up as they saw Will awake. "How do you feel?" Lyra asked, her voice full of concern.

"Drained," Will said. "But otherwise, I think I'm okay."

"We need to let him recover fully," Valenor said to the others. "We'll rest here for today, but if you feel up to it Will, we will continue tomorrow?"

Will took a deep breath and nodded.

The innkeeper brought in some food and drink, and they spent the day quietly in the room, planning their next steps and ensuring Will was well rested. Will continued to feel weak throughout the day, tiring early that evening and taking to his bed just after sundown.

That night Will had strange and disturbing dreams as his mind tried to process the enormity of the changes he had undergone. Late into the night, just before Dawn, he had a dream so vivid that it seemed almost more real than the waking world. He was standing in a vast, tranquil meadow under a sky painted with the warm hues of an eternal sunset. The grass shimmered as if dusted with gold, and a gentle breeze carried the scent of lavender and pine. Nearby, a rapidly gentle brook wound its way through the landscape, its soft burble soothing.

Standing at the centre of this dreamscape was a figure cloaked in radiant white and gold, his robes embroidered with intricate patterns that seemed to shimmer with an inner light. His eyes, a piercing blue, held an ageless wisdom, and his silver-streaked hair fell gracefully over his shoulders.

"Will," the figure greeted him like he knew him, his voice rich and resonant. "Welcome."

Will, who had been sitting by the brook, startled at the figure's presence but found himself oddly unafraid. Rising slowly to his feet, he took in the stranger's powerful presence. "Who are you?" he asked curiously.

"I am Eldran," the figure said, bowing slightly. "A mage from an ancient order known as the Path of the Burning Torch."

Will frowned, wondering briefly at the fact that he was completely unperturbed by the sudden appearance of this stranger in his dream. "Why have you come here? What is this place?"

Eldran gestured to the meadow. "I fabricated this place so that we could speak, I needed you to be at peace so I can impart some truths you must understand before the road ahead becomes too perilous. You are at a crossroads, Will, and your choices will shape the fate of this world... and yours."

Will mutely nodded for him to continue.

Eldran looked off into the distance as if recalling a memory. "My order follows the teachings of the Luminary Codex, for generations we have been using it's teaching s to help guide the people of this land on the path of light. It is a path of balance, of harmony with the world and with oneself. Yet there exists another codex—the Shadow Codex—championed by Malakar and his followers. It twists the truths of the Luminary Codex, perverting its wisdom to lead the people into darkness."

The mention of Malakar sent a chill through Will. "What does this have to do with me?"

Eldran's expression softened. "Everything. Both prophecies speak of a traveller who will shape the fate of this land—one who will gather the three great relics and unlock a power capable of saving... or destroying this land."

The weight of those words made Will's breath catch in his throat as he struggled to comprehend the enormity of what Eldran was telling him. "I don't understand. I am not even of this world. Why would I be in either prophecy?"

Eldran paused for a moment as if weighing up whether to even share the next bit, eventually taking a short breath and continuing. "We don't know why. What we do know is that it was the agent's of darkness who brought you here."

The revelation hit like a blow sending his mind reeling, his heart racing. "That can't be true. There has to be some mistake."

"There is no mistake," Eldran said gently but firmly. "This is why I have come to you now. Up to this moment, both prophecies have unfolded in parallel—your arrival, the gathering of the relics, all necessary for either outcome. I couldn't risk reaching out and causing a deviation. But now, you stand at a fork in the road. Your next steps will decide which path you take—for light or darkness."

Eldran could see the tension in Will and rested a hand on his shoulder to comfort him. "That is why I am here now, to guide you. Malakar's agents are everywhere. They will seek to influence you through deceit and manipulation, and they may appear as friends or allies. You must trust your instincts, Will.

You carry a light within you—a great light—but it is fragile. Your empathy is your strength, but it is also your greatest vulnerability. Guard your heart, and let it guide you."

Will digested everything Eldran had told him. He knew that he had to avoid becoming a pawn in the dark prophecy... but how? He looked at Eldran, who patiently waited, watching Will as he absorbed all this new information. "What can I do? How can I know what to do next?" he asked.

Eldran smiled at him. "The fact that you are asking these questions is a good sign. Seek out the Luminary Codex. It was lost to us many years ago and was last seen in the south lands, near the town of Candleford. Then you shall know your true path."

Will's ears pricked up at the familiar name that he heard Lyra speak of so often. He felt a sudden tug of his consciousness, seeking to pull him from this dream as his body awoke.

Eldran's form began to shimmer, the dreamscape fading around them. "Remember that there are no absolutes, you can take a wrong turn and still end up at the right destination. Our time here grows short, and there are things I must attend to."

Will had so many more questions, but he could tell that he was waking. "Will I see you again?" he yelled, unsure of whether Eldran could hear him.

As he felt his mind pushing up from the depths of slumber he heard Eldran utter one last phrase. "Our paths will cross again."

Will woke sharply and sat on the edge of the bed for a moment, his mind sluggishly trying to reassert itself into the waking world.

The morning light streamed through the cracks in the wooden shutters of the small room of the inn, casting streaks of gold across the floor. He yawned deeply and stretched, shaking off the remnants of sleep before rising. Pulling on his clothes, he laced up his boots and ran a hand through his hair. His reflection in the small, warped mirror on the wall caught his eye, and he paused. His face seemed different—wiser, more confident maybe. The reflection of the amulet pressed against his chest caught his eye and he held it briefly between his thumb and forefinger, feeling the connection he now felt with it coursing through him.

With one quick look back at the room to make sure he hadn't left anything, he placed the amulet back on his chest, and made his way down to the common room.

The scent of freshly baked bread and cooked bacon wafted up the stairs, guiding him toward the now familiar sounds of the busy common room. The innkeeper bustled about, serving steaming plates of food to the patrons seated at sturdy wooden tables scattered around the room. A fire crackled in the hearth, warding off the morning chill.

Lyra and Lolmig were already seated at a table near the corner, their heads close together as they spoke in hushed tones. Lolmig was digging into a plate piled high with food, while Lyra sipped from a steaming mug of tea, her gaze thoughtful. Valenor sat nearby, his pale face engrossed in the book on the table in front of him.

Will hesitated in the doorway for a moment, watching them. The dream still clinging to the edges of his thoughts, like a shadow lingering in the corners of his mind. He felt a sudden pang of worry as he looked across the room at his friends. Could they be trusted? Could anyone? The thought struck him unexpectedly, and he shook his head to dispel it. Don't let paranoia creep in. Trust your instincts, Eldran had said.

Forcing a small smile onto his face, Will crossed the room to join them. Lyra looked up as he approached, her expression softening as he face broke into a warm smile.

"Morning," she said. "You slept late."

"I needed it… I feel a lot better now though," Will replied simply as he slid into a seat. Lolmig grunted in greeting, too busy devouring his meal to say much else.

Lyra raised an eyebrow but didn't press him. "There's plenty of food if you're hungry. You'll need your strength for today."

Will nodded, though his appetite was far from his mind. As a serving girl brought him a plate, he resolved to find the right moment to tell them about his meeting with Eldran. For now, he would listen, observe, and try to piece together how this dream would shape the path ahead.

After breakfast the companions gathered their belongings, gave their thanks to the innkeeper and then left. After a brief discussion, Will proclaimed confidently that it was time to head to Candleford to check in on Lyra's family before making their way onto Shadowmoor. Happy to follow his lead and to have a destination, the others willingly agreed.

As they walked along the winding trail that traced it's way through the hills toward Candleford, Lyra's mood seemed to brighten with every step. Her voice carried on the breeze as she regaled the others with stories from her childhood. The farm where she had grown up sounded idyllic—rolling fields of golden wheat, the comforting bleat of sheep in the morning, and her family's old stone farmhouse nestled against a backdrop of gentle hills.

"There was this one time," Lyra said, her eyes sparkling with laughter, "when my brothers thought it would be funny to dye all the sheep bright pink. It was my mother's birthday, and they thought it would be a 'festive surprise.' She didn't find it nearly as funny as they did."

Lolmig let out a booming laugh, nearly stumbling over a loose rock on the road. "Pink sheep! Now that's a sight I'd pay good coin to see."

Will chuckled along, though he found himself more absorbed in watching Lyra's expression than the story itself. She was beaming, her cheeks flushed from the brisk pace and the excitement of returning home. His heart skipped a beat as he watched her, the morning sun framing her silver hair like a halo, her innocent energy seeming to radiate and warm him.

"And then," Lyra continued, "there was the harvest festival. Every year, my father and uncles would build a giant straw effigy, and the whole town would come to see it burned. It was supposed to bring good luck for the next season, but one year my little sister tripped and accidentally set it on fire before the festival even started." She paused, a wistful smile playing on her lips. "That was the year we all learned how much work goes into putting out a field fire."

"Sounds like Candleford has its fair share of adventure," Will said.

"More than you'd think," Lyra replied. "But it's not just the people there, although they are the heart and soul of the place. It's the feeling that I get when I am there—waking up to the sound of the rooster crowing, the way the sunset paints the hills. It's... home."

Her voice softened on the last word as her eyes grew distant, and for a moment, the group fell silent. The thought of returning to her family seemed to fill Lyra with a renewed energy, and she quickened her pace, urging the others to keep up.

"You'll love it," she said over her shoulder. "My parents will insist on feeding you until you can't walk, and my brothers will probably challenge you to some kind of ridiculous contest. Just wait—you'll see."

Her enthusiasm was infectious, and Will found himself looking forward to meeting her family.

As they continued toward Candleford, Will couldn't help but notice Valenor's unusual demeanour. Typically sharp-witted and quick to join in conversations, the elf now lagged slightly behind the group, his usually keen eyes fixed on some distant point on the horizon. His posture was stiff, his expression troubled.

Will glanced over at Lolmig, who seemed equally aware of the shift. The dwarf raised an eyebrow in silent acknowledgment but shrugging, said nothing, leaving Will to decide whether to press the issue.

Lyra, caught up in her excitement, seemed oblivious to Valenor's withdrawal. Will found himself splitting his attention—half-listening to Lyra's stories while also keeping a watchful eye on the elf.

Finally, unable to ignore it any longer, Will fell back to walk beside Valenor. "Everything all right?" he asked casually, keeping his tone light.

Valenor blinked, as though pulled from a deep reverie, and looked at Will. His expression was unreadable, his eyes shadowed with something Will couldn't quite place.

"I'm fine," Valenor replied curtly, but the tightness in his voice betrayed him.

"Doesn't seem like it," Will pressed gently. "You've been quiet all day. Not like you to pass up a chance to make a joke at Lolmig's expense."

A flicker of a smile tugged at the corner of Valenor's mouth, but it vanished as quickly as it appeared. He sighed, his gaze dropping to the dirt path beneath his boots.

There was something in his tone—something unspoken—that made Will's stomach knot. But before he could press further, Valenor picked up his pace, striding ahead to catch up with Lyra. His sudden burst of energy left Will standing there, wondering just what it was that the elf wasn't telling him.

The weather remained dry and overcast throughout the day and into the next as they traversed the hilly region between Crystal Lake and Candleford. As they drew closer to

Candleford, the scenery began to shift, and with it, Lyra's mood. Her expression grew increasingly troubled, her gaze darting anxiously over the changing landscape. Noticing her growing concern, Will glanced around to see what might be troubling her. The ground was barren and cracked, devoid of life. No trees or grass broke the monotony of the wasteland ahead—only a few skeletal, leafless trunks stood as bleak reminders of what once was.

"Is this not normal?" he asked.

Lyra shook her head mutely, her wide eyes darting left and right. "This was all farmland when I came north to Silverwood," she said in a quiet voice.

They had all come to a complete standstill, as another unsettling fact started to become apparent. It was deathly silent. Not one bird sang, no insects chirped. There were no signs of life here at all.

"What could have caused this?" Lolmig said, unnerved, making superstitious signs to ward off evil.

Valenor, who had been silent, finally spoke. "We must be close to the edge of Shadowmoor."

Will went cold all over at the mention of that cursed land. But Lyra looked sharply at Valenor. "You must be mistaken," she said angrily. "The edge of the moor lies many miles to the south from here."

Valenor looked apologetically at her, and after a moment, she took his meaning. She looked ahead at the ravaged landscape, the blood draining from her face. "My family!" she exclaimed and bolted ahead, running ahead of the others. They all looked at one another and then ran after her.

As the companions crested the next hill, they looked down into the valley where Candleford once stood. The sight that met their eyes was one of absolute devastation. The town that rested in the valley ahead lay in ruins, the buildings crumbled and weathered as if abandoned for centuries. The ground was arid and cracked, with no signs of life. Leafless, dead tree trunks dotted the landscape, the only evidence that life had ever existed there.

Lyra stood at the edge of the hill, her hands covering her mouth and nose, silent tears streaming down her cheeks. The complete desolation of her homeland was too much to bear.

Will approached her cautiously, his heart heavy with empathy. "Lyra..." he began softly, placing a comforting hand on her shoulder.

She shook her head, not taking her eyes off the ruins below. "How could this be? The edge of the moor was miles away from here!" she exclaimed. "How could it spread so far so quickly?"

Lolmig, visibly unnerved, cleared his throat uncomfortably. "We need to be careful," he said. "When the curse consumes a new area, it infects everything. We might encounter... them."

Valenor nodded gravely, but Will looked back and forth between them, unsure what they were referring to. "Them?" he asked.

Valenor's expression darkened further. "The creatures the curse creates," he explained. "Twisted perversions of the living that were consumed. Mindless, driven by the curse, they wander aimlessly, attacking anything that still has life, spreading the curse. We call them the Hollow."

# Chapter sixteen

Lyra looked desperately around at the others. "We need to check for survivors." she pleaded with them.

Lolmig looked down at his feet, unable to look on the pain in Lyra's face, but Will turned to her. "We can take a quick pass through the town and have a look." he said, looking around at the others.

Lolmig and Valenor exchanged uneasy glances. "The risk is too great," Valenor said, his voice low. "The Hollow aren't people anymore. They're dangerous, mindless—and worse, they're contagious. You don't know what you're asking us to walk into."

Will met his gaze steadily. "I know exactly what I'm asking. A quick pass through the town. If there's nothing, we'll leave. But we have to try."

They awkwardly looked at the ground, and Will could sense their reluctance. Finally, Lolmig sighed, muttering under his breath. "Fine, but let's be quick about it."

As they crossed the boundary into Shadowmoor, a palpable curtain of gloom descended over them. The light dimmed unnaturally, the sun's rays struggling to penetrate the dark haze that hung in the air like a choking veil. The very atmosphere felt wrong, as if the land itself resented their presence. Every sound seemed muted, dying at its source, leaving only an eerie silence.

The companions tread cautiously, their footsteps crunching against the brittle, ashen ground. The buildings of Candleford were little more than hollowed-out husks, decayed and ruined. The smell of rot hung in the air, mixed with an acrid tang that burned at the back of the throat.

A low, guttural sound broke the silence—a shuffling, punctuated by wet, animal-like grunts that sent a shiver down Will's spine. He froze, his hand instinctively moving to his weapon.

The group cautiously rounded a corner, and the source of the noise came into view. A group of Hollow staggered through the ruins, their movements jerky and unnatural. Their eyes were empty voids, devoid of life or recognition, and their twisted, broken bodies bore the marks of the curse.

Lyra gasped softly, her hand flying to her mouth to stifle a sob. Her wide eyes darted from one shambling figure to the next. "No..." she whispered, her voice barely audible.

Will felt deeply upset for her loss, and anger burned deep in his chest at the thought that this was all because of the arrogance and hate of one man.

"We need to find cover." he whispered.

"There," Valenor whispered, pointing to a small, dilapidated church at the edge of the square, its stained-glass windows cracked but intact, casting fractured colours across the ground. "We can shelter there until they move on."

Moving as quietly as they could, the companions began to navigate the ruined streets, skirting around the Hollow. The creatures shuffled aimlessly, their heads jerking toward every faint sound. Lyra pressed her hand against her chest, her breaths coming shallow and quick, but she followed without hesitation.

The church loomed closer, its heavy wooden doors hanging slightly ajar. With a final glance at the shambling figures behind them, they slipped inside, closing the door as quietly as possible. The sound of the latch clicking into place echoed in the silence, and for a brief moment, they allowed themselves to breathe again.

Inside, the air was stale but calm, the dim light filtering through the cracked windows casting muted hues across the stone floor. Will looked at Lyra, whose face was streaked with tears, and placed a hand on her shoulder. "We'll figure this out," he said firmly, though his own heart ached with uncertainty.

The interior of the church was in disarray, with broken pews and shattered stained glass littering the floor. The altar was cracked, and the once-beautiful murals on the walls were faded and marred as if by the passage of time.

Remembering the task that Eldran had given him during their meeting, he leaned close to Lyra. "Did Candleford have a library at all?" he asked, being deliberately vague.

Lyra's lips pursed pensively as she considered his question. "We didn't really have a library, but the pastor had many old books in his personal collection here at the church."

It seemed as though the prophecy was steering his every step, he mused to himself. *But which one?* he wondered with a wry smile.

He shared with the others the details of the book he was seeking. They exchanged puzzled glances, clearly curious about how he had come by this knowledge, but chose to hold their questions for now.

They spread out, carefully sifting through the debris. Will found himself drawn to a small alcove near the back of the church. He could hear the others moving around, gently turning over upturned furniture in their search. As he approached, he sensed a strange energy from the alcove and the amulet at his chest warmed against his skin... and then saw it; a dusty, ancient tome resting on a bookshelf, much older than it's neighbours. Gently, he picked it up and brushed away the grime and dust with the back of his sleeve, revealing the title: "The Luminary Codex."

"Over here," Will called softly. "I think I found something."

The others gathered around, peering at the book with curiosity. As Will turned back the cover, he felt a surge of energy, the pages glowing faintly with a soft, golden light.

The companions gathered around the Codex, its cover shimmering faintly in the dim light of the church. As Will carefully turned the first page, the codex seemed to come alive, emitting a soft, otherworldly glow that bathed their faces in pale radiance. The glow pulsed gently, as though the book itself was breathing.

The reactions were immediate and visceral.

Lolmig gasped audibly, staggering backward as his eyes filled with tears. His face crumpled, his hand clutching his chest as though a great weight had settled there. He stumbled into a corner, his shoulders shaking with barely suppressed sobs, the grief so palpable it seemed to echo in the silent air.

Lyra's breathing hitched, and her hands flew to her face as she let out a strangled cry of fear. Her wide, darting eyes scanned the church as though an unseen predator lurked in every shadow. She pressed her back against the nearest wall, trembling violently, her entire body poised for flight.

Valenor's reaction was sharp and violent. A low growl escaped his throat as his eyes burned with fury. His jaw clenched tightly, and he took a threatening step toward Will, his voice a harsh, venomous command. "Close it! Shut it now!" he bellowed, his face contorted in uncharacteristic rage. With a snarl, he lunged forward, his hand outstretched to grab the codex as if compelled to rip it apart.

Will's heart pounded in his chest as chaos erupted around him. "Stop!" he hissed, his voice urgent, his mind racing. He glanced toward the heavy wooden doors of the church, fearing that the hollow outside might hear the commotion.

"Valenor, get a hold of yourself!" he snapped, dodging the elf's grasp. In one swift motion, he snapped the book shut, the radiant glow disappearing instantly, plunging the church back into its dim, dusty stillness.

The change was immediate. Lolmig's sobs subsided, his breathing ragged as he leaned heavily against the wall, wiping at his face in confusion. Lyra's trembling slowed, though her wide eyes still flicked nervously toward the shadows. Valenor froze, the fire in his eyes extinguished as he took a step back, his face shifting to a look of bewilderment.

"What... what in the seven forges was that?" Lolmig muttered, his voice hoarse. He looked at Will as though searching for answers.

"I don't know," Will admitted, clutching the closed codex tightly in his hands. His pulse still raced, his palms damp with sweat.

Valenor exhaled sharply, as though trying to banish the memory of his outburst.

Will was still looking down at the book in his hands, reeling in shock from the violent reaction his friends had, "It felt like it was reacting to being opened here, in Shadowmoor."

"You don't know that for sure," Lyra whispered, her voice still shaking.

"No, I don't," Will admitted, glancing at the closed book, its surface now unremarkable. "But I'm not willing to test that theory again—not here, not now."

The companions exchanged uneasy glances, the echoes of their emotional outbursts still lingering in their expressions.

A cold breeze suddenly swept through the church, though there were no open windows, kicking up dust and papers from the floor as it passed. The shadows in the corners seemed to deepen, growing darker and more sinister. From those shadows, a voice began to whisper, low and malevolent, curling around them like tendrils of smoke.

"I can feel you..." the voice hissed, its tone sending a chill down their spines. "You tread in my domain, little insects. Leave now, if you value your lives."

"We're not afraid of you," Will said, his voice steady as he looked about the room, trying to see where the voice was coming from.

The whispers twisted into a sinister chuckle, echoing off the ancient stone walls, shaking the foundations. "Brave words... but empty. You have no idea what you face, boy."

Trying to sound bolder than he felt, Will stood up to Malakar's presence once more, "Then why don't you show yourself?"

"Soon enough, Traveller. But I have a surprise to finish preparing for before our meeting; a gift of sorts." Malakar said, his voice trailing off into chilling laughter.

As if in response to Malakar's mocking words, the air grew colder, and the wind began to howl outside the church. The whispering voice became a roar, echoing through the church, the very ground beneath them trembling with the force of it.

"Now Leave!" Malakar's voice thundered, the roar filling their ears, drowning out all other sound. The church's wooden beams creaked under the pressure, and the stained glass windows rattled as if they might shatter. The sky above darkened as storm clouds gathered out of nowhere, a violent tempest brewing directly overhead. Lightning flashed, illuminating the darkened church in brief, blinding bursts, followed by deafening cracks of thunder.

They could feel Malakar's power pressing down on them, a force so overwhelming it felt like it might crush them.

"We need to go," Valenor said, his trembling voice barely audible over the storm, all signs of his usual calm demeanour now gone, his eyes wide with fear.

Reluctantly, Will nodded. They had no choice. They weren't ready for a direct confrontation with Malakar.

With one last, defiant glare into the darkness, Will turned and followed his companions out of the church. The wind howled around them as they fled, the storm crashing overhead as if the sky itself was being torn apart by Malakar's rage.

Once they were a safe distance away, Will called for a halt. As they paused to catch their breath, he looked back at the ruins of Candleford, the church now shrouded in the swirling storm they had left behind.

"We need to figure out our next move," Will said, looking at his friends. "We have the codex, but I don't think we should chance opening it again until we understand it better."

Lolmig, his usual gruff bravado somewhat dimmed by their recent ordeal, said, "Let's get as far from here as we can before nightfall. The farther we are from this cursed place, the better."

They all agreed and continued moving further north, away from the town of Candleford and the awful fate that had befallen it. As they walked, they discussed potential destinations, but it seemed no one had any idea who could help them with the book.

They rode north for as long as there was daylight, and then stopped to make camp for the night.

Will sat silently, staring into the fire. He turned the events of his encounter with Eldran over in his mind. The time had come. "I think I know where we might look for answers," he said finally, breaking the silence.

The others turned to him, intrigued.

"What do you know of the Order of the Burning Torch?" he asked.

Valenor looked up from the fire sharply, a peculiar flicker of emotion crossed his face for a moment, but before Will could wonder about it, his expression settled, as if he were mulling the question over. "The Order of the Burning Torch is an ancient group of magic users who interfere in the affairs of men, elves and dwarves from time to time. They are very secretive, and I am not sure I would trust them."

Lyra shook her head, disagreeing with Valenor. "I've heard tales of their deeds. They are known to intervene in times of great peril, guiding those who fight against the dark forces. My people talk of them reverently."

Lolmig, who had been poking at the fire with a stick, added, "I've heard their name mentioned in old dwarf legends. They are respected amongst my people, but no one seems to know much about them, they tend to keep to themselves most of the time."

"The other night, at the inn, I had a dream—or, at least, I thought it was a dream," Will began. "A mage of the order named Eldran visited me."

Valenor's face darkened. "Why did you not tell us of this visit Will? Who knows what this mage's intentions were?"

Will shook his head. "I am not sure why I didn't mention it, but I got a real sense that he wants to help us. He told me about his order and their teachings, the Luminary Codex, and its dark counterpart, the Shadow Codex."

"Let me guess," Valenor interrupted, his tone sceptical. "He painted himself and his order as the saviours of light and truth, while the rest of the world teeters on the brink of darkness?"

Will's jaw tightened. "He told me about the dangers I face, the choices we all face, and that Malakar's agents are everywhere, trying to sway me to their cause. But more importantly, he said the order might have the answers we're searching for—about the codex, the relics, and what comes next."

Lyra looked uncertain, not sure what to believe. "If what he said is true, then they might be the only ones who can help us."

"Or they could be leading you into a trap," Valenor said, his voice edged with frustration. "I told you before, I don't trust the Burning Torch. Their secrecy is unnatural, and their agenda... it's too convenient."

"I know how it sounds," Will said, meeting Valenor's gaze. "But I believe him. Something about what he said felt... right. If we can find them, I think they can help us understand the codex."

Lolmig nodded thoughtfully, his face shadowed by the firelight. "Finding them is the tricky part. The Burning Torch doesn't exactly advertise their whereabouts. But there's one place that might have answers—the Great Library at Silver-wood."

Valenor sighed, rubbing his temples. "You're determined, aren't you?" he said, glancing at Will.

"I am," Will said firmly. "We need to know the truth, Valenor, even if it means taking a risk. This is bigger than any one of us."

After a long pause, Valenor relented with a resigned nod. "Fine. Silverwood it is."

# Chapter seventeen

The journey north took them several days, but the companions soon found themselves moving steadily under the golden canopy of the enchanted forest. This time, the forest did not test them, its enigmatic presence remaining tranquil. Whether the absence of trials was due to their prior success, the company of Valenor, or some deeper purpose, Will couldn't say. All he knew was that he was grateful.

The familiar sense of calm returned as they walked beneath the ancient boughs. Shafts of sunlight broke through the thick canopy, painting their path with shifting patterns of gold and amber. Despite the weight he carried, Will found himself momentarily lulled by the soothing presence of this magical realm, the almost melodic sounds of nature wrapping his burdens up and suppressing them slightly—the heartbreaking melody of nearby birdsong, the gentle babble of a nearby brook and the whisper of wind through branches, gently rustling the dried leaves on the ground, all contributing to the healing energy of this magical place.

After two days of steady travel, the spires of Silverwood came into view, rising majestically against the horizon, peeking out amongst the treetops.

As they approached the grand gates of Silverwood, they were greeted by guards clad in intricate armour, their expressions respectful as they recognised Valenor, who stepped forward, speaking in a melodic elvish tongue. The guards listened intently before nodding and stepping aside to allow them entry.

The city was a perfect embodiment of peace and tranquillity, and stood out in contrast to the bustle of human and dwarven settlements. On his last visit here Will had been overwhelmed, but this time he took the time to absorb it all and fully appreciate its beauty. The city seemed to grow naturally from the land—buildings of carved wood and stone blended seamlessly with the surrounding forest, their flowing designs adorned with flowering vines and glowing crystals that cast a soft, natural light.

The grounds were a vibrant display of nature, with lush gardens interwoven with the wild elegance of ancient trees. Streams of clear water meandered through the city, their gentle flow enhancing the serene atmosphere. The air was fragrant with the scent of blossoms, and a peaceful hush blanketed the city like a soothing balm.

Elves moved with quiet grace, their footsteps light and their voices low, as if unwilling to disturb the harmony of their surroundings. The delicate balance between civilisation and nature was seamless, the elves having long since learned to live in perfect harmony with their natural surroundings.

Valenor led them to the heart of the city, where the great library stood. Instead of entering through the council buildings, Valenor led them around to the public entrance. The Exterior of the building was if anything, more impressive than the inside. It's external structure of carved stone and living wood blended seamlessly into it's natural surroundings, its intricately carved wooden doors wide open in welcome.

"If we're quick here, we might be able to get in and out without alerting the council to our presence." he said as he led them through the doors.

As they made their way inside, and they found themselves at the place where they had first spoken with Valenor. It took Will a moment to recognise it as they had approached from a different direction, but that wave of recognition felt significant; they seemed to have come full circle since they were last here.

As Valenor assigned tasks to the others, a murmur of activity drew their attention toward the far side of the library. The grand doors swung open, and Elenion entered, his ceremonial robes sweeping the floor with every step.

"I heard whispers of your return," Elenion said as he neared them, his voice gentle and welcoming as his gaze swept over the group. "I thought it best to greet you myself."

Valenor stiffened, his posture betraying the tension that suddenly racked his body. Though he quickly schooled his features into something more neutral, Will could see the flicker of hesitation in his eyes. "We intended to report to you," Valenor lied, his tone steady but with an edge that betrayed his discomfort. "We've made some progress, but have not yet completed our quest."

Elenion's serene smile remained, his understanding gaze lingering on Valenor for just a moment longer than necessary. "I appreciate your diligence, Valenor. But there is no need for apprehension. The path of a quest is rarely straightforward. It's good to see you all in one piece."

Will stepped in, sensing Valenor's discomfort and wanting to shift focus. "We've come to seek information," he began, his voice confident as he addressed Elenion. "Specifically, about the Order of the Burning Torch. We need to locate them, and we're hoping your library holds the answers."

Elenion's piercing gaze shifted to Will, his expression curious as he looked at him, before softening again. "You've changed since we last spoke," he observed, his tone thoughtful. "There is... something... more peaceful, more confident in your eyes."

Will offered a faint smile, his hand brushing the medallion at his chest. "Change has a way of finding you when you least expect it."

Elenion gave a slow nod, a flicker of amusement crossing his face. "Indeed. As for your request..." He paused, his gaze drifting momentarily to the relics Will carried. "I would be curious to see the fruits of your journey thus far, but first things first. The Order of the Burning Torch... Yes, there may be something here."

He gestured toward the towering shelves behind him. "The section on ancient orders and their rituals is well worth exploring. It's deep in the east wing, and though much of it is fragmented or obscure, you may find what you need. If you like, I can assist."

Will exchanged a glance with Lyra and Lolmig, feeling thankful for the direction. "We'd appreciate your help," he said earnestly.

Elenion inclined his head. "Very well. Let us begin. Knowledge often hides in the shadows of persistence, and the light of understanding is earned through effort. Come."

Elenion led them through towering shelves lined with hundreds of weathered books, their spines etched with titles in languages both forgotten and forbidden. The scent of parchment and ink filled the air, mingling with the faint hum of ancient wards protecting the collection.

As they reached a corner of the library filled with tomes bound in deep reds and blacks, their edges gilded in silver and gold, they spread out and began searching through the shelves, occasionally pulling a book or scroll down from the shelf and flicking through it before returning it to it's place and continuing with their search.

They spent much of the afternoon searching, and Will had almost given up hope of finding anything when Lolmig called out from further down the row, his voice raised with excitement. "Here! I think I've found something."

The group gathered around him as he laid a thick, weathered book on a nearby table. The title, written in an ancient elvish script, translated to Orders of Flame and Shadow.

Elenion took the book and animatedly flipped through the pages, his brow deeply furrowed in concentration. Eventually, he stopped on a page adorned with the emblem of a flame encircling a torch. Beneath it, delicate script outlined the order's origins and purpose.

"Here it is," Elenion said. "It speaks of an island to the far north, protected by powerful enchantments and home to the Order's most sacred artefacts, including something they refer to as 'The Nexus'."

Elenion moved the book over to a nearby table and they all gathered round, looking at the weathered old pages as Elenion continued to read aloud. "To the far north lies a remote archipelago, only accessible by foot or by magical access. Thorn Island lies at the northernmost tip and is home to the Nexus of Light. The Order abides there to protect this sacred energy source and draw on its power."

Elenion looked up from the book a moment, looking at the others. "The Nexus of Light," he murmured. "I have heard of this during my studies. It is said to be a font of pure, untainted magic. A direct link to the light source of the universe."

Will felt something click deep within him at this news, a resounding sense of being on the right path. He remembered what Eldran had told him about trusting his instincts and he somehow knew that this was what he had meant.

He turned to Elenion. "The book spoke of magical entry to the island. Is that something you could help with?"

The others all turned to Elenion, hopeful expectation on their faces. He looked inward for a moment before looking back at Will. "I don't think so," he said apologetically. "A portal requires knowledge of the destination, an understanding of the endpoint. To create a portal without having a clear endpoint in mind doesn't bear thinking about. You could end up lost in between worlds. Your soul torn asunder for all eternity."

Will's shoulders slumped at that, having hoped to avoid a long arduous journey, and more importantly the lost time.

Elenion snapped his fingers suddenly as a thought hit him and disappeared off into the library without saying a word, leaving the others all looking at one another, bewildered. A moment later, he retuned carrying another book, banging it down on top of the other with a fevered look in his eyes as the excitement of hunting down clues ignited something within him.

He flicked through pages, scanning the information there as he searched for something, whilst the others waited with bated breath.

A few moments later Elenion exhaled sharply, startling the others. "Found it!" he exclaimed. "This book is one I studied when I was much younger, and I was always intrigued by this story... but I think it might be relevant."

Will waited a moment, but when Elenion left them wondering he spoke up, prompting him to continue. "Well? What does it say?"

Elenion looked at them, an excited look in his eyes. "Ah yes... The book is about the time before Aruna split onto two islands, when our lands here were connected to the woods on the southern tip of north island."

His eyes sparkled with barely contained excitement as he continued, his tone becoming more animated. "Many years ago, an elven scouting party discovered an abandoned temple, somewhere to the west of the human capital of Caeratheon." He gestured with his hands, as if painting the image before them. "At its heart was a massive, ancient portal. Its craftsmanship was unlike anything we had ever seen—neither elven nor dwarven, but something older."

Will straightened, leaning in further as a flicker of hope rekindled in his chest. "A portal?"

Elenion nodded, his enthusiasm infectious. "Indeed. The scouting party studied it for weeks, but it was inactive. No amount of elven magic could awaken it, and eventually, it was abandoned as our people moved on to other affairs." He leaned in slightly, his voice dropping to a conspiratorial tone. "But I always wondered about it. It never made any sense to me that it should serve no purpose. What if it was never for us elves to use?"

Lyra exchanged a glance with Lolmig, her curiosity piqued. "And you think it could have something to do with the Order of the Burning Torch?"

"It's possible," Elenion replied. "The portal's craftsmanship suggests an origin steeped in magic, and its placement—so isolated—seems significant. If it is connected to your order, there must be a way to activate it."

Valenor, who had remained silent until now, crossed his arms and narrowed his eyes. "If this portal exists, why did our people abandon trying to understand it?"

Elenion gave him a wry smile. "Not all mysteries are meant to be solved immediately, Valenor. Our people are nothing if not patient."

Everyone turned to Will, who was sitting quietly, deep in thought. Finally, he nodded. "If there's even a chance this portal is tied to the order, we should investigate further. If it turns out to be a wild goose chase, we'll reconsider our options then."

The others stared at him blankly, their expressions ranging from confused to outright bewildered. Lolmig furrowed his brow, breaking the silence with a serious tone. "I don't know what a wild goose is, but we'll certainly try and avoid chasing one... if that's a thing to be avoided, lad."

Will blinked at the earnest reply, then burst into laughter, the sound bubbling up uncontrollably. He clutched his sides, shaking his head as Lolmig watched him, his expression torn between confusion and mild offence.

"It's an expression from my world, Lolmig," Will managed between chuckles. "It means pursuing something that might not lead anywhere."

Lolmig stroked his beard thoughtfully, his eyes narrowing as if carefully considering this new information. "Ah, I see. So, we're chasing a goose that might not even exist? Sounds a bit daft, but fair enough. Lead on, lad. I'll trust your instincts."

Will laughed again, the tension in the room lifting slightly. "No goose chasing... I promise."

"Good," Lolmig replied, giving a firm nod. "Because I'd rather face a dozen hollow than a beast I can't even find."

Elenion, who had been watching the exchange with quiet amusement, finally interjected. "Then it's settled. You'll rest here tonight, and at first light, I'll prepare a map to the portal's location. May the light guide your steps, my friends."

Satisfied with the fruits of their labour, they followed Elenion back to his private quarters. Elenion called for a servant to bring food and drink, and soon the table was laden with a feast. There were roasted meats, fresh bread, an assortment of cheeses, and fruits from the Silverwood orchards. The sight and smell of the food lifted their spirits, and they eagerly sat down to eat.

As they ate, the conversation flowed easily. They talked about their journey so far, sharing stories and laughing at some of the more absurd moments. For a short while, the worries about the Shadowmoor and the challenges ahead were forgotten, replaced by the simple pleasure of good food and good company.

Will, who had been deep in thought since their discovery in the library, finally spoke up. "Elenion, do you think the Order of the Burning Torch will help us?"

Elenion paused as he considered the question. "I don't know is the honest answer. We know very little about the order. The history books mention them of course. They appear to mostly keep their own company away from others until times of great need in the world, when they venture out to shape events."

Lyra, who had been quietly listening, spoke up. "Valenor says they can't be trusted. What do you think Elenion?"

Elenion looked troubled as he gazed at Valenor, who didn't look up from his plate. "I am not sure where Valenor has gotten these ideas from, but all my people know of the order indicates that they are on the side of light."

Will's gaze shifted from Elenion to Valenor, his brow furrowed. "Valenor, you've been quiet about this. Why do you distrust the Order so much?"

Valenor's hand paused mid-air, holding his fork over his plate. He didn't look up immediately, but when he did, his eyes were guarded. "The stories of the Burning Torch are not all so glowing, Will," he said evenly. "They may call themselves an order of light, but their methods are... uncompromising. They see the world in absolutes, and in the past, their interventions have left destruction in their wake. I'm wary of anyone who claims to know what is 'right' for everyone else."

Elenion's expression darkened, but he kept his tone calm. "That may be so, Valenor, but history also shows that without their guidance during critical moments, far worse outcomes could have come to pass. Perhaps the destruction you speak of was the price for averting greater disaster."

Will rubbed the bridge of his nose, as the tension in the room made the air uncomfortable. "I hear what both of you are saying," he said carefully, looking at Valenor. "But Eldran reached out to me directly, and everything he said aligns with what we've discovered so far. I don't think we have the luxury of dismissing them outright."

Valenor leaned back in his chair, his eyes narrowing. "And if they decide that their vision of 'light' requires sacrifices you aren't prepared to make? What then, Will? Will you follow blindly?"

"No," Will replied firmly. "I don't follow anyone blindly. But we need guidance, Valenor. If the Order can provide it,

I think we have to take the chance. We'll proceed cautiously, but we can't afford to let mistrust paralyse us."

Elenion nodded approvingly. "Wise words, Will. The path ahead is treacherous enough without division among you. If there is any truth to the legends of the Order, then you must find them and judge their intentions for yourselves."

The room fell silent as the companions mulled over the conversation. The crackling fire provided the only sound, its warm light dancing across their faces as they wrestled with the uncertain path ahead.

As the evening wore on, their conversation moved back to lighter topics, until eventually the laughter and warmth of the evening slowly gave way to drowsiness. Elenion provided comfortable sleeping arrangements for them, and one by one, they retired for the night.

* * *

Before setting off on their journey the following day, they all met again in the library. Elenion met them there with the map and some provisions. "I have sent word to the captain of my personal vessel, moored just off the north coast," he informed them. "He will ferry you across to Caeratheon on north. May you have good fortune in your search."

Will and the others nodded in appreciation. "Thanks again, Elenion," Will said earnestly, clasping Elenion's hand warmly. "For everything."

With final words of gratitude, the companions turned and resumed their journey, leaving the comforts of Silverwood behind. They quickly made their way through the beautiful city, and in no time found themselves moving away through the forest. As they walked away, the elven city slowly receded into the distance, its tall, elegant spires vanishing behind the trees.

The journey to the coast passed quickly, the landscape blurring into a tapestry of greens and golds as the companions made their way north.

As they neared the coast, something began to stir within Will; a feeling he hadn't experienced since he first arrived in this world. Despite the lingering doubts and the heavy responsibility that had been placed on his shoulders, Will was suddenly filled up with a sense of excitement and wonder. The thought of the impending sea voyage, of setting sail into uncharted waters, ignited something primal within him; a sense of adventure that had lain dormant beneath his worries and fears.

This strange world kept throwing new scenarios at him. Some were terrifying, pushing him to the limits of his courage and resolve, while others were bewildering, leaving him struggling to find his place in a land so different from his own. But this—the prospect of a sea voyage, of exploring the unknown, this was different. It spoke to something deep inside him, something that had been yearning for a chance to break free. As the salty scent of the ocean reached them, carried on the wind, Will felt a strange sense of calm settle over him.

The sight of the coast, with the endless expanse of water stretching out before them, only fuelled his growing euphoria. And as they approached the small port where Elenion's vessel awaited, Will found himself almost overcome with that sense of adventure that made him feel alive to his very core.

The companions wove their way through the secluded seaport town, taking in the lively scene around them as the lowering sun painted the town in the golden hues of late afternoon. The streets were alive with the shouts of market traders, each trying to outdo the next as they hawked their wares to the passing crowds. The air was thick with the sounds of commerce, laughter, and the clatter of goods being exchanged. It was a place of energy and movement, where life pulsed with the rhythmic energy of trade and travel.

The town's population was a vibrant blend of cultures, woven together by the lure of the sea. Graceful elves sat beside sturdy dwarves outside taverns, sharing mugs of frothy ale and boisterous conversation. Humans moved through the bustling streets, some bargaining energetically with merchants, others steering heavily-laden carts through the lively crowd.

It was a sight unlike anything Will had encountered before. His journey across Aruna this far had shown him a world where the races often lived apart, wary of one another and clinging to their own traditions, which more often than not drove a wedge that divided them further. But here, it seemed different—a rare harmony where elves, dwarves, humans mingled freely, living and working side by side in apparent harmony.

Above them, gulls swooped and cawed, their sharp eyes scanning the streets below for any scrap of food they could snatch, their cries adding to the din. The smell of salt and brine was in the air, carried to them on the breeze, mingling with the scents of fresh fish, and the various spices that filled the market stalls.

Will felt a surge of excitement as they moved through the town, the energy of the place seeping into his bones. The sea was close, and with it, the beginning of a new chapter in their journey. The town was a crossroads, a place where paths converged and new ónes began, and he couldn't help but feel that their own path was leading them towards something significant.

As they neared the docks, the sounds of the town faded slightly, replaced by the creaking of ships' rigging and the distant calls of sailors readying their vessels for departure. The sea stretched out before them, vast and unknowable, and as Will looked out over the water, he felt a deep sense of anticipation.

They made their way to the wharf Elenion had described to them and quickly found his ship, as the captain of the ship made his way hurriedly towards the group, gesturing for them to hurry. "You're late!" he said bluntly. "We almost missed the afternoon tide."

The group mumbled their apologies as they hurried up the gangplank, feeling the eyes of the busy crew upon them. The ship was a hive of activity, with sailors rushing to and fro, each carrying out their tasks. No sooner had they set foot on the main deck than the hawsers were slipped, and the ship began to shift beneath their feet, gently moving away from the wharf. The captain, a stout man with a booming voice, began bellowing orders, his commands cutting through the air as the crew responded with the efficiency of those who work together every day.

The ship creaked and groaned as it came alive, the timbers protesting the sudden movement. Will could hear the rhythmic splash of the oars being run out, the blades slicing into the water as the ship began its ponderous journey towards the harbour wall. The noise of the busy seaport gradually faded into the background as the ship picked its way through the gauntlet of moored vessels, leaving the town and its vibrant, but chaotic energy behind.

Once clear of the harbour wall, the captain gave the order to unfurl the sails. The crew leapt into action, pulling ropes and adjusting rigging. The sails flapped wildly for a moment, catching the wind and snapping to full as they filled out. The sudden pull almost knocked the four companions from their feet, the vessel surging forward as the wind took hold, driving them away from the safety of the harbour and out into the open sea.

Will stood near the ship's aft railing, watching the town recede into the distance. The sails billowed high above, pulling them towards whatever lay beyond the horizon, and Will felt that same sense of adventure fill his heart and soothe his soul once again.

The first few days at sea filled Will with that same sense of adventure he had felt on first setting sail, but by the third day at sea the four companions started to settle into a routine of small tasks designed to pass the time and break up the journey; taking care of small repairs to clothing and armour that had been neglected whilst on the road, and spending many hours honing their weapons and reading, but mostly they would chat, sitting in their quarters or strolling on the deck.

Will especially enjoyed a late night stroll on the deck where he could gaze up and see the constellations in the crystal clarity of absolute darkness, the vast expanse of the night sky was a marvel Will could never have imagined. Every evening, after the day's tasks were done and his companions retired to their quarters, he would find himself drawn to the deck. The gentle rocking of the ship, the cool night air, and the rhythmic sound of the waves all provided a perfect soundtrack to the cosmic display above.

The constellations were unfamiliar to him, yet he felt a strange connection to them, as if they were part of a grand design that he was only just beginning to understand. Some nights, he would catch a glimpse of a shooting star streaking across the heavens, and it would fill him with a childlike wonder. There was something comforting about the vastness of the universe. It made his problems seem small and distant, like the stars themselves.

As he stood there, lost in thought on the fourth night, the door behind him creaked open, and Lyra joined him. She walked up beside him and leaned on the railing, her gaze also fixed on the sky.

"Beautiful, isn't it?" she said softly, her voice carrying a hint of awe.

Will nodded. "I've never seen anything like it."

Lyra smiled, her eyes reflecting the starlight. "My people believe the stars are the souls of our ancestors, watching over us. They guide us, protect us, and remind us that we are never truly alone."

Will considered her words. "Do you think they're watching us now? Guiding us?"

"I hope so," she replied. "But even if they're not, we have each other. That's something, isn't it?"

Will turned to look at her, feeling a warmth spread through him at her words. "Yeah, it is." he said, smiling warmly at her.

They stood in comfortable silence for a while longer, both of them soaking in the moment. Eventually, Lyra sighed and pushed away from the railing.

"We should get some rest, we should be approaching land in the morning," she said.

Will nodded in agreement, but as he followed her back inside, he couldn't help but steal one last glance at the stars. He made a silent promise to himself in that moment, that if he ever made it home that he would make some changes; to break free from the prisons he had built for himself. The stars seemed to twinkle in response, as if acknowledging his vow.

That night a storm hit with a sudden fury that caught everyone on board by surprise. One moment, the sea was calm, and the night sky clear — the next, the clouds rolled in from nowhere and the heavens opened up with a torrential downpour, the wind howling like a vengeful spirit. The ship lurched violently as if it were a mere plaything being tossed about by the tempest.

In their cabin, the companions clung to their bunks, their knuckles white as they tried to find some stability in the chaotic motion of the ship. The walls creaked and groaned under the strain, and the sound of the rain pounding against the portholes was deafening. Every now and then, a particularly large wave would slam into the side of the ship, sending it tilting precariously to one side before righting itself with a jarring thud.

Will sat up on his bunk, his heart racing with every crash of thunder that seemed to shake the very air around them. The dim lantern hanging from the ceiling swung wildly, casting erratic shadows on the walls that only added to their disorientation. He tried to calm his racing thoughts and churning stomach, reminding himself that ships were built to withstand storms, but the violent tossing of the vessel made it hard to hold on to that reassurance for long.

"Does this seem like a natural storm to you?" Will asked the others loudly to cut through the noise, remembering the violent storm that Malakar had summoned at Candleford.

Valenor looked at him, catching his meaning, but not daring to answer.

The ship lurched again, and a loud crack echoed through the cabin as something above deck splintered under the force of the storm. The sound was followed by the frantic shouts of the crew as they scrambled to keep the ship under control.

Will could feel the fear building in the pit of his stomach, a cold, gnawing dread that threatened to overwhelm him. He forced himself to focus on his breathing, trying to steady his nerves even as the storm raged on around them.

What they didn't know, was that the storm's fury had driven it wildly off course. As the wind howled and the waves pounded relentlessly, the vessel was dragged further and further from its intended path, pushed towards a jagged coastline obscured by the darkness and rain. Suddenly, a massive wave lifted the ship and slammed it down onto the hidden rocks below with a sickening crunch as the keel buckled. The timbers groaned and splintered under the force, the hull tearing apart as the already critically damaged vessel was mercilessly battered against the unforgiving stones by the shifting swells.

Inside the cabin, the companions were thrown violently from their bunks. Will hit the floor hard as the ship lurched again, the impact knocking the wind out of him and opening up a gash in his forehead, that immediately caused blood to run into his eyes, blurring his vision. Water began to pour in through gaping cracks in the hull, cold and relentless as it quickly flooded the lower decks.

"We're going down!" Lolmig shouted, his voice barely audible over the roaring storm and the creaking of the ship as it was ripped apart.

Scrambling to their feet, they grabbed their possessions as quickly as they could, their minds racing as they realised they had to get out before the ship was swallowed by the sea. The cabin was already filling with water, the floor tilting dangerously as the ship began to break apart.

They rushed up the narrow staircase leading to the deck, fighting against the rising water and the violent motion of the ship. When they burst out into the open air, the scene was one of utter chaos. The deck was awash with seawater, the sails torn to shreds, and the crew desperately trying to abandon ship.

Without a second thought, the companions joined the sailors who were already jumping overboard, leaping into the cold, churning sea. The water was frigid and rough, and the force of the waves threatened to drag them under, but they kicked furiously, struggling to stay afloat as they swam towards the distant shoreline. The shore was close, but every stroke felt like a battle against the relentless tide and the fury of the storm.

They swam with all their strength, driven by the primal need to survive as the remnants of the ship were consumed by the sea behind them.

# Chapter eighteen

After what felt like an eternity, they eventually reached the shoreline. With their muscles burning and lungs aching, they crawled onto the wet sand and collapsed, gasping for air. The relentless waves continued to crash and thunder against the rocks behind them, but for a moment, they were oblivious to anything except the sheer relief of having survived. They lay there, face down on the cold, gritty sand, letting the rain pelt down on their backs as they tried to catch their breath. The adrenaline that had carried them through the storm was rapidly fading, leaving only fatigue in its wake.

For a long while, none of them moved, their minds blank with the sheer intensity of their ordeal. Slowly, the pinpricks of light that had danced in front of their eyes began to fade, their vision clearing as their heartbeats gradually slowed.

Will didn't know how long they lay there on the cold, wet sand, but as he finally started to stir, the storm had begun to abate, its fury slowly dissipating into a distant rumble as it continued it's journey across the open water, and the eastern sky had started to blush with the faint colours of the approaching dawn.

With the first light of morning, they found the strength to move. Groaning softly, they pushed themselves up from the sand, their limbs heavy and stiff from the cold and exhaustion. The air was still thick with the scent of salt and seaweed, but it was now calm, the wind reduced to a gentle breeze that brushed against their soaked clothes.

As their eyes adjusted to the dim light, they could see shapes moving up and down the beach; other survivors from the ship, staggering and stumbling as they too began to recover. The shoreline was littered with the remnants of their vessel, random crates of cargo and bits of ship washing up on the shore, and dotted amongst those things, the occasional body of those who hadn't been so fortunate.

Will trudged up the beach, his feet pressing slightly into the wet sand with each step. The remnants of the storm still lingered in the air, a damp chill that clung to his clothes and skin. His mind was a whirl of thoughts as he scanned the shoreline, hoping to spot the familiar figure of the ship's captain among the survivors.

As he moved further away from where they had washed ashore, he noticed one of the sailors huddled by a large piece of driftwood, shivering as he tried to wring out his soaked clothes. Will approached him, recognising the sailor as one of the higher ranking crew members.

"Have you seen the captain?" Will asked, his voice hoarse from the saltwater he had swallowed during their desperate swim.

The sailor looked up, his expression grim. He shook his head slowly. "I haven't seen him since the ship went down. We lost sight of him in the chaos... a few of us were close, but when the timbers started breaking apart... it was every man for himself." His voice trailed off, thick with guilt and sorrow.

Will's heart sank at the news. He stood there for a moment, staring out at the tumultuous sea, hoping against hope that the captain would somehow emerge from the wreckage.

But the horizon remained empty, and the only sounds were the fading echoes of the storm and the crashing of the waves against the shore.

As Will stood shivering against the biting wind, his soaked clothes clinging to his skin, he assessed their situation. He quickly realised that their most immediate threat was the bitter cold threatening to sap their strength.

Turning back to the sailor, he gave some simple commands, realising that these soldiers would respond well to someone taking a position of authority. "Gather as many survivors as you can find. Search the wreckage for anything that can burn—wood, debris, anything flammable. We need warmth now."

The sailor nodded, setting off without hesitation, while Will turned back to where his friends huddled together, their faces pale and weary. "We need to build a fire," he said firmly. "Behind those tall dunes, where the wind isn't so harsh. We'll make it big enough to warm everyone and dry our clothes."

Lyra, still trembling, nodded and began gathering driftwood. Lolmig grumbled something about soggy conditions being worse than any battlefield, but he started moving.

In a short time, the effort bore fruit. A roaring bonfire sprang to life, its flames crackling and reaching skyward, bathing the survivors in much-needed warmth. Nearby, rudimentary shelters began to take shape, fashioned from what little they could salvage. Strips of torn sail and pieces of rope served as clotheslines, holding damp garments in front of the fire's heat.

The group gathered close to the blaze, steam rising as their wet clothing began to dry. Once they had gathered all the survivors and ensured everyone's immediate safety, they moved on to the next pressing issue.

"We need to find something to eat," Will said, addressing the group as he glanced around at the weary faces illuminated by the firelight.

Valenor stood, grabbing his bow and quiver. "I'll see if there's fresh game nearby. The forest beyond the beach might offer something."

"I'll go with you," Lolmig added, tightening his belt and pulling a knife from his boot. "Could do with a bit of proper exercise, eh? And my stomach's already growling like an angry troll."

Will nodded, grateful for their willingness. "Be careful. Stay within sight of each other."

As Valenor and Lolmig set off toward the treeline, their figures disappearing into the dim twilight, Will turned his attention to the wreckage along the beach. "Lyra, let's search through the debris. There might be crates of preserved food still intact from the ship."

Lyra straightened and grabbed a piece of driftwood to use as a makeshift pry bar. "Got it. And maybe we'll get lucky and find something else useful."

Together, they rallied the remaining survivors and returned to the shoreline. The sea was now much calmer, the waves gently lapping on the shore belying the chaotic experience of the night. The beach was a chaotic mess of broken planks, shattered barrels, and torn sails tangled with seaweed.

Will directed the group to work in pairs, scanning the piles for anything salvageable. "Look for barrels or crates—anything sealed. Even spoiled food could be boiled if we get desperate."

As the search continued, Lyra gave a triumphant shout. "Found one!" She and another survivor dragged a half-buried crate free from the sand.

Will rushed over and helped pry it open, revealing rows of salted fish, still relatively intact despite the battered condition of the crate. "This is good. Keep looking," he said, his voice edged with relief.

By the time the hunting party returned with a few small rabbits and a wild bird, Will and Lyra had unearthed two more crates containing hardtack biscuits and dried fruit. Though it wasn't much, it was enough to keep everyone going for the night.

Back at the fire, the survivors worked together to prepare a meagre meal, the scent of cooking meat lifting their spirits as the fire continued to warm them and dry their belongings. The air was alive with the sound of voices, the camaraderie of shared relief as they began to comprehend the reality that they had survived the shipwreck.

Once everyone had eaten and the immediate concerns of the group were addressed, Will and his companions moved a short distance away from the main gathering. They huddled together in the flickering firelight, their concern shifting to their next steps.

Lolmig was the first to break the silence. "Our biggest issue," he began, gesturing toward the dark horizon, "is that we don't know where in the gods' names we've landed. Could be anywhere along the southern coast, and that's a lot of ground to cover."

Will nodded, his arms crossed as he gazed out toward the faint, silvery line of the ocean. "We can't afford to stay put for long. If the weather shifts, we'll be exposed. We need to figure out our bearings at first light."

Lyra brushed a strand of hair behind her ear, her expression thoughtful. "We should scout the area. There might be a settlement nearby—or at least a landmark we can recognise."

For the first time in the discussion, Valenor spoke. His tone was unusually agitated, his words carrying an undercurrent of anger. "And what if there's no one to help us? Not every settlement is friendly."

Lolmig's brows furrowed, his voice tinged with irritation. "And what would you have us do, then? Sit here and hope for a miracle? I'd rather face whatever's out there than freeze to death waiting for the next disaster to come knocking."

Will raised a hand, cutting through the rising argument. "Let's stay focused. First, we need to know where we are. Everything else comes after that."

There was a pause as the group fell into a tense silence, each mulling over the situation.

It was during that silence that Will found himself observing Valenor more closely. Something had changed. Since retrieving the final relic at Crystal Lake, there had been a subtle but unmistakable shift in Valenor's demeanour—he had been irritable, less inclined to join in with group conversation, generally more withdrawn.

In the days leading up to that moment, they had all seemed to be working in complete harmony. Now, Valenor seemed frayed at the edges, his patience worn thin. Arguments had grown more frequent, his opinions veering toward the contrarian, his frustration bubbling to the surface with increasing regularity.

Will couldn't shake the sense that something was wrong with his friend. Was it simply the stress of what they had been through? Or was it something deeper, something more insidious?

He didn't know what to make of it, but it had him worried. For now, all he could do was keep an eye on his friend.

"That settles it, then," he said, his voice firm. "We'll rest here tonight and head out at first light to scout the area. With any luck, we'll find a way back to Caeratheon and pick up the trail from there."

The others nodded, though the tension lingered in the air. As they returned to the warmth of the fire, Will's thoughts remained fixed on Valenor, the faint shadow of doubt trailing behind him like a whisper in the night.

The four of them grabbed their packs from where they had left them drying by the fire and prepared their beds for the night, settling down near the fire that had now burned down to embers.

Will was the last to surrender to sleep, his eyes growing heavy as he listened to the crackling of the fire and the soft breathing of his companions. The events of the day all seemed distant now, like a bad dream fading with the dawn. As he felt his eyes close, he hoped that the following day would be more productive.

* * *

Will's sleep was deep but tormented, his mind dragged into a dream that was a grotesque distortion of reality. He was back on the ship, but it was no longer the same sturdy vessel that had carried them across the sea. The timbers were warped and blackened, oozing a dark ichor that bubbled and hissed as it dripped into the churning sea below. The sails hung in tattered shreds, their frayed edges clawing at a sky that boiled with blood-red lightning.

The air was heavy, suffused with the stench of rot and salt, and the ship lurched violently as waves surged up like grasping hands, clawing at the hull with unnatural intent. There was no horizon, no stars—only an endless abyss in every direction, the darkness swallowing the world.

Will stumbled across the deck, the planks beneath his feet slick and unsteady, his breath coming in ragged gasps. His companions were there, but they were grotesque parodies of themselves.

Lolmig crouched near the mast, reduced to a skeletal mockery, his skin pulled taut over hollowed features. His grin stretched too wide, revealing jagged, broken teeth that glinted in the dim, shifting light. His beard was now thin and matted, swaying as if alive.

At the helm, Valenor stood shrouded in darkness, the shadows clinging to him like a living cloak. His eyes glowed with an unnatural red light, piercing through the gloom. He gripped the wheel with skeletal hands, his expression twisted into a cruel smirk.

Lyra moved across the deck with serpentine grace, her hair a tangled mass of writhing, snake-like tendrils. Her hands, elongated into razor-sharp claws, left dark, smoking trails wherever they touched. Her face was contorted with rage, her glowing yellow eyes burning with an anger that seared into Will's soul.

Will tried to call out to them, to plead for understanding, but his voice was swallowed by the howling wind, the scream of the storm drowning him in a cacophony of despair. The ship groaned, tilting violently as the sea beneath them transformed into a black, viscous liquid that reached upward, clutching at the ship with writhing tendrils.

The others turned to face him, their eyes burning with accusation. Valenor stepped forward, holding the Shadow Codex. Its pages writhed like living things, their words glowing with a malevolent red light that pulsed in time with the storm.

"You brought us here, Will," Valenor said, his voice layered with an unnatural distortion, echoing and reverberating as though it spoke from the depths of the abyss itself. "You are the architect of our doom."

The deck beneath Will's feet began to splinter and crack, turning to a black quicksand that dragged him down. He struggled, clawing at the sinking planks, but his hands found no purchase. The darkness rose around him, cold and suffocating, seeping into his skin, filling his lungs with its icy dread.

Above him, the others loomed, their grotesque forms illuminated by the unholy light of the codex. Their laughter was a haunting chorus of malice that twisted in his ears.

"Join us, Will," they chanted in unison, their voices a symphony of mockery and despair. "Join us in the darkness."

As the black substance swallowed him whole, his vision was consumed by the codex. Its pages burned with an eerie flame, the words twisting and writhing like living things. One word stood out, searing itself into his mind, its meaning heavy with foreboding: **Betrayal**.

Will awoke with a start, his chest heaving and his body drenched in sweat. The echoes of the dream lingered, the word still burning in his thoughts like an unshakable warning.

The fire had burned low, and the forest around them was silent except for the occasional rustle of leaves in the wind. But the nightmare's grip remained strong, leaving him shaken and deeply unsettled.

He looked at his sleeping companions, their faces serene in the firelight, but the nightmare had planted a seed of doubt in his mind. Could he really trust them? The dream had felt so real, so vivid, that as much as he tried to put it behind him, the fear and distrust lingered, eating away at him.

He sat by the dying fire, staring into the embers, his mind racing, struggling to shake off the nightmare's influence. But no matter how hard he tried, the twisted images of his friends, the sense of betrayal, and the haunting words of the dream clung to him like a dark shadow, wrapping it's inky tendrils around his mind and festering there.

# Chapter nineteen

Their boots slipped in the wet mud of the trail as they travelled east the following day, but the air was fresh, carrying the unmistakeable scent of vegetation and wet earth that arrives after the rains. They walked in silence, the only sound the rhythmic patter of rainwater dripping from leaves all around them.

The weather remained dry and clear for the remainder of the day, but in the late afternoon the wind shifted bringing an arctic blast from the north, causing the temperature to plummet.

As their shadows began lengthening on the trail in the late afternoon sun, the companions spotted a farmer's cart coming toward them along the track. The cart was old and rickety, its wooden frame creaking with every bump in the road, and was being pulled by a tired-looking mare. The farmer, an older man with a weathered face, sat lazily at the front, holding the reins with one hand while chewing on a stalk of grain. The wheels of the cart churned up the muddy road as it rumbled closer, and the group could hear the farmer whistling a tuneless melody, seemingly lost in his own thoughts.

As the cart creaked its way down the road, the group stepped aside to let it pass. Will, spotting an opportunity, waved the farmer down with a friendly gesture.

"Afternoon friend!" Will called out as the farmer, an older man with a weathered face and a threadbare hat, gently pulled back on the reins to halt his tired mare.

The farmer tipped his hat, looking them over with a curious but amiable expression. "Afternoon to ya. What be bringin' a strange bunch like you lot out 'ere, then?" he asked, his voice rich with the rolling tones reminiscent of some of Will's own countrymen.

Will stepped forward, keeping his tone polite and approachable. "Our ship went down a couple of days ago off the coast. We've been trying to find our bearings since. Would you happen to know where we are?"

The farmer let out a low chuckle, shaking his head. "Ah, wrecked were ya? Proper unlucky that, but fair play to ya fer makin' it ashore. Don't reckon ye lost anyone?"

"Thankfully, no," Will replied. "But we're a bit turned around and could use some direction."

The farmer scratched his beard, his eyes squinting thoughtfully. "Well then, lad, ye've washed up in a better spot than most. Yer on the King's Road, see? Caeratheon's not far—hour's walk, maybe less if yer legs are keen."

A wave of relief washed over Will. "Caeratheon? That's good to hear. We weren't sure how far we'd drifted."

"Aye, Caeratheon," the farmer said with a nod. "Good spot fer a rest. Got plenty o' inns and a fine market square. If yer lookin' fer a bed, try the Silver Swan. Old Maisie runs it—she does a proper stew and keeps a tidy room."

"Sounds like just what we need," Will replied, smiling. "Thank you for the advice."

The farmer tipped his hat again, a twinkle in his eye. "No trouble at all, lad. Ye take care now, mind? These roads can turn strange-like after dark."

With a cluck of his tongue and a flick of the reins, the mare trotted forward, the cart rumbling away. The group watched as he disappeared down the road, his voice drifting back to them as he continued whistling his cheerful tune.

As the old farmer predicted, the tall, stone walls of Caeratheon came into view about an hour later as they crested the next hill, the city's towers and rooftops jutting skyward, framed by the gentle curve of the surrounding hills. The sounds of a bustling city carried to them on the breeze—the hum of voices, the rhythmic clatter of hooves on cobblestones, and the occasional bell of a town crier announcing the day's news.

The gates stood open, welcoming a steady stream of travellers, merchants, and townsfolk. On either side of the entrance, armoured guards stood at attention, their eyes vigilant as they observed the flow of people entering the city, their gazes never wavering as they assessed each person, ensuring no threats passed unnoticed.

Passing through the gates, the group was immediately swept up in the energy of the city. The streets were cobbled and narrow, winding between rows of timber-framed buildings with upper stories leaning precariously over the lanes below. Flags and colourful banners fluttered overhead, while laundry lines criss-crossed between windows, garments flapping in the gentle breeze. The air was alive with mingled aromas; roasting meats, freshly baked bread, fragrant herbs, and less pleasant scents from the alleys and gutters where refuse had collected.

The marketplace sprawled before them like a living tapestry of colour and sound. Stalls crowded every available space, their owners shouting over one another to attract customers. Barrels of apples, heaps of exotic spices, and bolts of shimmering fabrics spilled from their displays. The warm aroma of spiced cider mingled with the acrid scent of a blacksmith's forge, while a street performer juggled flaming torches to a small crowd's delight.

The companions moved through the throng, pausing at various stalls to replenish their supplies. Lolmig haggled cheerfully with a merchant over dried meats and hard cheeses, tossing in a few flasks of ale to the mix with a wink. Lyra lingered at a stall selling delicate jewellery, her fingers brushing over a pendant shaped like a crescent moon. Will found himself distracted by a bookseller's display, thumbing through titles with a wistful smile.

As they finished their errands, Valenor turned to the group, his tone casual. "The market's a maze, and there's plenty more to see. I suggest we split up and explore on our own for a while. We can meet at the Silver Swan by sundown."

Will frowned, something about Valenor's suggestion nagging at him. The elf's tone was off—too easy, too smooth. His gaze darted briefly to the side, as though avoiding Will's eyes. "Why split up?" Will said, his tone gently probing. "Surely it's better to stick together?"

Valenor shrugged, his expression composed. "We all have different needs, and it's more efficient this way. Besides, a little space might do us good after everything."

Will hesitated, glancing at Lyra and Lolmig. They seemed more preoccupied with the market than Valenor's suggestion. Reluctantly, he nodded. "Alright. Silver Swan at sundown."

As the group dispersed, Will lingered a moment, watching Valenor disappear into the crowd. Valenor's eagerness to separate didn't sit well with him, but he wondered if his lingering feelings of suspicion from his nightmare the night before might be influencing him. For now, he wandered the market, letting the sights and sounds momentarily distract him from the tension simmering just below the surface.

Will didn't really have need of anything, but he took the opportunity to wander through the bustling market. A bemused expression settled on his face as he passed the vibrant stalls, his mind drifting back to the day he'd first written the description of Caeratheon's market. Every detail—the leaning timber-framed buildings, the cacophony of street vendors, the mingling scents of spices and roasted meats—was exactly as he had imagined. It was uncanny, almost unsettling, to walk through a place he thought he had created in his mind. If they had the time to linger, he would have loved to lose himself in the winding streets, soaking in the city he had always dreamed of but never thought he'd truly see. He lingered for so long, soaking it all in, that when the sky began to darken and the torch-lighters came out, it took him by surprise, and he approached a vendor seeking directions to the inn.

The inn's common room was warm and inviting, with a roaring fire in the hearth and the smell of a hearty stew wafting from the kitchen. They secured a couple of rooms for the night and settled in.

The companions sat around a sturdy wooden table near the hearth, the fire crackling merrily beside them. The inn was bustling with life; patrons filled nearly every seat, their laughter and conversation blending into a pleasant hum that filled the air.

Will leaned back in his chair, a smile on his face as he sipped from his tankard of ale.

"This is just what we needed," Lolmig said, his voice content as he took another bite of his meal. "A hot meal, a warm fire, and a chance to catch our breath."

Valenor nodded in agreement, though his eyes were distant, as if his mind was turning over some problem. Lyra, seated beside him, seemed more at ease than she had been in days.

As the evening wore on, the inn grew even more festive. A group of locals at a nearby table broke into song, their voices rising in a cheerful chorus that spread through the room. Will found himself laughing along with them, getting caught up by the infectious atmosphere.

The door to the inn suddenly burst open, a cold draft sweeping into the room as half a dozen soldiers of the city guard marched in, their armour clinking ominously in the silence that followed their entrance. The music stopped abruptly, and the cheerful chatter of the inn's patrons died away as all eyes turned to the soldiers, wary expressions on every face.

The captain of the guard, a stern-faced man with a scar running down his cheek, stepped forward, his gaze sweeping the room until it landed on Will and his companions. His eyes narrowed, and he pointed a gauntleted hand toward them.

"There they are!" he barked. "Seize them!"

The soldiers moved quickly, advancing on the group with weapons drawn. The companions, caught off guard, leaped to their feet, instinctively reaching for their own weapons, but the soldiers were already upon them, surrounding them with a ring of steel.

"What is the meaning of this?" Will demanded, his voice steady despite the shock coursing through him. "We've done nothing wrong!"

"You are under arrest," the captain growled, his tone leaving no room for argument. "By order of the Lord of Caeratheon."

"What are we accused of?" Valenor said, his expression one of disbelief. "We've only just arrived in this city!"

"Save your explanations," the captain snapped.

Lyra's eyes flashed with anger. "This is absurd! We've been here all evening—we couldn't have possibly—"

The captain cut her off with a sharp gesture. "Enough! You will come with us, or we will take you by force."

Will glanced at his companions, his expression urging them to go quietly. Slowly, they allowed the soldiers to disarm them and bind their hands with rough ropes.

As they were led out of the inn, the stares of the other patrons followed them, some filled with fear, others with suspicion. The festive atmosphere had vanished, replaced by a tense silence.

The companions were marched through the dark, torch lined streets, the city's stone walls towering around them. Overhead, the moon was obscured by clouds, casting the world into darkness.

Will's thoughts were a jumbled mess, his heart pounding in his chest as the reality of their situation began to sink in. The clinking of the soldiers' armour and the sound of their boots on the cobblestone streets seemed to echo ominously in the quiet night. His breath felt heavy, the freezing air biting at his skin and constricting his lungs as he struggled to keep his panic at bay.

Lyra's soft whimpers beside him only made it worse. Will's protective instincts flared, but with his hands bound and surrounded by armed soldiers, he felt utterly powerless.

The streets were eerily silent at this hour, the sounds of merriment and laughter from the taverns faded into the distance as they were led deeper into the city's government district. The narrow streets seemed to close in on them, the tall stone buildings looming overhead, their windows dark and shuttered.

Will's mind raced, trying to piece together some way to escape this nightmare. He ran through countless scenarios in his head, but each one seemed more hopeless than the last.

His eyes darted around, searching for anything—an alleyway they could duck into, a moment of distraction where they might break free—but the soldiers kept a tight grip on them.

As they were marched farther from the market district, the streets grew wider, the buildings older and more imposing. The air felt thick with tension, and the fog of their breath hung heavily in the air, mingling with the mist that had begun to creep in as the temperature plummeted.

Finally, the soldiers led them into a dimly lit courtyard, surrounded by high walls that seemed to close off the world beyond. At the far end of the courtyard, a heavy iron door stood ajar, leading into what looked like a fortress or a prison. The captain gestured for his men to halt, and they roughly pushed the companions forward, forcing them to stand in a line.

"Wait here," the captain said, his stern voice leaving no room for argument.

With that, the soldiers stepped back, forming a perimeter around the courtyard, their eyes trained on the companions. The heavy door creaked ominously as it swung open wider, revealing a dark interior that seemed to swallow the light.

Will swallowed hard, his thoughts still in disarray. The terror of their situation threatened to overwhelm him, but he knew he had to keep it together.

The minutes stretched into what felt like hours, each second dragging painfully as Will's anxiety gnawed at him. The cold night air seeped through his clothes, chilling him to the bone, but it was the fear that made him shiver uncontrollably. His mind was a whirlwind of dark possibilities; visions of torture chambers, unjust trials, and executions played out in his imagination, each one more terrifying than the last.

Will cast a glance at his companions. Lyra was pale, her eyes wide and darting nervously around the courtyard. Valenor stood rigid, his face a stoic mask hiding his true emotion, but even he couldn't hide the tension in his jaw. Lolmig kept his gaze fixed on the ground, giving away nothing of his thoughts.

The silence was unbearable. Will's anxiety closed it's fist around his throat, making it hard to breathe. He wanted to say something, anything to break the tense silence, to reassure himself and the others that they would find a way out of this. But the words stuck in his throat, choked by fear.

Just when he thought he couldn't stand the waiting any longer, the iron door creaked open, its hinges groaning in protest. A tall figure emerged from the darkness beyond, flanked by two more soldiers. The figure was dressed in dark, formal robes, and his stern expression did little to ease Will's growing panic.

The man stepped forward, his gaze sweeping over the group with cold detachment. "Bring them inside," he ordered, his voice like steel. The guards moved quickly, their hands gripping Will and the others by the arms, pulling them toward the open door.

Will's heart sank as they were led into the dark interior of the fortress. The dim light of the courtyard faded behind them. The door slammed shut with a finality that echoed in Will's mind like the slamming of a guillotine.

They were in the hands of their captors now, and whatever fate awaited them, Will knew it would be out of their control. The dread that had been building within him settled into a cold, hard knot in his stomach as they were marched deeper into the darkness.

# Chapter twenty

The cell they were led to lay deep within the fortress, buried beneath layers of stone and shadow. As they descended the countless staircases, the air grew colder, the shadows darker. The flickering torchlight cast eerie shadows on the walls, adding to the sense of foreboding that clung to Will like a shroud.

He tried to keep track of the route they were taking, counting each turn, each step, but it soon became a hopeless task. The countless corridors seemed to twist and coil endlessly.

The further they went, the more Will felt like he could almost feel the weight of the fortress pressing down on him, and by the time they reached the cell, he had lost all sense of direction. All he knew was that they were deep underground, far from the world above, and far from any chance of escape.

The cell itself was a small, damp chamber carved from the stone. The door was made of thick iron bars, rusted but solid, and it creaked ominously as it swung open.

Will stumbled into the cell as he was roughly shoved inside, catching himself against the rough stone wall. The cold seeped into his bones immediately, and the air smelled of mildew and wet stone. A torch set in a sconce some distance back up the corridor emitted a small amount of flickering light, but it did little to dispel the gloom. The walls were lined with patches of moss, and water dripped steadily from the ceiling, forming small, dark pools on the uneven floor. Somewhere in the shadows came the squeak of a small rodent, followed by the skittering of tiny claws on the hard stone floor, fading off into the distance.

He turned to see his companions, their faces pale in the dim light. Valenor and Lyra had retreated to the back wall, but Lolmig quietly moved around, his eyes scanning every inch of the cell as if searching for weaknesses in the structure.

The sound of the key in the lock made a solid clunk as it effectively secured the only way out, and the guard grabbed the bars and gave it a pull to ensure it was properly secured before looking through the bars, "You should get some rest, you will have a chance to hear the charges against you and state your case in the morning." and with that he turned and walked away, the sound of his boots echoing off the close stone corridor walls, fading into the distance.

Will looked over to where Lolmig was still pacing around, scrutinising the cell, "Did you spot anything?"

Lolmig shook his head. "It's old, but there's no weaknesses."

"What are we going to do?" asked Lyra, a slight quiver in her voice.

Will paced around, frustrated at being unable to come up with any viable plans. He looked over at Valenor who was stood off by himself looking preoccupied, more withdrawn than usual. "I don't think we have any choice for now, let's try and get some rest and see what the morning brings." he said.

The four of them settled down and tried as best they could to get some rest, but the cold damp environment was anything but restful. The night seemed to drag on forever, the frustration over their unwarranted incarceration, and the physical discomfort of the cell allowing only occasional flashes of sleep. After a while Will gave up on sleep and paced the cell trying to figure out why they might have been detained.

As infinite as the night seemed though, it eventually came to an end and with the morning came the guards who informed them that they were to be led to the grand hall to be brought before Lord Tavar of Caeratheon for trial.

The guards marched them up through the labyrinth of tunnels, leading them away from the chill of the damp underground cells. The torches along the passage flickered faintly, casting jagged shadows that seemed to stretch and claw at the walls.

As they emerged into the courtyard, they were momentarily blinded by the sharp contrast of daylight. The morning sun hung low, its pale light doing little to melt the frost clinging to the cobblestones like shards of glass. A crisp breeze carried the faint scent of smoke and cold earth, biting at their exposed skin.

Across the courtyard loomed a grand building, its tall spires piercing the sky. The architecture was stately and imposing, with large arched windows reflecting the pale sunlight. Though undeniably beautiful, it radiated an air of stern judgment.

Will's eyes lingered on the intricate carvings above the heavy wooden doors—depictions of triumph and justice, no doubt intended to inspire reverence. Under different circumstances, he might have marvelled at the artistry or felt a flicker of excitement to glimpse the grandeur within. But today, the weight in his chest made it hard to appreciate the beauty, and all he wanted was to turn and run.

The guards ushered them toward the doors, their heavy wooden frames creaking open to reveal the grand hall beyond, where their fates would be decided.

Sunlight filtered through high, narrow stained-glass windows, casting fractured beams of colour across cold stone floors. Banners bearing the crest of Caeratheon hung from the vaulted ceilings, and a row of stern-faced guards flanked the hall, hands resting on the pommels of their swords. At the far end of the chamber sat Lord Aedrin Tavar, a middle-aged man with sharp, calculating eyes and a heavy crown of silver upon his brow.

To his right stood his advisor, a wiry man named Eramis, his robe of deep blue adorned with arcane sigils. His narrow eyes gleamed with the cold precision of a chess player about to claim checkmate.

Will, Lyra, Valenor, and Lolmig stood in the centre of the room, wrists bound. Their belongings, including their weapons had been seized the previous night and now rested on a table at the far end of the room.

"Will Preston," declared Lord Tavar, his voice reverberating through the hall. "You and those who travel with you stand accused of theft from the people of Caeratheon. On the day of your arrival, an ancient relic from our Hall of Antiquities vanished. Imagine our surprise when this very artifact was discovered in your possession."

With a flick of his wrist, Eramis signalled the guards. One guard stepped forward, reached into Will's pack, and pulled out a small, ornately carved jade idol, no larger than a man's hand. Gasps echoed from the gallery of onlookers who had gathered to watch the trial.

"Behold!" Eramis exclaimed with a victorious smile. "Proof that the accused is not only a thief but a collector of forbidden artifacts. Observe, my lord, the other relics he carries!" Eramis gestured broadly, his voice dripping with mockery. "What kind of man wanders the land hoarding powerful objects of legend? A thief. A scavenger. Perhaps a conqueror of things that do not belong to him."

A murmur rippled through the hall. The audience's gazes turned toward Will, filled with suspicion and doubt. But Will stood frozen, his mouth agape in disbelief. His mind raced, desperately trying to piece together the how and why, but no matter how hard he tried, he couldn't conjure a single plausible explanation for why the idol was in his pack. Will's eyes darted to Valenor, but Valenor stood quietly to the side, his eyes lowered, his face unreadable.

Lord Tavar leaned forward on his throne, steepling his fingers beneath his chin. "It is indeed troubling," he muttered.

"One man, a stranger to our land, in possession of so much power."

"Please, my lord," said Lyra, stepping forward despite the guards' warning glares. "Surely you must hear us out. You've listened to accusations, do we not get a chance to speak in our defence. Do the laws of Caeratheon not allow for that?"

Her plea gave Lord Tavar pause. He leaned back in his chair, his lips pressing into a hard line. "Speak, then. But know this—the evidence against you is damning."

Will took a deep breath. His heart pounded, but he knew this was his only chance. "My lord, I am not a thief. The relics I carry are part of a greater quest. These are not trinkets I've gathered out of greed. They are pieces of a puzzle meant to stop a force greater than any of us—Malakar."

The name sent a shiver through the chamber. People exchanged glances. Even the guards shifted uncomfortably.

"Malakar," Lord Tavar repeated, his brow furrowed in irritation. "A ghost story to frighten children."

Will stepped forward, eyes fierce, his voice unwavering. "Not a story, my lord. A threat. We have recently returned from Shadowmoor, and the curse is spreading faster than ever before. Malakar's agents are everywhere, and they seek to plunge this world into darkness. I carry these relics because I must. It is our intention to seek out this threat and end it once and for all!" he paused for a moment, looking at Lord Tavar with deep sincerity, "But I assure you that your idol has never be in in my possession, and I have no idea how it came to be in my pack."

A flicker of doubt passed over the lord's face, but before he could speak, Eramis interjected with a venomous sneer. "Lies from a silver tongue, my lord! The tale of every thief ever caught red-handed. He speaks of darkness but walks with it at his side, carrying the very relics that could tip the balance of power. Perhaps it is he who seeks to become the new Malakar!"

The words struck like a blade. The hall exploded into an uproar. Onlookers shouted, voices blending into chaos.

Lord Tavar raised his hand, and silence fell like a dropped curtain. His face was hard with decision. "Enough. I have heard all I need to hear. The four of you are to be detained until I decide your fate."

"Wait!" Will protested, but two guards were already stepping forward, gripping his arms. His eyes darted to Eramis, who stood with a satisfied grin, eyes gleaming with triumph.

It was then that something clicked in Will's mind. The Lord's gaze... it was too blank, too distant. The subtle look of a man whose will was not his own.

"He's under a spell," Will whispered to himself. His heart raced as realisation surged through him.

"Wait!" he called, yanking himself free from the guards' grip. "Lord Tavar is being controlled! The Lord is not acting of his own will—he's enchanted!"

The crowd jeered. "Desperate excuses from a desperate man!" someone shouted.

Eramis's eyes widened in panic for a split second before his mask of calm returned. "Guards, seize him!" he barked.

But Will was already moving. His fingers shot toward the amulet hanging from his neck, his will focused like a blade's edge.

"ENOUGH!" he roared. The amulet burned hot against his chest as he gripped it tightly. His eyes blazed with light as he channelled its power, summoning everything he had. A wave of golden energy exploded outward, radiating from him like a pulse of thunder. It passed through stone, metal, flesh, and spirit alike.

The guards stumbled back, eyes wide in confusion. Gasps echoed from every corner of the hall. Faces twisted in confusion as if waking from a long, hazy dream. The light struck Lord Tavar, and for a moment, his eyes shone gold. He clutched his head, gritting his teeth. Slowly, his gaze sharpened, clarity returning to his features.

"What... what have I done?" the Lord murmured, his voice thick with guilt and confusion. His eyes settled on Eramis, and in that moment, everything became clear. His eyes narrowed, and his jaw set with cold fury. "Eramis..."

The advisor stumbled back, hands raised defensively. "M-my lord, please, I was only acting in your best interests! You must believe me!"

"Seize him." Lord Tavar's voice was like iron.

Two guards moved instantly, gripping Eramis by the arms. His eyes darted wildly. "You fools! You have no idea what forces you're meddling with!" he hissed, his eyes briefly flickering with a sickly green light. "You think you've won, but you've only delayed the inevitable. He's watching. He's always watching!"

"Enough of your poison," the Lord said coldly, standing from his throne. "Take him to the dungeons. He will answer for his treachery."

As the guards hauled Eramis to his feet, his eyes, sharp as broken glass, locked onto Valenor. His lips curled into a sly, knowing smile. "Careful where you tread, old friend," he said in a threatening hiss just loud enough for Valenor to hear. "Paths have a way of crossing again when you least expect it."

Valenor's eyes narrowed, his face an impassive mask, but his fingers twitched at his side. Everyone else's attention remained focused on Eramis, faces locked in various states of shock and bewilderment at the sudden turn of events. None of them caught the exchange between Eramis and Valenor.

"Take him away," the Lord of Caeratheon commanded, his voice regaining its authority, no longer dulled with the enchantment's haze. Eramis was dragged from the chamber, his gaze lingering on Valenor until the doors shut behind him.

Will glanced at Valenor, catching the faintest flicker of tension in his stance. "You good?" he asked, still breathing heavily from the exertion of freeing Tavar from the enchantment.

Valenor's features softened into a grin. "Better than Eramis, I'd wager." He nodded toward the closed door, his casual tone betraying none of the turmoil beneath.

Lolmig grunted, cracking his knuckles. "One less snake slithering around."

"Indeed," said the Lord, his brow furrowed with shame. "I owe you all an apology. It seems I was blind to the poison in my own court. You have my gratitude for breaking his hold on me."

Will nodded but couldn't shake a sense that something still wasn't as it should be. Something lingered in the air like the distant rumble of an oncoming storm.

Valenor remained silent, his gaze fixed on the door for a moment longer before turning to the others. "So, what now?" he asked, his voice steady as stone.

Lord Tavar turned to the assembled crowd who were still talking loudly, the excitement of the events that had just unfolded giving rise to a level of disorder not usually seen in the grand hall. "I will have order!" he bellowed, and the din of voices gradually simmered down.

"You spoke of a quest, during that mockery of a trial." said Lord Tavar, returning to his seat after order was restored.

"That's right my lord." said Will.

"It seems we have wrongfully waylaid you in your righteous path. Please tell me if there is any way we might now assist you to make up for the lost time."

Will considered the offer a moment, but Lolmig pushed forward and whispered to Will, "You could see if he has any information on the exact whereabouts of that temple?"

Will nodded at his friend and then turned back to the dais. "There is something, my lord," he said, his confident tone carrying across the room. "We seek an ancient temple linked to the Order of the Burning Torch. We believe it lies somewhere to the west of here in the forest, but that is a large area to cover in a search. If you have any records, maps, or even rumours about such a place, it would be a great help to our cause."

Lord Tavar's brows lifted in thought as he leaned back in his grand chair, fingers steepled before his chin. He glanced to a steward standing by the wall. "Fetch the Keeper of Records. Tell him to bring the old surveys and cartographic scrolls of the western woodlands." The steward gave a swift bow and hurried from the hall.

Moments later, the steward returned with a gaunt, robed elf in tow — the Keeper of Records. He carried several scrolls bundled in his arms, his eyes darting to the companions with an aloof expression, as if he deemed these outsiders unworthy of his time.

"My lord," the Keeper said with a deep bow, setting the scrolls carefully on a table. "I have brought the tern woodland surveys, as you requested. Some date back over a century."

"Search for references to ruins, ancient structures, or unusual landmarks," Lord Tavar instructed. "This group seeks knowledge of an old temple linked to the Order of the Burning Torch."

The Keeper's face twitched at the mention of the name. "The Burning Torch, you say? Curious... I do recall something. A marker on one of the older maps, I believe. A symbol, not a name, but it might match what you seek."

He unfurled one of the scrolls, revealing a faded, hand-drawn map. His fingers, thin and spidery, traced the parchment, a slight tremor in his finger rhythmically tapping along the route. After a few moments, he tapped a point some distance to the west of the city, breaking the tense silence. "Here. This marking. It does not match any of the known settlements or trading posts."

Will leaned in, his eyes locking onto the symbol — a small circle with an outward burst of lines, like a sun or a star. It was faint, barely distinguishable from the surrounding topography, but it was there.

"That could be it," Lyra said, excitement bubbling in her voice. "It's in the right area, and it matches the information Eldran gave us."

"Could be," Will agreed, glancing at the Keeper. "Do you have any records of expeditions to this location?"

The Keeper shook his head. "None that I can recall. It lies deep in the heart of the woods, and most who venture there do so for hunting or gathering herbs. Few venture too far beyond the safe paths, as the ground becomes treacherous."

Lord Tavar stood, drawing their attention. "I will grant you supplies for your journey. It's not much, but it's the least I can do."

Will bowed his head deeply. "Thank you, my lord. Your aid means more than you know."

"I hope that it serves you well," Lord Tavar replied, his voice grave. "Dark forces are at play here in Aruna, and I have no doubt they watch you as you walk this path."

Valenor's gaze remained fixed on the map, his face unreadable as he traced the small, sun-like symbol with his finger, but said nothing.

Will glanced at him, noting his strange silence and the troubled expression he had worn since Eramis had been removed from the room.

# Chapter twenty-one

They chatted with Lord Tavar and his keeper of records for a little while longer. Lord Tavar had the cartographer make a copy of that region of the map, and delivered the supplies he had promised. After leaving the lord with some advice to seek the aid of the elves in binding Eramis, they gathered their things and left.

As they passed through the north gate of the city and left its heavy walls behind, a collective sigh of relief escaped the group. The tension that had gripped them since their trial began to ebb, though not entirely. They exchanged cautious glances, eager to put as much distance as possible between themselves and the imposing city, not quite trusting their freedom until they were a safe distance away.

Once they were beyond the city walls, the forest soon enveloped them, its canopy filtering the daylight into soft, shifting patterns across the path. The rustling of leaves and the distant call of birds brought a tentative calm, as the natural rhythm of the woods eased their frayed nerves. The cool breeze carried a freshness that seemed to wash away the lingering stench of the cells that stubbornly clung to them.

Will felt his shoulders relax as he took in the first breath of that soothing forest air, the tension in his chest giving way to a familiar sense of calm that he felt when travelling through the woods.

Lolmig glanced up at the trees, letting out a long breath of relief. "Aye, this is better." He glanced at the others with a grin.

"Don't jinx it," Lyra replied with a smirk, stretching her arms over her head as she walked. "I'm just glad to breathe fresh air again."

Will trudged ahead of them, his eyes forward. His fingers toyed with the amulet around his neck, his thoughts distant. Though he felt the same sense of freedom as the others, there was a lingering weight on his mind — The whole situation with Eramis felt off and left him with so many questions. How had he known they were in the city in the first place? He was left wondering how Malakar seemed to be tracking their every move, always one step ahead.

Valenor, for his part, was unusually quiet. He walked at the rear of the group, his posture rigid and his hand resting near the hilt of his blade, as though prepared for an attack at any moment. His jaw was tightly set, and the tension in his shoulders never eased, even as the others began to relax. When Lyra made a light-hearted comment about the forest's serenity, he didn't respond, his focus seemingly elsewhere.

"You've been quiet since we left the city, Valenor," Will said without turning around, his tone casual. "Everything alright?"

"I prefer silence in the woods," Valenor replied smoothly, his tone even. "Noise makes you a target. Every hunter knows that."

Will glanced back over his shoulder, eyes narrowing slightly. "True enough." He turned forward once more, his gaze sweeping the path ahead. "But sometimes, silence hides more than it reveals."

Lolmig glanced between them, one brow raised. "Bah, you're both too tense. No one's hunting us out here. Not yet, at least. Enjoy the quiet while we have it." He chuckled, patting the haft of his hammer. "Besides, if anything does come, it'll regret it."

"Careful, Lolmig," Lyra said with a grin. "You're starting to sound cocky."

The dwarf shot her a grin. "Confident, lass. There's a difference."

The group pressed on, weaving through narrow deer trails and over gnarled roots that criss-crossed the forest floor. Their pace was steady, and even with the difficult terrain, they managed to cover a lot of ground.

The sun dipped lower, casting long shadows through the trees. Their earlier invigoration from being back in nature had begun to wane as fatigue set in. Every step seemed to grow heavier, and although no one wanted to admit it, the sleepless night in Caeratheon had taken its toll.

"How much longer, Will?" Lyra asked, brushing a loose strand of hair from her face.

"Not long," Will replied, glancing at the sky through a gap in the canopy. "We'll camp before nightfall. A few more miles, just to put some distance between us and the city."

"Bah, I'd say that's distance enough," Lolmig grumbled, his steps slowing. "If something's following us, it won't matter if we're two miles or twenty miles out. We should stop soon, lad."

"One more hour," Will said firmly. "We push on."

Lolmig huffed but didn't argue. He knew Will's stubborn streak well enough by now.

The sun eventually dipped below the horizon, and the golden sky turned to shades of lavender when Will eventually called for a halt near a small brook.

They all gratefully dropped their packs and began their practised routine of setting up camp, and before the last of the colour faded from the sky they had makeshift shelters and all sat around a small campfire.

The fire crackled softly, its flames flickering against the bark of the surrounding trees, it's warmth chasing away the chill in the air. The rich smell of roasted herbs and bread filled the air as Lyra prepared a simple meal from the supplies that Tavar had pressed on them before they left Caeratheon.

Lolmig lay back against a mossy log, his arms crossed over his chest, his eyes half-closed. "This... this is more like it," he muttered.

Lyra handed him a piece of flatbread and sat down next to him. "Don't get too comfortable. We've got a long road ahead."

Will sat on the opposite side of the fire, eyes fixed on the flames, his amulet resting in his palm. The glow of the fire reflected off its surface. His thoughts were distant, as his mind wandered over the events of the past day.

Lyra's voice broke through Will's thoughts, soft and inquisitive. "What are you thinking about?"

Will didn't answer right away. He stared at the flickering fire, the flames dancing and casting fleeting shadows on the forest floor. Finally, he exhaled a long breath, his shoulders sagging slightly.

"I'm thinking about how things don't add up," he said, his voice low. He glanced at the others, their faces illuminated by the warm glow. "How did Eramis know we were in Caeratheon? It wasn't like we announced ourselves. And how does Malakar always seem to be one step ahead of us?"

Lyra frowned, her brow knitting together. "You think someone's feeding him information?"

Will shook his head. "I don't know. Maybe. But it's more than that. It's how easily he manipulates us—our actions, our decisions—even over vast distances. It's like he's always there, pulling the strings, making sure we're exactly where he wants us to be. And we don't even realise it until it's too late."

A heavy silence fell over the group as Will's words sank in. The fire crackled softly, the only sound breaking the silence.

"If he's that powerful," Will continued, his gaze fixed on the flames, "how are we supposed to stop him? Every move we make feels like it's playing into his hands."

The silence lingered for a moment longer before Lolmig broke it, his voice thoughtful. "Y'know, lad, maybe you're looking at it the wrong way," he said, leaning forward and resting his arms on his knees. "Malakar's pulling all these tricks, sure. But doesn't that tell you something?"

Will frowned. "Like what?"

"Like he's worried," Lolmig said, a hint of a grin tugging at his beard. "Think about it. If we weren't a threat, why bother with all the games and traps? He's trying to keep you on the path the Shadow Codex lays out, but you keep stepping off it. Whether you mean to or not, you keep making choices that lead you closer to the light."

Lyra nodded, her expression softening. "Lolmig's right, Will. You're not following Malakar's script, and that's what scares him. If he really was unbeatable, he wouldn't waste his time trying to manipulate us. He'd just crush us outright."

Will sat back, letting their words sink in. The idea that Malakar's relentless interference was born of fear rather than confidence hadn't occurred to him. It wasn't much, but it was a sliver of hope.

"And besides," Lyra added, her voice resolute, "once we reach the temple, hopefully we'll find a way to reach the Order of the Burning Torch and get some answers."

Will nodded slowly, his mind still clouded with doubt but grasping at the logic of their words. He glanced at Valenor, hoping for his input, but the elf was unusually quiet. He sat slightly apart from the group, his sharp features illuminated by the firelight, but his gaze was fixed on the shadows beyond their camp.

"Valenor?" Will prompted, his voice gentle.

Valenor didn't respond right away. His eyes seemed to pierce through the darkness, as though searching for something unseen. Finally, he shook his head slightly and muttered, "We should rest. We'll need our strength for the journey ahead."

The dismissive tone made Will's stomach twist, but he chose not to press further. Instead, he exchanged a glance with Lyra, who looked equally concerned but said nothing.

"Alright," Will said, settling back and trying to shake off the tension in the air. "We'll rest and move out at first light."

They slept well that night, exhaustion granting them a rare reprieve, but when they awoke just before dawn, the biting chill of the morning immediately pierced their rest. Sometime during the night, the temperature had plummeted, leaving a heavy frost coating everything in sight. The frost glinted and sparkled in the first rays of sunlight, beautiful but merciless in its reminder of the cold.

Will's breath came out in visible puffs as he sat up, his body stiff from the frigid ground. He rubbed his arms briskly, trying to chase away the numbness creeping through his fingers. Lolmig grumbled under his breath as he emerged from his bedroll, his beard frosted white at the edges.

"Blast it," the dwarf muttered, stamping his feet to get the blood flowing again. "Feels like I've been sleeping in a block of ice."

Lyra shivered as she bundled herself deeper into her cloak, her teeth chattering audibly. "I don't think I've ever been this cold. My joints feel frozen solid."

Valenor, stoic as ever, said nothing, but even he pulled his cloak tighter around himself, his breath misting heavily in the frosty air.

Packing up their camp was slow work, the frost clinging stubbornly to their gear. Ropes and bedrolls were stiff, making them difficult to handle, and every touch of the cold metal clasps sent a jolt of icy pain through their fingers.

"Let's get moving," Will said, his voice tight as he struggled to buckle his pack with numb hands. "The sooner we start walking, the sooner we'll warm up."

The group nodded, their movements sluggish as they prepared to set out. The forest around them was eerily quiet, the usual morning sounds muffled by the cold. As they stepped onto the frost-covered trail, their boots crunched loudly, breaking the fragile stillness.

"How far, you think?" Lolmig grumbled, adjusting his pack. He wiped a bead of sweat from his brow despite the cool air.

"It's close," Will said with certainty. His eyes scanned the trees ahead as if following some unseen guide. "We're on the right track. I can feel it."

"Feel it, huh?" Lyra shot him a sceptical look but didn't argue.

They pressed on, weaving through dense undergrowth and climbing over uneven ground. Occasionally, they stopped to catch their breath, drink water, and check their bearings against the map Lord Tavar had provided. The map's markings were vague — little more than landmarks and sketches — but Will's sense of direction never wavered.

As they neared a break in the woods, Lolmig held up a hand, signalling them to stop. He knelt low, eyes narrowing as he studied the ground.

"Tracks," he muttered, pointing at the faint indents in the dirt. "Deer, I think. Fresh. Could make for a good meal if we're lucky."

"Then let's make sure we're lucky," Valenor replied with a faint grin, drawing his bow. "Stay on the path. I'll join up with you later." Without waiting for a response, he slipped into the woods like a shadow, his footfalls barely audible.

"Shouldn't let him wander off alone," Lyra muttered as she watched him vanish into the trees.

"He's a hunter. He'll be fine," Will replied, his eyes fixed on the path ahead. "We'll keep moving. He'll catch up."

Sure enough, after another hour of travel, Valenor emerged from the trees carrying a small deer over his shoulders, its weight seemingly nothing to him. Lolmig let out a low whistle.

"Quick work, elf," the dwarf grinned. "I'll give you that."

"Don't praise me too soon, dwarf," Valenor replied, tossing the deer down near Lolmig. "You're the one skinning it."

They made camp briefly, just long enough to cook the fresh meat over an open fire. The smell of roasting venison lifted their spirits, and the warmth of the fire helped release stiff joints that had seized with the cold. After a quick meal, they put out their small cooking fire and continued.

It was past midday when they finally spotted it. The forest broke away into a clearing, revealing a crumbling stone structure partially swallowed by vines and moss. The temple was ancient, its once-pristine walls now cracked and weathered by time. Sections of the outer wall had collapsed, and nature had almost fully reclaimed it.

"There it is," Will said quietly.

They moved forward, stepping cautiously into the overgrown clearing. Birds took flight from the high stone ledges as the sound of their footsteps echoed softly through the hollow structure. The still air muffled everything, but the sound of their boot's echoed jarringly in the enclosed space. But as they drew closer, Will could hear something else — a deep, rhythmic thrum that seemed to vibrate through the stones beneath his feet.

"You hear that?" Will asked, glancing at the others.

"Hear what?" Lyra asked, frowning as she turned her head to listen.

"That... sound. It's like a heartbeat."

"I hear nothing lad, are you okay?" Lolmig said, tilting his head with concern.

The closer he walked to the centre of the temple, the stronger the sensation became. It was like walking in sync with something ancient and alive. His steps slowed as he approached a raised dais at the heart of the temple, framed by a crumbling stone arch. The arch was carved with strange runes that seemed to shimmer faintly as his eyes passed over them.

"This is it," Will said breathlessly, climbing the few short steps to the dais. "This is the portal."

His companions gathered behind him, gazing at the ancient structure.

"You sure?" Lolmig asked, tapping one of the stones with his boot.

Will didn't answer. His eyes locked on the pedestal at the centre of the dais. Set into its surface was a smooth, perfectly polished sphere of stone, its dark surface reflecting the glow of the sun like glass. It looked untouched by time, as if it had been placed there just moments ago.

He approached it slowly, his heart pounding in his chest. His fingers hovered just above its surface, and he felt the familiar pull of unseen energy. The thrum he'd felt earlier grew louder, more insistent, like the pulse of a living thing.

"Will?" Lyra's voice was cautious. "Be careful. We don't know what that does."

But Will barely heard her, his gaze still fixed on the sphere. His hands trembled, but he pressed them firmly against the stone.

The moment his fingers made contact, the runes on the arch flared to life. A pulse of light rippled outward from the sphere, travelling down the pedestal, through the stone floor, and up the arch. Each rune began to glow, first dimly, then brighter with each passing second. The air grew warmer, and the rhythmic thrum grew louder, vibrating in Will's chest.

"What's happening?!" Lolmig took a step back, his hand on the haft of his hammer.

"The portal..." Will said loudly over his shoulder. His hands remained on the stone sphere as his mind reached for something beyond himself. Instinct guided him now.

The energy in the portal spoke to him, deep within the recesses of his mind. He saw an image of a windswept island, surrounded by a tumultuous sea. At the centre of the island was a sphere of pure bright white energy encapsulated in twisted thorn vines that extended out, weaving through the fabric of the whole island. Instinctively, he locked his mind on that image and the space within the stone arch twisted and shimmered like ripples in a pond. The air grew heavy, and with a sudden whoosh of displaced air, the swirling void of the portal opened before them. It was a vortex of light and shadow, colours swirling and folding into each other like storm clouds caught in a whirlwind.

"By the forge-lord..." Lolmig breathed, eyes wide. "He did it."

Will took his hands off the sphere and staggered back, breathing heavily. He felt drained, as though part of his energy had been poured into the portal's creation.

"It responded to you," Valenor said quietly, his eyes fixed on the glowing runes. His gaze shifted to Will, his expression unreadable.

Will turned to his companions. "This is it," he said, breathless but steady. "This is how we get to Thorn Island."

"But is it safe?" Lyra asked, her voice filled with caution. "We don't know what's on the other side."

"We never do," Will replied, his eyes locked on the swirling vortex. "But we've come too far to turn back now."

Lolmig snorted, tightening his grip on his hammer. "Well, I'm not one for waiting around... Let's get on with it."

Lyra glanced at the portal, then back at Will. "Fine. But if something jumps out at us on the other side, I'm blaming you."

Valenor's eyes lingered on Will for a long moment, his face troubled.

Will took a deep breath, his heart steady now. He stepped forward, staring into the swirling light. Then, with one final glance at his friends, he stepped through.

# Chapter twenty-two

The journey through the portal was almost instantaneous, but Will felt pulled in a million directions, his mind filled with a flood of thoughts and emotions at once, as though witnessing the birth of a thousand worlds in an instant. A sudden rush of air spun around them as they stepped from the swirling chaos of the portal. For a moment, gravity seemed to lose its grip, and then, with a jarring lurch, it returned, and their boots hit solid stone. Will staggered forward, catching himself on one knee, his breath coming in shallow, ragged gasps.

The air was thick with the scent of ancient stone and stale air. The faint hum of the portal faded behind them, and for a brief, glorious moment, its pale glow lit the space. Massive stone columns loomed like giants in the flickering light, their surfaces etched with the same flowing runes they'd seen in the ruined temple. Vaulted ceilings arched high overhead, vanishing into shadow, and far-off echoes reverberated with a haunting, hollow quality.

Then, as suddenly as it had come, the portal winked out with a soft whoosh.

Pitch blackness.

The absence of light was absolute. Will blinked, as he struggled to force his eyes to adjust. For a moment, it felt as though he had gone blind.

"Everyone alright?" Lyra's voice came from nearby. Her breathing was fast, her voice tense.

"Still in one piece," Lolmig grunted, his voice gruff. "I'm starting to hate portals."

"I think I landed on something sharp," Valenor muttered, a faint curse following his words. "No... it was just a rock."

"Don't move," Will said, his voice steady despite the suffocating darkness pressing in around them. He stood slowly, his hand instinctively going to the hilt of his blade. Drawing the sword, he gripped the hilt tightly as he focused his thoughts.

"Let me try something," he murmured, his voice cutting through the silence.

Will closed his eyes, reaching for the well of energy that had become more familiar to him with each passing day. He let the connection flow through him, focusing on the blade in his hand. As had happened before, it slowly began to glow.

The light was soft and pale, and didn't reach very far, but it was enough for them to get their bearings, casting it's gentle glow over their immediate surroundings; the rough stone walls of the chamber, the faint outlines of ancient carvings etched into the stone, and the towering, time-worn arches above them. Massive columns loomed, their intricate designs now visible under the glow of Will's blade.

"That's better," Lyra said quietly, her voice filled with relief.

Will nodded, holding the blade aloft. Though the light barely extended beyond a few paces, it was enough to stave off the encroaching blackness.

"Look," said Lyra, pointing ahead. "There's a light."

At the far side of the room, framed within a stone archway, was a faint golden glow. It flickered like firelight from the room beyond, casting shifting shadows along the stone floor.

Lolmig squinted, noticing a movement in the archway, "We've got company."

A silhouette appeared; A figure draped in robes, his hood pulled low over his face. The figure moved with the slow, deliberate grace of absolute confidence. His hands were hidden in his sleeves as he stood at the threshold, as still as a statue.

Then, with an eerie calm, he raised one hand and spoke a single word, **"Ignara."**

The ancient word echoed through the vaulted chamber, taking on a life of it's own. Flame burst to life on the torches mounted to the wall on either side of him. The flames flared with a sharp whoosh and burned a brilliant, steady orange. One after another, torches along the length of the hall sprang to life, the light spreading like a wave, chasing away the darkness as it moved toward them in rapid succession. Shadows leapt and twisted wildly until the room was fully illuminated.

They stood at the centre of a grand chamber, larger than any hall they had seen before. The floor was polished stone, cut into a mosaic of interlocking geometric patterns. The vaulted ceiling soared overhead, supported by massive columns carved with depictions of figures in battle, mages casting spells, and the flow of stars and constellations. Arched passageways branched off in several directions, each marked with runes that glowed faintly.

But it was the figure at the far end of the room that drew their attention.

He stepped forward slowly, the folds of his robe swaying with each step. His face was now visible beneath the hood — an elderly man with a sharp, angular face lined with age. A long, pointed white beard framed his mouth, and his bright blue eyes, sharp as cold steel, shone with an ageless wisdom.

He stopped a few paces from them, his hands still folded calmly in his sleeves. His eyes scanned them one by one, lingering briefly on Will before his lips curled into a smile.

"I thought you would never make it," the man said in a deep, resonant voice, but tinged with a hint of playful mockery. "We've been waiting for you."

The companions tensed. Valenor's hand instinctively went to the hilt of his blade as Lyra narrowed her eyes, glancing toward Will, silently asking for his lead.

But Will stood frozen, his breath caught in his chest as a wave of recognition washed over him. He knew that face. He'd seen it before, in the vision he'd had back at Crystal Lake.

"Eldran," Will breathed, eyes wide with disbelief.

At his words, Eldran's smile widened, his eyes glittering with amusement. He pulled back his hood, revealing his full face. His hair was as white as snow, tied back behind his head.

His gaze swept over each of them in turn. "Make no mistake, your arrival here is not by mere chance. Every step you've taken has brought you to the edge of fate's precipice. This is the moment where paths converge, where the choices you make will ripple through the fabric of existence itself."

Turning to the others, Eldran's expression softened. "The prophecy foretold that the traveller and his companions would face unimaginable trials, that doubt and darkness would test their resolve. And yet, you have endured. That alone is no small feat."

Eldran's face grew serious, "For a time, I wondered if Malakar's schemes had managed to derail you entirely. His reach is long, his cunning unparalleled, and his ability to sow discord among allies is the stuff of legend. But here you stand—intact, united, and, most importantly, on schedule according to the prophecy."

"Malakar?" Valenor's tone was sharp. "What do you know of Malakar old man?"

Eldran's gaze flicked briefly toward Valenor, momentarily showing a flash of irritation, but his smile didn't falter. "More than you, I suspect. We know more than just about anybody on Aruna about Malakar, and how he can snake his way into the minds and hearts of even the strongest amongst us."

Will grew suddenly irritated by Eldran's cryptic words. "How do you know so much about us?" he asked, his voice tense. "I think it's high time for some answers Eldran."

Eldran nodded, "Yes, yes... all in good time, but now, the elders await."

Will looked around at the others who all looked back at him, waiting for him to make a decision.

Eldran was watching Will's face with an amused expression, as if he already knew how this would play out. "Come. I have much to show you. The pieces of the puzzle are beginning to shift, and you, Will, stand at the centre of it all."

Will glanced at the others. Valenor gave a subtle nod, but his eyes stayed on Eldran, watching him like a hawk. Lolmig and Lyra shrugged, indicating they would follow Will's lead.

"Fine," Will said at last, his gaze unwavering as he met Eldran's eyes. "Lead the way Eldran."

"Good," Eldran replied with a grin. He turned and walked back toward the archway, his robes flowing behind him. The light beyond the archway flickered and pulsed, illuminating glimpses of the large cavernous space beyond.

"Come along," Eldran called over his shoulder. "Time is short, and we have much to discuss."

Will glanced back at his companions, nodded once, and followed.

With every step they took towards the archway at the far end of the room, Will felt something powerful stirring within the walls, an unseen force that grew stronger as they neared the great chamber, immense, powerful. It washed over him like a tide, filling him up and coursing through his veins, as though it were probing, getting to know him. The sensation was profound, almost overwhelming, but it brought with it an unexpected calm. He glanced at the others, wondering if they felt the same, but their expressions gave away nothing.

Eldran watched their faces with a knowing smile as they stepped through the archway into the great chamber. Their reaction was exactly as he had anticipated—each of them stopped in their tracks, mouths agape, utterly awestruck by the sight before them. The vast chamber stretched out in all directions, its vaulted ceilings soaring high above. Shelves of intricately carved wood lined the walls, holding countless ancient, leather-bound books and scrolls. Mechanical devices and arcane artefacts were interspersed among the texts. A number of white robed mages moved about the space or sat intently studying at one of the many tables around the room.

But it was the centre of the room that held their gaze; the upper reaches of the ceiling were formed of the natural rock of the island above them. Through that rock protruded a writhing mass of massive thorned vines, seamlessly intertwined with the stone ceiling, and at its heart, a glowing sphere of pure light energy pulsated rhythmically, sending cascades of radiant light through the tangled vines. The light bathed the entire chamber in a gentle, etherial glow, its intense radiance raining down on them, constantly moving.

Valenor was the first to recover his voice. "What is that thing?" he gasped, still staring in disbelief.

Eldran, his expression reverent, looked at the sphere of energy as if it were an old friend. "That," he said softly, "is the Nexus of Light. It is the source of our order's power, our connection to the light source of the universe itself. We borrow its energy to weave our enchantments. And here," he gestured to the chamber around them, "we serve as its caretakers."

Eldran moved across the vast chamber, the others trailing behind, overwhelmed by the grandeur and power that filled the space. As they passed long tables where mages quietly studied, more than a few heads turned, and occasionally one of the mages would rise from their seat to offer a respectful bow as Eldran passed by. The others all exchanged knowing glances, each realising that their guide held a revered status amongst his peers.

"You seem to be well respected here," Will said, his voice intrigued as he looked over at Eldran.

Eldran gave a humble nod in response but didn't elaborate, his focus fixed on their destination.

At the far end of the massive hall, they approached a circular space that seemed to be a natural formation, as though the rock of the chamber had formed this specific area for a higher purpose. Around the perimeter were rows of galleried seating, hewn from the stone, while at the far side of the space stood a raised dais. Upon it sat five ornate thrones and seated upon the thrones were five elder mages, their white robes immaculate and distinguished by intricate vestments in vibrant colours, each symbolic of their particular pillar of faith.

As the group approached the council of elders, they were met with respectful nods. The elder seated in the centre, who Eldran had identified as the Elder of Light, spoke in a calm, resonant voice. "Welcome, travellers. We have awaited this day for generations. The time of the Codex is upon us, and we are honoured to be part of its fulfilment."

Will, feeling the ritual protocol of the moment, but unsure how to proceed, stepped forward, clearing his throat. "We appreciate your kind welcome, noble... um, mages?" His voice faltered, and his words hung awkwardly in the air.

A ripple of gentle laughter came from some of the mages seated in the galleries, though the stern gaze of the elders quickly silenced any further outbursts.

"We have travelled far and have many questions that we hope you can help us with," Will continued, a little more confidently this time.

The Elder of Light regarded Will and his companions with a patient, understanding gaze. "There is much you need to know before your quest can proceed. We will do what we can to assist you. But first, you must rest. Rooms have been prepared in the hive for you. We will speak more when you are ready."

At the mention of the 'Hive' Will's ears pricked up. Recalling the nickname for his workplace back in his own realm, but before he could linger on the thought, Eldran gently gestured for them to follow.

"Come," Eldran said softly. "You've earned some rest."

The others followed Eldran away from the great chamber, moving through a series of buttressed tunnels. The walls were bathed in the soft glow of magical torches, their light echoing the same ethereal radiance as the Nexus.

The tunnel Eldran guided them through widened abruptly, opening into a cavern unlike anything they had seen before. The scale of it was breathtaking—a vast expanse of stone that seemed alive with energy. The walls, towering high above, were covered in hundreds of tessellated openings, their geometric precision resembling a colossal honeycomb carved into the rock itself. Each opening was unique, some faintly glowing with a warm light, hinting at occupancy within.

At the chamber's heart stood a massive central pillar of stone, mirroring the same tessellated design of the walls. This monolithic core stretched skyward, its surface etched with countless openings that spiralled toward the ceiling above. Rope bridges criss-crossed between the pillar and the chamber walls, connecting platforms that jutted out like ledges in a living, breathing structure.

The air carried a subtle hum of activity, quiet but charged with energy. Unlike the grandeur of the Nexus chamber, this place felt intimate and soothing—a space where lives intersected, a blend of rest and quiet industry. It was a marvel of natural beauty and functional design, a hidden sanctuary shaped by nature and magic.

Eldran paused for a moment, allowing the group to take in the sight. "This is the Hive," he said quietly, his voice reverent. "It's where many of us live and study. You'll find peace here."

The others stood in awe, taking in the scale and intricacy of the Hive. Each alcove seemed to offer a private world of its own, a space carved out for contemplation and study. There was an undeniable hum of magic in the air, but it was gentler here, more subdued than the energy of the nexus.

Eldran led them toward one of the larger alcoves near the base of the central core. "These rooms are prepared for you," he said, gesturing toward the openings. "Rest for now. Tonight, the council will answer your questions."

Will stepped into one of the alcoves and found it simple but comfortable, with a bed carved into the stone and covered in a soft mattress and linens. The air was warmer here, carrying the faint scent of mineral-rich water. Soft, golden light emanated from enchanted sconces along the walls, casting a gentle glow that banished the harsh shadows of the larger corridors. The space was simple but elegant — smooth stone walls, polished floors, and a series of low, cushioned benches arranged around a central stone table. At the far end of the alcove, steam rose from a recessed stone bath, its water shimmering with a faint blue glow.

"Finally," Lolmig sighed, rolling his shoulders as he eyed the bath. "If that's not a sight for sore eyes, I don't know what is."

"I call first dibs," Lyra said, already unfastening her travel-worn cloak. "You can wait your turn, big guy."

Lolmig grumbled, but there was a grin on his face. "Fine, fine. But don't use up all the heat."

Lyra snorted as she vanished behind a stone partition for privacy. The sound of water splashing soon followed.

Will set his pack down and sat on one of the cushioned benches with a deep sigh, rubbing his temples. His body ached from their travels, and the lingering disorientation from the portal still buzzed faintly in his mind. "I think I could sleep for a week," he muttered.

"You'll get no argument from me," Lolmig said, stretching his arms over his head with a groan. "But a hot bath and a hot meal might just be the next best thing."

Valenor remained silent, his sharp eyes following the path they'd come. His gaze lingered on the archway, deep suspicion etched into his features.

"Relax, Valenor," Will said, leaning forward with his hands on his knees. "If they wanted us dead, they'd have done it when we arrived. They certainly had the chance."

"Or they're waiting for us to let our guard down," Valenor replied, his eyes narrowing. "They know what we're carrying, Will. I don't like it."

Will sighed, shaking his head. "I think you're wrong. The Nexus energy feels pure, and this place feels like a sanctuary, Val. You felt it too, I know you did." He gestured with his hands as he spoke, his eyes earnest. "I could feel it through the stone, like the ley lines themselves were flowing through that place. If this Order has malicious intent, then they're doing a good job of hiding it."

Valenor tilted his head, watching him. "Hiding it well is exactly what they'd want to do. That's how deception works, Will." He glanced at Lolmig. "Tell me you don't think this place is too clean, too prepared."

Lolmig scratched his beard, his eyes thoughtful. "It's... comfortable, I'll give you that. But I'm with Will on this one, Val. These folks seem like they're decent." He shrugged. "If I'm wrong, I'll swing my hammer, same as always."

"Convenient logic," Valenor muttered, his eyes drifting back to the entrance.

Lyra returned, her silver hair still damp but combed back neatly, her face looking far more refreshed. "Your turn, old man," she said, gesturing toward Lolmig.

"Don't have to tell me twice," the dwarf grumbled, grabbing a fresh tunic from a small pile of clothes folded neatly on a stone shelf and disappearing behind the partition, before quickly re-appearing. "Don't drink all the wine before I'm back," he added, disappearing behind the partition again.

"Wine?" Lyra raised a brow and sat down beside Will.

They sat and talked for some time, and for a moment, they felt like just a group of friends, enjoying each other's company.

Later, after they had all bathed, dressed in clean clothes, and settled at the central table, the aroma of a fresh meal filled the alcove. The acolyte, Eira, moved silently, placing bowls and plates in front of each of them. She was a young woman with plain features, her grey robes simple and unadorned. Her face was calm, her expression serene as she worked.

"Eat while it's warm," she said softly, her voice barely above a whisper as she quietly served, eyes downcast. She poured water from a clay pitcher into their cups, then stepped back, folding her hands in front of her.

"Will you not join us, Eira?" Will asked politely.

Her head bowed slightly, her eyes focused on the table, not his face. "I am here to serve, not partake."

Valenor raised an eyebrow but said nothing, though his gaze lingered on her longer than it should have.

The meal was simple but rich in flavour. A hearty stew of root vegetables and tender meat seasoned with herbs, and a side dish of spiced rice with dried fruits. The flavours were earthy but layered, every bite a blend of warmth, salt, and a subtle sweetness. Even Lolmig, usually a grumbler about "fancy cooking," nodded in appreciation.

"Better than anything we've had on the road," he said, scooping another mouthful of stew into his mouth. "They've got someone here who knows their way around a kitchen."

"Feels strange," Lyra said, dabbing her mouth with a cloth. "Being this comfortable. Warm food, soft clothes, hot baths. Almost makes me think we should stay."

"Almost," Valenor said, his eyes flashing. "Don't let your guard down, Lyra. Too much comfort dulls the senses."

"Yes, father," she muttered under her breath, rolling her eyes.

Will watched them quietly for a moment, turning over Valenor's words. He could see the logic in them, but it didn't match what his instincts were telling him. The Nexus had radiated an energy that felt... clean. Pure, even.

His eyes flicked to Valenor, his gaze thoughtful. He's pushing too hard this time, Will thought, wondering what had him so on edge.

"About the Nexus," he said aloud, hoping to shift the mood. "Did you all see those floating orbs of light? The way they spun around the centre like planets around a sun?"

Lyra nodded, her eyes lighting up at the memory. "I've never seen anything like it. It felt alive, like it was thinking."

"More than thinking," Will said, tapping his finger on the table. "I think it was aware. I could feel it in my bones. It knew we were there."

"Dangerous thing, being noticed," Valenor said, biting into a piece of bread. "Being seen means you can be watched."

"Not all watchers are enemies, Val," Will replied, staring directly at him. "Some are allies."

"Some are spies," Valenor shot back, his eyes narrowing as he shot a look over at Eira.

Tension hung in the air. Lolmig kept eating, his eyes down, while Lyra glanced between them like she was watching a storm roll in.

"Does it matter?" Lolmig finally said, his voice cutting through the quiet. He glanced at them both. "If they help us, they help us. If they turn on us, we deal with it. Just like everything else. Eat your stew."

"Lolmig, the voice of reason," Lyra teased, tossing a piece of bread his way.

He caught it with a grunt and stuffed it into his mouth.

"I'm just saying," Will continued, his eyes still on Valenor. "Until they prove otherwise, they've shown nothing but friendship."

Valenor leaned back, his face calm but his eyes hard.

Silence followed, but the air was thick with unspoken words.

Will glanced at Eira, still standing quietly in the corner, her hands folded in front of her, her gaze lowered. She hadn't spoken a word since the meal began, but she must be absorbing every word of their conversation.

# Chapter twenty-three

With their bellies full and the warmth of the room seeping into their bones, the companions lingered around the stone table, their usual wariness softened by the rare comfort of the moment. The gentle flicker of the enchanted sconces cast slow, lazy shadows across the alcove walls, enveloping the space in a soothing glow.

Lolmig leaned back against the wall, hands resting contentedly on his rounded stomach. "If every leg of our journey ended like this, I'd be far less grumpy."

Lyra raised an eyebrow, a playful smirk tugging at her lips as she absently twirled a strand of silver hair. "You'd still be grumpy."

"True enough," Lolmig conceded, closing his eyes with a satisfied sigh. "But I'd be a well-fed grump, and that's got to count for something, right?"

Will leaned back against the cool stone wall, his arms relaxed by his side. His gaze drifted upward, catching the faint flicker of the enchanted sconces, though his attention kept returning to Valenor. Even now, Valenor sat with one knee up, his sharp eyes fixed on the corridor leading back to the great chamber. His fingers tapped rhythmically on the hilt of his dagger, a constant, restless motion that set Will's nerves on edge.

"I wonder what they'll tell us," Will said finally, breaking the silence. His tone was light, almost casual, but his eyes stayed on Valenor.

Lyra glanced over, brushing a stray lock of hair from her face. "You mean the council?"

Will nodded. "Yeah. They were pretty cryptic earlier. All formal and measured. I couldn't really get the measure of them."

Valenor let out a low, disapproving grunt, his gaze still locked on the corridor's through which they'd arrived. "The real question is, do they know what we carry? And if they do, what's their angle?"

The fire crackled softly, but no one spoke.

Will tilted his head slightly, his expression deliberately neutral. He'd been watching Valenor closely since they entered the Hive, every offhand comment, every wary glance catalogued in his mind. Was it simply paranoia eating at Valenor, or was there something deeper—a shadow no one else could see?

Before he could pursue the thought further, a faint sound echoed from the corridor beyond the alcove — the soft, hurried tap-tap of boots on stone. The four companions sat up and paid attention to this new arrival.

From the corridor, a figure emerged — a young messenger, robed in the same simple grey attire as Eira. He moved quickly but respectfully, his eyes darting toward the companions only briefly before focusing on Eira. He leaned close to her and whispered into her ear, his words too soft for any of them to make out.

Eira listened, her face still and composed, nodding once before glancing briefly at the four of them. The messenger turned on his heel and disappeared down the hall, his footsteps fading into the distance.

The companions watched Eira expectantly, waiting.

Eira lowered her gaze to the floor, her hands folded neatly in front of her as she stepped toward them. Her eyes remained downcast, her voice respectful, but firm. "We have been summoned to return to the council." Her gaze briefly flitted toward Will, then back down to her feet.

"Summoned?" Lolmig echoed, his brow furrowing. "Like guests or like prisoners?"

Eira shook her head. "Guests," she replied, her tone unchanging. "The council is ready to receive you."

"And the prisoners were led to the gallows," Valenor muttered under his breath, just loud enough for Will to hear.

Will pushed himself off the wall and stretched his arms. "Better not keep them waiting, then." He glanced at the others. "You all ready?"

Lyra stood, pulling her cloak tight around her shoulders. "I've had worse invitations."

"Lead the way, Eira," Will said, gesturing forward.

The acolyte turned smoothly and began walking down the corridor, followed closely by the companions. Will walked beside Lyra, while Lolmig and Valenor hung behind.

The corridors of the Hive were quiet except for the faint hum of energy that resonated through the stone walls. Torches flared to life as they passed, one by one, illuminating the path ahead. Will felt it again — that same awareness he'd sensed in the Nexus chamber.

They descended a spiralling set of stairs, the air growing cooler and the pressure in the air thickening as Eira led them a different route to the one they'd taken from the great chamber, leaving them all wondering where they were being led.

"Feels like we're walking into a vault," Lolmig muttered, his voice low and gruff.

"Probably are," Lyra replied, her tone filled with an uncharacteristic note of suspicion. "The deeper we go, the harder it'll be to leave if we need to."

Valenor's eyes flicked to her, a hint of respect flashing in his gaze. Will just shook his head, realising that Valenor's paranoia was growing infectious.

The corridor opened into another great chamber, this chamber was perfectly circular, with a domed ceiling carved with constellations and ancient sigils. The companions stopped for a moment, marvelling at it. Pale blue lines of energy coursed between the constellations like ley lines connecting points on a map.

The chamber was smaller and more intimate than any they had seen yet. Rows of tiered stone seating encircled the room, each filled with figures in gray robes trimmed in various shades depending on the mages position within the order. Their faces were hidden beneath deep hoods, and faint whispers echoed from their ranks. The floor of the chamber was a vast circle of smooth black stone, polished to a mirror shine.

At the far end of the chamber, elevated on a broad platform, stood a semicircle of five high-backed stone chairs, and again, as in the great chamber, behind each chair hung a banner, vibrant in one of the five colours that symbolised the five Pillars of Faith.

Together, the five elders sat in solemn silence, their presence filled the chamber with an almost palpable energy—a reminder of the ideals their people had lived by for countless generations.

The four companions stepped forward, their echoing footsteps sounding very loud against the polished floor. He straightened his shoulders, forcing himself to look more confident than he felt. Looking around, he noticed that the galleries were now filled with onlookers. Word of their arrival had evidently spread, and it seemed the entire hive had come to witness the momentous conclave that was to take place. Hundreds of mages, students, and acolytes were seated in silence, their gazes fixed on the group, a hushed anticipation filling the air.

The elder of light, seated in the centre of the dais, rose slowly from his chair. He raised his hand, and the soft murmurings that had filled the chamber ceased immediately, leaving a profound silence that hung in the air. His voice, when he spoke, was calm, resonating through the chamber.

"Welcome once again, dear friends," the elder said. "This day has been awaited for generations, and this meeting is another crossroads in your journey, for some more than others. The time of the Codex is upon us."

The air in the chamber seemed to grow more intense at the mention of the Codex, as a ripple of murmurs broke the silence behind them, like the sibilant hissing of a hundred snakes in the shadows.

Lowering his hood, he revealed a face lined with the weight of countless years, but his eyes sharp and piercing belied his age. His gaze swept across the companions, lingering briefly on Will before turning to the gathered acolytes along the edges of the chamber.

"Before we commence, we must honour the tradition of welcoming the Nexus," the elder declared, his voice resonating with calm authority. It echoed through the vast hall, clear as a bell, cutting through the tense silence. Every whisper, every quiet murmur ceased at once.

All eyes turned toward the far wall, where a group of burly acolytes stepped forward. Their robes, though simple in design, bore faint silver sigils along the cuffs and collars, glowing with soft pulses of magic. Each one took hold of a large, brass wheel embedded into the wall. Their muscles tensed as they leaned into it, feet sliding briefly on the polished floor before their combined strength took hold. The wheel groaned, grinding slowly at first, then more steadily as ancient mechanisms hidden within the walls sprang to life.

Clunk... clunk... clunk...

A low, reverberating rumble echoed from above. Dust and fine grit rained down from the ceiling, followed by the distant groan of stone shifting against stone.

Will tilted his head back, his eyes narrowing as he followed the noise. His heart quickened as he spotted a thin crack forming across the ceiling high above. It started as a hairline fracture but quickly grew, stretching from one end of the chamber to the other. It widened of light, and with every inch it grew, the grinding noise grew louder.

"That's... not unsettling at all," Lolmig muttered, shielding his eyes from the falling dust. He shuffled closer to Lyra, his eyes darting to the mages above, searching for signs of concern.

Valenor's gaze was fixed on the ceiling, his hand resting on the hilt of his dagger, his eyes narrowing with suspicion.

At first, it was only a thin line of pale blue-white glow. Then it grew brighter, like the first rays of dawn peeking over the edge of the world. Lyra's gasped. "Look..."

The crack became a chasm, and suddenly, with a deep, resonating boom, the two halves of the ceiling split fully apart. Two vast slabs of stone, groaned as they slid slowly to either side, revealing the chamber above.

A rush of air poured down into the chamber, filling Will's lungs with a strange, electric sharpness that made his skin tingle. The companions squinted and shielded their eyes as the searing brilliance of the Nexus above spilled down into the chamber below.

Will's breath caught in his throat as he gazed up at the source of the light. He could sense it now. It was the same energy that hummed within the stones of the ruined temple, the same energy he'd felt in the amulet that now pressed against his chest.

His fingers curled around the amulet instinctively, and for the briefest moment, he thought he felt it thrum in response, like a heartbeat matching his own.

"By the ancestors..." Lolmig muttered, his voice filled with awe. His usual gruff cynicism faded as he turned around on the spot, gazing upwards. "That's... bloody impressive."

Valenor's gaze swept over the mages seated above them. His jaw tightened. "And here we stand... at the mercy of their power."

The elder of light raised both arms, palms facing upward. He tilted his head back, his face illuminated in the glow of the Nexus. "Behold the source of all paths. The light that binds, the veins of Aruna, and the heart of the world itself. Today, it witnesses us. Today, it judges us."

The mages all raised their arms in unison. The runes along their robes pulsed with the same light as the Nexus, as if they were drawing in its power. The glow traced the lines of the stone floor, forming sigils that hummed with energy.

Valenor stepped closer to Will, his voice low but firm. "I don't like the way this is going!"

"I know," Will replied, still staring up at the swirling glow. The energy seemed to press down on him from above, heavier than any weight he had ever borne. His arms felt leaden, his thoughts slower. His mind strained to stay sharp, like pushing back against the current of a river as the awareness of the nexus probed his mind.

The elder lowered his hands, his voice now softer but no less commanding. "Will of the shadow world, step forward."

The companions glanced at each other. Lolmig frowned. "Not liking this."

"Don't argue," Will said quietly. "We have to play along... for now." He stepped forward, his pulse quickening as his boots echoed on the polished stone.

The elder watched him with eyes like polished amber. "Will of the shadow world," he said again, his gaze unwavering. "The Nexus has felt your presence. It knows your journey. It knows your burden. And it knows the power you carry." His eyes flickered to the amulet resting on Will's chest, his lips pressing into a thin line.

"You stand once again at a crossroads," the elder continued. "The Nexus offers guidance to those worthy of it. So tell us, traveller of the shadow world," He leaned forward, his eyes narrowing. "Are you worthy?"

The glow of the Nexus intensified, filling the chamber with blinding, all-encompassing light. The constellations above flickered and shifted, aligning in patterns Will did not recognise. His breath quickened, his eyes squinting against the glare.

He could hear whispers.

They echoed from the edges of his mind, distant at first but growing louder. They came from all directions, hundreds of them, swirling around him in an unseen current. "**Worthy... unworthy... chosen... lost...**"

Will staggered, his hands moving to cover his ears, but the voices weren't coming from outside.

The elder raised his hands high. The glow intensified to a blinding crescendo.

And then, with a sound like a thunderclap and a blinding flash of light, the world went white.

When the light faded, Will found himself standing alone. The grand chamber was gone. The council was gone. The others were gone.

All that remained was the light — soft now, gentle as moonlight — and the voice.

"Why do you seek the light?"

The voice was calm but all-encompassing, like the weight of the ocean pressing down from every direction.

Will breathed slowly, looking down at his hands, then gazing up into the endless glow. He didn't know if he was still standing, still breathing, or even still alive. But he knew the answer.

"To stop him," Will replied, his voice clear, unshaken. "To stop Malakar."

The glow pulsed, bright and sharp.

*"And are you prepared to make the difficult decisions required to achieve that end?"*

Will considered that for a moment, reflecting deeply before answering. "I am."

"Then show me."

The light surged, wrapping around him, flowing through him.

Will stood in the radiant glow of the Nexus, his heart pounding against his chest as the voice returned, resonating from every direction.

"Your heart seeks light, but light alone is not enough. Courage, wisdom, and resolve will be your compass. Step forward, Will of the Shadow World, and face the truth."

The light shifted, coalescing into an iridescent barrier before him. A path formed in the brilliance, leading into an endless horizon of shifting light. With each step, fragments of memories surfaced—faces, voices, moments of fear, hope, and doubt.

Then the barrier shattered, and the world transformed.

"The light will test your will, but it will not make your path easy. Will you falter?"

Will gritted his teeth, his resolve hardening. "I won't."

The scene shifted. Now he was back in the chamber, the council watching silently. Their faces began to change—eyes hollowing, mouths distorting into cruel smiles. They rose, encircling him.

"Truth is heavier than fear. Will you carry it?"

The figures began to chant, their voices rising in a terrible cacophony. Will clutched the amulet at his chest, its warmth cutting through the chaos. He focused, his breath steady.

"I will carry it," he said, his voice unwavering.

The chanting ceased. The figures dissolved into light, and the Nexus spoke again.

"Then know the truth."

The brilliance around him coalesced into a shimmering display of fleeting visions that struck Will like physical blows. He saw himself standing at a precipice, the shadowy, faceless figure of Malakar looming ahead. The scene dissolved, replaced by a series of chilling images.

Valenor kneeling before a shadowy figure cloaked in dark magic—a disciple of Malakar. The disciple's voice was soft, persuasive. "A new world. A cleansed world. You can be part of its birth. Join us."

He saw Valenor, his face cold and resolute, meeting with the same disciple. Words carried on the wind reached Will's ears: "The traveller has arrived in our realm, he and the conduit will come to Silverwood. Ensure their path, guide their steps. Let them gather the relics."

The vision shifted. Valenor was aboard the ship to North Aruna, his hand pressed to the railing, lips moving in silent communion. The storm rose in response, summoned by Malakar to destroy them. Will's chest tightened.

Another image replaced the storm—the streets of Caeratheon. Valenor moving stealthily through the streets, meeting with Eramis. Words whispered: "The trial will force his hand. One act of darkness is all it will take to set the traveller on the path of darkness."

Will staggered as the images faded. The glow of the Nexus pulsed softly, its voice now solemn and heavy.

"The path of light is not easy, and even the brightest heart can falter. One among you walks a path of shadow, bound by loyalty not to you, but to the darkness."

The words hung in the air like thunder. Will shook his head, his heart rejecting the truth even as his mind grasped it. "No... you're wrong. He's saved us—he's fought with us!"

The Nexus pulsed again, a gentler wave of light enveloping him. "The light does not lie, Will of the Shadow World. He walks with you, but his steps lead elsewhere. You must confront this truth before you can proceed. Convert him back to the path of light, or bind him, for his allegiance to the darkness will surely destroy you."

Will's legs felt weak, his breath shallow. The visions replayed in his mind—Valenor's secret meetings, his unwavering gaze as he followed orders from Malakar's disciples.

"How can I... how can I face him?" Will whispered.

The Nexus flared brighter, its final words echoing with clarity. "With the light as your guide. Remember, the choice to change rests within all hearts. The question is: does his heart still hear the light?"

The light of the Nexus flared once again, and suddenly, Will stood back exactly where he had been. He sank to his knees, the weight of what he had seen crashing down on him. The voice of the Nexus leaving a lingering whisper in his mind: "Choose wisely, for the fate of Aruna rests in your hands."

Will blinked as his surroundings reassembled in his vision — the grand council chamber, bathed in the soft, cascading glow of the Nexus above. The golden beams of light trickled down like ethereal mist, illuminating the marble floors with a gentle radiance. The familiar warmth returned, but Will's heart felt cold. His breathing was slow, shallow, and his gaze swept the room with a new wariness.

Everything was exactly as it had been the moment he'd been pulled into the Nexus's vision. Eldran stood at the head of the council, hands clasped before him, his face serene. The elders seated around him sat in perfect stillness, as if not a second had passed.

The only difference was the Elder of Light, seated at the council's centre, was watching Will with a knowing smile. His eyes were sharp as crystal, clear as if he'd seen everything.

Will's heart thudded harder in his chest. The weight of the revelation from the Nexus still lingered, weighing down his soul with the knowledge of what must be done. His gaze flickered toward Valenor, taking him in with fresh eyes. Every movement, every glance, every small gesture — they all seemed different now. The ease with which Valenor had slipped away in Caeratheon, the moments where Malakar seemed to know their every move. The increasing arguments, the growing distance. It had all been there, right in front of him.

But now, it wasn't suspicion. It was certainty.

Will fought to keep his face calm. If Valenor noticed anything, it would be over. He lowered his gaze, taking a slow, steady breath. He could feel the eyes of the Elder of Light on him, expectantly scrutinising. Does he know? Will wondered. Did he see what I saw?

"Will," Lyra said softly, tilting her head. "You alright?"

He glanced at her, forcing a small smile. "Yeah. Just... it's a lot."

She nodded, her expression one of understanding. "Tell me about it."

Valenor raised an eyebrow at him, his eyes narrow with suspicion. "What happened?" Valenor asked, his voice steady, casual, but his eyes sharp. Too sharp.

Will hesitated for a breath too long.

"Just... another test," Will said, forcing calm into his voice. He shrugged, stepping forward to rejoin the others. "I'll fill you in later."

But his eyes flickered back to Valenor for just a moment — long enough to see Valenor watching him, his gaze calculating, as if measuring something unseen.

Will quickly looked away.

The Elder of Light stood, his hands raised, his voice carrying a weight of finality. "The Nexus has deemed you worthy, Will of the Shadow World. By its light, you are blessed, and your path is known." His gaze lingered a moment on Will. The smile returned, faint but clear. "Go with wisdom, and may your choices lead you true."

The words struck him harder than they should have.

May your choices lead you true.

He glanced at Valenor once more — and this time, he was sure of it. He wasn't looking at a friend. He was looking at a player on the board. And the only question now was who would make the first move.

Something had been troubling Will since they had first been brought before the council; something that had come up over and again. He turned to the assembled elders. "You keep calling me Will of the Shadow World," his face reflecting the worry he felt deeply. "what is meant by this? Am I deemed destined for darkness?"

The elder of light smiled, his eyes creasing at the corners as he regarded Will, twisting himself up over this question. "No Will... it is our firm belief that you will be the saviour of this world, and yours."

Will relaxed a little at that, but the Elder wasn't finished. "Have you noticed," the elder continued, "an increase in darkness and negativity in your own world? A rise in violence, despair, and cruelty?"

Will nodded, unable to bring himself to form the words to answer.

"Malakar the Twisted, in his madness, sought to link our world with yours, drawing in all the negativity, all the darkness and malevolence that plague both realms to amplify his power. This curse has infected us both."

The room had settled into an absolute silence as the Elder continued with his story.

"That is the influence of Malakar's curse, seeping through the veil between our realms. And you, Will...you have been marked by it. The Codex not only speaks of the curse but of you as well. You, whose empathy is so strong that you have absorbed the darkness of your world, carrying it across the divide to this realm."

Will's face paled as the weight of the elder's words sank in. "So...I brought this darkness here?"

The elder raised a hand, his voice growing softer yet firm. "No, Will. That is what the agents of darkness would have you believe—that you are a vessel of their will, spreading their malice. But we see the truth; your empathy, Will, is not a weakness. It is your strength. You have endured more than most could bear and still choose the path of light. It is that choice that makes you the perfect instrument of the prophecy."

As a hushed silence fell over the chamber and all eyes turned to Will, his thoughts spiralled, the pressure of it all crashing down on him like a tidal wave. A knot of anxiety tightened in his chest. He could hardly breathe under the weight of it. Why me? The question repeated in his mind, louder each time. He was just Will—a journalist for a newspaper that no one reads, living out his life in almost absolute obscurity. He dealt with targets and deadlines, not dark magic and ancient curses. How had his life taken such an incomprehensible turn? He realised that he had been swept up in this adventure without ever looking back and considering the consequences.

A list of his shortcomings reeled through his mind. He had poor health, anxiety, a life that was anything but heroic. He wasn't a warrior or a mage; he wasn't even particularly brave. The thought of bearing so much responsibility, for being the torch-bearer for a prophecy to some distant land felt like a sick joke.

He reigned in his wandering thoughts and paused a moment to collect his thoughts, before turning his gaze back to the elders. "Tell me more of Malakar" he said, realising he knew nothing of this shadowy figure that he was destined to face.

The Elder of Light leaned forward slightly, his face sombre as he considered Will's question. "Malakar's origins are... murky," he began, his voice echoing softly through the chamber. The gathered mages sat in rapt attention, and even those in the gallery seemed to lean in, hanging on his every word.

"No one seems to know much about his early history," the elder continued, his eyes flickering as he cast his mind back to recall the details of the tale. "He appeared from complete obscurity several decades ago. A prodigy, as many called him then. He was a promising student of our order, here on Thorn Island. As a child, he excelled in his studies, showing exceptional talent in the arts of light magic."

Will looked around at the others, who were hanging on every word, absorbed by the unfolding history.

The elder paused, as if measuring his words. "But something changed during his teenage years. Something dark," he said, in a troubled tone. "No one knows exactly what it was that led him astray. Some whisper that he found an ancient, cursed text. Others say that he ventured too deep into the forbidden places of this world... whatever it was, it began to consume him."

Will let his eyes wander briefly to Valenor, who was listening to the tale with a reverent look on his face, his adoration apparent in the look of zeal in his gaze.

From the dais, the Elder of light continued his tale. "He grew distant, withdrawn, obsessed with forbidden knowledge," the elder went on, his voice lowering. "And then came the day we discovered him. He was found in a remote cavern, practising a dark summoning ritual—one that sought to bring forth Moloch, lord of the underworld himself."

At this, a few gasps rippled through the gallery, and even the more composed mages showed signs of discomfort.

"The elders acted swiftly," the elder continued, shaking his head. "Malakar was banished for his transgressions, exiled from Thorn Island. He vanished without a trace for years. Most believed he had perished, destroyed by the dark forces he sought to control. But... he returned."

There was complete silence in the chamber now, as all eyes rested on the elder of light, each person there hanging on his every word.

"When he returned, he was no longer the boy we had known," the elder said, his voice grave. "Malakar was now a man, cloaked in an aura of darkness, wearing his power like a mantle. His eyes—cold, empty, soulless."

The room seemed to collectively hold its breath.

"He spoke only once," the elder said, his gaze darkening. "'You will pay for your folly,' he told the elders, before vanishing again."

The elders on the dais exchanged uneasy glances, squirming slightly in their chairs.

"Not long after," the elder continued, "the Shadowmoor appeared. A realm of twisted darkness, a blight upon our world consuming everything in it's path and perverting it into a dark, twisted version of itself."

The elder's eyes locked onto Will's, the weight of his words settling on everyone present. "Now, the darkness spreads, infecting both this world and yours."

# Chapter twenty-four

Eldran stepped forward, a look of sympathy on his face as he regarded Will. "Now Will, It's time for you to right a wrong before your quest can continue. You can delay no longer." he said, casting a meaningful glance at Valenor.

The air had grown cold, filled with a still tension as Will realised he could delay no longer. His heart pounded like thunder in his chest, but his hands stayed steady at his sides. Eldran and the elders watched from the dais, their faces like statues — still, calm, and completely devoid of emotion. Valenor stood across from him, his eyes narrow slits, his smile as thin as a dagger's edge.

"You know it's over, Valenor," Will said, his voice cutting through the chamber like a blade. "The Nexus showed me everything. Your meetings with Malakar's disciple. The messages you sent from the ship. The trap in Caeratheon. All of it."

Valenor's smile didn't fade. If anything, it grew wider. "Ah, so that's it?" he said with a soft laugh, his eyes wild with mirth. "The great Nexus shows you shadows and suddenly you think you know everything?" He took a slow step forward, arms wide. "You don't know half of it, Will."

"I know enough," Will shot back, his voice cutting through the tense air like a blade. "Enough to see you for what you are." He stepped forward, his gaze locked on Valenor with an intensity that made even the shadows around them seem to retreat. "You were supposed to be our friend." His voice cracked, raw with hurt and betrayal. "We trusted you, Valenor! Why? Why would you do this?"

Valenor's lips twisted into a bitter smile, his eyes gleaming with a dangerous fervour. "Trust?" he repeated, the word dripping with disdain. "You think trust matters? Trust doesn't win wars, Will. Power does. Control does. Malakar understands that. That's why he'll win."

He stepped closer, his voice rising, every word laced with conviction. "Look at the world around you—fractured, chaotic, ruled by weaklings who squabble over scraps of power while their people suffer. Humans, dwarves, elves... all of them clinging to outdated traditions and crumbling alliances. It's a broken system. A system that needs to be destroyed so something stronger can rise in its place."

Will's fists clenched at his sides, his heart pounding. "And you think Malakar is the answer? You think he'll bring peace?"

Valenor's eyes blazed, and he jabbed a finger toward Will, his voice a fevered pitch. "Not peace—order. A new world where the weak no longer hold sway, where those too feeble to lead are brought low, and the strong forge a future of prosperity. Malakar has the vision, the strength, to reshape this broken world. You call him a tyrant, but I see a saviour. He will tear down the old and build something better from the ashes. A world of discipline, unity, and progress."

Will shook his head, disbelief and anger warring on his face. "You're willing to betray us, betray everything we've fought for, for that? For him?"

Valenor's expression softened, a strange sadness flickering in his eyes. "I didn't betray you, Will. I made a choice—a choice to stand with the future. You're the one clinging to the past, to ideals that will only get us all killed."

For a moment, silence hung between them, heavy and suffocating. Valenor's voice dropped, quiet but unyielding. "You can't stop him, Will. You don't even understand the power you're up against. But if you join him... if you let go of this foolish fight, you might survive what's coming."

Will's breath caught, his mind racing. But as he looked into Valenor's eyes, he saw no hesitation, no doubt—only a fanatic certainty that left him feeling cold.

"You can still stop this," Will said, his voice filled with sorrow, pleading. "You can still choose."

But Valenor laughed. It was a bitter, hollow sound that echoed off the marble walls. "There is no choice, Will. It's too late for that." His eyes flicked toward the elders on the dais, his smile turning cruel. "You think they'll let me walk away now? You think they'll forgive me?" He barked another laugh. "No. No, it's too late for all of us."

He lunged, but Eldran was ready. He raised one hand, and in an instant, golden runes flared to life beneath Valenor's feet. His momentum died as shimmering chains of pure light wrapped around his wrists, his ankles, and his chest, forcing him to his knees. He thrashed and snarled like a wild beast, his eyes wild with rage.

"No! No!" he screamed, pulling against the chains, his muscles straining against the bonds of light. "You can't stop him! You think you've won? You've won nothing! Malakar knows! He sees everything!"

The guards stepped forward, their hands raised as they wove sigils in the air. The chains grew tighter, glowing brighter with each movement. Valenor writhed and spat like a feral animal.

"Shut him away," Eldran commanded, his voice filled with sorrow. "He has chosen his master."

"No!" Valenor howled, his eyes fixed on Will with pure hatred. "He's coming, Will! He's coming for you!"

The guards muttered a final incantation, and a circle of runes flared on the ground beneath Valenor. The air shimmered with power, and for a moment, Will could hear the hum of the Nexus grow louder, as though lamenting the choice that had been made. Valenor was lifted into the air, his limbs bound, his voice reduced to furious, incoherent screams.

The light surged, then snapped. Valenor was gone.

Will stood motionless, the fading light of the Nexus leaving a heavy silence in its wake. The space where Valenor had stood moments ago now felt impossibly empty. He clenched his jaw, trying to process the whirlwind of emotions that surged within him—anger, disbelief, and a bitter pang of loss.

"Where did he go?" Will asked, his voice tight.

Eldran stepped forward, his expression calm but weighted with sympathy. "He has been transported to our detention cells," he explained. "They are warded with light. He will not be able to contact his master."

Lyra and Lolmig stood nearby, mouths agape in absolute shock at what they had just witnessed. Neither of them spoke. Lyra's eyes darted to Will, searching his face as if looking for some sign that it hadn't been real, that there had been some sort of mistake. Lolmig's normally cheerful spirit was gone, his face pale, lips pressed into a grim line as he stared at the space where Valenor had vanished.

"By the forge..." Lolmig muttered, his voice hollow and brittle. "I knew he was a sullen bastard, but this..." He shook his head slowly, his hands curling into tight fists. "How did it come to this?"

Lyra's gaze hardened, her shock giving way to something more focused. Her voice was quiet, but there was steel in it. "He was with us the whole time," she said, her words slow and deliberate, as if each one had to be carefully measured to avoid breaking. Her eyes flicked toward Will. "All this time. He fought with us. Why?" She took a shaky breath, her shoulders rising and falling with the effort. "How could he betray us like that?"

Will turned toward them, his face still grim, his eyes distant as if still watching echoes of the visions the Nexus had shown him. "Because he believed it was right," he said quietly, his tone hollow with weariness. "Malakar doesn't just twist people with fear. He twists them with hope." His gaze lifted to meet Lyra's, his eyes filled with the pain of everything he had seen. "Valenor didn't think he was betraying us. He thought he was saving us."

"Trust is a blade," said Eldran, his voice soft but firm as he descended from the dais, his robes sweeping across the floor like waves on the shore. "It cuts both ways. Sometimes, it cleaves a path to unity. Other times..." He glanced at the spot where Valenor had been. "It cuts us deeper than any sword."

Lolmig let out a long, steadying breath, dragging his hands down his face. "Well, there's no taking it back now," he muttered, rubbing his eyes as if waking from a bad dream. "There's no chance this was all a mistake?"

Will simply shook his head, unable to form the words, "I didn't see it coming," he said, his tone low. "I trusted him. We all did."

Lyra placed a hand on his arm. "We did," she said quietly. "But whatever led him to this... it's on him, not us."

Will exhaled, straightening. "We have to keep moving," he said, his voice firmer now. "Malakar isn't going to stop, and neither can we."

The others exchanged silent glances before nodding in agreement. Though the sting of Valenor's betrayal lingered, Will pushed it to the back of his mind. There was too much at stake to dwell on it now.

Eldran looked back to where the Elder of light was, his amiable face starting to look impatient, and turned back to the others. "We still have much to discuss, it is a shame that Valenor chose as he did, but now we must look to the future by consulting the prophecy."

The elder of light gazed at Will with an expression of solemn gravity. "You seek to understand the prophecy, and so you shall. But know this—destiny is a path with many branches, and even we do not see them all clearly."

He gestured to the ancient carvings etched into the chamber walls, their intricate surface catching the glow of the Nexus's light. "Both the Luminary Codex and the Shadow Codex speak of you and your companions. In both, you are named 'The Traveller,' for it is you who walks between realms, the one who's path will determine the fate of Aruna. But the titles given to you diverge from there. In the Luminary Codex, you are called 'The Lightbearer,' the one who will banish the curse and restore balance. In the Shadow Codex, however, you are known as 'The Ender of Worlds.'"

Will felt a chill run down his spine. "Ender of Worlds..." he muttered, the words heavy on his tongue.

The elder's eyes moved slowly to Lolmig. "You, Lolmig, are 'The Father.' Your role is to protect and to guide, to be the steadfast shield that bears the brunt of the storm so others may endure. It is a heavy burden, and yet you have borne it well."

Lolmig's brow furrowed as he scratched his beard, his gaze distant. "Aye, 'Father' they call me do they? I suppose that fits well enough," he said, his voice gruff but his chest puffed up with pride.

The elder's gaze shifted to Lyra. "And you, child, are 'The Conduit.' You are the thread that binds the others together, the tether that anchors 'The Traveller' to his purpose. Without you, he risks drifting into despair, lost to doubt and shadow."

Lyra blinked, her lips parting as if to speak, but she remained silent. Her eyes darted to Will, her cheeks flushing. She absently pushed her hair behind her ear, looking to the ground to hide her momentary fluster.

Will looked back to the elder, a troubled look on his face as though he already knew the answer to his next question. "And Valenor? What role does he play in these prophecies?"

The elder's expression hardened ever so slightly. "Valenor is known as 'The Serpent' —a figure with a face that shifts like water, untrustworthy and cloaked in deception. What role he plays in the grand design is still unknown... his path is extremely unclear in both prophecies."

The elder paused for a long moment to allow them all the time they needed to digest what he had just shared. "You all have your roles to play. Be mindful of them, for the choices you make will echo far beyond this chamber."

The elder of light gestured toward Will, his eyes filled with expectation. "Now, Will," he said, "bring forth the Codex so that we might divine our path forward."

Will carefully retrieved the Codex from his pack. His companions watched in silence as he placed the ancient tome on a large table that stood in the centre of the council chamber. All five elders descended from their raised thrones and approached eagerly, their robes whispering against the stone floor. The air tense with the energy of the room—every mage and guest present seemed to hold their breath in anticipation.

Will, Lolmig, Lyra, and Eldran gathered around the other side of the table, eyes on the Codex. With a deep breath, Will opened it, the thick, weathered pages crackling under his fingers. They carefully flipped through the ancient text, skimming past prophecies that had already unfolded, past the trials and challenges that had led them to this very moment.

Excitement buzzed among the elders as Will finally turned to the last few pages. The page following this historic gathering were supposed to reveal the next steps, and they all eagerly turned the pages, expectant looks on their faces.

But when they reached the next page, their hearts sank. The pages before them were blank. Unwritten.

A stunned silence fell over the chamber. The elders exchanged worried glances, unable to disguise their expressions of disbelief and confusion. Will stared at the empty pages, his pulse quickening. The others leaned in, as if trying to will words to appear on the parchment.

"If the Codex does not dictate what comes next... Perhaps it is because the future is still unwritten?" suggested the Elder of justice.

The silence suddenly erupted into a deluge of voices giving a multitude of conflicting and increasingly unlikely reasons why the pages might be blank.

As the others stood around deliberating, Will's awareness began to drift, slipping away from the conversation that now sounded like distant murmurs in his ears. This detachment didn't alarm him, instead an overwhelming sense of purpose filled him—a clarity so profound as his mind flooded with the knowledge of what must come next, the energy from the nexus above pour directly into his soul.

He became aware that the room went silent as all eyes turned toward Will. His companions were looking at him with worried expressions. Lyra, standing closest to him, took a cautious step forward. "Will... are you okay?" she asked, her voice filled with concern.

His eyes began to glow, pulsing rhythmically with the light of the nexus above, a radiant energy syncing with his very being. Before he could answer, a force beyond his control seized him. The power of destiny coursed through his veins, overriding his thoughts, his consciousness pushed to the back of his mind as something far greater took over. The others watched, wide-eyed, as a supernatural wind stirred around them, swirling through the chamber.

Will's voice, now deep and resonant, echoed through the chamber, booming with the authority of the universe itself. "Behold, the last days of this prophecy are upon you."

As the words left his mouth, the Codex on the table began to shimmer. Its blank pages filled with glowing script, each word inscribed in tandem with his voice. The wind intensified, stirring the robes of the elders, lifting loose scrolls into the air as the chamber seemed to hum with ancient power.

"From the sacred isle of thorns shall the traveller venture forth in the company of the Father, and the Conduit to the realm of shadows. There shall the traveller become whole as his fractured aspects heal during the final conflict with the abomination."

The words flowed from Will's lips with undeniable finality, every syllable reverberating. The chamber seemed to pulse, reacting to the prophecy's unveiling.

As the last words were spoken, the wind died down, leaving an eerie stillness in its wake. Will's glowing eyes dimmed, and he stumbled slightly, catching himself on the edge of the table. As his own awareness returned, he saw the others staring at him, their expressions a mixture of awe and fear.

"What just happened?" Lyra whispered, breaking the silence.

Will, his voice now his own again, looked down at the Codex, seeing the newly inscribed prophecy that had just passed through him. He swallowed hard. "I think...we have our next destination."

# Chapter twenty-five

The companions spent the following couple of days hammering out a plan for how they might approach this final stage of their quest, learning all they could about the challenges they might face in Shadowmoor, and gathering what supplies they might need for their journey. Eldran, and the elders provided counsel when asked, but otherwise left them to their own devices.

Lolmig busied himself with inspecting their gear, sharpening blades and reinforcing straps. Lyra pored over maps of the region they would be travelling through and read anything she could get her hands on about the creatures of the cursed realm. Will, however, grew increasingly restless. He knew that they were delaying because, deep down, they knew that once they left this place, Valenor's departure from their number would be absolute.

Eventually, when it became clear they were simply procrastinating, Will called them together. "We've planned enough," he said firmly, his voice cutting through the lull in conversation. "We'll rest here for tonight, but we leave at dawn."

Lolmig gave a satisfied grunt, as if he'd been waiting for this decision all along. Lyra glanced at Will, her gaze studying his face. She folded up the map she was looking at with careful precision and tucked it away in her satchel.

As they prepared to leave the following day Eldran came to see them off, walking them to the portal room.

"We can create a portal at the site of an old temple near the coast, to the east of Stonehelm." he said apologetically. "That's as close as we can get you I am afraid, we have been unable to connect to any location within the cursed area of Shadowmoor ever since it was created."

Will nodded in understanding. "Thank you so much, my friend," he said warmly to Eldran as their group moved into the large portal room. "you've already done more than we could have asked."

Eldran smiled faintly, though his eyes held a trace of concern. "We'll monitor your progress from here as best we can. But within the Shadowmoor... our power is limited, if it exists at all. From that point, you'll be on your own."

The air around them hummed, vibrating with energy as the portal shimmered into view, a swirling mass of light and shadow contained within the huge stone disc.

Before stepping through, each of them took a moment to embrace Eldran, expressing their thanks for the hospitality of his people and for all he had done to prepare them for the journey ahead. Lyra stepped through first, vanishing into the portal's swirling depths. Will lingered for a second, exchanging a final glance with Eldran.

"We'll see you after this is all over," Will said quietly, offering a reassuring nod before stepping into the portal.

Lolmig was the last to approach. He hesitated, squinting his eyes as if bracing himself. "Here goes nothing," he muttered under his breath, then, with a resigned sigh, stepped through.

They materialised on a raised stone platform just as the first rays of the sun broke over the horizon, casting a golden glow over the ancient ruins that surrounded them. For a moment they stood still, letting the calm of the dawn settle over them as the portal behind them flickered briefly, before collapsing into itself with a faint rush of wind.

Will, steadying himself, looked around. The temple ruins surrounded them—crumbling stone columns, remnants of once-magnificent arches, and scattered debris from a civilisation long past. The air smelled faintly of the sea, the temple situated high on a coastal bluff, overlooking the eastern waters.

"Nope... I still don't like it," Lolmig muttered, adjusting his pack and taking a deep breath.

Will moved slowly through the crumbling halls, his fingers trailing lightly over the cool, weathered stone. The ruins bore the same elegant, sweeping arches and intricate carvings that he had seen in the temple on North Aruna, and again in the great vaulted chambers of Thorn Island.

He crouched near the base of a shattered pillar, wiping away the dirt with his hand to reveal a sigil beneath. The mark was identical to one he'd seen in Thorn Island's council chamber, a symbol of balance encircled by ancient glyphs.

"How many more of these do you think there are?" Will said, his eyes narrowing in thought. He glanced around, taking in the ruins from a new perspective. "The order must have had a presence everywhere — a whole network of these portals, hidden across Aruna. But why are they all abandoned now?"

He rose to his feet, eyes scanning what was left of the vaulted ceiling. Whatever had happened here, it had left scars. The mystery of it all intrigued him, and he promised himself he would investigate it further... once this quest was complete.

The warm sea air blowing in from the coast was soothing, a calmness that seemed to seep into his very bones. The distant sound of crashing waves echoed through the ruins, blending with the soft rustle of ferns and the heavy coastal grass that surrounded the place, still wet with morning dew.

The scent of the sea breeze, mingled with the fresh smell of warm vegetation filled his lungs. He closed his eyes and turned east, facing the sea and the rising sun. Its warmth spread over him, a gentle radiance that seemed to melt away all the tension he carried. For a moment, he allowed himself to simply be—just a man in a forgotten place, bathed in the light of a new day.

As he stood there, eyes closed, enjoying the warmth of the sun on his face, he felt a small hand slip into his. He opened his eyes and looked to his side to see Lyra standing there, her expression uncertain as she searched his face for a reaction. He smiled softly, squeezing her hand in silent reassurance, and then closed his eyes again.

Her hand felt warm, comforting. There was something in her touch that stirred an emotion within him. Reassured by his response she leant in closer, leaning her head against his shoulder.

Soon after, they gathered their belongings and moved out from the ruins, heading generally south along the coastline. The rising sun bathed the path ahead in warm, golden light, and the sounds of distant waves crashing against the shore and the stiff dune grasses whispering in the wind blocked out the noise in Wills head that haunted him in the quiet moments. The closer they got to Shadowmoor, the more his old friend self-doubt crept in, fortifying his fears that he was rushing headlong towards certain doom, although he could sense he had changed since this all began. He still carried those worries, but now instead of spiralling into the darkness and letting his own self-loathing consume him, he would accept that difficult times lay ahead, and prepare for it as best he could.

As they left the temple ruins and turned inland from the coast, the landscape transformed into rolling meadows that stretched endlessly under a pale blue sky. The tall grass swayed gently in the breeze, rippling like a golden sea.

The air was unnervingly still, and the usual chorus of birds and rustling underbrush was absent. Here, so close to Shadowmoor, even the boldest wildlife seemed to keep its distance. The occasional flutter of wings overhead or the distant scamper of a rabbit offered brief signs of life, but they were rare and fleeting.

They pressed onward for several hours, the endless expanse of meadows seemingly almost indistinguishable from one another. Time and again, they paused to double-check their bearings on the map, a creeping uncertainty gnawing at them as they feared they might have strayed from their intended path.

"We should be getting close," Will said under his breath, more to himself than the others.

"You've said that twice already," Lolmig grunted, pushing aside a low-hanging branch. "I hope you're right this time."

As they crested the next rise Will spotted something in the distance, "Look." He said, pointing ahead to a low ridge rising up ahead of them. Jagged stones jutted from its face, broken and weather-worn, but there was something unnatural about the way they leaned. "That's one of the markers Eldran mentioned — a broken crown of stone. Right?"

Lyra shaded her eyes with one hand, peering at the ridge. "It looks like it."

Confidence returned with that confirmation, and they quickened their pace. As they crested the ridge, they sensed a shift in the very quality of the air, and the feel of the land around them as the vibrant grasslands gave way ahead to arid, barren earth.

Lyra shuddered, her eyes scanning the increasingly desolate landscape before them. "Well... that's starting to look a lot more like Shadowmoor."

"Close enough," Lolmig said, his voice low. "Smells like it too."

They were close now, but this transitional area still showed evidence of the most resilient forms of life, struggling to exist against all odds, as the darkness that was stalking across the landscape indiscriminately obliterated everything in it's path.

As they walked, Will found his thoughts drifting back to the moment at the ruins when Lyra had taken his hand. The warmth of her touch still lingered in his mind, and the connection they had shared, however brief, filled him with an unexpected excitement. Despite the impending challenges they inexorably marched toward, his heart raced and fluttered as he replayed the moment; the way she had looked at him, the subtle smile that had passed between them.

There was a spark of something deeper, something that stirred in him a passion that seemed to hold back the darkness that surrounded them. He found himself grinning foolishly, the excitement bubbling up inside him, making him feel giddy and light, like a lovestruck schoolboy.

She was wilful, passionate, and undeniably beautiful, and somehow, without him even noticing, she had quietly but effectively slipped into his thoughts, and his heart, now occupying them entirely.

Lost in these musings, he cast a shy glance toward Lyra, wondering if she felt in any way the same, finding that she was already looking at him, her gaze soft and searching. Will smiled warmly, and when she smiled back, it was like a fire in his chest—a warmth that made him feel alive. It was a moment of pure connection, and for the first time in what felt like forever, he allowed himself to believe in the possibility of a future beyond the darkness that lay ahead.

The terrain grew gradually harsher beneath their feet as they ascended into the rocky peaks that surrounded the centre of the curse, the last vestiges of life that were clinging on behind them giving way to jagged rocks and uneven ground.

The inky blackness of the Shadowmoor stretched across the horizon like a storm frozen in time, its roiling gloom moving with a sluggish, malevolent convection, churning in slow, deliberate waves, obscuring everything in an impenetrable haze.

No landmarks were visible beyond the cursed boundary—nothing but the all-consuming darkness. The light-hearted conversation from earlier in the journey had evaporated, replaced by the heavy silence as the sudden reality that their quest was drawing to it's conclusion, dawned on each of them.

As they pressed on through the rugged mountain paths, the terrain grew increasingly unforgiving. Jagged rocks and steep inclines slowed their progress, and the increasingly oppressive atmosphere that surrounded them in a perpetual gloom started to affect their mood.

Whenever they paused to rest, Will took the opportunity to hone his newfound abilities. At first, it was slow progress. He would sit cross-legged on a flat slab of stone, his breathing steady and controlled. His hands hovered just above his knees, fingers splayed as if ready to grasp something unseen.

"Focus on the current," Eldran had told him once, back on thorn island. "It's always there — like a stream beneath the surface. Don't try to pull it, just let it flow."

Eldran's words echoed in his mind as he sat still, eyes closed, searching for that elusive current. It wasn't a physical control, like wielding a weapon or climbing a cliff face. This was something subtler, a force that required a nuanced patience. Always before, when he had called on the magic, it had been impulsive, but he knew that if he was to stand any chance of defeating Malakar, he would need to learn to wield deliberate mastery over the light. He breathed in slowly, feeling for the hum that lay just beyond sensation. It started faint, like a thread of warmth curling at the edge of his mind.

His hands tingled.

A faint glow emerged, a shimmer of pale gold encircling his fingertips. The energy felt warm but weightless, like sunlight on his skin. Slowly, he willed it to grow, pushing it outward. The glow intensified, pulsing in rhythm with his heartbeat. The soft light danced around his hands, casting flickering shadows on the stone walls behind him.

"Not bad," Lolmig rumbled, sitting on a nearby boulder, his arms resting on his knees as he watched. "Bit more focus, and we might make a decent lantern out of you."

Will cracked one eye open, smirking at the dwarf. "A lantern, huh? I was thinking something a bit more useful than that."

Lyra looked over from where she crouched, keeping watch on the path behind them. Her sharp eyes scanned the trail, ever wary of the dark things that roamed these outer reaches of the Shadowmoor. "We should keep moving. I don't like how quiet it's gotten."

"Another minute," Will said, his voice distant as he returned his focus to the glow in his hands. "I almost have it."

He took a deep breath and visualised the glow taking shape. No longer a wild pulse of energy, but something sharper, more defined. His mind reached for the memory of the rune symbols he'd seen back at the Thorn Island chamber — the way the glowing runes had been so precise, so perfect. He pictured one of them, letting the lines form in his mind's eye. His fingers traced the shape in the air, the glow following his movement like ink on parchment.

It worked. The rune hung in the air before him, faint but distinct — a curved line with interlocking arcs, its glow steady and unbroken. Will's breath caught in his chest, his eyes wide with awe. He reached out, half-expecting it to vanish at his touch, but it held.

Lyra turned to look, her eyes narrowing with intrigue. "Well... you don't see that every day," she said, rising to get a closer look.

"Don't jinx it," Will muttered, beads of sweat forming on his brow. The glow flickered but held. The glow from the rune pulsed, radiating out, pushing back the darkness that surrounded them and warming their souls against it. Will's heart swelled with pride, though he tried not to let it show.

"Not bad at all, lad," Lolmig said, nodding with approval. "But don't get too cocky."

"Yeah, yeah," Will said, letting out a slow breath as he released the rune. It dissolved into a soft rain of golden sparks before vanishing completely. His hands fell to his sides, trembling slightly from the strain. "But I'm getting better."

"You've come a long way" Lyra said, her warm smile lighting up his soul far more than the magic he was wielding. "You still have a long way to go though before you're ready to face Malakar."

"Agreed," Will said, pushing himself to his feet. His legs felt stiff, but he ignored it. "Let's keep moving. I'll practice more when we camp tonight."

As they moved, the hum of energy remained with him. It wasn't as loud or insistent as before, but it was there, just beneath the surface of his mind. The warmth had settled into his chest, always with him now, a comforting presence.

They stopped only once more before they would enter the deepest part of Shadowmoor, finding a narrow outcropping that gave them a decent view of the path below. Will sat on a flat stone, this time with Lyra beside him. She was sharpening her dagger, the soft shhkt, shhkt of steel against whetstone filling the air. Lolmig sat on a nearby boulder, chewing on a strip of dried meat, his eyes scanning the trail for movement.

Lyra glanced over at Will as she worked the edge of her blade, her eyes flicking to the amulet around his neck, which pulsed faintly with light. "So, what is it you've been practising?" she said casually, her tone curious. "That enchantment you keep weaving?"

Will straightened slightly, glancing at her and then down at his hands. "It's a protection charm," he said, his tone humble. "We're going to be in the curse's grasp for a while this time, and I need to make sure none of us fall under its influence before we can finish this."

Lyra paused in her sharpening, tilting her head to study him. "You've been casting it on us since we got here, haven't you?" a look of realisation dawning on her face.

Will nodded. "I have. Subtly. It's more like a shield, a buffer to fortify against the worst of the curse's effects. I didn't want to worry anyone, but I also didn't want to take any chances."

Lolmig grunted from his perch. "A bit more useful than a torch after all," he said, tearing off another bite of jerky. "Good thinking, lad."

She paused to blow a few metal shavings from her blade. "Just let us know if it starts draining you too much."

Will returned her smile briefly. "Thanks. I'll manage. For now, it's holding, and that's what matters."

Will and Lyra grew closer with every passing mile. After their long days of trudging through rough terrain, they would sit side by side, their shoulders touching, and eventually, Will would pull her into his arms. She would lean into him, her head resting against his chest, and they would stay like that for hours, finding solace in each other's presence.

There was an unspoken understanding between them, a quiet connection that needed no words. Every glance, every touch, seemed to say more than they could express. As the fire crackled nearby, Will felt a warmth in his heart that rivalled the power of the light he was learning to harness. In Lyra's embrace, the weight of the world—and the looming prophecy—seemed just a little lighter.

After a few more gruelling days in the rugged mountains, the terrain finally began to ease as they descended toward the lowlands near Candleford.

# Chapter twenty-six

As they entered the what remained of Candleford, Will's heart sank. The transformation was now complete—the curse had grown more intense, more malevolent since their last visit. Shadowmoor's creeping edge had swallowed Candleford further into its grasp, leaving even what previously remained of the town unrecognisable. An unnatural dark mist stalked the narrow streets, its cold, shadowy tendrils curling around their feet, shadowing their every move. The chill cut through their cloaks and into their very bones, carrying with it an eerie stillness that seemed to whisper of despair.

In their absence, the curse had been festering, concentrating its dark energy, twisting the natural world it had already devoured into something far worse than they could have possibly imagined. The land was no longer just blighted; it had been grotesquely mutated into a living nightmare.

Where once twisted flora and roaming Hollow haunted the landscape, now every inch of this cursed realm seemed sentient, dark, and malevolent. Trees loomed like sinister sentinels, their blackened trunks contorted in unnatural angles that defied reason. Dark ichor dripped from their branches; limbs that writhed and reached out as if seeking to consume anything that came near. The air was thick with an unnatural miasma, each breath a struggle against the corruption surrounding them.

The Hollow had undergone horrific transformations as well. What had once been pitiful husks, recognisable as having once been living beings, were now abominations—horrific, misshapen creatures formed from twisted, tortured limbs that defied the laws of anatomy. Their flesh pulsed with dark energy, oozing the same vile ichor that bled from the trees. Limbs dragged unnaturally across the ground as they moved, each one more grotesque and unpredictable than the last. The companions moved cautiously, keeping their distance from these creatures but every now and again they would see the huge form of a twisted silhouette moving about in the distant shadows, unnatural sounds emanating from it.

The clock tower from the old town hall floated eerily in mid-air, its broken face eternally frozen at an undecipherable hour. Pieces of the surrounding buildings hovered and drifted aimlessly, as if gravity had lost its grip. The remnants of the old church, where they had once sought refuge, flickered in and out of sight like a haunting mirage, shifting between solidity and illusion.

It was as though the curse had not merely infected the town but had begun to unravel its reality altogether. The very air hummed with the dark energy, as if the land itself were on the verge of tearing apart, dragging whatever remained into the abyss.

The group could feel the unnatural pulse of the curse deep in their bones as they cautiously moved forward, all conversation between them now hushed into silence as their wide eyes maintained watchful vigilance.

"Who thought this place could have gotten worse?" Lolmig muttered, his eyes narrowing beneath his bushy brows. His hand hovered near his hammer as he scanned the mist-shrouded alleys. "Curse must be spreading faster than we thought."

Will could feel it — the curse pressing against his senses all around, like a vice pressing in, trying to crush his soul. The tingling on the edge of his mind was more intense than it had been before, like an itch beneath his skin that he couldn't scratch. There was a presence here, as if something unseen was watching them from the mist, just beyond where they could see. He glanced toward Lyra, who was walking a few paces ahead, her eyes darting toward every shadow, her hand never far from the hilt of her dagger.

"It wasn't like this last time," Lyra said, her voice low.

"Feels like something's watching." Lolmig rumbled, his eyes scanning the upper windows of the buildings.

"Let's keep moving," Will said firmly, his eyes darting from one shadowy alley to the next. "I feel it too... there's something out there and I doubt it's intentions are friendly."

"Agreed," Lyra said, her eyes scanning the rooftops as she kept pace with him. "We're too exposed here."

They moved quickly but cautiously, staying close together as they navigated the winding streets. Their footfalls echoed off the cobblestones, far too loud for Will's liking. Every creak of a shifting shutter or distant thump of unseen movement set his nerves on edge. He glanced up at what remained of the buildings looming on either side of them, their twisted and shattered remains silhouetted against the thick, dark mist.

"Keep your eyes sharp," Will said, his voice low but commanding. "If anything moves, you call it out."

"Don't have to tell me twice," Lolmig muttered, his heavy warhammer now firmly in hand, his grip tight on the worn handle.

They turned a corner into the town square, and Will was sickened by what he saw. The fountain at the centre had previously been a thing of beauty, now perverted by the curse. Twisted black onyx formed screaming faces and nightmarish creatures. Thick black slime dripped from the cracked stone mouth of a long-dry spout. The cobblestones around it were stained with dark streaks that looked too much like old blood. Rotting crates and overturned carts lay scattered across the square, their rusted frames all that remained, their timbers having long since decayed to dust.

They pressed on, their way obscured by the warped remnants of a town that no longer obeyed the laws of nature. Progress was slow, every step a careful, deliberate, as they communicated through silent gestures, keenly aware of the dark forces lurking all around them. They moved as one, eyes sharp, senses heightened, knowing that any misstep could draw the attention of the horrors roaming the land.

A shape moved at the edge of Will's vision. He spun, eyes narrowing on an alley just to their left. For a moment, he thought he saw a figure — a person, small and hunched, peeking out from behind a crumbling wall. But as he locked eyes with it, it darted back into the shadows, it's movement's unnatural. His heart thudded in his chest.

"Something's there," he hissed, pointing toward the alley.

"I saw it too," Lyra said, eyes sharp as she unsheathed her dagger. "It looked... almost, human?"

"Shadowmire spirits like to wear faces, sometimes," Lolmig muttered grimly, his eyes locked on the alleyway. "Don't trust it if it calls for help."

"Keep moving," Will said, his voice low. "Don't stop. If it follows us, we deal with it then."

They continued forward, eyes darting to every shadow, every darkened doorway and fog-drenched alley. Candleford felt less like a town and more like a hunting ground — and they were the prey. Will's fingers twitched at his side, itching to summon the light, but he forced himself to wait. If something attacked, he wanted to be ready.

They reached the edge of town, where the crumbling buildings gave way to an empty barren expanse beyond. Will breathed a sigh of relief as his boots crunched on grey, cracked earth instead of stone.

He glanced at Lyra, who hadn't looked back once. Then at Lolmig, his knuckles white from the grip on his hammer. They all felt it, they were deep behind enemy lines and knew almost nothing of what foul creatures even existed here.

Above, the murky sky churned with inky black clouds. Every so often, the upper reaches of the atmosphere were split by flashes of silent lightning, jagged arcs of energy discharging from one place to another. There was no rumble of thunder, no crackling energy—just flashes that illuminated everything for the briefest of moments before plunging it back into deeper shadow.

Time stretched into a disorientating blur as they trudged through the desolate, twisted landscape. The boundary between reality and nightmare began to fade, their senses betraying them. Strange noises—a whisper of wind that sounded like voices, or the distant crack of something underfoot that echoed unnaturally—all encroached on their awareness, fraying their nerves.

Shadows moved in the distance, huge and menacing, the distorted figures of the twisted creatures that had claimed this place.

Will's mind fought against the creeping sense that reality was ebbing away, trying to stay focused on the path ahead. He could feel his companions growing restless, their nerves as frayed as his.

The attack was so sudden, none of them saw it coming. The still, dead air of the Shadowmoor muffled the sound of the beast's approach, and it was upon them before anyone could react. Unlike the hollow, who moved sluggishly, these nightmare creatures moved with a fluid, terrifying speed.

The creature was massive, a twisted amalgamation of shadow and flesh, dripping black ichor that hissed as it hit the ground. Its form was barely recognisable as anything natural, limbs bent at unnatural angles. Its face—or what passed for one—was a gaping maw of jagged, uneven teeth, from which a deep, guttural howl escaped, reverberating in the pit of their stomachs shaking them to their core.

For a heartbeat, they were frozen, terror locking their limbs. The beast's glowing, soulless eyes bore down on them, and for a moment, the companions were utterly dwarfed by the monstrosity.

The panic that gripped them was fleeting. Their shared battles and experiences these past months had honed their instincts, and they moved as one. The beast's lunge was met with an immediate counter-response, the companions shifting into their roles with practised efficiency.

Will quickly focussed his energy to send out a pulse of light. It sent up a shimmering wall of protection around them that slowed the beast down, and it imbued his friends weapons with light energy.

Lolmig, recovering from the initial shock, roared as he drew his war hammer, the enchanted weapon now glowing faintly in the cursed darkness. He charged forward, meeting the beast's massive limb with a devastating swing. The blow landed with a resounding crack, momentarily staggering the creature as black ichor spattered across the ground, quickly soaking into the arid earth, but as quickly as the limb was destroyed, the beast spawned a fresh one.

Lyra, with her nimble reflexes, flanked the beast. Her daggers gleamed with the faintest touch of light as she moved in swift arcs, aiming for the tendons in its hind limbs. She struck fast and true, the blades sinking deep into the dark flesh, but the creature seemed barely slowed by the attack.

Will felt the surge of light welling up inside him as he joined the battle. He stepped forward, his eyes glowing faintly as he extended his hand toward the monster. The pulse of energy that had been building within him was now like a blazing inferno, ready to ignite. "Ignis!" he shouted, as a beam of light shot from his palm, searing through the beast's torso.

The creature howled in agony, staggering backward, its form sizzling where the light had struck. But it wasn't down yet. Dark energy rippled through the air as the creature regrouped, its eyes locking onto Will, now recognising him as the greatest threat.

Multiple faces undulated just below the surface of the creatures chest, each seeming to fight for its position before fading away to be replaced by another, as limbs seemed to spring forth from the torso at will. Now the beast had it's sight locked on to Will it moved with lightning speed and was upon him, slashing and clawing in a frenzy. Seeing the creature approach, Will had drawn his sword, but the ferocity and speed of the attack took him off guard, and he stumbled backwards. Before the beast could bare down on him though, Lolmig had swung a mighty blow to it's ribcage, knocking it sideways causing it to turn its rage upon Lolmig. The change of direction was so sudden that they didn't have time to react and the beast lifted their friend up off the ground, throwing him back to the earth with so much force that the ground shook.

Lolmig's body lay crumpled and limp on the ground where the beast had thrown him, his chest unnervingly still. A trickle of crimson traced a path down from his ear, glinting in the dim, cursed light. Will's heart clenched at the sight, but the monstrous creature still loomed before them, its breath hot and fetid, claws raking the air.

There was no time to rush to Lolmig's side. Will's grip on the Sword of Light tightened, and he forced himself to focus on the immediate danger. "Lyra, keep it busy!" he shouted, his voice cracking with urgency.

Lyra darted forward, her blades flashing as she aimed for the beast's exposed flank, drawing its attention away from Will. Despite her agility, her expression was strained, her movements filled with desperate determination.

Will's thoughts screamed at him to run to Lolmig, to shake him awake, to do anything but fight. But he knew the only chance they had to help their friend was to bring the beast down—and fast.

The momentary pause gave them the opening they needed to turn the tide, Will unleashing a barrage of blows with his imbued sword at the beast as Lyra continued to attack it's flanks.

The beast, now enraged and desperate, became more erratic in its movements. Its grotesque, undulating torso writhed as new limbs emerged from its mass, swiping violently at anything in reach. The faces trapped within its chest contorted in agony, a chorus of silent screams etched across the grotesque surface.

Will's heart pounded in his chest, fear threatening to overwhelm him, but he pushed it down. He had no choice. He reached deeper into the power of light coursing through him, channelling it with more intensity than ever before. His hands glowed brighter, the energy within him threatening to burst forth uncontrollably.

His eyes blazed as he focused all his energy into his blade, and a huge lash of blazing light energy emerged from the tip of his sword. With a shout, he swung the blade towards the creature, the beam of energy slicing cleanly through it. The creature went immediately silent, its body convulsing as the light seared through it, burning away the dark energy that held it together.

The creature let out a final putrid breath, its form collapsing into a heap of blackened, oozing flesh. The faces within it pulsed once more, and then faded, the limbs twitching before falling still. Silence settled over the battlefield.

The victory was bittersweet. As the adrenaline began to fade, their eyes turned to Lolmig's still form. Lyra rushed to his side, a small whimper escaping her lips as she knelt beside her fallen friend.

"Lolmig... please..." she whispered, her voice tight with fear as she knelt beside him, desperately checking for signs of life. Will, his chest still heaving from the exertion of the fight, staggered over, his heart sinking as he saw his friend lying so still.

Will placed his hands on Lolmig's chest, his expression tense. "Come on, old friend. Not like this," he muttered as he began to channel healing magic, his hands glowing faintly.

But as he looked down upon Lolmig's ashen face, he knew that his efforts were in vain.

In that moment of realisation the world seemed to stand still for the briefest of moments, everything frozen in one perfect harrowing moment before devastation washed over them, grief tugging at their stomachs and obliterating all rational thought.

Lyra, kneeling on the other side of their friend, let out a choked sob, her hand covering her mouth as tears spilled down her cheeks.

Will's vision blurred as tears welled in his eyes. "I... I'm sorry, my old friend." he choked out in broken bursts, his voice barely audible over the rising storm in his mind. He wanted to say more, but the words wouldn't come. All he could feel was the crushing weight of loss.

The world seemed to shrink into a narrow, suffocating stillness. Will knelt by Lolmig's lifeless form, his hands trembling as he reached out to touch the dwarf's shoulder. The warmth that should have been there was gone. His eyes, so often filled with mirth, were closed now, his face forever still. The battle was over, but the price had been far too high.

From where she knelt nearby, Will could see Lyra's face streaked with dirt and blood, her body wracked with silent, shuddering sobs. She covered her mouth with one hand, but it couldn't stop the sound of grief from escaping. Her other hand hung limply by her side, her dagger still clutched in her fingers like she'd forgotten it was there. Tears streamed down her face, cutting pale tracks through the grime. Her gaze never left Lolmig. She didn't dare blink, as if afraid that if she did, he might be gone for good.

The fog of Shadowmoor coiled around them like a serpent, slithering across the ground, the cold bite of it pressing into their skin, seeping through their clothes. It moved unnervingly, slow tendrils snaking across the ground, feeding off their emotions, inching toward Lolmig's body. Will noticed it, almost too late. The curse was already reaching for their fallen friend, eager to claim its prize. A flicker of rage flared in Will's chest.

"Not him," he growled, his eyes hardening with sudden clarity. He shoved his hands forward, fingers splayed, his mind reaching for the light within himself. Not him. You can have nothing from me.

A warmth bloomed in his chest, surging through his arms like fire in his veins. The amulet at his neck pulsed with brilliant light, a wave of golden energy burst forth, like a shockwave, pushing back against the darkness. The fog recoiled instantly, as if seared by unseen flames. It hissed and pulled away from Lolmig's body, curling back into the shadows like a beast denied its meal.

As they knelt by the still form of their fallen friend, Will remembered what the elder of light had said, back at thorn island. He had called Lolmig 'The Father', and that felt quite fitting in this moment. The elder had told Lolmig that his role was to protect and to guide, to be the steadfast shield that bears the brunt of the storm so others may endure. That line had filled Lolmig with so much pride, but in that moment, in the wake of his loss, it felt like a cruel mockery that almost made Will Surrender to the darkness.

He knelt lower, placing his hands on Lolmig's chest. His breathing was shallow and broken by deep convulsive sobs, his gaze distant and unblinking as he reached for the magic, knowing that he didn't want his friend consumed by this curse. The light flowed from him into Lolmig, not to revive him, but to preserve him, to protect him from the corruption and decay of the curse. His fingers tingled with the sensation of it, and he could feel the world around him slow as the magic took hold. The glow spread like cracks of gold across Lolmig's armour, faint lines of light that pulsed in rhythm with Will's breath.

"They won't have you, Lolmig," Will muttered under his breath, his voice hollow with exhaustion. "We're not leaving you here. We're not leaving you here."

The light seeped into every inch of Lolmig's form, wrapping him in a protective glow, like a faint golden shell just beneath his skin. It shimmered faintly for a moment, then dimmed, leaving only a soft glow that lingered in his beard and hair. Will's hands fell away, drained of strength. His arms felt like lead, his breath came in shallow gasps, but it was done.

Lyra stepped forward, eyes wide with disbelief. "What... what did you—?"

"He's safe," Will said hoarsely, his head bowed, eyes closed. "The curse won't touch him now. His body will remain whole, until we can return." He let out a long, shuddering breath. "We'll come back for him. I swear it."

Lyra sank to her knees beside Will, fresh tears falling freely now. Her hands hovered over Lolmig's still form, hesitant, as if she feared touching him might undo the spell Will had cast. Slowly, she reached forward, brushing her fingers gently through the dwarf's wild, unkempt hair. Her breath caught in her throat.

"I thought he'd always be with us," she said, her voice barely a whisper. "He was supposed to make it. He always made it."

"We carry him with us," Will said, his voice low, like steel being sharpened. He stood slowly as the initial wave of grief started the pass, his gaze cold and sharp as flint. His hands still glowed faintly, the after-image of the magic sparking along his fingertips. "He stays with us, every step of the way. We'll finish this. For him."

Lyra nodded, wiping at her face with the sleeve of her cloak, her expression hardening into something resolute. She glanced down at Lolmig one last time before pushing herself to her feet. Her eyes burned, heavy with grief, but her voice came steady as stone.

The fog loomed just beyond their circle of light, shifting with unnatural patience. It had been denied its prize, but it hadn't left. It never left. Will could feel its cold awareness on them, silent and unseen, waiting for them to break.

"Let it wait," Will muttered under his breath, staring into the fog with pure defiance in his eyes. "It'll get nothing from us."

# Chapter twenty-seven

Will held Lyra close for a moment, feeling the warmth of her tears soak into his tunic as they each found solace in the embrace from their shared grief. He gently rested his chin on her shoulder, offering what little comfort he could. But the moment of solace was short-lived.

The deep, bone-rattling howl that echoed from beyond the shrouded perimeter sent a tingling chill down his spine. Then another howl, closer this time, followed by a third from the opposite direction.

Their eyes snapped up, meeting each other's gaze in shared terror.

"The light from my enchantment," Will said, his voice tense, "It must have alerted them to our presence." He tightened his grip on Lyra for just a second, then released her, urgency overriding the moment of tenderness. "Let's move... quickly," he said, his voice low.

The darkness of Shadowmoor seemed to close in tighter around them, and the unravelling landscape twisted in unnatural ways as they hurried through the uneven terrain.

The howls grew louder, more menacing, moving closer with frightening speed.

Will led the way, his mind raced as they picked up their pace, darting between jagged rocks, trying to stay ahead of whatever monstrous creatures were hunting them. The ground beneath their feet seemed to pulse with dark energy, and every shadow felt like it was watching, waiting for them to falter.

"Stay close!" Will called back, glancing over his shoulder. Lyra was right behind him, tense and alert.

Another howl pierced the air, closer still, accompanied by the thunderous pounding of enormous feet carving a path parallel to the course they were on.

"We're running out of time," Lyra called. "They'll be on us any moment."

Will gritted his teeth, pushing forward, desperate to find some cover, a place to regroup. As they rounded a bend in the path, he spotted a narrow ravine up ahead, its rocky walls providing some protection. "There! In the ravine!" he shouted. They scrambled toward it, hearts pounding, knowing the beasts weren't far behind.

Once inside the ravine, the air around them settled into an eerie stillness. The narrow passage of jagged rock walls distorted every sound, making it nearly impossible to track the creatures' movements.

Will signalled for them to slow, and they came to a stop, huddling together to catch their breath. His pulse pounded in his ears, louder than the faint sounds of the creatures moving around above, apparently trying to re-acquire their trail.

The only sound was the occasional clatter of loose gravel raining down into the ravine, displaced by the hulking beasts that prowled above.

Will glanced up, eyes scanning the jagged walls. The creatures were close. Too close. "They're searching," he whispered. "I think we're beneath their line of sight."

The distant grunts and growls of the beasts echoed above, accompanied by the sharp clatter of loose stones skittering down the cliff face. Dust swirled lazily in the air, stirred by the tremors of heavy footfalls from above. Each clatter of gravel making them flinch.

Will pressed his back against the cool rock, trying to control his breathing, trying to remain as still as possible. His eyes darted to Lyra, crouched a few feet away with her cloak drawn tightly around her, her eyes locked upward. Her gaze flickered to meet his, her lips pressed into a thin, determined line.

Another shower of loose stones fell from above, rattling down the cliff face in bursts of clinks and clatters. Will clenched his jaw, watching the cascade with a grimace. He glanced up, just barely able to make out the hulking silhouette of one of the beasts as it moved along the edge of the ravine. The creature's shape was indistinct in the gloom, but the sheer size of it was unmistakable. Its heavy breath came in deep, guttural snorts that rumbled like distant thunder.

They're hunting us, Will thought, his stomach twisting in knots. They know we're here.

He turned his head slowly, inch by inch, and caught Lyra's attention. He raised his hand, palm down, then moved it in a slow, deliberate line, the signal to move cautiously. Lyra gave a single nod to indicate she understood.

Will eased himself forward, keeping his movements as fluid as possible to avoid shifting the gravel underfoot, his eyes flicking between the path ahead and the ridge-line above. Every muscle in his body felt like a coiled spring, ready to react at the slightest sign of danger. His fingers hovered near the hilt of his sword—not that it would do much good against the creatures if they all attacked at once, but it made him feel a little less helpless.

Lyra followed in his wake, moving with the grace of a shadow. Her footfalls were softer than his, her steps precise and deliberate. Will glanced back to check on her, and she raised an eyebrow at him as if to say, Keep moving.

He exhaled slowly through his nose and turned forward. Stay focused. One step at a time.

Above them, one of the beasts let out a low, guttural growl that echoed through the ravine like a roll of thunder. Will flinched, his pulse spiking, but he kept moving. Another rain of gravel fell behind them, and he whipped his head around in time to see a large paw grip the edge of the ravine above. Thick claws scratched at the dirt, sending more rocks tumbling down.

The beast's snout appeared next, sniffing the air, its breath coming in short, sharp snorts displacing clouds of dust from the dry, arid ground. Will's forced himself to stay perfectly still, hoping the sound of his pounding heart wouldn't give them away. He could see the creature's nostrils flaring in the dim light, the glint of the rows of sharp teeth behind its curled lips.

For one agonising moment, it seemed as though the beast's gaze settled directly on him. The hair on the back of his neck stood on end, every nerve in his body tingling. He could see every detail—the unnatural skin, the multitude of twisted limbs, the dark, glassy eyes that stared straight into him. *Does it see me?*

His muscles tensed, ready to bolt if it lunged, but the beast's attention shifted. Its head turned, its ears twitching as if catching some distant sound. Slowly, it withdrew its paw, vanishing back over the edge.

Will let out a breath he hadn't realised he was holding. He glanced over at Lyra, who looked just as shaken as he felt. She gave him a sharp nod, urgency flashing in her eyes. *We can't stay here.*

He nodded back. *Move.*

This time, he didn't look up. He didn't dare. His steps became faster, though he kept them as quiet as possible, his focus now entirely on getting out of this death trap. Every crunch of gravel felt like a hammer blow against the stillness, but he forced himself forward, step by step. Lyra was right behind him, her every movement controlled, her breathing quiet and steady.

Minutes passed like hours, their progress painstakingly slow. The ravine walls loomed high on either side of them, pressing in like the jaws of some massive stone vice. The growls and snorts of the creatures above continued, growing fainter the further away they moved.

They reached a narrow bend in the ravine where the path widened just enough for them to breathe a little easier. Will paused, leaning a hand against the stone to catch his breath. Lyra crouched beside him, glancing back the way they'd come. Her chest rose and fell in silent breaths, her eyes sharp and watchful.

"Still with me?" he whispered, his voice barely a breath of sound.

"Always," she replied softly, her gaze not leaving the ridge above. Her eyes darted to him briefly. "You think they've given up?"

Will shook his head. "No. They're still moving about out there, but we have put a little distance between us." He wiped the sweat from his brow, the cold air chilling his damp skin."

Lyra glanced toward the narrowing path ahead. "Then let's keep going."

Will nodded, steeling himself for the next stretch. Every muscle in his body ached from the tension, but he couldn't afford to feel it. He glanced up one last time, scanning the ridge for any sign of movement. His heart rate was finally slowing, but his nerves were as taut as a bowstring.

He drew in a deep breath, letting the cool air fill his lungs, then turned back to Lyra.

"Stay close," he said.

"I'm not going anywhere," she said, eyes narrowing.

The distant grunts of the beasts became harder to hear with each step. Occasionally, the faint sound of claws scraping stone reached them, but it was farther now—higher up, more distant. Will's breathing steadied as the tension slowly unwound from his chest. He glanced back at Lyra, her eyes still sharp and watchful but her posture less rigid than before. The flicker of exhaustion was plain on her face, and he knew she could see the same in him. Days of travel had worn them down, and this chase had sapped whatever strength remained.

"They're pulling back," Will said, his voice low. "I think we've shaken them."

Lyra's gaze lingered on the ridge above for a moment longer, her brow furrowed. "Maybe," she said cautiously.

They quickened their pace, each step more deliberate but less cautious than before. The crunch of gravel underfoot sounded louder than it had earlier, but they pushed through it.

They moved more quickly now, trading caution for distance. The walls of the ravine rose sharply on either side, jagged black rock that jutted like broken teeth through the dark hazy gloom.

Every time the path widened, they took advantage of it, jogging for short stretches to put more distance between them and the ridge above. The ravine twisted and turned unpredictably, forcing them to slow when sharp bends obscured their view ahead.

The sheer cliffs on either side began to lose some of their height, the jagged peaks flattening into slopes of loose rock and dirt. For the first time, it felt like they were moving toward an exit.

Will slowed to a stop at a wider part of the path, his chest rising and falling with steady breaths. His hands rested on his hips as he turned to Lyra, who pulled back her hood and swept damp strands of hair away from her face. Her eyes scanned the heights one last time before finally looking at him.

"Think we lost them?" she asked, her tone lighter than before but still edged with doubt.

Will tilted his head, listening. The only sounds now were the faint rustle of wind through the crags and the pounding of their hearts. He frowned, still unconvinced, but his instincts told him they had gained enough ground to breathe.

"For now," he replied. "But we need to push forward. I will feel better when we get out of this ravine."

Lyra nodded, pulling a water-skin from her pack. She took a quick drink and offered it to him. "I'll feel a lot better when we get out of Shadowmoor."

Will took the water-skin, tilting it back and letting the cool water wash away the dry ache in his throat. When he handed it back, he glanced up at the ridge once more, his features relaxing.

The closer they moved to the centre of the curse, the more distorted the landscape around them became. After a while it became clear that there were no further signs of movement past a certain point. Even the twisted perversions of creatures that roamed the perimeter of Shadowmoor seemed to have abandoned this place.

As they continued on, the land grew darker still, colours draining from their surroundings until it seemed the world existed only in shades of gray and black. The sky above, if it could still be called a sky, was a swirling vortex of dark clouds, shot through with veins of lightning.

Time was meaningless in this strange place where nothing made any sense. Will had no idea how long they had been travelling through the darkness, but he started to get the sense that they were nearing their destination.

The pulling sensation Will had felt since entering Shadowmoor was growing with every step now, and there was something almost familiar about it, but it was a familiarity that he couldn't quite put his finger on. The strange familiarity gnawed at the edges of his consciousness, teasing his memory like a word on the tip of his tongue, but just out of reach. Whatever it was, he felt compelled by it now, sensing that whatever it was, was nearby.

They crested a ridge, and as they looked down into the hollowed out basin below, Will froze. At the centre of the basin lay a colossal structure, a twisted black monolith rising from the shattered earth. Black tendrils of the curse wrapped around it, pulsing with dark energy, and above it, the sky seemed to warp and twist as though the very fabric of reality was being drawn into its vortex.

The sensation in Will's mind sharpened into clarity.

"This... I've seen this before," he said, his voice trembling slightly.

There was a powerful aura of energy surrounding this region. So powerful that the air seemed to ripple and distort in a perfect sphere around the monolith, extending out in a huge radius, miles wide. As they approached, huge chunks of the twisted, arid earth began to break away at the edge of that aura and spiral around it, creating a wall of projectiles, blocking any further progress.

The ground trembled beneath their feet as rocks and debris were sucked into the vortex, spinning faster and faster. Lyra squinted through the chaos. "It seems Malakar doesn't want guests." she said wryly.

Will stood at the edge of the cyclone, his heart pounding. The pull inside him grew stronger, urging him to step closer despite the danger. His eyes locked onto the monolith at the centre, its dark form pulsing with energy, calling to him.

"We can't get through that," Lyra shouted over the roar of the spinning debris. "It'll tear us apart!"

Will looked into the swirling maelstrom, the wind whipping around him, tugging at his clothes. Every instinct told him this was the moment he'd been preparing for.

Instinctively, he knew what he needed to do. He stood before the cyclone of swirling projectiles, and looked inward and a plan started to take shape in his mind's eye.

He looked at Lyra who was looking at him with such trust in her eyes that his heart filled. "I am going to try something, but don't follow me. If I am right, I will come back for you."

She nodded, unquestioningly.

He drew in a steady breath, centring himself. His hands moved with slow, deliberate precision, palms pressed together before his chest. Light flickered between his fingers, faint at first, like the first glow of dawn on the horizon. But as his focus sharpened, so too did the light. It gathered at the point where his palms met, a flickering mote of pure energy that pulsed with a steady rhythm, matching the beat of his heart.

With a slow, measured movement, he pulled his hands apart. The mote of light stretched with them, thinning and widening, growing into a small, molten sphere of energy. It hovered between his hands, spinning slowly, radiant tendrils of golden light arcing off its surface like miniature solar flares. His eyes, now glowing softly with the same golden light, snapped open with sharp focus. He shifted his stance, planting his feet firmly as if to anchor himself to the ground.

His fingers spread wide, and he thrust his arms out to either side, palms facing outward.

The sphere of light exploded in a soundless flash, not a burst of destruction but an expansion. The glow surged outward, sweeping away the darkness with a rush of warmth and brilliance. A perfect sphere of shimmering golden energy formed around him, smooth as glass but unyielding as steel. For a moment, Will marvelled at it. The light hummed in harmony with him, a part of him.

It will hold, he thought. It must.

The cyclone raged ahead, a twisting storm of jagged rock and swirling debris. Stone shards the size of his head whipped through the air like leaves caught in a gale. The roar of it was deafening, relentless.

With slow, deliberate steps, he started moving towards it.

As he neared the edge of the maelstrom, smaller shards of stone slammed into the surface of his shield with sharp tinks and pings, like hail striking glass. Larger chunks followed, crashing into the glowing barrier with thunderous cracks. But the shield didn't falter. The golden energy shimmered brighter with each impact, a ripple of light that travelled across its surface, absorbing the force and dispersing it harmlessly.

Will's gaze remained locked on the centre of the storm. Lightning arced through the cyclone in jagged forks of white-blue energy, lighting up the swirling wall of destruction. The air was thick with pressure and the tang of ionized energy, but Will pressed on. His muscles screamed from the exertion of maintaining the shield while walking forward, but he continued on, his face set.

The light of his shield blazed brighter as the maelstrom's fury increased. Shards the size of boulders slammed into him, splintering into dust on impact. The sounds were deafening — cracking stone and grinding metal.

Focus, he reminded himself.

He kept walking. One step. Then another.

A jagged slab of stone spun through the air, hurtling straight for his head. For an instant, Will's heart clenched, but his shield flared with blinding intensity, and the stone cracked clean in two, each half spinning past him on either side.

Lyra's voice echoed faintly behind him, barely audible over the roaring storm. "You've got this Will!"

Her words were cut off as another thunderclap echoed through the cyclone, but he didn't need to hear her to know she was there, watching. She believed in him.

He believed in himself.

The closer he got to the centre, the denser the storm became. Chunks of debris the size of tree trunks battered against the shield, each impact draining him a little more. The golden glow flickered for a heartbeat, but Will grit his teeth and willed it to hold. The storm would not break him. He refused to be broken.

With a roar of defiance, he pushed forward, his steps quickening. Faster. Stronger. The golden light surrounding him pulsed, matching the rhythm of his heart. Step. Pulse. Step. Pulse. The light beating back the storm.

The cyclone screamed its fury, the wall of spinning death pressing in on him from all sides. Sparks flew as stone scraped against the outer edge of his shield. Lightning cracked against it, sending jagged forks of light arcing across its surface. The ground beneath his feet quaked, but still, he moved forward.

At last, his foot stepped free of the maelstrom's inner wall. The swirling wall of debris spiralled behind him, a violent tempest of unrelenting chaos. But as Will stepped though to the eye of the storm, he felt a shift in the energy holding the maelstrom together.

The storm trembled, and with a final shudder, it collapsed. The wall of flying debris losing all momentum in an instant and dropping to the ground with a deafening crash. Silence fell. Pure, perfect silence.

He took a slow, steady breath, letting the calm settle into his bones. His body ached from the exertion, his limbs heavy with exhaustion. Behind him, he heard Lyra's footsteps crunch over the settling debris. She stopped just behind him, her breath catching in her throat as she took in the stillness.

# Chapter twenty-eight

Will stood at the edge of the basin, gazing out at the monolith that loomed at its heart like an obsidian titan. Its surface shimmered with faint runic light, pale blue-green glyphs pulsing in a slow, steady rhythm, like the heartbeat of an ancient god. He took a deep breath, his gaze absorbing the scene laid out before them. This was it. Every trial, every loss, every hard-won victory had led to this moment.

No more doubt. No more second-guessing.

His heart, once ravaged by a storm of uncertainty, now beat with the steady rhythm of clarity. It was an eerie feeling, like standing in the eye of a hurricane, where everything beyond the calm was chaos. The curse pressed in around him, the weight of it ever-present, but it couldn't reach him now. Not here. Not with this sense of purpose blazing within him.

It was only now, in the eerie quiet that had settled over them in the wake of the maelstrom, that he was able to fully take in the scale of what lay before him.

What he saw stole his breath.

The basin wasn't just a hollowed-out crater of cracked stone and arid soil. A vast, sprawling city covered the distance between them and the monolith. Towers of glass and steel jutted up from the ground like the shattered bones of a fallen giant. Skyscrapers, shattered and ruined, leaned precariously against one another, their steel frames exposed like the ribs of some ancient beast. Streets were cracked and crumbling, choked with dust and debris. Vehicles sat rusted in the streets, their husks twisted and deformed by time and decay.

"This... this isn't right," Will muttered, stepping forward slowly, unable to reconcile his mind with what his eyes were showing him. His eyes darted across the wreckage. "This shouldn't be here."

Lyra moved up beside him, her eyes wide with disbelief. Her gaze followed the lines of the broken towers, the derelict vehicles, the hollow shells of streetlamps and toppled power lines. She turned slowly, her voice quiet, awestruck.

"What is this place?..." she trailed off, her awestruck voice barely audible. "I have never seen anything like this before."

"It's something that shouldn't be here at all," Will said, his voice harder now, more certain, "This is a city from my world." He gestured to the buildings in the distance, their jagged silhouettes like broken teeth against the horizon.

A heavy silence fell between them, broken only by the distant creaks and groans of warped metal slowly shifting and settling.

His eyes were locked on the monolith now, its glow steadily increasing as they drew closer. Subtle streaks of energy flickered across its surface, like veins of molten fire running through stone. It seemed this Monolith served as a convergence point, a place where realities bled into each other. He could feel it now, every inch of his skin tingling as he drew closer.

"The Ender of Worlds," he muttered, his voice distant, eyes fixed on the crimson threads lacing through the stone.

Lyra shot him a glance. "What?"

"It's what they called me," Will said, his jaw tightening as he kept walking. "In the Shadow Codex." His fingers flexed at his sides, his hands curling into fists. "They call me The Ender of Worlds."

Lyra fell silent for a moment, keeping pace with him, eyes flicking nervously to the distant skyline. The ruined city, the broken towers, the scorched streets — it appeared to be the very vision of an ending of worlds.

She looked at Will, her gaze searching his face. His expression was calm, his eyes sharp, the light from the monolith flickering across his features. Not the face of a man resigned to fate, she thought. The face of a man prepared to challenge it.

"What next?" she asked, her voice tense.

Will stopped at the edge of what looked like it had once been a park, the wide-open space lined with crumbling stone benches and the shattered remains of rusted play equipment.

"I guess we go and find out what's at the centre of this curse, and end it. Once and for all!" he said, his tone matter-of-fact.

The two of them walked down a cracked, overgrown street, the overwhelming silence amplifying every sound. Shadows lingered in the doorways of the empty buildings, and Will could feel the faint pull in his mind growing stronger as they moved closer to the monolith at the city's heart. The familiarity of the place unsettled him—this wasn't just any city; there was something about it... something he couldn't quite put his finger on.

Will's heart ached as he took in the ruined buildings and vehicles around him. He couldn't comprehend the extent of the curses reach, but this city from his world, being here made him realise he had drastically underestimated Malakar's power. The curse's tendrils had stretched far beyond Aruna, far beyond the borders of any one world. It had reached his world... and he shuddered to think how many others.

The familiarity of it made the curse's corruption feel personal in a way it never had before. He had seen Shadowmoor's blight twist forests into tangles of blackened thorns, seen it choke the life from peaceful villages and turn it's people into horrifying beasts. But this was something else entirely. A warning carved in rust and ruin that seemed personally tailored to him.

He stood there for a long moment, the sharp winds of the basin tugging at his cloak, the faint hum of the monolith pulsing in the distance, calling to him. His eyes tracked the skyline, moving from one broken tower to the next. They had once stood tall and proud, symbols of progress and possibility. Now they were hollow, gutted by ruin, their skeletal frames leaning like old bones too brittle to stand.

"Will," Lyra's voice pulled him from his thoughts. She was watching him closely, her brow creased with concern. "We need to keep moving."

He exhaled slowly, eyes still locked on the distant monolith. "I know," he said quietly, his voice hollow, almost mournful. "I know."

He forced himself to look away from the skyline, from the memories it stirred. Keep moving forward, he told himself. *What is gone* is gone. The future can still be saved.

But as they pressed on, a single thought haunted him like a shadow at his back.

How much of my world has already fallen?

The growing sense of familiarity that was welling up in Will suddenly reached a certain point and something clicked. He looked sharply at Lyra, silently grabbed her hand and led her quickly though streets, winding his way towards a destination that he suddenly knew would be there.

Amidst all the decay and darkness stood a familiar house with a light on in the window. The house stopped Will in his tracks. This couldn't be, it made no sense... but yet here it was. The street of suburban houses, almost unrecognisable in this place, but even here, the sense of familiarity that washed over Will nearly knocked him to his knees.

He stood frozen, staring at the house that should not exist. The home where he'd grown up, untouched by time, standing against the backdrop of devastation. The light in the window flickered, casting a warmth that looked out of place in this cold colourless environment. His heart raced as he tried to reconcile the impossible sight before him.

Lyra squeezed his hand gently, her voice soft and cautious. "Will... what is it?"

"It's my parent's home," Will said, his voice barely audible, as if speaking louder might shatter the fragile reality of it. "The home I grew up in, as a boy."

Without another word, he stepped forward, leading Lyra through the rusted gate, the creaking of the seized hinges unnervingly loud in the stillness. Every detail of the house was hauntingly familiar—the worn path to the front door, the chipped paint on the porch, the smell of earth and grass somehow clinging to the air despite the corruption.

As they approached the front door, Will hesitated, his heart pounding. His mind was awash with confusion and memories, emotions long buried suddenly rising to the surface. He feared what he might find on the other side of that door, but something was pulling him inside—something stronger than the fear.

Lyra, sensing his turmoil, stepped closer. "You don't have to do this alone," she whispered, her hand still in his, steadying him.

He looked at her with a smile, and then with a deep breath, he turned the handle, and the door creaked open. As he stepped through, the door suddenly slammed shut behind him with a violent force, locking Lyra on the other side.

"Lyra!" Will shouted, spinning around and grabbing the handle, but it wouldn't budge. He pounded on the door, his heart racing. On the other side, he could hear Lyra doing the same, her fists beating against the wood.

"Will!" she called, her voice strained.

Will threw his weight against the door, trying to force it open, but it wouldn't give. "It won't budge!" he shouted back.

He pressed his forehead against the cool wood, frustration gnawing at him.

"Will..." Lyra's voice came through, softer now. "It's no use. You have to go on. Try to find a different way out. I'll wait here and meet you when you get out of there."

He hesitated, torn between not wanting to get separated, and knowing she was right. "Are you sure?" he said, his voice thick with concern.

"Yes. I'll be fine. Go. I'll find you."

Will stood there for a moment longer, pressing his forehead to the door, before reluctantly stepping away. "I'll come back for you," he promised.

"I know," she said from the other side.

With one last glance at the door, Will turned and moved further into the house, searching for another way out.

The interior of the house was like a time capsule pulled from the depths of memory and left to rot. He stepped inside, his breath catching in his chest. The air was thick with the faint, lingering scent of his mother's cooking. It was impossible, but there it was. The same smell that used to greet him every day after school.

His eyes swept over the familiar layout, and his heart twisted with a mix of conflicting emotions. The old wooden furniture was exactly as he remembered it; the low coffee table where he'd done his homework, the overstuffed armchair his father claimed every evening. But the effects of the curse touched even this place. The table was warped and splintered, signs of significant rot and decay having long since claimed it. The armchair sagged in the middle, its fabric torn and leaking tufts of stuffing like exposed bone.

Long, curling strips of paper peeled from the walls like dead skin. A thin layer of grime coated every surface, dust motes drifting lazily in the stagnant air.

His parents had remodelled this house years ago. He remembered the summer his parents tore it apart to 'modernise' it, remembered the smell of fresh paint and the sharp chemical tang of new carpet adhesive. All this had been gone for decades. But here it was, eerily whole, like the Shadowmoor curse had dredged it up from his childhood memories and brought it into this world, only to leave it to rot.

At the centre of the living room, sitting in an old armchair with her back to him, was a figure, it's permed hair visible above the chair back.

"Mom...?" he whispered, his voice trembling.

The figure stirred, slowly rising from the chair. She turned, and though her face was shadowed, Will could feel her gaze upon him. A chill ran down his spine. Something about the way she looked through him wasn't right.

"Will," the figure said, her voice soft but distorted, like an echo. "Where have you been? I called you in ages ago. Now be a good boy and go and set the table for dinner." and with that, the figure shuffled off to the kitchen, leaving the radius of warm light and vanishing into the shadows.

Everything about this place made Will's skin crawl and every fibre of his being wanted nothing more than to run.

As he was about to leave the room and search for another way out, something else caught his eye. He moved around the chair to get a better look only to see the back of a young boy of about eight years sitting on the rug in front of the fire. The boy was playing a very involved imagination game with some small toys in front of him and seemed oblivious, but as Will stepped closer a floorboard creaked and the boy stopped suddenly and the silence was broken by a chilling voice that shook the foundations of the house.

"You finally made it here Will. I have been waiting for you for a very long time." the voice of Malakar reverberated throughout the place, rattling the windows and shaking loose items from the mantle.

The young boy stood from where he was playing in front of the fire and turned to face Will, looking at him directly in the eyes for a moment, before running off through the opening that led to the kitchen. The warm light in the front room vanished and plunged Will into darkness where he stood, completely shaken for a moment, weighing up his options.

Will stood frozen, breathless, as the darkness closed in around him. His mind raced, trying to process the strange scene.

"Malakar?" Will called out, his voice shaky. But the house gave no answer—only the deep silence that wrapped around him like a suffocating blanket.

He looked around the darkened room, his eyes struggling to adjust. His instincts screamed at him to leave, to run, but something compelled him to stay. He took a deep breath, steeling himself.

He cautiously moved toward the kitchen, where the boy had disappeared. His heart pounded in his chest as he crossed the threshold, the old wooden floor creaking under his weight. The kitchen was just as he remembered it from his childhood, yet unnervingly distorted. The table was set, but the plates were chipped, covered in a fine layer of dust, the food there turned to unrecognisable putrid rot, filling the air with the smell of decay. Again, his instinct's screamed that he was in terrible danger, and he had to suppress an overwhelming urge to turn and bolt.

"Come, Will," Malakar's voice echoed again, this time softer but just as unnerving. "You've come this far. Don't turn back now."

Will's hand instinctively tightened around the hilt of his sword, unsure whether it would be of any use here, against these strange echoes of his past. Still, it seemed prudent to be prepared to defend himself so he drew his weapon.

He moved cautiously through the twisted, decaying hallway, his sword drawn and glowing with a brilliant light. Yet, even the intense radiance of the blade couldn't fully pierce the suffocating darkness that clung to the corners of the house. Shadows seemed to swallow the light whole, leaving it to illuminate only a narrow, flickering path in front of him.

Malakar's voice, cold and seething, echoed from every direction. "You left me, Will. You turned your back, abandoned everything we could have been."

Will tightened his grip on the hilt of his sword, its warmth offering little comfort in this place. His mind raced, trying to make sense of Malakar's accusations. "What are you talking about?" he called out, his voice filled with confusion.

A growl reverberated through the house, the walls trembling with Malakar's fury. "Excuses! We were destined to change everything, but you ran. You let fear steer your path, and left all our potential to the cold void."

Will shook his head, his heart pounding as he struggled to grasp Malakar's words. "I don't know what you mean!" he shouted back, stepping carefully over the creaking floorboards.

Malakar's laugh rang out, harsh and bitter, filling the house like a suffocating fog. "You'll remember soon enough. All that light you cling to won't save you from the truth, Will. You belong to the darkness now."

The last line came from directly behind him, so close that Will could feel the chill of Malakar's presence prickling his skin. He turned sharply, fear flooding his senses at the horrifying realisation that he had been effectively ambushed.

As he spun around, his glowing sword trembling in his grasp, he found himself face to face with the younger version of himself. The boy hovered in the air, sheathed in a pulsing aura of swirling shadows. Tendrils of darkness coiled around his small frame, flowing like a dark river. The boy's eyes were now inky black voids, and the same dark aura seemed to be emanating from them, spilling out in thick, smoky tendrils. The sight of his own youthful face twisted by Malakar's corruption sent a wave of nausea crashing over Will.

The boy tilted his head, studying Will with a mixture of curiosity and contempt, his face twisted unnaturally as

Malakar's voice spilled from his tongue. "You see now, don't you?" the boy whispered, his words dripping with malice. "You can't escape who you are. You can't escape me."

Will's heart pounded in his chest, his pulse deafening in his ears. For a moment, he was paralysed, torn between disbelief and the overwhelming urge to flee. The sword in his hand flickered, struggling against the encroaching darkness, its blazing light dimming as the aura of shadows pressed closer, overwhelming it's energy.

"I... I don't understand," Will said, his voice barely audible. "What are you?"

The boy scowled, his aura pulsing with his inner rage. "I am what you left behind."

The young boy lunged forward with terrifying speed, his shadowy form pushing Will backwards with immense force. The impact should have knocked him into the wall behind him, but where he should have met resistance, Will stumbled back through the wall, disorientated, as the world shifted around him.

He found himself suddenly standing in his old bedroom on the upper floor. There was an area over near the window bathed in a pool of warm, soft light, casting a golden glow over the small writing desk that lay before it. Sitting at the desk was yet another version of his younger self, slightly older this time, absorbed in scribbling on a piece of paper, completely oblivious to the chaos that had just unfolded.

For a brief second, a rush of nostalgia flooded wills senses, the familiar scent of his old bedroom and the sound of pencil scratching paper. But as he stood there, the warm nostalgia was pierced by Malakar's voice, cold and filled with venom, hissing through the room once more.

"After you abandoned me, Will," Malakar growled, his voice carrying through the walls of the house like a relentless storm, "I drifted alone, lost in the void. Forgotten. Nothing but a shadow of what I was. A mere fragment of a memory."

Malakar's words continued to strike him, like unseen blows. "Until," Malakar continued, the anger palpable, "I found a memory strong enough to latch on to. *This* memory, Will. Do you remember this moment?"

Curious now, Will moved over towards the writing desk to see what the young boy was scribbling away at. He leaned over the desk, his breath catching in his throat. It was unmistakable; the rough, childlike lines forming a map—the first map he had ever drawn of the land he now found himself in. The rivers, the mountains, the places he had only imagined as a boy. His mind swirled as the memory flooded back to him, of nights spent dreaming of this strange, magical place, imagining noble quests and heroic characters.

"The first time I drew this land..." Will whispered to himself, his voice barely audible. His words trailed off, tangled in the flood of memories that washed over him. He remembered how excited he had been, how his imagination had run wild with dreams of adventures, dangers, and treasures hidden away in distant lands. But now, standing in the corrupted nightmare born of Malakar's hate, he found it hard to imagine the beautiful land that he had created.

"You created this place," Malakar hissed, his voice sharp with accusation. "You gave it life, and then you left me here. You left us here."

The boy at the desk remained still, absorbed in his task, but the room grew darker around them, the air thick with Malakar's growing rage.

Suddenly the room was plunged into absolute blackness, as if all the light in the world had suddenly vanished, extinguished by the hate radiating from this powerful mage.

Malakar's voice echoed through the void, venomous and laced with bitterness. "But you see, Will," he continued, his tone almost mocking, "I needed you. When I settled here, I devised a plan to be reunited. To finish what we started."

Will's heart raced as the words sank in. "Finish what we started? What are you talking about?" he called into the darkness, trying to steady his breath, though the cold tendrils of fear gripped him tightly.

Malakar ignored his question, his voice simmering with years of resentment. "It took me years, Will. Years to master the arts of magic, to hone my craft. But those fools at Thorn Island—they stifled me! They were too afraid of what I could become. Too afraid to let me develop to the level I needed." There was a pause, and the anger in Malakar's voice grew. "And then, of course, they exiled me. Left me to rot, just as you had."

Will's mind raced, trying to think of some way out of this situation as he realised Malakar's rage was building. "I didn't abandon you, Malakar. I didn't even know—"

"Liar!" Malakar's voice erupted, shaking the very air around Will. "You left me, just like everyone else."

The darkness around Will was suddenly interrupted by a vision, almost like a living memory projected on a screen before him as Malakar continued to explain his story to Will. He told of his mastery over magic, how he had made a deal with the lord of the underworld; Moloch, who allowed him to wield the most powerful dark magic, and how ultimately he had unleashed the curse of Shadowmoor.

"All to lead to this moment Will," Malakar's voice echoed in the void. "the curse was designed to bring you to this place."

"But why?" Will shouted into the void. "What do you want with me?"

Will's breath caught in his throat as a figure materialised before him, a reflection of himself so similar that he thought for a moment he had stepped in front of a mirror. But this figure, like the boy downstairs was cloaked in darkness, radiating malice.

Malakar's voice reverberated in the air, filled with venom and triumph. "Don't you get it yet, Will? I am you. The part of you that you discarded all those years ago, when you stopped believing in magic. When you left me behind."

Will shook his head, his mind spinning. "No...," he muttered, taking a step back. "I'm nothing like you!"

"You were once," Malakar snarled, stepping closer, his dark aura flaring. "You were full of dreams, full of power. But when reality rejected your dreams, you rejected me. You abandoned everything we built together—the magic, the belief, the potential, and in that moment you cast me into the void."

Will's sword glowed faintly in his hand, but it seemed feeble against the intense darkness surrounding Malakar. He gripped it tighter, trying to steady his thoughts, but Malakar's words gnawed at him. Memories of his younger self—the adventures he dreamed of, the magic he once believed in—all came flooding back. He had buried that part of himself deep, let it wither as he grew older, but now it stood before him, twisted and hateful.

Will's confusion turned to anger, his grip on his sword tightening. "I didn't abandon magic. I didn't abandon you!" He shouted back, the fire in his chest rising. "You chose the darkness. You made this curse. You caused so much pain and suffering in this land. Maybe you were once a part of me, but if so, what you have become sickens me!"

Malakar's dark reflection only smirked, stepping closer. "I am your darkness, Will. You can't escape me."

Will's mind raced as he tried to process it all, but just when he felt it might all overwhelm him, as the realisation of his involvement in the horrors that had been unleashed on this land struck him, and his mind began to spiral into that all-too-familiar anxiety attack, a face surfaced in his memories. It was the face of the woman he had saved in the woods south of Silverwood—or, now that he thought about it, she had actually saved him. He had been lost, aimless, and she had given him a path, a purpose. The prophecy called her 'the conduit' and he understood that now. She had been his grounding force, always steady, always there, and now she was counting on him to end this, to break the curse.

The realisation struck him like a bolt of lightning—he would do anything for her. To keep her safe, to make her happy. He loved her.

That love swelled in his chest, pushing back against the fear, the hate, the darkness, filling him with a strength he hadn't known was there. As his heart surged with that pure, undeniable love, the sword in his hand began to glow brighter, pulsing with energy. The light grew, searing and intense, until it became too much to bear. Will shielded his eyes, unable to look directly at the radiance that now burned through the shadows.

When the brilliance finally subsided, the darkness around him had been dispelled completely. The suffocating void that had clung to him moments before was gone. Blinking away the last of the light, Will looked around, taking in his surroundings.

Both he and Malakar had been transported, and now stood on top of the monolith at the heart of Shadowmoor. The area stretched out in a wide area of perfectly flat smooth basalt, it's surface reflecting the flashes of lighting that occasionally flickered through the churning colourless skies above them.

Will could feel the immense power of the place. An immense power, twisted and corrupted by Malakar's dark magic, crafted and moulded into a perverted dark reflection of reality. And there, standing across from him on the monolith's surface, was Malakar, staring back at him with fury and hatred, the dark aura surrounding him flickering and unstable.

"You think you have the power to stand against me, Will?" Malakar spat, his voice trembling with barely contained rage. "You think that your light magic will save you? Save her?"

Will raised his sword, the light still burning in its core, and met Malakar's gaze. "I don't know," Will said, his voice steady, filled with resolve. "But I have seen darkness and hate gain too much ground, and I think it's about time someone did something about that."

Malakar's face twisted in anger, and with a roar, he drew his own blade, shrouded in shadow and lunged forward, tendrils of darkness swirling around him as the battle between them began.

# Chapter twenty-nine

Will stood, feet planted on the monolith, the winds howling around him, whipping his cloak and gently tossing his hair. Yet, despite the chaos of the storm raging in the skies above and the ominous darkness swirling below, he felt an absolute calm wash over him. Every moment of his journey—the trials, the losses, the triumphs—had led him here. He was no longer the man who had stumbled into this world, burdened by fear and self-doubt.

The power of the relics at his side, the steady pulse of light magic in his veins, and the quiet strength that had grown within him—all of it had honed him into the person he was now. He was no longer just Will, the terrified and reluctant visitor from another world. He was the instrument of fate, standing at the edge of destiny.

As Malakar's dark form emerged from the churning shadows, a tide of intense energy rolled forward, like a shock wave ahead of him. But Will felt no fear. He closed his eyes for a moment, taking a deep breath that seemed to resonate with the rhythm of the universe itself. The final door in his mind opened, and in that instant, he became one with the light.

It surged through him, brilliant and pure, not as a tool, or an extension of him, but as a part of him—instinctive and boundless. He didn't have to think about wielding it; it simply was, as natural as the air in his lungs or the beat of his heart. A serene smile curved across his lips, and he opened his eyes, their glow matching the radiance of the sword he now raised to meet Malakar's attack.

Malakar bore down, his voice a thunderous roar that shook the heavens, but Will remained completely unfazed, finally accepting his fate and stepping forward to meet it without fear or expectation.

"Come then," Will said softly, his voice resolute. "Let's end this."

The initial clash of their meeting sent a shock-wave rippling outward, a violent explosion of energy that split the sky like a storm unleashed. Sparks rained as their blades met, the brilliance of Will's light clashing with the oppressive darkness emanating from Malakar's heavy sword. The force of their battle reverberated across the polished basalt surface beneath them, cracks forming where the energy spilled over, light and shadow battling for supremacy.

They danced around each other in a deadly rhythm, each strike met with a deft parry or a calculated dodge. Between the flurry of their blades, they unleashed surges of raw energy—arcs of searing light and torrents of inky blackness colliding mid-air with deafening discharge of energy. At one point, Malakar lifted his blade high, its edge pulsing with malevolent power. He brought it down with such force that it would have split Will in two, but Will instinctively summoned a radiant shield of light, the air around it warping with intensity. The blow deflected, sending another shock-wave rippling across the battlefield.

Their duel continued, back and forth, with neither willing to yield. But Will began to feel the strain creeping in—his muscles burning, his breath coming in ragged gasps. Every movement required more effort, and still, Malakar pressed on, his strikes as unyielding as they had been at the start. It was as if their prolonged exchange had absolutely no effect on him.

As Will deflected another devastating blow, his eyes caught something—a faint flicker of energy stretching from Malakar into the monolith itself. He adjusted his focus, his senses expanding, and then he saw it clearly: four beams of dark energy, tethering Malakar to the four corners of the monolith. The realisation struck him suddenly. The monolith was more than just the centre of the curse—it was the source of Malakar's strength.

Between strikes, Will reached out with his mind, following the threads of power as they pulsed with concentrated shadows. He could feel their immensity, their roots stretching deep into the earth, tapping into the heart of Shadowmoor's curse. The monolith was a conduit, drawing from the cursed land and feeding its power into Malakar, bolstering him, sustaining him.

Will's grip on his blade tightened as he dodged another slash, his mind racing. He understood now that the key to defeating Malakar wouldn't just rely on brute force—he would need to sever those tethers. He feinted to the left, buying himself a moment to glance toward the monolith's edges, where the beams converged with the ground. He could feel the corruption seething through them, like veins pumping venom into the heart of their enemy, venom that empowered and enraged him.

Will dropped back, his chest heaving, as he tried to focus his mind through the haze of exhaustion. He needed a plan—something to counter Malakar's overwhelming speed and strength. It was clear now that he couldn't outmatch his foe in raw power, but as Malakar lunged forward again, his blade slashing in a wild arc, Will saw it; the unchecked fury burning in Malakar's every movement. His attacks, though devastating, were driven by rage, not precision. Rage could be exploited.

Will parried the blow, twisting his blade to deflect the strike, and danced back a step. The movement felt less like retreat and more like setting a trap. He let Malakar come at him again, his snarling fury pouring into a reckless overhead strike that Will sidestepped with ease. The opening it left was fleeting but enough. Will's eyes darted toward the nearest tether of dark energy, and he struck.

His blade, pulsing with light, slashed through the tether. The impact wasn't immediate; for a heartbeat, nothing happened. Then, with a sound like a thunderclap, the tether snapped, unleashing a wave of force that rippled through the battlefield. The shock-wave knocked them both from their feet, the ground beneath them trembling as the reverberation echoed across the distant mountains.

Will rolled and scrambled to his feet, his sword raised defensively as he scanned the battlefield, watching for his opponent's next move. Malakar rose slower, his eyes blazing with a fury that seemed even more unstable now, his movements wilder. The severed tether left a faint void in the air where it had been, and the remaining three pulsed more intensely, as though struggling to compensate for the loss.

Will took another steadying breath. The plan was working, but each tether would come at a cost. He shifted his weight, ready to goad Malakar into overextending again.

The battle shifted. Malakar's fury no longer translated into reckless aggression. Instead, his movements became calculated, his strikes more measured as he realised what Will was trying to do. The advantage of exploiting Malakar's rage had waned, and his growing caution made each tether harder to reach.

Will pressed on, weaving and feinting, drawing Malakar's attention with quick jabs and feigned retreats. Each step closer to a tether felt like pushing against an unyielding tide. Malakar blocked Will's path at every turn, his blade meeting Will's with relentless precision, the clash of their weapons ringing out like the toll of a bell.

Finding a brief opening, he drove Malakar back with a sudden surge of light magic, forcing Malakar to recoil. Seizing the opportunity, Will dashed toward another tether and struck with everything he had.

The blade connected, slicing through the dark energy. The tether snapped with a sound like an explosion, sending out another wave of concussive force. Both Will and Malakar were hurled to the ground, the impact shaking the monolith and scattering loose shards of polished stone.

Will struggled to his feet, his entire body aching from the repeated blasts of raw energy and the exertion of the battle. Malakar rose slower this time, his movements more laboured, the dark energy feeding him was faltering, but he was still far from defeated.

As they squared off again, Will could feel the exhaustion creeping in, his muscles screaming for rest. But he knew he needed to continue. He summoned the strength from the nexus to fortify his spirit, taking the edge off the exhaustion slightly. Through gritted teeth, he parried another of Malakar's brutal strikes and lunged for the next tether.

The third tether fell, shattering with the same deafening roar, the wave of force nearly blinding in its intensity. Will hit the ground hard, pain lancing through his side. For a moment, he couldn't breathe, his vision swimming. But when he forced himself up, he saw Malakar on one knee, the weight of the severed tethers beginning to show.

For the first time, they stood apart, neither pressing the attack, their chests rising and falling as they struggled to catch their breath. The sky above churned with swirling energy, the lingering echoes of their titanic clash still rippling through the air.

Malakar's lips twisted into a mocking sneer, his blade resting lightly against the polished onyx floor. "Look at you," he said, his voice dripping with disdain. "The so-called chosen one. The great hope of Aruna. Tell me, Will—does it feel good to know how easily you've been played?"

Will narrowed his eyes, refusing to rise to the bait. "What are you talking about?"

Malakar's laugh was a cold, cruel sound, echoing ominously. "Oh, so clueless. Every step you've taken, every so-called 'choice' you've made, has been according to my design. The curse wasn't some random blight, conjured by chance. I devised it as a means of enacting my purpose. It's primary purpose was to thin the veil between our worlds—to drag you here."

Will's grip tightened on his sword. "Why?"

Malakar tilted his head, feigning curiosity. "Why not? You're the perfect pawn. A nobody in your own world, desperate for meaning. The curse whispered in your dreams, lured you with visions of grandeur and heroism—feeding your desire for purpose, and when the time was right, it brought you to me."

Will's jaw clenched. "You still haven't answered my question."

Malakar's sneer deepened, his glowing eyes narrowing. "Why? Because I needed a way back. Because once I've killed you here, I will take your place there. Step into your life, wear your face, walk among your people. And they'll never know the difference."

The words hit Will like a physical blow. His mind raced with the implications.

Malakar's expression darkened, as he continued, his voice growing colder. "Here, I have my limits; other magic users who curtail the scope of my potential... but there— a world without magic, defenceless against my power. Your people will bow before me, and your world will be mine."

The depravity of Malakar's plan made Will feel nauseous. But beneath the dread, something else stirred—a spark of defiance. He raised his blade again, stepping forward. "You think you can break me with your words, Malakar? I'm still standing. I'm still fighting. And I'm going to stop you."

Malakar's laughter echoed again, but this time there was a flicker of doubt in his eyes. "Bold words, Will. But let's see if your courage lasts when I snuff out your pathetic little light."

With a flick of his wrist, Malakar vanished in a burst of shadow, the air distorting where he'd stood. Will's senses screamed in warning. Instinct took over. He spun, raising his sword just in time to catch Malakar's strike, sparks erupting as steel met steel. The impact jarred Will's arms to the bone, but he gritted his teeth and shoved Malakar back, forcing distance between them.

Malakar sneered, his sword trailing shadows like wisps of smoke. "Your reflexes are fast," he said begrudgingly, circling him again. "but are they fast enough?"

Will tightened his grip on the hilt of his sword, the glow from the blade pulsing in sync with his steadying breaths. He held his ground, his eyes fixed on Malakar, anticipating his next move. Then, Malakar teleported again, his figure dissolving into shadow. This time, however, the attack came faster—too fast. He reappeared to Will's left, but before Will could fully pivot, Malakar vanished again, leaving only the faintest wisp of darkness.

A chilling realisation struck Will a split second before the pain did. Malakar materialised behind him, his blade cutting through the air with merciless precision. The dark steel bit deep into Will's side, tearing through leather and flesh with ease. He gasped, a sharp intake of breath, as the pain overwhelmed his senses. Blood spilled from the wound, warm and wet, soaking his hand as he clasped it to his side in a desperate attempt to stem the flow.

Malakar stepped back, his laugh low and filled with mockery. "Did you really think you could best me?" he taunted, his voice cutting through the charged air like a blade. "You're nothing, Will! A mere pawn in a game far beyond your comprehension."

Will stumbled but managed to stay on his feet, his breaths ragged. His vision blurred for a moment, the edges darkening as the pain threatened to drag him under.

Malakar tilted his head, feigning pity as his lips curled into a cruel smile. "Look at you," he said, gesturing with his shadow-wreathed blade. "Bleeding, broken, and still clinging to that absurd hope. Do you truly believe you're destined to stop me? Even now? Fate doesn't care for the weak, Will. It only rewards the strong."

Will gritted his teeth, his mind racing through the haze of pain. He tightened his grip on his sword, summoning the light within him to cauterize the wound. He felt it burning in his side, searing the wound and stemming the flow of blood.

Malakar's eyes narrowed at the sight. "How quaint," he sneered, taking a step closer. "Still defying me, even as you crumble. You're nothing but a flickering candle in the storm,

Will. Let me snuff you out and put an end to this charade. Just another fool who thought he could fight fate."

Will met his gaze, eyes calm, unwavering. "You're right about one thing, Malakar," he said, voice steady. His arms tensed as prepared to make his move. "You can't fight fate—"

A surge of light radiated from Will's core, flowing into his blade. Malakar's eyes widened in realisation as the glow intensified.

"You rewrite it."

Will shoved Malakar back and lunged at the remaining tether, striking it with a flash of blinding brilliance, light exploding from the point of contact. Malakar staggered, sliding across the cracked stone as wisps of shadow peeled away from him like smoke caught in a strong wind.

Will took a step forward, his chest heaving as he struggled to catch his breath. "It's over, Malakar," he said, his voice heavy with exhaustion. "End this madness."

Will didn't know what to expect next, but Malakar let out a low, chilling laugh. The sound echoed in the stillness, a mocking, mirthless sound that sent a chill though Will.

"Give up?" Malakar's voice was filled with derision as he lifted his head, his eyes burning with dark fire. "Why would I give up now, when you just walked directly into my trap?" He gestured to the shadows around them, which began to swirl and thicken, coalescing around his fallen form. "You fool, you've done exactly what was needed. You've freed me from the curses bonds."

Will's heart clenched as he took a step back, his grip tightening on his sword. *No... this couldn't be right. Had he really just been played... again?*

Malakar pushed himself to his feet, his body trembling with the effort. "Just as the shadow codex ordained; my ascension to glory will be preceded by the ender of worlds breaking my bonds. Now you have sealed your fate!"

Even as he spoke, the shadows around them surged towards him, coalescing and flowing into his body like a river of darkness. His form began to shift, twisting and contorting as the dark energy poured into him. His limbs stretched and thickened, his body growing larger and more monstrous by the second. Black scales erupted across his skin, claws sprouting from his hands and feet. His face elongated into a grotesque snout, rows of jagged teeth protruding as his eyes glowed a malevolent red.

Will watched in horror as Malakar's transformation completed, his now grotesque form radiating an unholy power. The creature let out a deafening roar, the sound shaking the ground beneath them, and Will felt the force of it like a blow.

Instinctively, Will channelled the power within him, allowing it to flow through him and transform his body. His form began to expand, his muscles rippling with energy as the light enveloped him, his entire being glowing brighter and brighter until he stood as a towering, radiant figure of pure energy.

"Malakar, please!" Will called out, his voice echoing with a power that resonated through the very air around them. "Don't take this any further!"

But Malakar, now fully consumed by madness, let out a deep, rumbling growl that seemed to shake the ground beneath them. His eyes, glowing with an intense rage, were fixed on Will, his expression twisted with hatred. He began to circle Will, massive claws digging into the hard stone surface of the monolith as he prowled, his dark energy swirling around him like a storm.

"There is no turning back now!" Malakar roared, his voice a guttural, bestial sound. "I have given every ounce of myself to bring you here at this moment! I will not be denied what is rightfully mine!"

With each word, Malakar's form pulsed with dark energy, the shadows around him thickening and twisting, reaching out like grasping hands. He moved with a terrifying speed, lunging forward, claws outstretched, seeking an opening in Will's glowing defences.

Will staggered back, the ground cracking beneath his feet as he struggled to hold his ground. He swung his sword, the blade of light cutting through the shadows that swarmed around Malakar's claws, but the beast was relentless, his attacks coming faster and more furious.

Malakar he laughed—a chilling, hollow sound that sent chills through Will.

"You can't stop me, Will!" Malakar snarled, his voice dripping with venom.

With a surge of determination, Will swung his blade in a wide arc, the radiant energy of his sword colliding with Malakar's dark aura. The impact sent both of them skidding back, the force of the clash reverberating through the air.

Malakar howled in fury, his monstrous form thrashing as the light scorched him, burning away at the dark energy that swirled around him. But he only seemed to grow more frenzied, more desperate, his movements erratic as he lunged at Will again and again, each strike more ferocious than the last.

Will stayed focused, his breath steady despite the relentless onslaught. Malakar's movements bore the telltale signs of his growing frustration. His strikes came faster, harder, but with a recklessness that betrayed his desperation to crush Will once and for all.

Parrying another devastating blow, Will side-stepped just in time to avoid a clawed hand swiping where his head had been a moment before. He kept moving, keeping his distance, his glowing blade a constant barrier against Malakar's fury. He could feel the strain in his arms, the dull ache in his muscles, but he remained calm, his focus unshaken. He knew Malakar would make a mistake. He just had to be ready when it happened.

And then it came—a split-second misstep. Malakar raised his massive arm for a crushing downward strike, but he over-rotated, shifting his balance forward. The hulking beast's clawed paw momentarily slipped on the polished floor, his stance faltering as he adjusted to regain control.

Will's instincts kicked in. He darted to the side, using the opening to pivot behind Malakar in a blur of movement. Summoning every ounce of strength and precision he had left, Will drove his blade low, the sword flaring with a brilliant, golden light as it struck. The energy of the light coursed through the blade, slicing cleanly through the shadowy aura that cloaked Malakar's monstrous form and severing both of his Achilles tendons in a single, decisive strike.

Malakar roared in agony, the sound reverberating through the air as he collapsed. The ground shook beneath them with the force of his fall, and the air seemed to ripple with the raw energy of his pain. With his loss of focus his form shifted back to the dark mirror image of Will, and in response, Will too shrank back to his normal size.

Will took no pleasure in this victory, but he knew that he needed to finish it. He made his way over to where Malakar lay, writhing about on the ground, his blood running in rivulets on the cold stone surface beneath their feet.

His heart ached as he looked down at the twisted reflection of himself, now stripped of its monstrous facade and reduced to a pitiful figure writhing in pain. Malakar's face twisted in pain and fury as he clutched at his ruined legs, dark blood pooling around him. His eyes, still blazing with hatred, locked onto Will's as he struggled to lift himself, only to collapse back onto the cold stone, his strength failing him.

Will's voice was calm, but filled with sadness as a wave of overwhelming empathy for his fallen foe washed over him. "It doesn't have to end like this, Malakar," he said, his sword still glowing softly in his hand. "You can yield. This can be over. I don't want to fight you anymore."

For a moment, the darkness in Malakar's eyes seemed to waver, as if some part of him was struggling against the hatred that had consumed him for so long. But then he bared his teeth, a snarl twisting his features. "Yield?" he spat, his voice a hoarse rasp. "You think I would yield to you? After everything you've taken from me?"

He tried to rise again, but his legs gave out beneath him, and he fell back, gasping in pain. His hands clawed at the ground, trying to drag himself towards Will, but the effort was futile.

"You don't understand, Will," he said, his voice trembling with anger and desperation. "You never understood."

Will looked at Malakar now with pity, his resolve wavering as he looked at the broken figure before him. "I never wanted any of this," he said softly.

Malakar laughed, a harsh, bitter sound that echoed through the silence. "Regardless... your pathetic fragility led you down a sorry path, and you left me to die."

He coughed, his body shuddering with the effort. "But I didn't die, did I? I survived. I grew stronger. And now... now I have the power to take back everything you stole from me."

Will shook his head, his heart aching at the bitterness and pain in Malakar's words. "This isn't power, Malakar. It's destruction, it's pain. It's not what you really wanted, and you know it."

"Don't pretend to know me!" Malakar roared, his voice cracking with the strain. "You don't know anything about what I want!"

He tried to rise again, but his limbs refused to cooperate, and he slumped back to the ground, gasping for breath.

Malakar closed his eyes, a shudder running through his body as the last of his strength drained away.

Will felt a pang of sorrow deep in his chest. "I don't want you to die, Malakar. We can put an end to this."

But Malakar only shook his head, a faint, bitter smile on his lips. "You don't get it, do you? I'm already dead. I've been dead for a long time."

He coughed again, his body convulsing, and for a moment, Will thought he would pass out. But then Malakar's eyes opened, and they were filled with a fierce, burning light. "But I won't go alone," he said with a snarl.

Malakar's body suddenly tensed, and a surge of dark energy erupted from him, lashing out like a wave of pure hatred, all directed at Will. But Will was ready.

As the surge of dark energy burst from Malakar, Will didn't raise his sword to strike back or defend himself. Instead, he opened himself up to it, letting the dark energy crash into him. He grasped the chaotic force with his own light energy, and a blinding light flared from his hands. He felt the searing hatred and anguish that Malakar had carried for so long flood into him, threatening to overwhelm him. But he didn't flinch. He held steady, channelling all of that darkness into the burning fire of pure light within him, merging the two energy streams into one.

Malakar's eyes widened as he realised what Will was doing. The pain etched on his face began to ease, the anger and hatred transforming into something else; relief. The dark energy pouring out of Malakar slowed, then stopped, as Will drew it all in, taking the darkness, the pain, the bitterness—all of it—into himself.

The light around them grew brighter, almost blinding, as Will's power surged, transforming the darkness, absorbing it. Malakar's body, once writhing with torment, began to dissolve, the shadows that had clung to him lifting and dissipating like smoke in the wind.

Malakar's face softened, the anger and hatred that had twisted his features melting away. For the first time, there was peace in his eyes. "Will..." he whispered, his voice barely a breath. "Thank you."

And then, in a final, gentle pulse, the last of Malakar's essence flowed into Will, merging with him, filling the emptiness that had existed within him for so long. The light around them flared one last time, then faded, leaving only Will standing alone on the cold stone monolith, the sword still glowing softly in his hand, remembering the words of the Luminary Codex: There shall the traveller become whole as his fractured aspects heal during the final conflict with the abomination.

He took a deep, shuddering breath as the reality of what he had done settled over him. He looked up at the sky, the darkness of Shadowmoor now fading, slowly being replaced by a gentle warm glow as the sun rose on this land for the first time in years. The curse had been lifted, and he could already feel the fibres of magic returning to their natural course, now their purpose was no longer being corrupted.

"Rest now, Malakar," he whispered softly. "We're finally free."

And with that he fell to his knees and wept as a flood of emotions washed over him.

# Chapter thirty

An unnatural calm settled over the battlefield in the immediate wake of the encounter with Malakar. Or maybe Will was simply numb to his surroundings as he tried to come to grips with the physical and emotional changes that were happening within him. Waves of memories, emotions, and sensations surged through him as his fractured parts struggled to find a way to coexist within his mind. Malakar was the embodiment of the part of himself that he had buried and tried not to look at, but suddenly all that pain, anger and bitterness was laid bare. Now, with the veil torn away, those feelings lay raw and exposed. It was as if someone had overturned a stone that had rested in the earth for years, revealing the writhing insects beneath. They scurried and swarmed, clawing at his consciousness, demanding attention and reckoning.

Taking a deep, shuddering breath, Will raised his head. His hands trembled as he wiped his face, feeling the heat of the tears he hadn't realised he'd shed. Slowly, deliberately, he let the waves of emotion wash over him, no longer resisting. He didn't try to suppress them or push them away. Instead, he allowed them to exist alongside the light, seeking balance in the chaos.

As the moments passed, the chaos within him began to settle. He could feel the edges of his mind smoothing out, the sharp contrasts between light and dark blending into something more harmonious. There was still a long road ahead, he knew that, but for the first time in a long time, he felt like he was walking it as his true self—complete, unbroken.

Will took another deep breath, his gaze drifting over the now tranquil landscape of Shadowmoor. The heavy darkness that had once choked this place was slowly receding, replaced by a gentle, dawn light that had just begun to cascade over the land like a cleansing wave, chasing the last of the dark curse into the small pockets of shadow that still remained.

He closed his eyes, letting the peace wash over him. He had been through so much, lost so much, but here he stood, on the other side of it all, with a future that was finally his to shape. He imagined what his future might look like and he smiled as his mind automatically went to Lyra.

Lyra!

His eyes shot open, heart pounding in his chest. She was still down there — still somewhere in the city. A surge of panic flooded him, and he reached deep into himself, calling on the light. But this time, something had changed.

He felt it instantly, like a second heartbeat resonating in his core. The familiar warmth of light magic was there, but so was something else. It wasn't the suffocating cold of shadow magic he had fought so hard against. It wasn't something he needed to reject or push away. It was... part of him now.

No longer two opposing forces, but one. Light and shadow, order and chaos — they were no longer enemies, but simply two sides of the same coin, as they always had been.

This revelation only held him for a moment. The air shimmered around him, and with a twist of his will, reality folded in on itself. His vision blurred as space bent like rippling water, and with a pulse of quiet power, he was gone.

He reappeared in the living room of the house that looked like his childhood home. Even here, evidence that the curse was receding existed. The sunlight streaming in the window had begun restoring colour and life where before there had been only rot and decay.

But none of that mattered.

"Lyra!" he called, his voice echoing off the hollow walls. Too quiet. There was no reply. His heart pounded in his chest. "Lyra!"

He stepped into the hall, thinking to check outside the front door, where he had last seen her. The front door stood wide open, but there was no sign of her. His senses reached out instinctively, following the faint currents of magic that flowed through the world around him. He focused, listening for her essence, for the familiar rhythm of her presence.

It was faint, but it was there.

He turned around. The door to the basement was ajar.

He didn't have time to wonder how she had gotten in right now, he needed to find her. He could sense something wasn't right.

"Lyra..." he whispered, his throat tightening with worry.

Will hesitated at the threshold, his fingers tightening on the splintered door-frame. The air emanating from below was unnaturally cold, carrying with it a heavy, oppressive weight that seemed to press against his chest. Peering into the basement, he was met with a suffocating darkness that pooled at the bottom of the stairs like spilled ink, so thick and impenetrable that even the faint light behind him seemed unwilling to touch it.

His pulse echoed in his ears like a distant drum. The malevolent energy was sentient, hungry—a remnant of the curse, clinging stubbornly to this natural refuge of darkness, its presence slithering and undulating below.

The faintest trace of Lyra's essence lingered below, and his stomach tensed as he realised the shadow was feeding off her light; consuming it to sustain itself. His jaw clenched as anger flared in his chest.

Will stretched out his hand as he summoned the light from deep within. He felt its warmth flow through his veins, filling him up. He released it as a steady current of energy that flowed outward and illuminated the darkness below.

The shadow recoiled at the sudden intrusion, writhing violently, twisting into unnatural shapes as it lashed out in anger. The air filled with an ear-piercing screech of rage and despair that reverberated through the confined space.

He concentrated harder, guiding the light with every ounce of focus, feeling it grow stronger, brighter, and more insistent. The shadows flailed against the relentless glow, shrinking and dissipating like fog under the morning sun.

With a final, defiant roar of energy, the light surged forward, vaporising the darkness in a blinding wave. The screaming ceased abruptly, leaving a deafening silence in its wake.

And there she was.

Lyra lay on her side, still and unmoving. Her arms were curled close to her chest, her face pale. For a split second, fear gripped him. He flew down the stairs, his heart in his throat.

"Lyra! Come on, no, no, no, not like this..."

He dropped to his knees beside her, gently rolling her onto her back. Her head lolled limply to the side, her eyes closed. Will's breath came in short, frantic gasps as he pressed his hands to her shoulders, her face, searching for any sign of life. His fingers pressed against her neck, desperate to feel the rhythm of a pulse.

There it was.

Faint. But there.

He inhaled deeply with relief, releasing it in a slow, shaky breath. She was alive. Barely, but alive.

"Hey, hey," he whispered, his voice cracking as he brushed a strand of hair from her face. "Come on, Lyra. Wake up."

Her eyelids fluttered as she drew a deep shuddering breath.

Her eyes opened slowly, clouded with confusion. She blinked a few times, her gaze unfocused, searching. When her eyes finally settled on him, her lips twitched in the faintest hint of a smile.

"Will...?" Her voice was weak, barely above a breath.

"Yeah, it's me," he said, his voice thick with emotion. He fought to keep it steady, but every word felt like it could shatter at any moment. "I'm here. I've got you."

Her eyes darted around, taking in her surroundings. "Did we... did we win?" she asked, her voice hopeful.

Will glanced up at the ceiling, sensing the air around them. A surge of emotion welled up inside him and bubbled to the surface. He blinked back tears as the emotions briefly overwhelmed him, constricting his heart.

"Yeah," he said, his gaze softening as he looked back at her. "Yeah...we won."

Tears welled in her eyes, and she let out a quiet, exhausted laugh. Her head leaned into his chest, her breath warm against him. "Took you long enough..." she murmured, her voice trailing off into a sigh of relief.

Will sat there for a moment, holding her close, feeling the steady rise and fall of her breath. It was real. She was safe. They were safe.

But as they held each other, the ground beneath their feet began to tremble violently, a deep rumble building into crescendo of absolute chaos. Fear gripped them both, and they scrambled to their feet, racing up the stairs. The house groaned and shuddered around them, dust and debris falling from the ceiling as they burst through the door and into the open air.

The city outside was in chaos. They turned their eyes toward the monolith at the heart of the city that appeared to be unravelling, its dark surface splintering and disintegrating. The absence of Malakar and his curse had left a vacuum of power, and the monolith was collapsing into itself, its very essence imploding.

Will froze, his senses struggling to grasp the sheer magnitude of the event. He could feel the ripple of energy radiating outward from the monolith, tendrils of unseen force stretching across the ruins. These tendrils seemed to claw at the world around them, pulling everything—rubble, debris, and even the air itself—toward the collapsing centre.

The buildings closest to the monolith began to fracture and break apart, their stones and timbers being drawn towards the centre of the forming vortex. Shards of glass and twisted beams flew through the air, spiralling toward the heart of the destruction. The noise was deafening as the curse of Shadowmoor continued its inexorable collapse.

"We have to move!" Will shouted, grabbing Lyra's hand.

She looked up at him nodding, her eyes wide with fear and confusion.

With a single, focused thought, he teleported them away, the world around them blurring as they vanished from the collapsing city.

They reappeared outside the outer limits of the city, the ground beneath their feet stable and solid. Will looked back, his breath catching as he took in the sight before his eyes. They could still feel the ground shaking and hear the devastation unfolding, but it was less intense from this distance.

"Is it... is it over?" Lyra asked, her voice trembling.

Will shook his head slowly, still staring at the distant chaos. "I don't know." he said. They continued to watch as more of the city was pulled into the ever-expanding vortex, the twisted structures and debris vanishing into the spiralling void.

As they stood there, witnessing the collapse of the city, a shimmering portal appeared a short distance away. A moment later, Eldran stepped through the portal, his robes billowing in the gentle breeze that swept across the plain as the portal behind him closed. He looked around, his eyes scanning the scene before landing on Will and Lyra.

"Well done," Eldran said, his voice carrying a genuine tone of relief and admiration. "Your actions here this day have saved countless thousands of lives."

Will's gaze shifted to Eldran, his body still tense from the intensity of the battle. "Are you sure it's over?" he asked, his voice filled with uncertainty.

Eldran nodded, stepping closer. "Yes, it's over. The curse is unravelling as we speak, and Shadowmoor will soon be nothing more than a memory. Already, the effects of the curse have started to reverse."

Lyra looked up, her eyes wide with hope. "My family?..."

"The afflicted in some areas returning to normal," Eldran explained, a smile spreading across his face. "I can't say for sure that your family are amongst them... but it looks promising."

Will felt a surge of relief, he let out a huge sigh as a weight lifted off his shoulders. "We can finally start to look to the future." he murmured, glancing over at Lyra.

But Eldran's expression shifted, a pained look crossing his face. Will caught the change immediately.

"What is it?" he asked, his voice concerned.

Eldran hesitated looking down at his feet, then spoke reluctantly. "Before I opened a portal and travelled here, the elders at Thorn Island were monitoring the collapse of the curse. They witnessed something... unexpected." He took a deep breath, his gaze steady on Will. "The minute the curse was lifted, the Luminary Codex began inscribing a new passage. It seems this unstable vortex at the centre of the collapsing curse is more than just a void. It's a huge portal back to your own world."

Will felt as if the ground had been pulled out from under him. "My world?" he said, echoing Eldran's words in a hollow voice.

Eldran nodded solemnly. "It will continue to grow and collapse, consuming everything in it's path until there is nothing left, until..." he paused, an apologetic look on his face.

Will shook his head, not understanding Eldran's meaning. But a tight knot had started to form in the pit of his stomach as he got the sense that what was coming next wasn't good, "Unless what?"

Eldran reached out a hand and grasped Will by the shoulder. "I am so sorry my friend, it seems so unfair after everything you have done for us... The vortex will vanish once you return to your own world."

The words hit Will like a physical blow. After everything he had been through, the thought of leaving this world, leaving Lyra... it was almost unbearable. He looked over at her, seeing the realisation dawn in her eyes, the shock and sorrow that followed.

"No," she said, her voice trembling. "No, there has to be another way."

Will's heart ached as he stepped closer to her, his hands reaching out to gently cup her face. "If there was any other way, I would take it, Lyra. You know I would."

Tears welled in her eyes, and she shook her head, her hands grasping at his arms as if she could hold him here by sheer will alone. "But we were supposed to have more time."

"I know," he said, his voice thick with emotion. "I know. But if I stay, everything we fought for could be lost. I can't let that happen. The only thing more painful than having to leave you would be knowing that you had been consumed by that vortex, and I could have stopped it!"

They stood there for a long moment, holding on to each other, the world around them fading away as they shared what they both knew would be their last embrace. Finally, Will pulled back, his own eyes wet with unshed tears.

"I will always love you, Lyra. Nothing will ever change that," he whispered in broken sobs, his cheeks wet with warm tears.

"I love you," she said quietly, barely able to speak the words through the pain.

With a final, lingering kiss, Will turned away, his heart completely broken.

"Take care of each other," he said to Eldran, who nodded solemnly. As he started to leave, he turned one last time, his eyes finding Lyra's. He tried to memorise every detail of her face, every nuance of her expression, before he steeled himself and turned towards the vortex. He covered the distance in the blink of an eye, calling upon the magic to transport him there, even as his heart shattered. He stood for a moment on the threshold of the vortex, resisting the pull, second guessing his choice. But again, he realised there was no other option and he let go, allowing himself to be drawn into the swirling chaos.

And then he was gone.

# Chapter thirty-one

B eep.
  Beep.
Beep.

Will squinted his eyes, not wanting to wake up and face the world just yet, but the alarm on his mobile phone persistently sounded off, until eventually he rolled over with a deep groan to silence the noise. As he reached out, his arm came into contact with a bed rail that made the whole bed shake. He blinked a few times, trying to clear his eyes and figure out what was going on when he heard a young man's voice, calm and reassuring. "Welcome back Mr Preston, you had us all very worried there for a while."

Will jumped, startled, wondering who was in his bedroom, but as his mind slowly rose up from the depths of his slumber, he realised that he wasn't in his bedroom at all. His head was fuzzy and his throat hurt, but he managed to croak out a single phrase. "Where am I?"

His gaze darted around, taking in the sterile surroundings, the relentlessly beeping machines, the intravenous drip attached to his arm.

"You're in hospital Mr Preston." The young man was dressed in scrubs and was moving about his bed, taking readings and checking his vitals. "You've been unconscious for nearly a week. The paramedics said they found you collapsed at your home. Do you remember that?"

Will shook his head weakly, not really able to take any of this in. The pain of separation from Aruna and the people he loved there was squeezing his chest, making it hard to breathe. *Was it all just a dream? Had it all been some elaborate fabrication of his mind?*

But the pain of leaving them, of leaving her, felt too real. He could still feel the heat of Lyra's kiss on his lips, the crushing ache in his heart as he'd said goodbye. *How could that be just a dream?*

The nurse finished his checks and smiled. "It's good to see you awake, Mr. Preston. The doctor will be in shortly. She'll want to run some tests and check on your recovery, but it's a good sign that you're awake."

Will nodded numbly, his thoughts a mess. He needed to understand what had happened, needed to find some way to make sense of it all. But as the nurse left the room, closing the door softly behind him, Will could do nothing but stare up at the ceiling, his mind numb from shock.

If this was real, then what was the other world? A hallucination? A coma-induced fantasy? He reached up with a trembling hand to rub at his eyes, but then he stopped, staring at his fingers.

There was a faint, lingering warmth there, like the echo of light. His breath caught in his throat as memories flooded his mind. He flexed his fingers, willing that light to appear again, desperate for some sign, any sign, that it had been more than just a dream.

But there was nothing. Just his hand, trembling slightly.

Will let his arm drop back to the bed, his heart aching with the loss. "What's real?" he whispered to himself, his voice barely audible.

He felt tears prick at the corners of his eyes, but he fought them back. He had to be strong, even if he didn't know why anymore.

Over the next few hours, the doctors ran what felt like dozens of test on Will, but eventually, completely dumbfounded, they had to concede that he was well enough to return home.

"We'll keep you in for one more night for observation Mr Preston, but tomorrow morning you can go home." Said the elderly doctor that had come to give him the test result. "We'll want to see you back here for regular check ups, there'll be a letter in the mail with details. We don't know what caused your collapse, and we would like to get to the bottom of it to make sure it doesn't happen again."

The doctor's words seemed to echo distantly, barely breaking through the fog clouding Will's mind. He nodded again numbly, though he wasn't sure what he was agreeing to. His body felt foreign, as if it belonged to someone else, and the clinical sterility of the hospital room only made the feeling worse.

"Thank you," he managed to mumble, though the words felt hollow. The elderly doctor gave him a sympathetic smile, patted his arm, and left the room, leaving him alone with his thoughts once more.

He glanced around, his gaze settling on the window. The sun was beginning to set, painting the sky in shades of orange and pink. It was beautiful, but it felt like a cruel reminder of everything he'd lost. Lyra would have loved this, he thought, the memory of her smile making his chest tighten painfully.

He clenched his hand into a fist, frustration and despair welling up inside him. How was he supposed to just go back to his life here? How was he supposed to pretend that everything was normal, that he was just Will Preston, some ordinary man who had collapsed in his home for no apparent reason?

His eyes stung with unshed tears, and he squeezed them shut, trying to hold himself together. But the weight of it all was crushing, suffocating. He wanted to scream, to cry, to do something—anything—to release the pain that was tearing him apart. But he couldn't. He had to be strong. He had to—

A soft knock on the door pulled him from his spiralling thoughts. He quickly wiped his eyes and turned his head as a nurse stepped in, carrying a tray with dinner.

"Hi, Mr. Preston," she said gently in a kind voice. "I've brought you something to eat. You should try to get your strength up."

Will nodded absently, not really looking at the tray. The nurse set it on the small table beside his bed, then paused, her eyes searching his face.

"Is there anything else I can get for you?" she asked, her tone laced with concern. "Someone you'd like to call? A family member, maybe?"

Will shook his head slowly. "No... no, there's no one."

The nurse hesitated, then gave him a sympathetic smile. "Alright. Well, if you need anything, just press the call button, okay?"

"Thanks," he said quietly, watching as she left the room, the door closing softly behind her.

He glanced at the tray, his stomach churning at the sight of the food. He knew he should eat, knew he needed to keep his strength up, but the thought of putting anything in his mouth made him feel nauseous. Instead, he leaned back against the pillows, staring up at the ceiling.

The tears finally broke free then, silent and hot, trailing down his cheeks as he lay there, feeling more alone and lost than he'd ever been.

He turned to lay on his side and felt something fall off his chest, only to stop short as it got hung up on something around his neck. He reached down inside his gown and pulled out a pendant. As he tried to focus his burning, tear-filled eyes on the pendant trying to see, it slowly came into focus and his heart skipped a beat, as his eyes took in the unmistakeable intricate designs on the face of the Amulet of Purity.

Will held the amulet tightly in his hand and closed his eyes as hot tears of joy welled up. A surge of emotions swelled within him—relief, sadness, and, above all, a profound sense of gratitude.

A tear slipped down his cheek, but it wasn't a tear of sorrow. It was a tear of acceptance, a release of the regret that had been crushing his soul since waking up in this strange, familiar world. He gently traced the intricate patterns engraved on the amulet's surface, feeling a connection to the magic that had woven through every moment of his time in Aruna.

He laughed softly, the sound shaky. It felt strange to be so happy and so heartbroken all at once. He wished he could see them again, just once more, to tell them how much they meant to him. But perhaps, in some way, they already knew.

"I'll never forget you," he whispered to the empty room, as tears of joy streaked down his cheeks.

In the days and weeks that followed, Will continued to attend his appointments and the doctors continued to find nothing wrong with him, and he had honestly never felt better. He smiled more now, saw more hope in the world around him. He reconnected with his friends and family that he'd pulled away from before, making time to fit them into his life.

The biggest change came on his first day back at work once the hospital had discharged him and deemed him fit for work again. It came as a complete shock to even him, but he walked in to his cubicle, sat down, and wrote out his resignation letter. Those two weeks of his notice period felt like a dream. For so long, he had been trapped in a prison of his own making, locked in the same never-ending cycle that slowly killed his soul, one depressing day at a time. But something had changed. He'd changed.

His final shift at the hive passed without ceremony. No grand speeches. No obligatory farewell party with stale cake. He'd said his goodbyes in his own way, thanking the few people who had been more than just colleagues. Then, as he walked out of the building for the last time, he didn't look back. He didn't need to.

The sun was setting when he got home, its warm, golden light filling his small home. It too felt different now — not just a place to sleep between shifts. The kitchen table was still cluttered with his old notes, pages filled with sketches, ideas, and half-finished thoughts he'd scribbled down long ago but never had time to pursue.

He stood there, just looking at it for a moment. The pile of old dreams. He picked it up and started placing the pages into a box, but then he paused... his fingers lingering over the map and the town of Candleford, a small lump forming in his throat.

He was suddenly filled with such a desire to breathe life into those pages once again. He pulled out his chair, opening his laptop, and shifted the notes in front of him. For the first time in years, he felt the pull — the irresistible call to create, to shape something from nothing. He hadn't felt that in so long that he'd almost forgotten what it was like.

His fingers hovered over the keyboard, hesitation creeping in. What if it's not good enough? What if I fail?

He closed his eyes, taking a steadying breath. I've faced worse than this, he reminded himself. I've grown, I've fought, I've risen—and I'll rise again.

The first keystroke was like striking a match in the dark. Then came the second. The third. Each one a tiny flame, a spark of something greater. Words flowed from him, not perfectly, but honestly. He didn't stop to edit. He didn't stop to doubt. He simply wrote.

He wrote of a magical land, vast and wild, filled with windswept coasts and towering forests that whispered secrets to those who listened. He wrote of a brave young hero, burdened by doubt but driven by a sense of purpose even he didn't fully understand. There were companions — fierce and flawed but bound by friendship. And, at the heart of it all, a looming curse that had crept across the land like a shadow that couldn't be outrun.

He wasn't just writing a story. He was pouring himself onto the page. His doubts, his fears, his dreams — all of it found its way into the ink of his world.

Hours passed in a blur. His fingers moved with a rhythm he hadn't felt since he was a kid dreaming of writing epic tales that captivated and enchanted his audience. Somewhere in the background, the soft hum of city life echoed through the window, but it felt so far away, muffled. Here, in his world, it was just him and his story.

When he finally stopped, it wasn't because he ran out of ideas. It was because his eyes were heavy, and his fingers ached from typing. He glanced at the time. 3:42 AM.

His heart was still racing. His mind buzzed with scenes yet unwritten, conversations between characters that only existed in his head, and moments that he needed to capture.

He leaned back in his chair, stretching his arms, exhaustion finally settling in. But it was a good kind of exhaustion — the kind that comes after doing something that mattered.

He glanced down at the screen. 4,327 words. Not bad for a night's work.

His eyes scanned the first few paragraphs. The prose wasn't perfect. It never was on the first pass. But it was real. It was his.

For the first time in a long, long while, he felt like he'd done something that mattered.

And he smiled.

THE END